THE
FAIRGROUNDS

A THRILLER

BOOK I MESSAGE IN A BOTTLE

BLAKE ALB

World Castle Publishing, LLC
Pensacola, Florida

Copyright © Blake Alb 2022
Hardback ISBN: 9798410961714
Paperback ISBN: 9781956788600
eBook ISBN: 9781956788617
First Edition World Castle Publishing, LLC, February 21, 2022
http://www.worldcastlepublishing.com

Licensing Notes

Cover Art: John Davies
Editor: Maxine Bringenberg

Table of Contents

CHAPTER 1
FEASIBILITY AND CHANGES OF HEART

Main Character: Shawn Schroeder
Setting: Backyard of Shawn's Home, inside privacy fence
Date: May 9, 2019, Thursday afternoon

> To whom it may concern (if anyone),
> Consider this to be my suicide note. Sadly, they don't teach you how to properly pen one of these in school, in the same manner, they instruct and give direction on the proper sections, styling, or formatting techniques of a cover letter, thank you note, or letter to a friend. As such, you will need to forgive any lapses in proper form or rhythm. But I think you will get the point, and the picture, as evidenced by the unsightly view of my body dangling from this very apple tree. After all, necessity is the mother of invention. Or is it really the other way around? Oh, my precious Emeril, my beloved! They say that parents should never outlive their children. But alas, in my situation, this is not the case. And it is for this very reason, I believe, that life just isn't fair. There is no justice in the world! Like they say, the apple doesn't fall too far from the tree.
>
> ---------------*unused suicide note*

At just before five in the afternoon on this Thursday, the mid-fifties and divorced Shawn Schroeder was pacing around his twenty-seven-year-old Whitney crab apple tree in Alexandria, MN. He had heard the last of his immediate neighbors go into their humble abodes of picket fence suburban ramblers after what seemed to him like an eternity. The smell of mesquite was permeating the air as the last of them was putting away his Weber barbecue grill. Shawn mused at the irony of how such a scent would normally rekindle his own nostalgic revelations to pull out his own grill and do the same. But today was not that day.

By now, he had already dug a two-foot grave for his time capsule of his deceased nine-year-old son Emeril, containing baby pictures, the boy's favorite jacks and marbles, fourth-grade class photo, various school awards and knick-knacks, and his favorite stuffed teddy bear "Nettles." He decided to bury the metal box underneath the apple tree as if he could take such possessions with him into the realms of the next life, like in the tales of ancient Egypt. *How long does it really take to put away your stupid backyard barbecue equipment?* he thought to himself. He also wondered if the privacy fence was high enough to block any visible vestiges of what might transpire within the dark hour. He walked towards the wooden and rusty old park bench he had purchased at an antique shop some three years ago and pulled it closer to the apple tree. With a brute force method, he finagled it under one of the sturdier branches, about eight feet above the freshly cut lawn below. Hobbling to the garage, he retrieved the old dirty tow rope that he used to pull cars from ditches in winter. Tying the knot required more than one trip to the Internet via his cell phone, no small feat for a less than computer-savvy gentleman such as himself. After all, this certainly wasn't your grandfather's Windsor knot or the pleasant sort of "tying the knot" that oft accompanied marrying one's true love. To get the height just right, he had to wind the rope a few times around the branch.

And all the while, he thought about his nine-year-old son and all the joyous times they had spent together, particularly their escapades involving their matching yellow metal detectors and all the precious coins and metals they had unearthed in the most unlikely of places. But these thoughts quickly diminished as the look of Emeril's dying face took precedence, like faces suddenly appearing from background to foreground like phantoms in the night or the famous face/vase illusion.

Shawn stepped on the bench and put his head into the hole of the rope, like a child inserting his head into a cardboard cutout at the county fair. *Ah, I almost forgot*, he thought to himself as he snapped his fingers, took off the rope, and stepped off the bench as if merely forgetting one's keys for work. After a short jog back to the 1964 rambler, he snatched the envelope containing the suicide note from the top of the deep freeze. Two seconds later, the envelope found its way into his breast pocket. Returning to the apple tree, he mounted the old rusty bench, placed his head back into the circle of the rope, and slowly tip-toed off the bench as if he were a bashful child stepping off a diving board into a deep swimming pool.

"Shiiiit," he mumbled with a guttural sound, his legs flapping and flailing like a marionette puppet. He noticed that this was every bit as painful as it looked in the movies. He also found himself having second thoughts, or "second feelings," to be more apt. The rope was the killer but also his safety net as he grappled for the top of the rope with both hands and pulled his legs back onto the welcoming safety of the bench. It took a moment for his breath to return. And then he tried again. But this time, the pain was even more intense than before. His body was so numb and weak that he was barely able to dismount from this rather lackluster carnival ride. It took even longer for his breath to return to a calm and collected rhythm. After untying the rope from the branch and tidying his collar, he pulled the bench back to the shadows from whence it came, and untied the noose from his neck and put it back on its reserved hook on the wall of the garage as if it had never left. With a hard toss, the suicide note from his breast pocket found its way into the metal garbage can in the corner of the garage. After this bout of drama, he didn't "love life" any more per se, but he sure feared the pain of death that much more. And that was enough motivation to keep our Shawn alive, at least in the interim.

Leaving the garage, a thought ran through his head. *Maybe this rope is better suited for saving the lives of stranded cars.*

· —

CHAPTER 2
"TERRA INCOGNITA"

Main characters: Shawn Schroeder and Nathan Dickson
Setting: Alexandria Hospital's "Food for Thought" cafeteria, Children's Cancer Wing
Date: May 11, 2019, Saturday, 10:00 am

And the killer beekeeper, not to be confused with a keeper of killer bees, the fractious Amrak, has apparently been up to his zany old hijinks once again, reprising his role as lord of karma in yet another act of depravity, his death toll now reaching fifty people. This includes the seven people he killed in 2017 when he re-enacted the 1929 St. Valentine's Day Massacre and the twenty-six people he killed in 2018, each having a name starting with a different letter of the alphabet. He has just claimed his seventeenth victim this year alone and the second one in April. This time around, he has taken it upon himself to wreak havoc on the old, senile, and decrepit. Seventy-year-old Justin Thompson from Louisiana was found dead in his trailer home on Sunday afternoon five days after he was released from federal penitentiary for killing his stockbroker in 1989 for giving lackluster financial advice. After inundating his home with killer bees, Amrak and several of his cronies barricaded Thompson's door with a large bronze statue of himself, a six-foot man in beekeeper's regalia, waving a flag with the name "Amrak." The body was found just over a week later, and police found yet another philippic at the scene. It was pinned to his body with a flagpole, what has become his usual formal censure to highlight the victim's wrongdoing. The note read as follows. 'Young or old, rich or poor, male or female, or any other classification you can muster, you will get what you deserve! I am not a killer. This man's sin is what killed him. I am just the messenger. And we all know what not to do with messengers!'

----- *from Vigilante Vignettes, May issue, 2019*

"Is life fair?" asked Shawn Schroeder to his friend of thirty years, Nate Dickson, as the formerly mentioned homo sapien closed the magazine and set it on one of the dining room tables in the Alexandria Children's Hospital. On this particular day, Shawn was dressed in black jeans, Rockport hiking boots, and a lambswool Fair Isle sweater. He was reading what was intended to be a feel-good article about a Shetland sheepdog being rescued from a well. Nate was wearing a wildlife fleece jacket with a Northwestern moose on the front, black dress slacks, and Tony Lama western boots.

Today was the annual open house for the Alexandria Hospital Cafeteria's "Food for Thought." There were buffet tables encircling two of the walls, and today's amenities were free (free will donation requested). The foodstuffs included such things as mixed nuts, Little Smokies with barbecue sauce, crackers and cheese, and desserts like macaroons, snickerdoodles, caramel rolls, scotcharoos, and toffee bars. There was a large blue ribbon dangling from the ceiling, which said in bold letters, Food for Thought: Not Just Hospital Food.

And while a hospital cafeteria may not be one's usual haunt for top-shelf dining, this cafeteria had a better reputation. This particular cafeteria, as many locals would surely attest, was just as much about distraction as it was about the food. After all, they knew full well that a hospital can be the stuff of birthing rooms and convalescence, or it can also be the middleman to the mausoleum. And like any hospital perhaps, this one was known to represent the very dichotomy between life and death and everything in between. In many ways, the dining hall was similar to any other hospital cafeteria, with its sterile industrial kitchens, portable wooden tables and chairs, and various booths scattered haphazardly around the room amidst a smell of the cross between foodstuffs and disinfectant cleaners. The place could seat fifty if some elbow room was compromised.

While many hospitals may be notorious for lackluster foodstuffs, this hospital was locally known to be a cut above the rest in the local vicinity. This reputation held so steadfast that there were rumors of occasions where people would come to the cafeteria for the sole pastime of repast, their lack of medical necessity notwithstanding. And when impugned by non-locals about whether quality of food was really a top priority in a medical facility, they would simply remind such nay-sayers that quality of food was not to be taken lightly, especially for an expedient recovery. "It's good for the morale of the infirm and their families," some would say. Or, "If chicken soup is good for the soul, just imagine what sorts of feelings a mid-west hot dish could conjure with all its visceral power." Or so the theory goes.

But there were several enticements that set this cafeteria apart. One, it had large pane-glass windows overlooking the sunny view of Lake Winona. And two, it had a stellar menu with more options than any other hospital in the tri-state area, including the aforementioned iconic midwest desserts. As for main dishes, the foodstuffs consisted of midwest fare, things like hot dishes, meat/potatoes, burgers/fries, and even funeral potatoes.

It was early enough that Nate and Shawn were the only ones in the room, save for an elderly couple in one of the booths across from them. They each had their paper plates adequately stuffed with the open house amenities, to the point where various foods were encroaching over each other to make room. Shawn was armed with a concoction that consisted of one part French vanilla creamer and four parts dark roast coffee. Nate had chosen an unsweetened peach iced tea.

"Is that a rhetorical question?" asked Nate Dickson as he considered Shawn's question. He took a long drink of his tea and clanked his mug on the wooden table.

"Let's just suffice it to say that I am being quite serious," repeated Shawn, taking a short sip of his coffee. "Do you think life is fair in your heart of hearts?" He took a napkin from the dispenser and dabbed his mouth.

Shawn was genuinely curious in this equally curious manner of incisive inquisition, further evidenced by the steadfastness of his piercing gaze and the way he positioned his elbows on the table, placing his chin on the knuckles of his clenched hands. One might think that Shawn had just asked Nate, "Are you now or have you ever been a communist?"

***

To offer but a moment of brief backstory, Shawn was a tall fifty-five-year-old gentleman of German and Polish descent. He was born and raised in the typical manners and fashions endemic to the local Midwest traditions of "MN Nice" and Puritan Work Ethics. And while he might on occasion gossip about his neighbor, he wouldn't hesitate to help him or her should they ever find themselves stuck in a ditch in winter. His occupation was one of "bank manager," for more than twenty years, from the time he was twenty-five to the time he was forty-nine. And during that tenure, one could say he was almost betrothed to the profession, out of a combination of necessity, penchant for the familiar, and even a genuine liking for the trade. Be it from exhaustion or sudden dearth of passion, he had resigned from the bank about five years ago to work at the local rare coin shop "Treasure Island," for a substantial pay decrease. And while the nature of both of these employments was quite disparate, the passing of coins was the common thread. He was most fascinated with American history, most notably all manner of American currency, and even on his own time, he had been an avid and astute coin collector since the day of his ninth birthday. He owned several metal detectors and had amassed an impressive coin collection over the course of his life. And while the pay was not surreal at his new job, he likened himself to a pirate of sorts, and such embellishment, hyperbole, and small use of humor and fantasy helped make his rather boring place of employment seem all the more exciting.

But an actual pirate, he was not, as he was as honest as the bust of Lincoln on that aforementioned penny. And in similar accord, while he knew virtually everything there was to know about counterfeit money, his knowledge was more tantamount to making sure he could spot it and avoid it at all costs, especially in his coin collecting pursuits. But make no mistake, his love of money mustn't be confused with a love of making it. His connection was with the rich history, craftsmanship, and the aesthetic aspect, the "flip-side of the coin," as it were. It could be said he had just as much love for a nickel as he did for a diamond. "How much would you pay for a bust of Abraham Lincoln?" he would ask. "Five hundred dollars, you say? As for me, I wouldn't pay more than a penny!"

But his pride and joy was his childhood stuffed animals. He had them sitting on three layers of wall shelves in his bedroom quarters of his rambler. And near the shelving was a very large bookcase, with volumes upon volumes of daily planners, one for every year, since February of 1980. Each daily planner served as a diary, which was rather befitting to his organizational spirit. His manner of routine was to write at least three sentences about his day, right before bedtime, a habit he very rarely deviated from. Occasionally he would even have conversations with his plush friends and jot down the gist of the conversation in the journals. He had an entire bookshelf dedicated to these tomes. And what fun it was for him to take out a volume, from whence he was twelve, twenty, or even twenty-five, and relish and reminisce in the nostalgia, memory, and sentiment of it all. Even the "bad memories" stirred up a sort of wistful longing of his halcyon days of youth, as if simply being that young again, notwithstanding the drama of the day, was promise enough of the zest and zeal of a brighter future!

***

Nate donned a crooked grin. He bought a moment of time by stealing another sip from his iced tea. "I would much rather wax small talk regarding your growing coin collection. I am still waiting to see your three-legged buffalo. Nuff said. Done and dusted."

"So how about it, fair or unfair?"

Nate cracked a small smile. "Now that is what they used to call a cavalier question."

"That I don't dispute. I know it runs counter to my usual shy disposition."

"Might be a loaded question," said Nate as he cracked

his knuckles. "First, we gotta make sure we are on the same page of what exactly fairness even means. Are we talking equal opportunity or equal outcomes? Happiness or pursuit of happiness? Equal but different?"

"Let me put it like this," said Shawn as he moved condiments around the table like a war general positioning models of troops on a map. "Does everyone have a purpose? Or are we just stuck with what or who we are? You are either a mustard bottle or napkin dispenser, and you gotta make the best of it? Is there a rhyme or reason for what everyone goes through?"

Nate considered him for a moment, squinted his eyes, and took a long sip of iced tea as if reading him. H set down his cup with a loud thud and licked his lips. "But maybe the answer about life being fair isn't so black and white. Maybe it's a matter of degree? Maybe the answer is more like 'maybe'? Or 'sometimes'?"

"Perhaps," Shawn said with a nod as if talking to himself just as much as to Nate. "See, I got to thinking about this lately with all the news these days about this Amrak fellow — you know, the 'Karma Killer,' among other things."

"Yes, I have heard of him," said Nate. "Who hasn't. Not that I want to give him the time of day. Or the time of night, for that matter."

"Although he is a convicted criminal, he has his fans, mostly from the pro-vigilante camp," said Shawn. "Let's just suffice it to say that there are many who believe that his victims got what they deserved and deserved what they got."

Nate rubbed his eyes. "So what exactly are you saying now?"

"Well, fairness, like morality, may have a subjective element," continued Shawn. He picked up the Time magazine and a book of crossword puzzles from the stack of books on the table and tossed them in front of Nate, where they made a loud thump. "Take this hospital, for example. We are taught to think that hospitals are hospitals and libraries are libraries. But if you think about it, libraries have first-aid kits, and hospitals also have magazines. There is a small area of overlap, like those Venn diagrams that used to litter my textbooks back in school. Even disciplines that seem incongruous may have a common element, even for the likes of, say, politics or religion. Art and science. Good and evil. Fair and unfair."

"So the answer to whether life is fair, then, is sometimes," said Nate. "I couldn't agree more. Nuff said. Done and dusted. Let's move on."

"Perhaps," said Shawn, as he picked away at a hangnail on his finger. "Still, even if life is sometimes fair at best, there has got to be a reason for such a less-than-ideal arrangement. And I don't see why we have to be okay with the way things are without complaint."

Nate rested his hands on the edge of the table. "But this still begs the question, why this line of inquiry in the first place?"

Shawn tapped on the window until the horsefly standing on the other side took flight. "Well, Nate, despite all the well-wishes and sympathy cards, condolences, and commiserations, my son hasn't been doing all that well in the last four months." He turned to face Nate. "Let's not beat around the bush or tiptoe around the elephant in the room. At some point, somebody's gotta point out that the emperor is not wearing any clothes."

For a bit of backstory, Nate was freshly retired at sixty-seven. He had just stepped down from his seventeen-year stint as the chief game warden for the MN Game and Fish Department (after another ten years west of the Red River as a Game Warden in ND). He was born and raised in Bismarck, ND, and he had recently moved to Alexandria only a year ago to be closer to his work, not to mention the fringe benefit of residing closer to his best friend and confidant Shawn Schroeder. Despite his enduring tenure for the Game and Fish Department, though, he seldom did any fishing or hunting on his own volition.

Shawn paged through the magazine some and settled on the crossword puzzle. "What's an eleven letter word for justice?"

Nate paused. "Hmm, comeuppance?"

"Well done," said Shawn as he took the pencil from behind his ear and wrote in the word. He then set the pencil and magazine aside, folded his hands, and gave Nate his undivided attention. "Now, back to Emeril."

"Now now, don't get all morbid on me," said Nate as he began fiddling with his napkin. He looked around from side to side, trying to avoid making eye contact with Shawn.

Shawn grunted. "Well, this is a hospital, isn't it?"

"Well, that's not the point," said Nate. "We gotta be strong, you know, not for our sake, but for Emeril's. What you are alluding to here, in not so many words, questioning the gods and the like, is tantamount to blasphemy round these parts. Such talk is best reserved for homeless philosophers who have far too much time on their hands. We have no choice in the matter. Fair or unfair, we have to be here for Emeril until he breathes his last breath, heaven forbid. The way I see it, 'fairness' is a moot point. A privilege even."

"'These parts' are starting to sound mighty bleak if you ask me," said Shawn. "And if the translation of that poignant little soliloquy of yours is 'suck it up,' save it for the coffee." Shawn pushed Nate's cup towards him as some sloshed out. "Besides, blasphemy is quite therapeutic, if I say so myself."

With that, Shawn took a long and loud sip as if such an impertinent gesture was the stuff of righteous protestation. The display lost some of its dramatic zest and zeal, however, when he winced from the pain of the hot coffee.

"Yeah yeah, I told you they have hot coffee here," said Nate. "No need to show off."

"There are better ways to show off than chugging hot coffee, rest assured," said Shawn. "But since you mentioned lips, I am not into any of that 'stiff upper lip' lip service or any of that macho posturing, which is more often than not meant for the comfort of those that do not wish to hear such complaints or grievances. For them, such cloaked well-wishes are more about their own comfort."

Nate put up his hands like a traffic cop indicating to slow down. "Now now, I should really take offense that you think so little of your old chum sitting in front of you. I wasn't accusing you of being weak in any way, make no mistake."

"Well, that is something," said Shawn, wiping the spilled coffee with a new napkin.

"I have no intent to be sanctimonious here," said Nate.

Shawn's voice grew louder. "The Boy Scouts can have their 'Always Be Prepared' nonsense. AA can shove their 'It works if you work it' platitudes. And the marines can keep their 'Pain is weakness leaving the body' euphemisms. Truth is, I have never really considered Murphy's Law to be cynical, just proactive, even if I don't follow it to the letter—"

Nate interrupted. "Well, I don't always want to think about how things might go wrong. What I am really alluding to, in not so many words, is that sometimes it helps to be stupid. I am not talking about malingering or playing dumb. I am talking about the real McCoy. Actually, being stupid. Not playing. And being none the wiser for it. We need to find our 'irrational courage,' the kind born from dumb luck and fool's hope."

"As if placing a cherry on top of the insipid ice cream will somehow make it taste like sweet ambrosia," murmured Shawn as he gazed out the window with a dead blank stare.

"What do you mean by that, pray tell?" asked Nate, squinting to see what Shawn was looking at.

Shawn returned his gaze back to Nate. "One can put a positive, or even delusional, spin on just about anything, I suppose. My brother Jacob, the one that's a janitor, one time he was taking his lunch break, in the bathroom of all places, and he placed a bit of his ice cream on the urinal cake and even put a maraschino cherry on top. The picture was posted on the Internet, and he called it 'Toilet Humor: Commode à la mode.' But what I took out of it was that just because you put a cherry on top, it doesn't necessarily make everything better. I suppose there is a difference between making the best out of something or merely deluding yourself that everything is fine."

"Who says toilet humor has to be about popular bodily fluids?" laughed Nate.

"Speaking of which, I suppose you see your fair share of

animal bodily fluids managing all those habitats and wildlife reserves."

"Indeed I do," said Nate, sitting back in his chair, taking a swig of his tea. "You are really missing out."

By now, there were about a dozen people in the cafeteria, and the air was filled with the murmurs of nervous conversation about the status of loved ones.

The pair enjoyed a moment of silence until Shawn pulled out a small square sleeve containing a three-legged buffalo nickel from his pocket and slid it towards Nate like a curling stone, and it stopped just as it reached the edge of the table. "At any rate, we all have our defenses, eh?"

Nate slapped it with his palm. He held it up and stared at it. "Wow, that's three legs all right." He handed it back.

"And they say emblazoned imperfections can't be beautiful," said Shawn. "Sometimes flaws become the most highly coveted features."

"Say what you want about circus sideshows, but those so-called flaws bring in money and crowds," said Nate.

"Flaws or not, everyone has worth," said Shawn. "It's one of the reasons I carry it."

"Just don't let anyone steal it," Nate said, sliding it back to Shawn. Shawn stopped it dead in its tracks by slapping it with his palm just as Nate had done prior. He wiped it with a napkin as if it were sullied with Nate's hands before putting it back into his pants pocket.

"So is life fair?" repeated Shawn once again, more to himself than anything.

"My own life?" said Nate as he fiddled with the napkin dispenser. "Certainly not. And definitely not yours either, if I may speak freely and frankly. No offense."

Shawn leaned in closer. "I am not talking about just my life or anyone else's life. I mean life in general, the human condition, the matters affecting your average Joe. It's not fair, is it? Nobody's life is fair."

Nate laughed as he nodded to himself. "You know how

many times people in the world, over the course of thousands of years, had this very conversation? Utter waste of time if you ask me. Nuff said. Done and dusted."

"Indeed, but repetition of said line of questioning has naught to do with the veracity of the question's answer, now does it? To put it another way, the reason this theme crops up in conversations of the world, on occasion, is because it's an unresolved inquiry. As such, it should not be asked less. It should be asked more. The technology of the world grows at an exponential rate. Look at how computers evolved since the mid-seventies."

Nate smiled. "Yes, and you still don't know how to use one."

"Even still, we are still in the Stone Age when it comes to the big picture, the truth of truths, the very reason we are having this very conversation at this very moment. We know nothing more than the old world philosophers knew ten thousand years ago. Maybe less."

Nate leaned in closer until their faces were only about four inches apart. "Very poignant, if not a bit paranoid. But why worry about things you can't control?"

Shawn positioned his face even closer so that Nate could feel his breath against his cheek. "Why not?"

"I asked you first," said Nate, as they both resumed their leisurely positions.

Shawn sighed and allowed his muscles to relax in resignation. "Isn't that the very definition of worry? Fear of the unknown? The unexpected? How can one not worry about things like death, the very crux of uncertainty and unfamiliarity? It would be counter-intuitive not to worry about such things if you ask me."

Nate rubbed the tired from his eyes. "You make it sound like life itself is one of the grand mysteries of the world."

"Well, isn't it? One minute we are enjoying the company of those we love, and the next minute they are gone like a foggy morning come afternoon, with not a glimmer of evidence that we will ever see them again."

"If only game wardens were privy to top-secret information outside the scope of conservation reserve programs."

"So bigfoot and aliens are not in the purview of the Game and Fish Department?" asked Shawn. "What a shame." He followed it with a long drink of his coffee.

Nate shook his head. "I like to see humans as just bees in a hive. Mere animals. The same quest for survival, competition, scarce resources, and the like. 'The human race,' it even sounds like a marathon. It's not rocket science. It's just the stark truth. Game wardens know about such things. And it's not just about kill or be killed. There is also overpopulation to worry about."

Shawn removed a piece of lint from his sweater and fiddled with it between his fingers. "Spoken like a game warden. Oh yes, and you guys are the ones that have to come up with hunting bag limits for deer every year."

"Many people, including yourself, I suspect, think those limits are heartless," said Nate.

"You are more right than wrong there," returned Shawn. "Nature is a heartless beast."

"But without it, we face the threat of overpopulation. By the end of the day, I still think life is a miracle, don't forget it. Even if I don't think life is always fair."

Shawn watched an elderly couple bickering about the expense of a medical bill. He continued as he watched them. "But not all miracles are pleasant. A person gets struck by lightning. Now that too is a miracle. Just not a very good one. A rust-laced silver lining in the clouds."

Nate coughed into his hand. "Well, not when you put it like that, I suppose."

"Funny how we reduce trauma to natural disaster, abuse, or war," muttered Shawn, returning his gaze back to his friend. "What about losing our loved ones?"

"Well, I suppose that much we can agree on," said Nate, taking a sip. "In the end, it's all about survival. Like all the locals bragging about how many points they can get on their buck's antlers. More 'buck for your bang,' as the locals like to say at the Vermilion Iron Range."

Shawn shook his head. "Ah yes, as if the hunter or angler's ability were the sole determinant in antler point size or length of walleye. As if the fish that bites the hook or the deer that wanders by has naught to do with it."

Nate smiled. "I suppose you might have a point buried in there somewhere. But you might not want to tell the locals that."

"I will keep that in mind," said Shawn, looking towards the kitchen.

A lanky forty-something woman from the kitchen, a certain Hannah Rogers, approached their table and set a caramel roll down for each of them. They were heated up, each with a pat of butter placed haphazardly on top, starting to melt. Shawn shoved his brown briefcase out of the way to make room.

"Thanks a bunch," said Nate with a nod as he eyed up his foodstuffs from side to side with fervent anticipation.

"Don't mention it," said Hannah. "This place will pick up very soon, on account of the open house."

"We never miss it," said Nate.

"You know I only heat up the rolls for you two. But don't feel too flattered. I expect a tip just as handsome as you darlings!"

They both smiled as Hannah sashayed back to the kitchen.

Shawn's smile turned to a subtle grimace. "You know what the expressions 'icing on the cake,' the 'proof in the pudding,' and the 'cherry on top' all have in common?"

"They all involve decadent desserts?" asked Nate, pointing his thumb towards his caramel roll. "Ever notice how most of your colloquialisms involve food or money?"

"Well, if you mean to say 'just desserts,' you might not be too far off the mark," said Shawn as he unfolded his silverware from the black cloth napkin. "What all these allude to, in not so many words, is a certain 'crux,' or 'bottom line.' What our Patron Saint of Caramel just said about tips is much more than a mere jovial quip. It's a hard truth. THE hard truth. Waitresses aren't nice because they care. They have an agenda, and it's not all that hidden or subtle."

"Such blunt interpretation is often taken for cynicism," said Nate. "Which is somewhat out of character, even for you." He nodded towards the waitress, who by now was in the kitchen behind the counter. "But you gotta give her credit. She knows the situation with Emeril. And that's part of her motivation. Hell, this isn't even a restaurant. We are probably the only people she bothers to serve around here."

"Outside of her husband's divorce papers at least," said Shawn as he patted the butter down on his roll with his fork until it was melted, evenly distributed, and dripping down onto his plate. "She's a good person, I suppose. I don't mean to sound flippant or unfair."

Nate followed suit and got his pat of butter properly melted. "And there is that word again, 'fair.' Going back to your question, I would say that some folks' lives are more fair than others." Nate wiped the caramel off his hands on the nearby napkin and yanked a new one from the dispenser.

"More fair or less fair, I suppose," said Shawn, "but still not fair." He used his fork like a knife and tore a chunk off his roll, and plunked it into his mouth.

"I suppose you are right, but we gotta keep playing positive, or playing dumb, as the case may be," said Nate, as he also started in on his roll. "Do I believe all things happen for a reason? Sure I do. But that doesn't mean life is always fair. One thing I know from being a game warden is that people are still part of the food chain. Eat or be eaten and all that. A person could drive himself crazy over such rumination. Caramel rolls are more fun than karma. Just accept the way of things and move on."

"Prefer caramel to karma, eh?" asked Shawn with a slight embarrassed smile. "I think you accidentally did some alliteration or consonance. I don't remember which."

Nate ran his fingers over the stubble on his chin. "I like seeing your smile just the same."

Shawn drummed on the table. "Well, even if I did accept such a shameful state of affairs, I would do so only begrudgingly at best."

"But your situation with Emeril," continued Nate, pointing his butter knife towards Shawn, "It's—well, definitely not a blessing in disguise. It's not even a curse in disguise. It's a curse in plain view. And no, life is not always fair, no matter which way you slice it or dice it. After seeing how animals treat each other in the wild, I don't think it's meant to be either."

"At least you seem to agree that this life business isn't always a picnic or walk in the park," said Shawn, turning his gaze to Nate. "It sure beats us bickering all day."

"Well, yes, I suppose so. I take a lesson from the wild. Animals know life isn't fair. And they don't expect it to be as such. Survival requires constant vigilance. You make do with what you have and what you can muster. Fairness is not given. It's something to strive for. And even when you can't achieve it, you gotta remember that happiness doesn't require fairness as a prerequisite. Make no mistake. A person can still be happy in an unfair world. Expecting fairness, now that will set you up for failure. You gotta cheat the system. When life tells you that you are supposed to be miserable, you smile in its face as if such a gesture were an act of rebellion or the middle finger. That is the lesson I have learned from the wild. And always look behind you from time to time."

"Happiness is the best revenge," said Shawn, as he looked back at the window, noticing the horsefly fly off. "If only I could believe it. Speaking of animals, I think I lost my faith in the world in fits and spurts starting when I was seven, and then twenty-three, and then thirty-four."

"Those are some specific years," said Nate, raising a brow. "What happened, if I may ask?"

"Oh, it's nothing," muttered Shawn. "I don't know what I'm going on about. Just some random years, I guess. I guess I expect more from the world than you. I am not one to just roll over and be all complacent and sanguine about it all." Shawn looked around the cafeteria. "I find it a rather sad place. And I don't just mean this hospital."

Nate wiped a splotch of caramel off the table with his napkin. He leaned against the table, putting his elbows on it. "In my line of work, I can clearly see that animals don't play fair. Not that there are any rules, to begin with. Rams butting heads on a mountaintop is hardly the stuff of civilized conversation and olive branches. Not that your typical job interview is much different, mind you. It's just that instead of clashing horns, you clash your assets a bit differently, using work experience and academic prowess. But the competitive element is still there. It might appear a bit more civilized on the surface, but these are merely appearances."

Shawn continued. "But with human-folk, I guess our legal system is meant to level the playing field, at least a little bit. So at least there's that."

Nate nodded. "With that said, there is nothing your son could have done short of genocide to deserve cancer if that's where this conversation is headed."

"That's precisely my point, Nate," chimed Shawn. "I mean, who deserves anything? I have asked you for your viewpoint about karma. But you want to know what I think?"

Nate smiled. "Do I have a choice in the matter?"

Shawn continued. "I have decided recently that fairness, karma, or whatever you want to call it is horse hockey. What I mean to say is that if there is anything remotely related to fairness or justice in this world, as we know it, it would have to take place in the next life, sure as hell not this one. Truth be told, I am not sure if I ever believed in it."

Nate leaned back and took a deep breath. "One thing I learned about fish, geese, deer, elk, pheasants, or any other kind of wildlife, is that they are very instinctual. Geese fly south for the winter and never miss a beat. There is very little room for error or ability to stray from this beaten and well-worn path. And they have survived for thousands of years, no matter how tiny their brain. And I don't think people are really all that different. If an animal is treated badly, it will fight back. It will return all that negative energy back into the world. The same goes with people."

"Is this energy you allude to karma?"

"Well, now that I think of it, maybe the energy humans and animals put back in the world is a kind of karma, in a way. It's just simple math and science. What goes around comes around, as they say."

Shawn smiled. "So you believe in some level of fairness after all."

Nate chuckled. "Well, I didn't say that exactly. I am just referring to the basic rules of survival. You know, habitats, instincts, and the like. Parasites vs. hosts. That sort of thing."

Shawn yawned and stretched. "So you think people operate on instinct like animals?"

Nate laughed so loud the nearby couple gawked at him. "I do think people have some wiggle room to make choices, compared to our animal brethren. I know this every time I catch someone fishing or hunting without a license!"

Shawn turned the honey bottle around and pointed at the bear on the Mello Honey bottle. "Perhaps, but as a game warden, surely you are familiar with anthropomorphism."

Nate guffawed. "I said I was a game warden, not an English teacher!"

Shawn folded his hands on the table. "If overestimating human characteristics in animals is called anthropomorphism, what is it when we underestimate the animal characteristics in people?"

Nate looked at the ceiling and mumbled the question to himself to better wrap his brain around it. He looked back at Shawn. "Fair enough question, I suppose. A shame I don't have an answer, though."

"I just wonder if we sometimes expect too much from the human race," continued Shawn. "Maybe we are no better than sheep, grazing, mating, and busying ourselves during the day."

Nate nodded. "With people, the rules of competition and survival of the fittest still apply." Just then, the story on the television in the corner of the cafeteria caught Nate's eye. He pointed at the screen. "Wow, speaking of karma, take a gander at that. It's this Amrak fellow again." Shawn turned around and faced the screen. They leaned in to hear past the noise of the increasing number of patrons in the cafeteria. There was a news story about the Karma Killer Amrak. The headline at the bottom of the screen read, "The unremitting Karma Killer Amrak claims yet another victim, this time in our good old MN."

The female reporter went on to say, "Jake Olmstead, known as the 1987 'Infant Killer,' was released from prison this very morning. And as he was being transported to an unnamed Minneapolis homeless shelter by his case manager, Amrak was waiting in the parking lot, posing as a homeless vagabond. Amrak greeted them and indicated that he was the welcoming committee for the shelter, and part of his community service was to help new people get acclimated. As soon as the case manager left, an eyewitness from the shelter spotted the man chloroforming him from behind and stuffing him in a run-down rusty van. By the time the terrified witness mustered enough confidence to run out, they were squealing away from the lot. His body was spotted in the van nine hours later by a search party. Needless to say, Olmstead was not the life of the party. His body was among swarms of killer bees, with stings all over. Amrak's trademark red flag also pinned down another note. The note simply said, 'A sting for a sting.'"

They watched the entirety of the three-minute segment before turning towards each other.

"Wow, right here in our Minnesota," said Shawn.

"And regarding karma no less," said Nate, facing him. "And what a tasteless journalist, cracking jokes at a time like that."

Shawn shook his head as if disappointed and ashamed of what the world has come to. "Makes you wonder if karma itself turned on that damn TV."

"Now, don't get all superstitious on me," said Nate. "You seem jumpy the way it is today—one might think you had just seen a ghost."

"Well, haven't I? Amrak is a rather odious fellow, to be sure. Shame that he's such a punitive vigilante, caring more about punishment than reward."

Nate shook his head. "Well, I wouldn't hold your breath that this Amrak fellow will work in any soup kitchens anytime soon."

"Well, every good little demagogue knows how to prey on the emotions of his constituency," said Shawn. "And the best creeps know how not to look suspicious while doing so."

"Well, at least there is a hefty reward for finding the cretin," said Nate. "A shame it's not 'dead or alive.'"

"A reward?" asked Shawn, raising his eyebrows. "I didn't know that."

"If I didn't know better, I'd say you seem almost interested," said Nate. "Taking up bounty hunting now? Finding old coins wearing thin? I'm afraid I can't give you a hunting license or bag limit for bounty hunting."

"Nah, not interested," mumbled Shawn with a faint smile, shifting his gaze to the edge of the table. "I just found it curious, is all."

By now, the place was filled with the hustle and/or bustle of people, a conglomeration of local and non-local. There were peals of laughter in the air, and it was becoming increasingly more difficult to maintain a conversation.

Nate checked his Seiko SKX007 diving watch. "Well, maybe we should go somewhere and do something more relaxing and, well, fun."

Shawn remained silent, checking the length of his stubble in the napkin dispenser. "Done shining the old philosopher's stone in this morbid cafeteria so soon? What do you have in mind?"

"Well, we could watch one of your boring documentaries on coin collecting," said Nate. "I can bring some beer to make it more tolerable for me."

Shawn checked his gold-plated gear-operated pocket watch. "Sounds like a plan."

As they were preparing to leave, Hannah spotted them and rushed over. "Now, you boys be careful, and come back again."

"Will do," said Nate. "Good luck with the open house."

Shawn nodded in her general direction as he got up and gathered his briefcase.

By the time Shawn drove his 2014 Ford Fusion back to his 1964 brown rambler, it was just past 11:15 am. Nate arrived fifteen minutes later in his 2017 Kia Sorento with a case of Grain Belt in tow. Shawn let him in, and Nate took his boots off and left them in the entryway. The house was tidy, and this room at least fairly formal, as evidenced by several pieces of antique furniture, including a Bergere chair, Ashley leather davenport, Wentz coffee table, and a chaise lounge.

Adorning the wooden walls were various framed coins, historical knick-knacks, and monetary artifacts. In the corner near the television was also a large windowed China cupboard, showcasing all manner of collectible coins, paper bills, and artifacts made from precious metals. Perhaps most notable was a framed thousand-dollar bill from 1932 in the living room depicting President Cleveland.

The rest of the house was mostly tidy and clean but not as meticulously arranged or eloquent as the living room. After all, our Shawn spent the lion's share of his time in the latter.

Shawn had already closed (and locked) the door to where he kept his daily journals and plushy friends before Nate came with his refreshments, a ritual he had grown accustomed to on those rare days when company would come over. He had also already put on the third episode of season 1 of his favorite reality show "Pedal to the Metal," a show about two rowdy college-aged guys and a girl armed with metal detectors and cheap wine, and how they would sneak onto people's private property and see what they could "dig up" in the more literal sense of the word. Episode one was entitled "Dredging Up the Past." He also had a cheese, cracker, and cold meat tray on the coffee table to count as lunch, despite having their danishes at the "Food for Thought" cafeteria earlier.

"I just can't get enough of this program," said Shawn as they both entered the living room. Shawn sunk into the davenport as Nate handed him a cold one. He took one for himself and set the rest on the coffee table, along with his cell phone. Nate let out a heavy sigh as he hunkered down into the Bergere chair.

"Let's have a look-see," said Nate, watching the program.

"I have seen the entire series multiple times," said Shawn as he took a drink. "Although it's probably not your usual cup of Long Island iced tea."

"Yes, well, I think they are starting to run out of ideas for reality TV," said Nate. "They will probably do a reality show on the life of reality show producers before you know it. But I have seen an episode or two of this before, mostly just to see what is so exciting about coin collecting—you know, to understand you a bit better."

"Thanks, I think!"

Nate continued. "And while the subject matter may not entice me so much, these guys are absolutely bonkers."

They watched the rest of the episode, hardly saying a solitary word, partly due to the fact that they were tired after their meal at the hospital. By the time the episode was over, they had both drunk their first bottle.

"Let's let the next episode play," said Nate. "I want to see if they find actual bullet casings from the Civil War." The next episode, "Bullet Point," played on.

"That works for me," said Shawn, as the opening theme song started to roll for the next episode. "But I'm afraid that when you hear my big secret, you may not want to hang out with me ever again."

Nate reached towards the coffee table and grabbed the remote. He fished around for the pause button. "And what secret is that? There are good secrets and bad secrets, you know. Buried treasure vs. finding out that I'm actually adopted. In all seriousness, I had a feeling you were keeping something from me ever since the hospital."

"Let's just suffice it to say that my question about fairness back at the *Food for Thought* was slightly rhetorical. Yes, I wanted your opinion. That much is true, but I'm afraid my mind had already been made up before I even asked the question."

Nate gave up looking for the pause button and set down the remote back on the coffee table, allowing the episode to continue. He reached over and took another beer from the cardboard carrier and twisted the cap with the bottom of his fleece jacket. "I must admit you are making me a tad bit worried with this particular line of conversation. I would probably sit down for this if I wasn't already sitting. You are okay and everything, right?"

"I met with the doctor just shy of three hours ago," said Shawn. "Before we even had our rolls."

"Oh, geez," said Nate, scratching his neck as if he had an itch. "It's some more bad news, isn't it?"

"I guess you could say that," said Shawn as he uprooted himself from the sofa to fetch another Grain Belt. He sat back down with a sigh. "But I suppose it depends on who you ask. Even Emeril himself might consider it good news, considering how much pain he had been in as of late."

"Okay, now that sounds a bit vague," said Nate, taking a long drink.

Shawn looked flat and apathetic. "What I mean to say, in not so many words, is that Emeril has already died."

"What the hell?" asked Nate, a small gruffness in his voice. "So why didn't you tell me at *Food for Thought*? Some damn midwest macho pride thing?"

Shawn sighed. "No, no, nothing like that. You know how it is, these kinds of conversations just make both parties feel awkward, and people don't know how they are supposed to act or what they are supposed to say. Three days ago, the doctors told me he would not come out of his coma, and he would die very soon. And just this morning, he died. It is what it is. I found out as soon as I got to the hospital."

"Say no more," said Nate, leaving his chair to sit next to Shawn on the davenport. He slapped Shawn's knee a couple of times. "How people take it is not for you to worry about it. That's everyone else's problem. And people who really care don't need to worry about what to say because they are already worried and saying what needs to be said. And I am here for you. Is there anything I can do in this dire time of need? I may not know what to say, but maybe you know what I can do. And actions speak louder than words."

"I appreciate the sentiment. I really do," said Shawn with tenderness in his voice. Just then, he proceeded to rub his neck. As he did, Nate noticed some redness on the upper half.

"What, pray tell, is wrong with your neck?" asked Nate.

"Ah, nothing really," returned Shawn, lurching back and positioning his sweater in an attempt to cover the wound. "I slept wrong last night. Or just getting older, I guess. The old parts not working like they should."

Nate pulled the collar of Shawn's sweater so he could get a better look. Shawn acquiesced and didn't put up a fight.

Nate's volume increased. "What the hell, did you try hanging yourself or something, you asshole?"

Shawn faced him. "I'm assuming you mean 'asshole' in the nicest sense of the word."

Nate took a deep breath. "Please don't mistake my anger for a lack of compassion. Quite the contrary, if you must know. It's just that I would be quite pissed if you offed yourself. And not just for your sake. But for mine. But why in God's name didn't you just tell me?"

"Oh, I don't know," said Shawn as he made a sweeping motion with his hand, "You know how it is. I didn't want to burden anyone with my troubles, I suppose. I know that's a trite answer. But there it is. It was two days ago. I thought my visible wounds would have healed over some by now. I guess I was wrong."

Nate sighed. "So what stopped you, if I may ask? You know, from finishing the job? You were never one to leave a project half-finished."

"Well, pain for one," said Shawn. "The chair was still there as I was dangling, and I managed to stand back on it and change my mind. Simple as that."

"Say no more. I just thank God you didn't kick the chair over. Or I would probably be at your funeral right about now."

"It was an old park bench, if you must know, not a chair," said Shawn. He left the sofa to sit on the Bergere chair. "Hard to tip something like that over."

Nate let out a chuckle. "My mistake, you pedantic fool! You gonna be okay now? Maybe I better stay with you for the night."

"It's okay," said Shawn, his eyes becoming moist. "Really. Just this morning, I discovered something that took the suicide ideation right out of me."

"I'm all ears, friend," said Nate, getting off the sofa to fetch a church key in Shawn's kitchen drawer. "And this time, you better spill your guts. And I don't mean hara kiri or seppuku."

Nate fished around in the drawer, making quite a bit of racket in the process. He resumed his seat on the sofa and opened up his beer.

Shawn took a breath as if preparing for a speech. "To clarify, I noticed something peculiar this morning, but I actually received the bill itself when I took out some money from Bremer Bank, some three months ago now. I am not sure why I hung onto it—these two-dollar bills are not all that rare, to begin with. But just this morning, I thought I noticed a watermark on it as I was organizing my coin collection. I thought it was counterfeit, as two-dollar bills lack the UV security threads or color-shifting ink of five-dollar bills or higher. But everyone knows two-dollar bills don't have watermarks. And it clearly wasn't done with cylinder mold or dandy roll."

Nate glared at Shawn. "Everyone knows that? Are you delusional? Not everyone is a coin collector, you know!"

Shawn continued as if Nate had not said a word. "But when I finally put my glasses on, it turned out it's just a slightly faded out stamp someone put on the bill."

"Your imagination got the best of you once again, I see,"

said Nate. "I keep telling you about that little problem of yours. The world isn't nearly as exciting as you would like it to be."

"Well, I was part of the counterfeiter's club in college," said Shawn.

"I still think that sounds like a right nefarious operation," said Nate, gazing at the Surgeon General Warning on his bottle. "Hard to picture you of all people into that."

"Oh shush, you know it was just a hobby, to see how closely we could do it," said Shawn. "Just a bit of harmless fun. Like the folks that try to create phony UFO sightings. Our money club only disbanded after that one guy actually tried to spend his counterfeit money to get out of a money jam."

"Well, serves him right," said Nate. "Why don't you just let me see it already?"

Shawn wiped the residual moisture from his eyes with his sleeve and fetched his briefcase that he had placed on the armrest of the davenport. After some rifling, he pulled out the two-dollar bill. He handed it to Nate.

Nate took it with his right hand and put his glasses on with his left.

"Notice anything odd about it?" asked Shawn. He hovered over Nate's shoulder to get a closer look.

"I must admit, I haven't seen one of these in quite some time," said Nate as he studied it closely. "Even I know that these are not all that rare. What am I supposed to be seeing here? You are the coin collector. Maybe you should just tell me."

Shawn pointed at the QR code just up and to the left of the face portrait of Thomas Jefferson.

Nate got up and walked to the window to get more light. He held it up against the windowpane. "Yes, I can see something here. It just looks a bit faded out."

Shawn went to the window. He stood next to Nate and peered over his shoulder. "At first, I didn't know what that mark was. But this morning, before I went to the hospital, I took the bill to the bank, and the woman at the counter said it was a QR code. I didn't know what that was, so she used her Smartphone and scanned it for me. She revealed a secret message. She was about to put her phone away, but something told me to read it, so I insisted that I borrow her phone. She was a bit impatient, but I didn't give the phone back until I had read every word. And I also insisted on getting my bill back."

Nate snapped his fingers towards the phone, gesturing for Shawn to fetch it for him. "Funny that someone would put one on money, though. Probably just a punk kid with computer skills."

Shawn snatched the phone almost before Nate could finish the sentence and thrust it into Nate's left hand. Shawn continued to peer over his shoulder.

Nate held the bill with one hand and proceeded to open his QR scanner app on his phone. "You may know currency, but your tech skills are hardly savvy."

"Well, thanks, I think," said Shawn.

"What are friends for?" said Nate, pausing for a moment. "You gotta get with the times, buddy," said Nate, getting back to the task at hand. He opened his app and aimed the lens over the QR code, and adjusted it this way and that, trying to grab a reading from the rather faint and dim QR label.

"I just recently learned how to text message," said Shawn. "Give me a break."

Nate struggled to get a reading, so he moved the phone closer to the QR label. "That's no excuse. Cowboys have been text messaging with the telegraph before it was cool, way back in the 1800s. Although I don't think they had emojis or gifs."

Shawn crept in for a closer look. He put his hand on Nate's shoulder and peered at the screen. Even though he had already read the message, he was excited to see Nate's reaction.

"Hold your horses," said Nate, just as he locked onto a reading. Nate held the phone as still as he could, like an angler waiting for the perfect time to pull the line. After about twenty seconds, the scan brought up a secret message with very strange letterhead. The letterhead showed what appeared to be a dollar sign composed of three snakes. One snake with two heads was made into an "S" shape. There were two vertical snakes, each with two tails, intersecting with the other snake to finish the dollar sign.

"A creepy letterhead," said Nate, as they both took their place on the sofa.

"Well?" asked Shawn, rubbing his hands together.

Nate adjusted his glasses and took a deep breath. "Complete with a hidden message."

_ ˙

CHAPTER 3
SURVIVAL OF THE FITTEST

Setting: Anodyne Research Labs (affixed to Anodyne Hospital),
Winnipeg, Canada
Time: June 4, 2019
Main characters: Mark Anderson and Darl Tanner

April 17, 2019 (Observation): It goes without saying that
catastrophes and disasters disrupt many people's lives. And
it always goes without saying that criminal acts wreak havoc
in communities. This much is obvious. But what about how
seemingly innocuous events can also play out in disaster? I can
only think of the Butterfly Effect, where even seemingly small
decisions, including complacency, can have a very significant
impact on the framework of the world. I have taken to calling these
small events that have major consequences "key events." And
such key events need not be large events in and of themselves.
It is the outcomes of these events that are most important. These
are the incidents that are popular with stories of time travel, as
changing the course of them can save many lives. And this is why
the idea of an "innocent bystander" is nothing short of a myth.
Bystanders are guilty of complacency. Each one of us has the
potential to save many people from death. It is not only crimes
that take lives. Sometimes it is not what we do, but rather what
we don't do, that plays a hand in human tragedy. As they say, if
you are not part of the solution, you are part of the problem. And
while I hesitate to castigate the person that fails to call off school
during a blizzard as a murderer, the tragedy and outcome can be
essentially the same if a person should die in the carnage of the
blizzard's wake.

April 17, 2019 (Fear experiment): I did some more Parkour today. Well, not exactly. But I did another dangerous stunt to prime my fear response. One of the maintenance men at the Richardson Building let me onto the roof for a small bribe of fifty dollars. Of course, I didn't tell him what I had planned. He thought I was doing an aerial sketch of the Winnipeg skyline. But the truth is, right now, at this very moment, as I am writing this very note, I am sitting on the edge of the skyscraper! But that is only half of it. Just ten minutes ago, I was dangling off the side of the building like Wu Yongnin. And I was wearing my invention, "Project Madcap," the entire time, measuring the objective amount of fear in my body as if merely taking my temperature. And when I checked the reading, the high numbers actually seemed to match with my subjective feeling, some of the most gut-wrenching terror I have ever felt! Needless to say, my invention appears to be working splendidly. Call it my way of commemorating the fiftieth-year anniversary of the building.

April 17, 2019 (License Plate Synchronicity" experiment). I wasn't planning on doing any license plate experiments today. But I kind of fell into one. I was into the comic book and game shop and had a bout of deja vu coupled with an intrusive thought that I would see something dire. Lo and behold, the very next license plate I saw had the number 248, the number of my apartment. What does this mean? Is it a portent? Coincidence? Foresight? Did I affect the universe? Or did the universe affect me? What does it mean? Best not take any chances. I didn't even enter the shop. Fuck. And to think they had a sale on Gloomhaven!

----------------------*From Mark's Journal of Existential Musings, April 17, 2019*

The tall and gangly forty-three-year-old Mark Anderson lumbered his way through the heavy metal doors of Anodyne Research Institute, a highly coveted research facility in Winnipeg, Canada. It was adjoined to the Anodyne Hospital. It was within these walls where the men and women of the mortuary sciences took fresh and intact cadavers, just after they flatlined and were declared dead, from the hospital, to see if they could re-animate any of them. This was a not so far-fetched proposition, given that they were successful on two occasions, albeit both subjects flatlined soon after resuscitation.

Mark was wearing a not-so-usual suit and tie, tied in a Windsor knot. His black Oxfords had a sheen and shine from only being worn to the scant few funerals he had attended over the course of his years.

Once inside, he went to the receptionist station in the center of the large room. The entire enclosure was completely encased by glass windows. There were two cupid fountains and non-native palm trees, planted in large engraved wooden brown pots, scattered in random spots around the shiny marble floor.

Mark faced the twenty-something young lady, out of breath from the burning and churning feelings of trepidation lingering in his gut. After all, this was the day of his job interview.

"Are you okay, dear?" asked the woman, wearing a fleece vest emblazoned with the "Anodyne Research" patch, depicting a snow owl in flight holding a bundle of wheat in its talons. The splashing sound of the fountains made it difficult to hear what she said.

Mark took some deep breaths. "I sure hope so. I am here for the interview."

"Oh yes, Darl is expecting you." She pointed up the curvy stairwell. "Just go upstairs and to door 247."

Mark took another deep breath for the road and mustered some confidence by imagining he was a food inspector entering an eatery. This thought made him feel more in charge. He wasn't working for Darl. Darl was working for him!

It didn't take long for Mark to stumble his way to office 247. He raised his hand and stopped just before knocking. With a soft and rhythmic tap, he knocked four times on the heavy oak door with the consistent rhythm of a metronome. It was so soft that nobody heard or answered.

Just as Mark raised his hand to try again, an older man with a scruffy beard, in his early fifties, barged out, almost shoulder checking Mark. Mark looked at his fist and brought his arm back down to his side.

"Excuse me, young man, I am so sorry!" said the bearded man, putting his hand on Mark's shoulder.

"It's all good," said Mark. "No worries."

"Can I help you?" asked the bearded man.

"I am looking for Mr. Darl."

"Come in!" said the man. "You came to the right place! Mr. Darl is right inside. You go on in there and give him a hard time." He pointed inside the door. With that, the man left towards the stairs.

As Mark entered, he was greeted by three seated people, Darl behind his desk. Mark noted he must have been in his early sixties, and he took that as further evidence that he was undoubtedly quite seasoned in his adventures concerning life, liberty, and the pursuits of happiness.

Is this an interview or an interrogation? he asked himself as he noticed all three of them holding clipboards. *Let's just hope the Hawthorne effect works in my favor.*

"Have a seat," said the thirty-something woman as she nodded towards the brown leather chair.

Mark did as he was told.

Mark looked around. The room screamed of "wood," with oaken desk, chairs, and cabinets. Mark couldn't help but wonder why there was a china cupboard filled with china and what purpose it could possibly serve, other than utter ostentatious posturing. There were several ivory elephants poised in different poses on the desk.

"We each have a copy of your resume," said Darl, looking at each of his cohorts in turn. "And we all agree it is most impressive." The others nodded in agreement. "Usually, we like to have folks with masters degrees or higher. But in my book, having three separate bachelor degrees is just as impressive."

"Especially in three fields such as psychology, philosophy, and mortuary science," said the youngest of the three, a gentleman on the right of the woman, wearing the same fleece vest as the receptionist downstairs. "And to think that you had your Capstone experience at the well-renowned mortuary in Vancouver. Don't they actually do research there also, with the cadavers and such?"

"Yes," said Mark. "Nothing like here, though. They just study things like how long it takes certain body parts to decay compared to others. Nothing like Frankenstein or anything. But I still enjoyed it very much."

"Don't sell yourself short, young man," said Darl. "Very few mortuaries do any kind of research." Darl stared at the woman. "Still, in our line of work, the term 'human resources' takes on a whole new meaning, doesn't it, Polly?" All three of them laughed.

"Indeed," said Mark, chuckling while he fiddled and fidgeted with the edge of the chair.

"You are so bad with introductions," said the woman, looking at Darl. "Don't you think we should let our Mark here know who we all are?"

"Yes, yes," said Darl, drumming his fingers on his knees. "I suppose you are right as rain. Still, you gotta admire any conversation where Frankenstein comes up before introductions," added Darl. "He gets points for that." He looked at Mark. "Okay, Mr. Mark, I am Darl Jacobs."

"And I am Polly Sanderson from HR," said the forty-something woman.

"And last but not least, I am Douglas Richards," said the young man, who appeared to be in his early twenties.

"I noticed you included a section on your resume about your personality," said Polly. "That is rather unusual."

Mark nodded. "One of my professors once told me that job interviews are essentially personality tests since you already know our resumes before we get here. What we are doing now is basically a judgment of character."

"A man that gets to the point, addresses the proverbial elephant in the room, and doesn't mince words. I like that," said Darl.

"In addition to these lovely elephants," said Mark, pointing towards the ivory elephants on Darl's desk.

"Right as rain," said Darl as the three of them smiled.

Polly squinted and gazed closely at her copy of the resume before looking up at Mark. "I see here that you cite something called the *OCEAN Model of Personality*. And it appears you do not hesitate to share some of your quirks and eccentricities."

"Honest to a fault, I'm afraid," said Mark. "But honesty is the best policy, eh?"

"I, for one, find it refreshing," exclaimed Darl. "Most job applicants are veritable con artists, lying through their teeth, crossing their fingers, and wearing their most out-of-character clothes."

"I must say that I find that refreshing to hear," said Mark, followed by a play-acted deep sigh as he made an exaggerated motion of wiping sweat off his brow.

"It also suggests that you do not have the proclivity to bite the hand that feeds you," said Polly, eyeing up Darl and Douglas. "That's the kind of respect for the employer that is missing in this day and age."

"Care to elaborate regarding the neuroticism?" asked Douglas. "I am not trying to pry. I just want to know if there is anything we can do to help."

"Full transparency, that's what I like to say," said Mark. "You know how in statistics you choose a confidence interval, as in how much risk you are willing to take so that your results are not due to chance, but rather the treatment effect itself?"

"Absolutely," said Darl. "This is a research firm, after all. We would be quite remiss if we were insufficient in such knowledge." Polly and Douglas nodded in agreement.

"Okay, well, I kinda feel that way in my everyday life," continued Mark. "Unless I feel 95% confident about something, I tend to stew, ruminate, and otherwise obsess on all manner of things, even trivial. But rest assured, it doesn't affect my productivity. Only my personal life. Just a nervous disposition, you know. I was told by my psychiatrist that I had a rather serious case of apophenia."

"No worries," said Darl. "We are just naturally curious, you know."

"Naturally," said Mark. "Regarding your penchant for admiring laying it out all out on the table, I hope you didn't find my last page of the resume particularly off-putting."

Polly cleared her throat and looked up. "I must say, in all my years working here, this is the first resume I have ever seen where the applicant dedicated some room to their legal blemishes and blunders." She sniffed the paper with an audible sniff. "And all written with confidence on scented Southworth paper, no less."

"Well, I figured with all the dead bodies around here, it might be nice to use scented paper," said Mark.

"I like your morbid sense of humor," said Darl, followed by a belly laugh.

"Kind of refreshing, literally, in a world where HR departments seem to look down on using scented resume paper," said Polly. "I am not a fan of sending thank you notes, though. I find them manipulative."

"I will keep that in mind," said Mark. "When you think about it, you are not really saying 'thank you' so much as 'please,' as in 'Please give me this job!'"

"I can already tell I like this guy," said Polly, looking at Darl.

Darl perused Mark's legal problems on the final page with a careful eye. "Yes, you pretty much laid everything out there." Darl read the following, all identified with bullet points: public urination, public intoxication, and one DUI, under the heading "Legal Blemishes."

Mark smiled. "Well, I could have added 'potty trained' to my credentials, but I figured that would just be overkill."

All three of the members of the "welcoming committee" laughed once again as they looked at each other.

"Small potatoes compared to the skeletons we dig up on some of our folks — these are hardly deal-breakers," said Polly.

"Still, we would like to be reassured that you have since learned your lesson."

"Absolutely," said Mark frantically. "Those are from like five years ago."

"And you don't mind doing grant work?" asked Darl. "Or grunt work, as we like to say around here?"

"Not at all," said Mark. "I come from the camp that says that having a job is a privilege, something to be grateful for. After all, it's our meal ticket by the end of the day. Mustn't bite the hand that feeds you, eh?"

"Not your typical flippant attitude," said Darl. "A rare thing in our era of entitlement. You have no idea how many people march in here and make it seem like we work for them, not the other way around."

"Humility is a virtue," said Mark, posing with his nose up in the air.

"One last thing," said Darl, looking at his Bulova Octava watch. "Under 'Accomplishments', you listed that you were working on a groundbreaking invention of sorts. What's that all about? Care to elaborate? I mean, that narrows it down to anything between the atomic bomb and the McCormick Reaper."

Mark cleared his throat. "Well, you know how the great scientists of old predicted the existence of cells and atoms before we had the technology of microscopes to view them?"

"Well, sure," said Darl, as he looked at each of his colleagues. "What about it?"

"Well, we assume that emotions exist, but nobody has ever actually seen them," said Mark.

"What do you mean?" asked the youngest. "I see them every time my wife has her period!"

Polly laughed with some hesitation. "Come now, Douglas, that's hardly appropriate for a job interview—or ever for that matter!"

Doug smiled. "I couldn't resist. Many apologies, Polly."

Mark continued. "But Doug is talking about behaviors. Behaviors are the aftermath of emotions. What I am talking about is more akin to being able to record raw emotion as raw data. The intangible feelings that you can't see, touch, or feel."

"That's most fascinating," said the woman. "But I'm afraid unless it has something to do with working here, it probably won't do much good other than make for good convo around the water fountain."

"Come now, Polly," said Darl, making a gesture for her to keep mum. "I was the one that brought it up. I, for one, find it most fascinating. And it shows a steadfast dedication to just the kind of scientific rigor we want to see around here."

"Or rigor mortis, as the case may be," added Mark.

Darl guffawed as he pointed at Mark. "See, Polly and Douglas? This guy will fit right in."

Darl stood up, and Mark followed suit. The two of them walked towards the door. As Darl opened the door, he gave Mark a very firm handshake. "We will be in touch."

"We are touching right now," said Mark, looking at their handshake.

"A wise guy in more ways than one," said Darl with a smile. "Thanks again, Mark. You will hear from us within two days."

Mark went home and went straight to bed. And not one day later, Mark's cell phone buzzed, and his "The Prisoner" theme song ring tone played. Mark let it go for a few seconds so as not to seem too eager. He then snapped up the phone and put it to his ear.

"Is this Mark?" asked the voice. Mark couldn't recognize it, and it didn't sound like anyone from the facility, including the receptionist.

"Yes," said Mark with a forced calmness.

"While your resume and interview were both most impressive, I regret to inform you that you did not get the position at this time. But we will keep your information on file, as you made the top of the list."

"I understand," said Mark. "And thanks for considering me."

"We will call you if anything comes up," said the gentleman with a sympathetic tone.

Mark slowly put his finger over the red button and hung up the phone. With a slow and deliberate gait, he went to his computer and proceeded to watch some Death Hag videos in the comfort of his messy but spacious bedroom.

After his moment of distraction, and at the end of the day, he wrote in his "Journal of Existential Musings." He dated the page 6/4/2019. He then drew a large Venn Diagram on the page, with three overlapping non-concentric circles. On each circle, he wrote: Psychology, Philosophy, and Mortuary Science. In the shared area in the center, he wrote terror management theory, evolutionary psychology, primordial matters, and biology. After a moment of hesitation and tapping the back of the pen against his chin three times, he also scribbled the words "Project Madcap" slanted across all three circles. And then he chucked the notebook against the wall.

..

CHAPTER 4
STURM AND DRANG

Date: May 11, 2019, 1:30 PM
Location: Shawn's rambler

As Nate read the secret message, Shawn was also reading his body language.

To whom it may concern,

I hope this letter finds you well. The reason you are reading this is because I went through the trouble of discovery that often accompanies one's disgust with the unfairness that is life. Why a two-dollar bill? For most, the rarity would not be sufficiently suitable to justify any manner of safekeeping, lest you be a patron of the treasury or have a niche penchant of rare coinage. They are just rare enough to garner a closer scrutiny but not so rare that it would be taken out of circulation. Either way, you are reading this. And that is enough. So please entertain me with an audience in which to elucidate. This is my reverie, bared to the world.

For most of my life, I expected fairness in the world. And not surprisingly, I saw fairness all around me. Persons committing crimes would pay in full for what they did. And the blessings and burdens of an entire generation could be counted and tallied with a steadfast alacrity behind the scenes of the world's great curtain. Starving artists starved only because their craft was superfluous and unnecessary. And people were only homeless because they didn't want or choose to work. People got what they deserved and deserved what they got. Why did the Titanic sink? It must have been punishment for all the wealthy on board. And even when things didn't make sense, I assumed the universe must have had a good reason, even with incidents such as the Radium Girl, Great Plague, Challenger, Chernobyl, the Mataafa storm of 1905, the Escape Room Fire Tragedy, Pompei, and the tragic death of Barbara Paplior. Or the scores of natural disasters of all shapes and sizes.

In my mind, it was all the stuff of cosmic calculation, a patchwork of planned and intentional repercussions in a myriad system of cosmic checks and balances. And even when the punishment didn't seem to befit the crime, I held on to faith that all things happened for a reason, in the grander scheme of things.

And realizations such as these only solidified my steadfast belief in fairness and accountability, or dare I say, karma. And so my world made sense, the existential furniture in my mind arranged neatly, in a row and all in place, as the world should be. And life really did feel like a modest series of ups and downs, good days and bad days, balancing out in the end, as things are and ought to be.

When you really think about it, life, in its deconstructed bits and pieces, is about "degrees of freedom." Like mahjongg solitaire, there is a balance of luck and skill. And your options for mobility are limited by certain constraints, such as your health, financial reserve, nepotism, laws of nature, one's networking abilities, and the confines of friction and mortality itself.

I have been touched by tragedy. My dad died when I was two. And my dear mommy Tessa died just a month ago at the hands of a killer with the epithet of Amrak. My house burned to the ground, leaving only my PT Cruiser sitting in the driveway unscathed. What did I do to deserve such a dire fate?

The tragedy in my life allowed me to view the karma police differently. No longer were they about fairness. And their punishments did not befit the crime. They were a blight and destined to make my life, and many other lives, miserable. It was the karma police that killed my mother and father. The very universe was out to get me.

Long have I wondered about and considered the nature of our world. Of all the billions that have come and gone, there is not a single one who has survived death. And this stark and wretched truth weighs on me nightly. It is a macabre realization that provides little solace, and yet I cannot help but wrack my brain with a morose intellect. There is hardly a morning that goes by where I do not at least hesitate, if only for a moment, and allow dark thoughts to swell through my mind like a passing cloud regarding the manner in which I will die. Will it be infirmity? Murder? Natural disaster? Old age? Plucked from a crowd? Alone in bed? Will it be painful? Unexpected? An audience of onlookers and last rites? And while old age may be a solid predictor of one's waning mortality, it is far from sufficient, as a person can die at any age, as the lambs on their graves can attest. Even these very tombstones and effigies cannot withstand the elements, as they weather and wear with the passing years. And when they finally go, even the memories and stories die with them, as even these monuments and monikers no longer serve their purpose.

And even those who live relatively calm lives, they still have many burdens to bear. How many billions have walked this very earth, only to lose all manner of loved ones, friends, family, or acquaintances? How many stories have been told, how many people have been missed? Pick a random date—how about February 23, 1649. Every person trudging along in the world had a motivation, something driving their lives.

And what does it all mean? Such a trite question. Even asking it at this very moment feels like a waste of time. But let us ask it again, as if for the first time! Let us gaze at the ineffable universe, the very abyss, as a stranger in a strange land looking into the vastness of an endless forest. What is this place? What is life? I beseech you, and entreat onto thee, what the hell is this place? I am but a reformer, and how I long for a better and reformed world, a reformed world where we can see the decedents rise from the tomb, once again.

But it is not just fear that many of us hold, but a wistful and plaintive longing embedded in a deep-rooted nostalgia. Every time a person dies, a lifetime of memory, and one person's version of history, dissipates like morning dew. The rise and fall of civilizations. Where do all the forgotten memories go? And will they ever be told again? And if only one person remembers, that memory is not dead but very much alive. If a person falls and there is nobody left to remember him, did this person exist at all?

And then there is education. People are born. They become educated, acquiring the vast knowledge bases of reading, writing, and arithmetic. History. Technology. The arts and crafts. The sciences. But even renaissance men die. And what becomes of their knowledge? Their brains rot away and are staved to waste, and they are reduced to simpletons, suddenly having less education than a walking stick, an illiterate corpse, a rag doll. But then their kin must carry the torch! To learn all of it over again. But how much of history is accurate after it has been filtered and re-filtered over and over again?

And death. Billions of decedents. Human and animal alike. And who should maintain the lion's share of culpability of such oblivion, the one who kinetically pulls the trigger or the one who invented the concept of death in the first place? We are moribund the day we are born, as we age but a little, day by day, with little clocks poised above our heads, little time-bombs attached, with unknown dates of detonation.

People are immured to existence. They do not consent to being born. Nor do they (usually) consent to death and oblivion. Life and death are the nature of the beast that is existence. And while beauty is in the eye of the beholder, so too is ugliness. And while some may cherish the earth-tone hues of the trees in Autumn's bitter chill, we mustn't forget that this is the color of death. It is the color of a leaf's dying days.

And then there is "love." People match and mate, and the human race goes on. People humor a certain notion that the objects of their amorous affections are somehow "meant to be," dropped from the very heavens like sweet ambrosia, as if the stuff of serendipity, kismet, and all manner of Divine Providence. But what if you could measure and ascertain, from the billions of those who have walked these soils, only to discover that one's true "soul mate" might actually have been from a different place or time. What if Person A in Japan in the year 1496 is the soul mate to Person B in Massachusetts in 1877? Surely proximity and pragmatic factors play a part. And never will I understand how humans can drivel on and on about the "miracle of life," jutting out their baby pictures to the masses, as if such offspring were dropped from the very heavens by an entourage of angels or storks, and in the very same breath, their forked tongues will denounce, decry, and impugn the act of copulation that produced such "little miracles" in the first place.

My counselor in group talked about the Gambler's Fallacy and the just world hypothesis. And while they insisted that these were biases, or "cognitive distortions," as she called them, it is my contention that these are not necessarily irrational but rather adaptive. Both of these "biases" seem to point towards an inherent belief in fairness and karma and that somewhere under the tumultuous turmoil that is life, there exists an expectation for a fair world, something to believe in. But the world is but a room viewed only through a keyhole. Perhaps that is what Goethe meant when he compared life to an old-fashioned raree show.

The despondent truth, as I have discovered, is that good things do happen to bad people, and bad things do happen to good people. Many in this world believe what they want to believe. And sadly, this wistful longing can blur one's vision based on nothing but a fool's hope. Like lightning rods, there are some in this world who carry the onus of bad luck. I have taken to calling people like us "chaos magnets." We don't find trouble. Trouble finds us. One dilemma after another, until others accuse us of "wanting it this way" or that we somehow "crave" or "deserve" such drama and misfortune in our lives. And yet, even as I sit down and pen this missive, I can't help but wonder if in a previous life I must have done some very grave things indeed.

Why are some people beautiful while others can't find a mate to save their lives? Why are some wealthy and others in abject poverty? Some are free, and others in jail? Why is one twin sometimes rewarded while the other punished, living completely different trajectories? The list goes on and on.

One thing I have come to know, from my very own musings and misgivings, however anecdotal, is that all the motivations of the world can be reduced to avoiding pain and seeking pleasure. After all, such is the pleasure principle. And if there exists this life force called "karma," how can it possibly be fair? It is my contention that they are far from solicitous.

As a reformer, I often find myself feeling an ominous compassion fatigue, a sort of Weltschmerz, feeling the world's pain and making it my own. It is nothing short of an insidious war of attrition, waged on my very conscience.

The line that hangs between hedonism and abnegation is a mighty fine one indeed. Some behaviors produce immediate and indolent gratification, while other "random acts of kindness" are merely sagacious investments to bear future fruit. And while the latter may require an element of impulse control, both are every bit as self-serving, and neither is the stuff of spartan living. Even so-called "pious acts" are rife with hidden agendas.

I do not pretend to be reticent. I have a deep need to know why things happen the way they do. If whoever is reading this message shares my ardor and curiosity, please consider my invitation to join me in this endeavor. And let us make an accord to get to the bottom of the sheer absurdity of existence, like a film or play that dares to break the fourth wall. It is time to expose the Man Behind the Curtain!

And if there is no karma or entourage of angels watching behind the scenes, then we as people must take the mantle and create fairness ourselves. My therapist claims that expecting fairness in our cold world is a cognitive distortion, a delusion of sorts. As a natural-born reformer, and to the chagrin of my therapists, I impugn and reject this notion wholeheartedly. I am not the one that is pathological. It is they!

And much like the grim reaper has put a personified face to the existential concept of death itself, or Cupid and his arrows has put a face to one's amorous affections, I have claimed certain liberties to do the same with the karma police. I have taken to calling him "Jack." Like a Jack in the Box, existential events, whether painful or pleasurable, will jump out at you when you are most unawares. Could be a promotion. Could be a death in the family. A blessing or a curse. Or any event in between. Only Jack can think outside the box or see beyond the big picture. Only he knows when and where the unknown will come knocking on your door like an uninvited guest. The existential postman could arrive with a singing telegram from a love-struck paramour. Or the message may be the one that alerts you that your soldiering son has just fallen in battle. Jack is an unpredictable and austere sort indeed. But one question remains. If Jack is the incarnate harbinger of karma, then who is it that turns the crank? And who do the gods answer to?

Karma alone will play a hand in who reads this memo. The only prerequisite, as I can tell, is that you must be at your wit's end. And you must believe in your heart of hearts that if things were up to you, and left in your hands, and to your own devices, you would create a more fair world. At least more fair than the one we have been given. But if we meet, we must adopt, at least partially, the ideas of serendipity, nostalgia, apprehension, hope, and Will.

And though I have not listened to your story firsthand, your tragedy has not fallen on deaf ears. You have been a fugitive of life's cold stare. And while I cannot save you from those experiences, we have the gift of the future. We will get to the bottom of this cruel world! We need to forget all the biases and lies that we have been taught, like a snake shedding its skin. We need to erase our Tabula Rasa and see the world anew with fresh eyes, sharpening our focus on the raw data, before it gets filtered by all the illusions of the world.

I would be remiss to claim that these questions come from curiosity alone. The crux of the matter is, as I see it, is that all this intellectual obfuscation has at its very core a certain element of fear. An unreachable itch, as it were. And such is the stuff of Mimento Mori. Indeed, I am afraid! And why shouldn't I be? Death is but the mystery of mysteries. Long have I scoffed at the supposed hubris of the pretentious and elitist posturings of academics and philosophers. And yet, as I pen this very letter, I have discovered that these questions come not from elitist posturings but rather the humility of a child.

If you feel so inclined, I will harbor all of you from atop the precipice that couches the beacon of hope. It will cast a net of light for those caught between a rock and a hard place. It is near a dangerous castle that we will find sojourn from the harsh elements of our own great storm. Allow me to be your port of call! We will need over a month to do our noble work. Every day we will congregate, whoever shall come, for our plenary meetings. Come at 10:00 PM sharp, on Friday, September 13, 2019. We will disband at 10:00 PM on Halloween. I have already blocked five rooms for the occasion, not knowing how many, if any, will come. Oh yes, and meet me at the guardrail, cliffside.

I understand that the location I have just described is rather delphic. But considering the gravity of our "rocking the boat," we mustn't split hairs over trivial matters. Like a superior lighthouse in the night, we must entrust karma and karma alone to guide the way, assuming it exists in the first place. This mission must be kept at least somewhat nebulous for security purposes. We will also need ample time for the two-dollar bill to make its rounds and circulate. Our goal is to attract at least three of the king's men, including myself. But do bring whatever scientific talents, gifts, and skills you can muster for our grand experiments. I am not sure exactly what our objectives will be, but I know what they won't be. No longer will we sit idly by and let the gods play dice with us clueless humans. Long enough have we suffered in silence. I am a reformer, and I want a better world!

I ask that before you make your holy pilgrimage, please place this bill back into circulation. There are others that must find it. I would suggest using a change machine, purchasing a food item at any convenience store, or making a bank deposit. Find a place that will disperse the bill far and wide. Karma will do the rest, like a message in a bottle cast at sea. As they say, all you have to do is "follow the money." And yet, I can't help but feel like a ship in a glass bottle with all sails raised, poised for adventure but blocked by the bottleneck. How ironic it is that the more motivated and driven I feel, and the higher I lift the masts and raise the sails, the harder it becomes to actually find egress from the bottle! Like a Chinese finger trap, the harder I fight, the harder my mission becomes. All I can see is the tunnel vision proffered by the bottleneck. But the question remains. What lies beyond the confines of the bottle?

The fact that you have read this far must mean that I have piqued your curiosity. If you can empathize with any of the contents of this rather discursive letter, come join me on the precipice at 10:00 PM. Can you stomach the FairGrounds? If so, please consider this humble requisition, and do not be 'dismissive of this missive.'

Sincerely,
XX
March 14, 2017

P.S. Bring your three most thought-provoking or self-defining movies, books, and albums. Such things are very telling of someone's personality, don't you think? I also have a tiny little favor to ask of you. But due to its sensitive nature, I cannot talk about it now. But we will have ample time, should you arrive.

***

When he was finished, Nate flopped down on the davenport and let out a heavy sigh. Shawn sat down beside him and did the same. Shawn took the phone from him and clutched it as if it were some mysterious ancient artifact.

"Well, that was certainly something," said Nate.

"Oh, spare the MN Nice," said Shawn. "What do you really think?"

"Do you really want to know what I think?" asked Nate.

"Do I really have a choice in the matter? I have a feeling you will tell me eventually, one way or another."

"I think whoever wrote this is obviously 'cuckoo for Cocoa Puffs,'" said Nate. Shawn's smile diminished. "This person probably suffered a loss, very similar to your own, and they are too fragile, much too broken, to face reality. Probably just some forlorn poet, looking for some sort of meaning, something bigger than ourselves."

"So that's it?" snapped Shawn. "You are going to write all this off as some type of fringe movement conspiracy theorist?"

"I wouldn't say that," returned Nate. "Don't get me wrong."

Shawn nodded his head and started to get up from the sofa. "I don't think you need the Rosetta Stone to make it any more clear. I guess I got your opinion one way or another. I have better things to do than to be mocked by my best friend."

"No, no, please sit down," said Nate as he put his hand on Shawn's shoulder and guided him back to a sitting position. "I am just being a tad bit facetious here. I really mean no disrespect. I am just a bit worried about you, is all. I think part of you is trying to deny what's going on with your son, that's all. I'm no shrink or anything, but it just seems painfully obvious. You are trying to make sense out of things you can't make sense of."

Shawn sat down in fits and spurts, feeling somewhat skeptical, wondering about the veracity of Nate's empathy skills. "You are my best friend, right?"

"Last time I checked," said Nate. "As long as you will have me." He picked up the "Coin-Age" magazine on the coffee table near the drinks and leafed through it as if to assuage his awkwardness.

Shawn rubbed his eyes and set the phone down on the coffee table.

Shawn put one of the well-worn couch pillows behind his head and stared at the ceiling. "Don't you ever wonder, Nate, what it all means? If there really is a rhyme and reason to the things of this world? That bill, which you so callously wrote off, actually saved my life. That bill may have saved my very life. This is my chance to really test the waters, to test the reality of this message. I deserve an explanation for what happened to my son. We all deserve an explanation. Every last living and breathing organism on this planet. We all deserve to know the truth. People are far too willing to stumble through all the madness without question. No more secrets. No more cloak and dagger skulduggery. I am resolved to find out, one way or another."

Nate tossed the magazine back on the table and raised his voice. "Are you seriously considering this person's request?"

Shawn made eye contact and didn't say a word. His face was chiseled, determined, and steadfast, his silence speaking volumes.

Nate sighed. "What can I say? You seem resolute in your convictions. I thought there must have been something to your odd questions about fairness at the hospital. But why is the meaning of life so important anyway? Most of us are content being confined to simple daily pursuits—food, water, shelter, survival, employment, romantic troubles, and the odd simple pleasures of name-brand cereal."

Shawn went to the window and peered out. The garbage truck was outside, collecting his garbage. "It's not necessarily the meaning of life I am after, per se."

Nate raised his voice. "What is it then? I mean, why worry about things you can't control?"

"Why not?" asked Shawn, turning around.

"I asked you first," said Nate.

"You want to know what I think?" asked Shawn, putting his hands on his hips like an upset parent.

"Do I have a choice in the matter?" retorted Nate.

Shawn continued. "I think most people are too *afraid* to care first, and that leads to being too *busy* to care. People allow themselves to be so encumbered by life's silly and trivial trifles they don't, won't, and can't stop and think. And they like it that way. Less time to think about our inevitable and futile mortality. It's easier to embrace mindlessness and join the herd. You know, establishment and all that. Some people join the masses because they don't know any better. Others join the herd because they fear the repercussions of revealing their true colors. Some of us free thinkers long to become independent from the masses and powers that be, even if we are afraid."

Nate picked up the phone and perused the secret message. "You have always been an independent sort and stubborn to boot."

Shawn paused. "More than you know. And more than I care to let on."

"But who is this mysterious guy? Is this even safe? It could be a practical joke for all we know."

"Or an impractical one at that, as the case may be," retorted Shawn.

"Still, we mustn't forget that the note is over two years old. Who knows if this nut is still serious about any of this?"

Shawn approached Nate and gestured to him to hand over the phone, and he handed it to him. Shawn skimmed over the letter again as he stood near Nate. Shawn scrolled through the message. "Wow, now that's peculiar."

Nate stood up and careened his head over for a look. "And what is that, praytell? What is peculiar now?"

Shawn spoke without shifting his gaze from the letter. "If you rearrange the letters of these five values in the memo, they spell Shawn."

"What were the five values again?"

Shawn spoke at a half pace. "Hope, Serendipity, Nostalgia, Apprehension, and Will."

"Well, how about that!" said Nate. "You are more right than wrong, at least in this matter. You could have been a detective in your better days."

"Better days? Thanks, I think."

"Well, you know," said Nate.

"But strange, eh?"

"A wee bit," said Nate, making a hand gesture denoting a very small amount.

"Only a wee bit?" asked Shawn.

"Okay, a wee bit more than a wee bit."

"Thanks for the vote of confidence," said Shawn.

Nate put his hand on Shawn's shoulder. "Still, sometimes

we choose to interpret coincidence as nothing short of miracles."

"So you still think I am crazy," said Shawn, brushing Nate's hand off.

"No, crazy in the good way, like a 'wild and crazy' frat-boy and all that," said Nate. "Or crazy like a fox."

"Nice save," said Shawn.

Nate put his hand back on Shawn's shoulder. "Shawn is a common name, and those are common values, so it could just be a coincidence. That's all. I'm not saying you are wrong or anything. Just entertaining other ideas. Alternative explanations and the like."

"Well, thanks for at least entertaining my silly ideas," said Shawn.

Nate walked to the wildlife calendar on the wall and perused it. "Hey, this is my kind of calendar. And a fox, no less. Wow, I can't believe it's May already, and we let another winter go by without snowshoeing."

Shawn was lost in thought, reading the message yet again, this time mumbling as he went along.

Nate turned from the calendar. "So you really are gonna try and meet this person?"

Shawn did not reply. In fact, he didn't even hear him. He just continued looking through the message as if trying to decode its mysteries.

"Shit, if I had known you would get silly ideas in your head, I wouldn't have even let you read the message."

"Come now, Nate, you know I have to," said Shawn, finally looking up from the screen. "And you know I'm going to, one way or another. You are not going to stop me."

"Hold on just a minute," said Nate, wagging his finger. "I refuse to let my friend get stabbed by some nutcase."

"You are talking to someone who was just about to hang himself," said Shawn. "I think I can handle some one in a million chance that this person is some sort of axe murderer. But thanks for the concern and all that, I think."

With shaky hands, Nate ran his fingers through his hair.

"Can't we just plan a snowshoeing trip or something instead?"

"I wouldn't enjoy it even if we did," said Shawn. "In the words of Jackson Frank, 'the blues run the game.' I could be on a hammock between two palm trees and still feel miserable at this point. Besides, the note makes it clear to come alone. But make no mistake. I have to go. And I will go. It's the only thing that is derailing my plans to take my own life. With Emeril gone, I have nothing left to lose. The worst that could happen is he can kill me. That's what I was gonna do anyway."

Nate went back to the couch and flopped down. "Obviously, that pains me to hear, but how can I put a wedge into such a steadfast ambition? If I had to choose, I would much rather tell you to go on this trip than to take your own life. That goes without saying. The lesser of two evils, and all that. But this person doesn't even make it clear where to meet."

"It sounds like the writer of this secret note is talking about some sort of light source of some kind. After reading it a few times, there seems to be some plays on words, such as the use of the word 'harbor.' I also think there may be a lighthouse involved."

Nate took a deep breath as if preparing for a speech. "That's all fine and good, but there are literally dozens, if not hundreds or thousands, of lighthouses permeating the far reaches of this God-forsaken world. How do you know which one this clown is rambling about?" Nate snatched the phone and began re-reading the memo. After a moment, he continued. "Although you are right, there do seem to be clues in here about where to meet, I am obliged to admit."

"That's what I think also," said Shawn. "Maybe you can do some sleuthing on that smartphone of yours?"

Nate began Googling. "I really shouldn't be humoring you like this...."

Shawn glanced at the clock near the doorway to the kitchen and saw that it was running out of batteries. The second hand was creeping ahead and back again as if stuck in a time loop. He got up and rifled through the kitchen drawer for some new batteries to replace the old ones. He took down the clock, inserted the batteries, and set it to 4:17 p.m to match the time on the microwave.

"Hey, do you got a pen and paper?" asked Nate.

"Sure I do. What kind of question is that?" said Shawn as he took a pad and pen from his antique stationery desk sitting in the living room across from the coffee table and sat back down on the davenport next to Nate. "Why don't you tell me what to write, and I will write it."

"Yes, you can be my scribe," said Nate. "Okay, one, it sits atop a precipice. Two, it mentions a castle. Three, it references a 'rock and a hard place.' Four, it mentions a superior lighthouse. And Five, it mentions a 'great storm.'"

"Okay, okay, slow down," said Shawn, scribbling to keep up. When finished, he put the pen behind his ear.

They both sat thinking and repeating these five hints to themselves.

Not only does it sit right next to Lake Superior, but the great storm is a reference to Mataffa, the tragedy that led to the creation of the lighthouse, to begin with. And the 'dangerous castle' is referring to a nearby community in that area called "Castle Danger."

"Maybe do some more Googling?" asked Shawn.

"I told you that you should have upgraded that old flip phone," said Nate. "You are lucky I have a smartphone. You are younger than me for crying out loud."

"Yeah, yeah, point taken and duly noted," said Shawn. "Well, what are you waiting for? Get Googling!"

"You are also lucky I was a game warden," said Nate. "You forget that I know ND and MN quite well."

"You know what lighthouse they are talking about?" asked Shawn. "You gonna tell me or just sit there and play dumb."

"So I am playing dumb now? That's an improvement over when you say I really am dumb."

"I get it, I get it," said Shawn. "Settle down."

"Okay, I cross-referenced, and I think I got something.

And I think it's fairly obvious. It's clearly talking about Split Rock Lighthouse, a very common tourist trap right here in our very own MN. Not only does it sit right next to Lake Superior, but the great storm is a reference to Mataffa, the tragedy that led to the creation of the lighthouse, to begin with."

"Well, how about that," said Shawn. "Nothing beats an outdoorsman with a smartphone."

"They also referenced Barbara Paplior," said Nate. "That name sounds somehow familiar too, come to think of it."

"Look her up!" said Shawn.

"Well, it appears this woman was all over the news in the early 90s for her tragic death on the Aerial Lift Bridge, which just happens to be another famous Duluth landmark."

"What can I say? I am so thankful to have you here with me right now, despite your smart ass," said Shawn. "What I lack in tech-savvy you make up for in your knowledge of the great outdoors."

"Well, thank you kindly," said Nate. "But personally, I would have picked a more land-locked lighthouse, such as Trowbridge, which is also nestled on Lake Superior."

Shawn slapped his knees. "Nonetheless, the very proximity of Split Rock in our very own Minnesota only adds to my confidence that my excursion is more than meant to be. With a couple more drinks in me, I might even entertain the very idea of fate or karma."

Nate finished off his third beer. "Well, how about that. But I don't think he meant the riddle to be all that hard to figure out, just hard enough to keep the riff-raff away. Like a security question on the Internet to prove you aren't a robot."

"Almost sounds like one of those science fiction movies," said Shawn. "At any rate, he may have just added the riddle for no other reason than to make things more exciting. Isn't that what life is all about? Escaping reality? What is a dream, be it figurative or literal, but the brain's ability to create virtual reality?"

"No, that sounds more like you, a natural born poet," retorted Nate. He got up, gathered up the empty beer bottles, and went into the kitchen to throw them in the trash for Shawn.

"Oh, you know, necessity is the mother of invention, and all that," shouted Shawn.

Nate tossed the bottles, returned, and stood in the doorway between the kitchen and the living room. "But do you know what else I think?"

"Do I have a choice in the matter?"

"I don't think you have to worry about keeping the riff-raff at bay."

"And why is that?"

"Well, I think he's the riff-raff. The person in the letter, I think he's the one we may want to avoid!"

"You may not be too far off the mark there," said Shawn as he put his pillow back on the couch where it belonged.

Nate sat in the chair. "But all humor aside, I think I should come with you, just in case this is an unsavory fellow."

Shawn sighed. "I know you mean well, I really do, but the note made it clear to come alone. But I can arrange to keep my phone with me at all times and respond to any texts or calls within the hour. Does that sound fair?"

"I suppose it will have to do—I know there is no stopping you at this point. You have always been a stubborn fool, with all due respect."

"Thanks, I think," said Shawn.

Nate perked up. "What do you say we watch another episode of those crazy metal detecting boneheads?"

"I don't mean to be rude, but I think I would rather start planning my quaint little egress to Split Rock come September."

Nate looked at the newly energized clock. "Yeah, I suppose I gotta tidy up my house anyway." Nate went to the main door and began putting his boots on as he stood on the welcome mat.

Shawn put his hand on Nate's shoulder, and the latter turned around. "Nate, I really must thank you. If it weren't for you, I would have never gotten that message."

"That's what I'm afraid of," returned Nate. "But thanks for the sentiment."

"I felt alive today, like one of the Hardy Boys, as if we were playing some sort of mystery game. I guess that's why they call you a game warden, eh?" said Shawn with a laugh.

Nate laughed. "Something like that. You are too kind. But you gotta call me. Keep me in the loop. That's the condition for not having me come along."

"You know I am hardly a voluble spokesman, but I will heed your warning and chat you up occasionally, if only because it would hurt you more than it would hurt me."

"What would, pray tell?" asked Nate wearing only one boot.

"My dying."

"Ah, come now, don't talk like that," continued Nate as he put on his second boot. "Or I will have to make it a point to come along."

Shawn was misty eyed. "Thanks, friend."

Nate gave him a tight hug, slapping his back in the process. "Many heartfelt apologies about Emeril."

..

CHAPTER 5
CAVEAT EMPTOR

Setting: Winnipeg, Canada
Time: June 7, 2019, Friday, 2:30 p.m.
Main character: Mark Anderson

"The sagacious Amrak's handiwork has been witnessed yet again, his death roster just this year now claiming over twenty people by May's end. And while he has been difficult to track, what can be confirmed is his ongoing enmity for targeting ex-felons with murder charges. And in each case, they were found dead within a week or two of their release. He also seems to have a different theme to each year of his harvesting. In 2017 he recreated the 1929 St. Valentine's Massacre, and in 2018 he killed twenty-six people, each person's name starting with a different letter of the alphabet. It is currently unclear what his pattern or agenda is for 2019, other than the fact that people are dying in his wake.

His newest victim, a Darren Lichmon from Wisconsin, died in his fishing house, once again from stings from the Africanized bee, also known as the killer bee. Police indicated that Amrak sealed the man in the fish-house with tow rope while the man slept and funneled the bees into the house through the makeshift chimney in the roof. As per Amrak's MO, a flagpole waving the message "Karma's a bitch" was jamming a note into the body. The note read, "Darren may have had friends in high places, but in their high and mighty posturing, they failed to see the bottom feeder coming from the depths. Justice is blind, and I will keep it that way. Nobody has yet to catch me in the act. Simon got what he deserved. As such, I feel no compunction. I did what karma instructed me to do. And karma, my fellow Americans, is the master to whom I bow."

----- from Vigilane Vignettes, June issue, 2019

Mark yielded at the fire hydrant. He was wearing a pitch-black suit-coat over a "Steins Gate" tee. The left sleeve had been expertly cut by a seamstress at the local dry cleaner, so the coat had one short and one long sleeve. He also had a pair of equally pitch black jeans, this time with the right leg cut short, by his own hand and sheers, so that the left side looked like pants and the right side shorts. His mismatched Converse red high top on his right foot and low cut black on his left seemed a natural fit. In general, our Mark more or less welcomed the occasional "conformist" stares, as he called them, as he saw conformists as a type of con-artist of sorts.

For the purposes of his experiments, he always carried the same weather-beaten and well-worn beige Chrome Industries denim messenger bag that his mother had given him some five years prior. He had since sewn "Stein's Gate," "Death Note," and Claymore patches onto it, and he did not hesitate to boast to his teasing friends that his home-economics class he took was not all for naught. Today he was feeling particularly ambitious and was hoping to do some license plate synchronicity tests, a randomness test, a fear-laced parkour experiment, a basic brute force pain experiment, and a pleasure experiment, along with any general observations he may feel inclined to record. He used his "Journal of Existential Musings" more for initial thoughts, and he entered the actual quantitative data from his research, including actual pain measurements from his "Project Madcap" helmet, into his computer files at home. Project Madcap was his secret invention and pride and joy, a device that could literally read a person's pain states as if simply taking one's temperature.

With his shaggy brown hair, Faber-Castell pen, and green Mead notebook in tow, he walked along the street, taking note of the cars parallel-parked along the road some five blocks from his own place of residence. He was also wearing his "Project

Madcap" helmet to record his pain and pleasure states during key moments of his experiments. He induced an emotionally charged incandescent thought into his head: "If I see the number 472, something dire will most certainly happen." Next, he walked by the line of vehicles. He wrote down the license plate numbers: 592, 844, 236, 843, and 473. He analyzed them to see if he could find any pattern, rhyme, or reason to them. After a moment of lucubration, he saw a couple of peculiarities. He thought it somewhat strange that the second plate, 844, was only one up from the fourth plate, 843. He also thought it was noteworthy that 236 was exactly one-half of his feared number 472, and the fifth plate 473 was only one higher than his target number as well. A bit strange, he thought, but overall, nothing tantamount to what could be construed as metaphysical or supernatural. He decided to chalk this one up to sheer coincidence. *Better luck next time*, he thought. *Or worse luck, as the case may be.* He put the notebook and pen back into his messenger bag and closed it with a loud "zip." With such lackluster results, he didn't even bother writing any of this down in his journal. He also didn't even bother to take off his Project Madcap helmet.

He strolled along to gear up for his second little experiment. He revealed from the large side pocket of his messenger bag one of those "map pulling" rods with the hook on the end, used in many academic classrooms. With a steady rhythm, he tapped the top of the fire hydrant no less and no more than forty-three times. He paused for a moment afterwards, almost as if he were waiting for something to happen, like a magician tapping his hat before a rabbit hops out. Or the parting of the Red Sea. He unzipped the bag, took out his notebook, and wrote:

06/07/19 (Randomness Test): Was this the first time in the history of the world someone tapped a fire hydrant with a map hook exactly forty-three times? Can you even still call it a map-hook when it wasn't used as such and transcended its "functional fixedness?" But the question remained. Will this act of randomness send a ripple through space and time, catching the attention, much like SETI, of the universe or the gods that be? Events are either random, or they are not. Or perhaps it's more nebulous than all that. Perhaps some life events are random, and others are not.

"You okay?" asked a tall woman around forty-five walking her poodle along the broken and cracked sidewalk next to the hydrant, as he had just finished his notes. "Do you work for the fire department? By the way, I like the helmet."

Mark risked making eye contact. "Yes, no worries. I mean, yes and no, in that order—yes, I am okay, unless I have a terminal illness I don't know about. And no, I don't work for the fire department. It's just an OCD ritual. Oh yes, and thanks regarding the helmet, I think."

"Wow, aren't you all blunt and honest," said the woman, trying to keep her poodle on the sidewalk.

Mark smiled at how his mention of a psychological aberration stirred such a reaction in the woman as he put his map hook back inside the back flap of his messenger bag.

The woman waited as her dog was sniffing around the vicinity of the fire hydrant. "Well, have a nice day, and good luck with all that business."

Mark stood in front of her. "You are not so strange for a stranger."

"Thank you kindly, I think," said the woman. "By the way, my name is Aiyanna. And this here is Kyle."

Mark nodded. "I am Mark."

Aiyanna began walking, but her plans were circumvented when Kyle decided to mark his territory on the very same fire hydrant.

"Sorry about that," said Aiyanna, followed by awkward laughter.

"No worries," said Mark. "Take your time."

"Maybe you should say it to Kyle here."

Mark smiled. "Take your time Kyle. You mark that territory. You gotta be vigilant in this world. Take what's rightfully yours.

It's a dog-eat-dog world out there."

Aiyanna smiled. "Well, when you put it like that, Mark, you almost make it sound like a noble gesture."

They both laughed. When Kyle finished, Aiyanna tugged gently on his leash, and they walked away. Mark watched them for a moment and then sat down on the grass next to the fire hydrant. Feeling an observation brewing in his head, he got it down in his journal.

6/7/19 (Observation). Swearing an oath: What is swearing anyway? What gives these words their power? Arbitrary assignment? If I write "fuck" twice, is it considered twice as bad as if I wrote it only once? What if I say the word but don't mean it? Does that take its "evilness" away? What if I say it only once but savor it and take an entire minute to spit it out? F-u-u-u-u-u-c-k! Is that still only half as bad as if I swore twice but quickly? What if I wrote it in twenty-four-point font. Is that twice as "bad" as twelve point? Or what if I decided a swear word isn't bad at all? Do I have the power to make that decision? What if I decide not to give it its visceral power? Who decides what a "bad word" is in the first place? How can a one-calorie word in a movie be considered worse than an act of violence or a brief moment of nudity? How dumb are people, anyway?

6/7/19 (Observation). Could Project Madcap theoretically examine Arthur Schopenhaur's contention that the absolute value of a prey's pain exceeds the absolute value of the predator's pleasure?

With that, he put the notebook back away into his bag. The open pockets were zipped with great haste, making an even louder swoosh sound. After a short trek, the nearby eight-level parking garage came into view, a perfect spot for some parkour or stunts. The elevator took him to the top-most floor, and the stairs took him the rest of the way. He walked to the nearby balcony, peered over the edge, and noticed that the top of an apartment complex was just below and not too terribly far off into the distance. A note was made in his journal.

6/7/19 (Observation): The gravity of the situation. Isn't it amazing how much higher eight stories seems when you are topside? If your velocity remained constant when you jumped, it probably wouldn't be so bad. But the problem is the acceleration — 9.81 meters per second squared, to be exact. That's ultimately what kills you. Not the height, per se. How many people have died due to gravity, and how come nobody directs their anger at gravity for being such a strong causal factor in a great many decedents? Are natural disasters somehow beyond reproach? But I mustn't waste too much time waxing philosophical. I have a jump to do!

After literally returning his thoughts to more "down to Earth" matters, and after some cautious musing and planning, he put his journal and pen away. He was already wearing his "Project Madcap" helmet, so he could record his fear states. As if throwing a shot-put, he tossed his bag over to the building below. Going back a ways to get a head start, he took a run for it. Without looking at the concrete below, he leaped off the edge of the parking garage like a cheetah.

The good news was that he cleared a large distance. The bad news was that he didn't quite make the clearing, and he barely secured the hard landing on the balcony below, hurting his left leg. Arms flailing, he couldn't regain his balance, and he fell from the balcony. His instincts grabbed the side of the balcony with both hands as he fell. Flailing his legs, he pulled upwards with all the adrenaline he could muster until he rolled over onto the balcony and flopped on the cement below. He laid still, staring dolefully at the sky. He couldn't help but think about poor Wu Yongning and what he must have thought and felt during his descent. And why the powers that be didn't opt to save him or anyone else that shared such a dire fate. After catching his breath for a moment, he took down some notes.

6/7/2019 (Fear experiment). I did some parkour today.

Well, more of a stunt, really. Just as with the Richardson Building, my subjective fear that I felt during the jump seemed to match the objective fear measured by Project Madcap (with a pain rating of -65.73 meta grams). Not only that, but the fear measurement was even higher than when I did this same stunt on the fourth story of this parking garage about a month ago, suggesting higher fear sensations associated with being higher in the air.

But our Mark was not quite done, for he still had his pain experiment and pleasure experiment to do before he could call it a day. Last week he had used a staple remover, the kind that looked like the jaws of a snake, to "bite" the flesh between his toes. Today he was bent on upping the ante. He took off his left shoe and sock. Next, he unzipped one of the small pockets on the side of the bag and revealed some firecrackers. He unraveled four from the bunch, smoothed out the fuses, and gently placed them between his toes on his left foot. The fuses were long enough he was able to tie them together into a sort of roughshod chain, hoping he could light the entire mass and they would all go off in a mad bang frenzy. After having the fuses tied, the mass looked like some sort of electrical circuit.

He mused about how he was not doing this out of some sophomoric double dare, fit of macho overconfidence, or even sheer stupidity. He knew full well that he was utterly terrified of this stunt. And that was partly why he felt it was so important. But he was tired of beating around the bush. A moment later, his punk was lit and allowed to smolder. He laid down atop the apartment building, back to the pavement, and took a deep breath. His shaky hand brought the punk to the fuse. As soon as it was lit, he thought, "What did I just do?" and closed his eyes as tight as he could.

The firecracker exploded, and the pain was far worse than he had anticipated. He was by now screaming at the top of his lungs, and oddly enough, nobody heard or bothered to care to come to his aid. There was blood coming from all five of his toes. The pain was so intense he had to check to make sure all his toes were still there. He noticed that one of the firecrackers didn't go off, the one all the way to the left, between his little toe and the one to its right. He felt relieved by this, as he wondered if that little piggy may have gone to market if the firecracker had indeed gone off. He kicked it away with his foot in the event the fuse still had a chance to be lit.

The Project Madcap was still on his head. He remained on the roof for a good fifteen minutes, taking deep breaths, until the pain died away at least somewhat. The next thing on the docket was tidying the wound with some gauze and double socking it. Looking at the pain reader on Project Madcap, he was quite pleased with the results. Not only did the device measure a very high pain value during the explosion itself, but it also showed a fairly high level of pain just before the explosion, suggesting just how painful anticipation anxiety could be. Despite still feeling a high level of pain, he took down some notes.

6/7/2019 (Pain Experiment): I am in pain as I write this very note, but in some respects, pain has never felt so good. The subjective pain I felt from the firecrackers was dramatic, to say the least, but it seemed to match the objective pain measured by Project Madcap (with a pain rating of -78.11 meta grams). This made the staple remover incident seem like child's play. Thankfully I was terrified, as Project Madcap was also able to detect the anticipation anxiety I felt just before the firecracker went off. As I lay here bleeding, I can't help but feel all warm and fuzzy inside. But I gotta be careful, as I could have quite literally blown my socks off and my toes with them.

Mark was still feeling lots of pain, so he once again seized the opportunity. He pulled out his little "morphine kit" he saved for such occasions as this. He gave himself the injection and self-monitored the subjective experience as he also monitored the readings from Project Madcap. He took down more notes.

6/7/2019 (Pleasure/Relief Experiment): I took the injection. It did not take long for the subjective sensation of pain to go away. And in tandem with this, the readings from Project Madcap likewise seemed to follow. However, something interesting happened. Just as my physical pain seemed to go away and return to baseline, the pain readings from Project Madcap also approached zero. But after that, with the over-abundance of morphine in my system, the pleasure seemed to exceed the relief, and I even got some pleasure readings above zero with a (+) valence (showing a rating as high as +23.58 meta grams).

Mark noticed the blood from his foot had become less voluminous than before. He didn't want to wait a moment longer, so he took out his first-aid kit and wrapped up his foot in gauze and put his sock and shoe back on. At that point, he put everything away in his bag and used his hands and knees to help himself up. Noticing a stairwell leading to the ground floor, he hobbled over to it and tried the knob. It was a massive relief to know that the door was not locked from the outside. He limped downstairs and took the elevator back to the safety of ground level.

He began his journey home with a leisurely gait and thought about his randomness studies. And while he generally didn't wear "Project Madcap" during his randomness studies, he found these studies to be equally important. It was his mission objective, at least once every day or so, to set out to "do something truly random, something never done before, in the history of the world." Last weekend he'd purchased a lawnmower blade and used it to spread cottage cheese on the side of a rain gutter, trying his best to legibly write the words "Lignite Buttons" with the cottage cheese and a twig. And about a week before that, he'd used a glass eye he's ordered on Amazon a year ago to tap "waffles and fire detectors" on his television screen in Morse Code a total of four times. A month ago, he'd purchased an ink cartridge for a printer, spread peanut butter on it, and placed a toy army man on the makeshift quagmire. And he engaged in dozens of truly random, one of a kind events, hopefully never done in the history of the world over the course of thousands of years and billions of people. And since his less-than-auspicious call-back from Anodyne Research, he was dedicating even more time to his "odd" pursuits of happiness. His aim was to "catch the attention" of the rulers of the universe, as if SETI calling the attention of other worlds, to let them know that he wasn't just an average Joe member of the hoi polloi, but someone that was not about to be manipulated by the powers that be, whoever they might be.

He made it home at last and entered the main security door that led into the main hallway. He trudged up the faded-out red-carpeted steps and found his way to apartment 248. It was a one-level apartment on the second floor and was located in the dark green, five-story tall "Veranda Flats" building near the Shell gas station.

Mark burst into the less-than-tidy quarters, as evidenced by the random bits of dust, grime, and/or grit he had emblazoned on the most unlikely of places, such as bare walls, tops of doors, and lamp-shades. The apartment still smelled of movie theatre popcorn that he had made in the microwave this morning prior to his little pilgrimage and run-in with the alpha-poodle marking his territory.

Mark did not live alone. He shared the apartment with Gavin, his younger brother by two years, and also his similarly aged friend Sandy Larson. And while he wasn't a neat freak by any stretch, the tidiness of his surroundings had definitely taken a hit since his parents died a year ago.

Their quaint apartment consisted of a living room, kitchen, bathroom, and a small hallway, leading to the two bedrooms — Gavin took the liberty to crash on the sectional. The carpet was old and had a sort of threadbare, haggard grayness to it, indicating that at one time in its glory days, the half-length shag was brown. And where Gavin attested that such battle scars gave it character, Mark carried the conviction that such well-worn quality did no such thing and even told Gavin once that "If this carpet could talk and tell a story, it actually wouldn't say much, it would just stare at the ground with misty eyes and a loss for words."

Two of the walls extended out about four feet from the floor and served as shelves. One of these "shelves" had two layers of Funko Pop! figures of a various anime, sci-fi, and video game variety. The other shelf contained various figures or statues courtesy of Nendoroid, Figure Arts, Figma, and Weta Workshop. There were two anime wall scrolls as well, of Full Metal Alchemist and Death Note. One corner of the room had a bookshelf containing graphic novels, many of them by DC Vertigo (such as Demo, We3, and Enigma). One of the shelves contained various board games, such as Pandemic, Catan, and Shadows Over Camelot. The kitchen was equipped with a standard electric oven, a vertical fridge, a brown tile floor, an old-school dial microwave, and a circular glass table with a poly-stone statue of Gandalf the Grey as a centerpiece. And while none of the appliances matched in color, they matched in their layers of residue and filth. Even some of the lightbulbs were burned out, and at least in this point in time, everybody was either too lazy or too depressed to change any of them.

Sandy Larson appeared from the kitchen wearing an oversized long sleeve Nirvana shirt sagging over nothing but her underwear. She scowled at Mark. "Welcome back. What was it this time, crop circles?"

"Crop squares," said Mark as he limped around the living room, picking up several newspapers from the floor and crumpling them all up as he gathered them, grumbling and mumbling all the while. He never even bothered to take off his shoes like usual, on account of his bloody foot from his pain experiment.

Sandy shook her head. "Smartass much? And what's with the limp?"

"Oh, I just fell outside," Mark replied. He was happy that by the end of the day he didn't actually lie. After all, he did fall. Still, he knew full well that the manner in which he fell wouldn't bode well for Sandy so that part he edited out. But he was glad Sandy didn't berate him about his shoes, at least.

Sandy Larson was a childhood friend from the fifth grade;

they'd only lived together for just over three years. She was exactly one year older than him, as they shared the exact same birthday. And while their respective families had known one another for years in Winnipeg, it was this mutual birthday that really brought the two children together above and beyond mere "acquaintance" status (Mark had made it a point to approach her in fifth grade just to theorize about the sheer coincidence of the affair). Sandy had a political science degree and worked as a notary public in Manitoba after passing her exam. And while very few kindergarteners would ever dare say "notary public" when asked what they would like to be when they grew up, on most days, she felt the role rather befitted her no-nonsense temperament and fascination with routine, structure, and/or parliamentary procedure.

Gavin was sprawled out on the green garage-sale sectional, his head propped up on the armrest, lost in his own virtual worlds. This time he was playing Nine Hours, Nine Persons, and Nine Doors on his DS. He was wearing an orange hi-pile fleece hoodie with the hood up so tight only his eyes, nose, and mouth were visible through the small opening. He didn't even notice Mark had come home. He was a certified public accountant and currently did the bookkeeping for two different restaurants in Winnipeg—and he worked mostly from home. He also did taxes for people during Canadian tax season in April for some quick extra cash.

"Thanks for the concern and worry," said Mark in reply to Sandy's perceived aloof manner of inquisition, as he tossed the papers he had collected into the already-full garbage bin on the right side of the flat-screen television, leaving one of the papers to roll back down again from whence it came. "Would you greet me in such a manner if I were mugged or kidnapped?"

"Drama much?" asked Gavin as he glanced up from his game. As soon as he made eye contact, he returned his gaze back to his game.

"Thanks for the backup," said Mark. "So much for brotherly love."

"Chalk it up to 'brotherly tough love,'" said Gavin. "Besides, you made me mess up in my game."

"Oh yes, blame it on me," said Mark as he picked up Gavin's partly opened umbrella from the floor, closed it, and put it in the basket near the door. "By the way, it's bad luck to have an umbrella open in the house."

"It probably opened on its own," said Gavin as he played. "Even I'm not that untidy."

"Mark Anderson, ever the Drama King of Winnipeg," said Sandy. "There are two kinds of people, those that can detect sarcasm and those that can't. You are definitely in the latter."

"I second that motion," said Gavin, without bothering to look up. "He's incorrigible."

Mark perked up his eyebrows. "And here I thought the only kinds of people were those that love Krull and those that don't."

Without any cue, Sandy snatched one of the couch cushions and tossed it at Mark. He fumbled with butterfingers trying to catch it, but to no avail, and it just sort of thumped against his hand and fell to the floor. Mark groaned and sighed, in that order, picked it up, and tossed it right back at her. She caught it with one hand.

"What can I say?" chimed Gavin, shaking his head. "He's incorrigible."

"And you are out!" Sandy shouted.

Mark didn't say a solitary word.

"So what's up?" asked Sandy as she tossed the cushion atop Gavin's legs. Sandy waited for a moment for a pithy comeback, but he didn't even seem to notice. Sandy turned her attention back to Mark. "You seem a bit flustered and possibly even bewildered. Something happen out there in the wild jungles of the real world?"

Mark flopped himself into the equally worn brown La-Z-Boy near the sectional and let out a long-winded sigh. "I actually did have a bit of a rough day, if I too may be frank."

Sandy snagged the red floor chair from in front of the TV,

turned it towards Mark, and slowly lowered herself down and plopped onto it.

"I always thought Frank suited you more than Mark if I too can be frank," returned Gavin. "In fact, let's all be frank!"

"The only man in history to be both a wise-ass and a dumb-ass at the same time," said Sandy.

"What can I say? It's a gift," said Gavin as he kicked the couch pillow back towards Sandy, her catching it once again.

Sandy looked at Mark and raised her eyebrows. "But only a bad day, eh?"

"Well, maybe a bad week. Give me a break—I just got that damn joy-kill callback from Anodyne a few days ago, if you even care to remember."

"It's not just that," continued Sandy. "And yes, I do care to remember. I might venture that you had a rather rough May and so-far June. It's painfully obvious, just in your melancholy and stressed out and sometimes annoying demeanor. You have been unemployed for about half a year now. And it seems like the tiniest slights these days are enough to provoke your tantrums and fits." Sandy opened her mouth but then almost bit her tongue as she recalled how her aloof nature had a nasty way of raising the ire of our Mark's already irascible and insecure natures.

"I second that motion," said Gavin. "He's been a pain in the ass for months!"

"Said the pot to the kettle," said Mark. "It takes one to know one, Mr. 'work from home.'"

"I second that motion," said Gavin. "I am not disagreeing with you there. Truth be told, I have probably been a thorn in your side as well."

Mark pulled the lever on the chair and reclined into it until he was laying down at about a forty-five-degree angle. "Geez, Gavin, will you stop saying 'I second that motion'? It doesn't make sense. It's not a motion of any kind."

"Rest unassured. This game requires much more than mere thumb-twiddling," said Gavin with an exaggerated voice of confidence. "As they say, 'Idle hands' and all that! Besides, who's the one lounging in a chair dubbed as an 'easy chair' and/ or 'Lazy Boy?'"

"Point taken and duly noted," said Mark, lifting his index finger. "I guess I am still moping because I didn't exchange numbers with this lady just outside walking her dog, that's all."

"Well, let's hope that Lazy Boy helps your hurt ass," returned Gavin.

"Still, such little trifles never used to get you so riled up," Sandy added. "I think all these 'little things' might merely be the straws that are breaking the camel's back."

"Now, are we talking dromedary or bactrian camels here?" asked Gavin. "It makes a difference, you know."

"Just play your damn game," said Sandy, to which Gavin just smiled. Sandy squinted her eyes towards Mark. "I mean, sometimes what we think is bothering us is just a surface layer to something deeper. Feuding couples may fight about the garbage, but it's never about the garbage, is it?"

"I guess not," admitted Mark. "But why be so patronizing about it? Your motivation for being inundated with such a barrage of concerns is not because you care about me. You just care about how you are being affected by it all."

"Cynical much?" asked Sandy. "Yes, you can be annoying sometimes, but I also care about you, you dumb, sad bastard."

Mark rubbed the sweat from his palms on the armrests of the chair. "I really am fine, really, message delivered, rinse and repeat. Loud and clear. Would you rather me go back to sitting on the couch eating Little Debbies in a fetal position? At least I applied and got interviewed at Anodyne. That's a helluva lot more than I would have done a month or two ago."

"Little Debbie? Damn that vile and evil temptress!" said Gavin as he continued punching buttons on his DS. "If she gives me a heart attack, I will sue her from beyond the grave."

"And I thought such litigious meanderings was strictly an American affair," said Sandy.

"What exactly are you getting at, Sandy?" asked Mark as he nervously slid his fingernails back and forth across the wooden handle on the right side of the Lazy Boy.

Sandy sighed as she struggled to get up from the floor chair. She stretched, reaching her arms straight up towards the ceiling. "I just think losing your job at that creepy mortuary six months ago is taking its toll, that's all. You are building up walls faster than a construction contractor. And yes, I care, despite my ironic and iconic carelessness of my lip service!"

"I like lip service," said Gavin. "At least the French kind."

"Enough!" shouted Sandy and Mark in unison.

"Well, I hate to be pedantic, but I was working at a funeral home, not a mortuary," said Mark to Sandy. "Rookie mistake on your part. Most funeral homes don't provide cremation services. I haven't worked at a mortuary since my Capstone experience in Vancouver."

"Kinda like how not all Dairy Queens have a grill," said Gavin.

"Yeah, exactly just like that, Gavin," said Sandy, putting her palm on her forehead and shaking her head.

"See, I can tell when Sandy is being sarcastic," said Gavin, making a bit of a racket as he punched the buttons on his DS. "Well, if it's any consolation, I find funeral home staff to be rather two-faced."

"How so?" asked Mark, perking up his eyebrows. "Not that I disagree, mind you."

Gavin paused his game and looked towards them. "Well, take our cousin, Randalph, like when he died like five years ago or whatever. Remember how that weird funeral conductor guy put on some sort of phony sad face when he talked to us? He even got some of the details wrong at the actual funeral, like where Randalph worked or how long he was married. He even got the name wrong and called him Randy. Everyone who knew him knew that he hated being called Randy! Poor guy must have turned in his grave — well, I mean coffin, as he wasn't in the grave quite yet. Bottom line he pretended to care. And don't get me started on that lame little gift shop, playing with our grief like a cheap fiddle, offering little trinkets, souvenirs, and keepsakes, as if our loved ones were just excuses to make more money off them, even after they were dead. No thanks. When I die, you can cast me out to sea for all I care."

"I just might take you up on that, Gavin," said Sandy. "Be careful what you wish for."

"I said 'cast me out to sea,' not to the dogs!" Gavin retorted. "And I don't mean killing me yourself and disposing of the evidence either!"

Sandy laughed. And even Mark let out a faint smile.

"Well, mortuary science happens to be my wheelhouse, I'm afraid," said Mark to Sandy. "But Gavin here is partially right about some of that, I must reluctantly admit."

"So, back on point?" asked Sandy.

"We all have our defenses, I suppose," said Mark in a quiet and tired voice. "You have yours also, Sandy. Don't deny it."

"I already know what mine is, and I own up to it already," said Sandy as she took the remote from the cheap coffee table and turned it on to the Sci-Fi channel. She remained standing as the 60s Outer Limits episode, "The Hundred Days of the Dragon," was playing.

"And what defense is that, Sandy?" asked Mark. "Are you thinking of the same one I am thinking of?"

Sandy went to the couch and forcibly slid Gavin's legs off it, and sat down, keeping the remote with her.

"Hey! I almost died!" said Gavin.

"Oh, shut up. That's a point and click adventure," said Sandy. "You can't die in those games. It's hardly a bullet hell schmup, now is it?"

"You're a schmup," said Gavin, sitting in an upright position and continuing with his game.

Sandy looked at Mark and pointed her thumb towards Gavin. "Damn, I think he thinks he just won the argument with that answer."

Gavin smiled.

With her remote, Sandy turned the volume down on the TV until it was almost completely silent. She used the remote as a fidget as she continued. "Well, Mark, my defense. Why don't you venture a guess if you know me so well?"

"You better get this question right, Mark," said Gavin, "and within three guesses. You just might end up in the doghouse if you don't."

"Doghouse?" asked Mark. "Sandy and I are not a couple, Gavin. That sort of thing only applies to married doormats."

"Careful, Mark," said Sandy. "Gavin knows me better than you think! And who says friends can't end up in the doghouse?"

"Well, color me pedantic," continued Mark. "But for one, we don't have a doghouse—or a dog, for that matter. Besides, dog houses have become quite nice in recent years. Some of them are even heated."

Gavin hit pause. "I just wanna know, if dogs live such a great life, then doghouses must not be so bad. I should consider getting one. It's probably better than this sectional."

"Maybe you can live in a tent like that girl in *Party of Five*," said Sandy.

"Maybe I will," continued Gavin. "I can go glamping and keep my Keurig in there."

With a loud ratchet noise, Mark extended the footrest on the La-Z-Boy. "Okay, okay, but I just know we all have defenses of some kind. Another brick in the wall and all that."

"Give up?" said Sandy, looking back at Mark. "It's my sarcasm and facetiousness that our Gavin here has just been pointing out. You know, the very things you never seem able to detect. But that's how I cope with the harsh elements of the world. And while most of it is rather self-aware and tongue in cheek, I know that occasionally it can be a bit caustic, and it can hurt people's feelings."

Sandy stood up, and Gavin seized the opportunity to throw his legs back up on the couch where she had been sitting.

Sandy walked around the living room, dramatically and loudly snatching up additional random cups, pudding containers, plastic forks, cardboard boxes, and snack wrappers and waving them around with wide sweeping motions. She stomped her

Converse shoe into the trash can, freeing up more space. She put the garbage in, including the paper that had fallen from the mountain of trash earlier.

"Like this," said Sandy, pointing at the garbage. "You used to be a neat freak. You would have never settled for this mess a year ago. You were the one picking my shit up if anything. Hell, I got cleaner over time because of you."

"Honestly, I have seen nary a solitary pep in his step since he got let go from the funeral home."

"First of all, I didn't get 'let go,'" said Mark as he shot his eyes at Gavin. "I quit that job on purpose, so I could work more on my invention."

"Sure you did," said Gavin as he folded up his DS and set it on the coffee table.

"Gavin!" shouted Sandy. "That's a bit much, even for you."

"Well, it's true!" said Gavin.

"You were the one that was let go from work if I am not mistaken," retorted Mark.

Sandy shot her gaze at Gavin. "He's got you there, Gavin. Weren't you the one hitting up random rich ladies back in the day when you were working as a tax preparer?"

"Well, yes, but that was only that one time. And besides," said Gavin, as he straightened himself up prim and proper. "You were my friend back then; you could have stopped me. I contend that I was completely blameless in the matter, given my highly amorous disposition."

Sandy laughed. "And it's somehow my fault that I didn't put a wedge in your little love affairs?"

"Sure, why not," laughed Gavin. "Young love and all that. *Romeo and Juliet* and the like."

Sandy turned to Mark. "So is what Gavin said true? Is this just a case of the ol' sweet lemons and sour grapes? I was kinda led to believe you were let go from that job also."

"Yes and no," said Mark, after a pause. "I quit the job, that much is true, as I did want to free up more time for my invention.

However, after the fruits of my own labor rotted and spoiled, I regretted this decision wholeheartedly."

"Don't mind Gavin," said Sandy. "We are worried about you." She glared at Gavin. "Aren't we, Gavin?"

"Sure, sure," said Gavin. "That goes without saying."

"Well, say it then!" snapped Sandy, slapping his thigh.

"I apologize for my rather prickly demeanor lately," returned Mark. "You are right, Sandy. There are lots of things going on with me, deeper things than pesky ladies walking poodles in the park."

"Wanna chat about it?" asked Sandy. "A little venting, perhaps?"

Mark put down the footrest and put his chair back in its normal position. He left the comforting nest of his easy chair and went to the large window behind the television, across from the sofa, and stared outside. There was a heavy deluge of rain beating loudly against the pane. "As you all know, I have nary had a solitary relationship in my entire life, at least any that lasted more than a month. And while some may have mistaken me for a lone wolf, I'm afraid I was never that cool. I was, and am, a bit of a virgin. Ever since college, I coped with this less than savory state of affairs by adopting the existential position that what the human race likes to call 'love' is merely a spell of sorts that provokes humans to copulate — an evolutionary cheap trick, as it were. My contention was that the only reason sex feels good is to con people into having children." He turned around to face them. "Do you really think the world would have this many people if this were not true?"

Gavin and Sandy looked at each other as if being accused of something. They raised their shoulders, almost in unison.

Mark resumed his gaze out the window. "Person A admires how person B looks, and person B admires how much money or power person A has, and we have the audacity to call it love. If you ask me, it's naught to do with love at all but has all the makings of a business arrangement. This mindset may seem cynical to some, but I think it saved my life, as it helped me from getting my hopes up too high. I would rather not believe in love at all than believe I am unlovable and lonely. It may have been a bittersweet Pyrrhic Victory, but it was a victory nonetheless. The old Scylla and Charybdis. You can call it sour grapes or sweet lemons." Mark turned to face them. "I call it reality."

Gavin looked at Sandy. "And they say chivalry is dead. Leave it to Mark to suck the romance right out of Casablanca."

Sandy stood up and turned off the TV. "It must be hard. Is that a third-world problem or a fourth-world problem?"

"Well, thanks for the understanding, you guys," said Mark. "It's most appreciated."

"Perish the thought. I was being sarcastic," said Sandy with a sweeping hand motion.

Mark and Sandy both looked at Gavin as if he was next in line for further comment.

"Leave me out of this," said Gavin. "Still, I have had my fair share of heartaches in the game of love and the 'Victim Olympics.' But where is my plaque?"

"On your teeth," said Mark. "Consider it a consolation prize."

"Hey, I thought you were on my side!" said Gavin. "Still, in my defense, without sex, the world as we know it would end. Just like what Mr. Mark just said. So what many of us consider sordid behavior is actually necessary for our very existence. But the real question is this: is it worse being the dumpee or the dumper?"

"So even Gavin here is engaging in the act of critical thinking," said Mark. "A Socratic question no less. Dumpee, no contest."

Gavin finished off the half-full can of Mello Yello that was sitting on the coffee table since yesterday with a series of loud gulps.

"That's disgusting," shouted Sandy. "In more ways than one."

"Well, let's just say you are not just speaking to the choir, but you are shouting at him," returned Gavin as he slammed the empty can down on the coffee table. "As much as I am loathe to admit, I am partial to agree."

Mark went to the coffee table where Gavin had set his can. He picked it up and set it down again with a loud thud. "But it really all just begs the question—if you place a can of pop on a coffee table, is it still a coffee table?"

"Don't confuse being smart with being a smart-ass," said Sandy. "The bigger question remains—do you choose to see the old can of tepid pop as half full or half empty?" She exchanged looks with Gavin and Mark.

"Chalk it up to pop psychology," said Mark. "Take that, nature vs. nurture debate."

"I found it rather refreshing," said Gavin.

"That makes one of us," said Sandy, shaking her head.

Mark took a seat on the red floor chair where Sandy had been sitting earlier. He rocked back and forth as he spoke. "Point being, people are inclined to believe what they want to believe, simple as that. What we want to believe is more important than what is really true."

"Well, not everyone cares about psychology, mate selection theory, or philosophy, and least of all mortuary science," said Sandy. "I'm afraid that's all you."

"Not so, Sandy," continued Gavin, raising his index finger. "I, too, like me some mate selection theory, especially the hands-on experience portion of the class."

Mark shook his head. "And don't forget studying abroad. That's a classic."

"It's the little things," returned Gavin. "I try to stay on Cloud 9."

Mark stopped rocking and looked at Sandy. "If his life is anything like Cloud 9, I would sure hate to see what his 9th rung of hell looks like."

Mark and Sandy stared at Gavin, not saying a word.

"What?" asked Gavin, looking from one to the other.

"I guess we were expecting some sort of innuendo," returned Sandy.

"I got nothing," said Gavin. "I hate to disappoint."

"Hey, who's up for something fun?" said Sandy, going up to the plywood bookcase near the left side of the flatscreen. "Let's play some more of that 'End of the World' role-playing game again since we all sort of know how to play it by now. Which kind of apocalypse do we want to pretend we are in, zombies, gods, aliens, or machines?" She didn't even wait for an answer. She removed the "End of the World: Revolt of the Machines" role-playing rule book from the top shelf of the four-layered bookcase and sauntered into the kitchen.

"It doesn't sound like we have much say in the matter," said Gavin, standing up and stretching.

Mark and Gavin followed Sandy into the kitchen. Assuming the role of Game Master, Sandy had already placed a stack of character sheets and a pile of six-sided dice on the table in front of her. She also had the educational math puzzle game Twenty Four on the table, as she liked to use that for the in-game computer hacks. Mark took his seat on one of the padded folding chairs at the glass round table. Gavin opened the fridge and put a six-pack of Mello Yello on the table near the Gandalf poly-stone statue and set the box containing half a pizza on the counter, along with a small stack of paper plates. He also grabbed a K-cup and a mug from the cupboard and fired up the Keurig. After it was done, he put a generous helping of hazelnut creamer in it. He fixed a plate of pizza for Mark and Sandy and set them down next to them, and they indicated thanks. He made himself one as well, and with his coffee, he took a seat at the table. Mark reached for a Mello Yello.

Sandy handed Mark and Gavin a character sheet. "Remember, we play ourselves in this game. So try to choose attributes that mesh with your real-life talents, shortcomings, or fears." Sandy held up her character sheet and showed it to Mark and Gavin. "We get one point in all six sub-categories. And we also get ten additional points to split up over the physical, mental, and social categories. This includes dexterity, vitality, logic, willpower, charisma, and empathy. Oh yeah, and remember to come up with a positive and also a negative feature of your personality. And lastly, try to think of at least one real-life trauma you are comfortable sharing that could negatively affect you during a real-life apocalypse, like a phobia or fear of some kind. And since we are still learning the game, I think we can forego the formal rules on voting in our final character choices. I know the GM probably shouldn't have a character sheet, but I will also forego that rule and create one for myself since we only have three of us."

Mark gazed at his character sheet. "I think I could use the fact that I am cautious and open-minded as an asset." He started to lift his last slice of pizza to his mouth.

"Yes, to a fault," said Gavin.

"And what is that supposed to mean?" asked Mark, holding his pizza mid-flight,

Sandy made eye contact with Gavin. "Gavin is right. I mean, those are laudable traits, to be sure. But I just think sometimes you read far too much meaning into things. I know you are particularly fond of the fact that we share the same birthday, and you often cite it as a sort of sign of fate, kismet, or some sort of divine providence playing a hand in our friendship. And I am flattered you feel that way. I truly am. But in the grander scheme of things, sharing a birthday isn't all that strange."

Mark huffed and let his slice of pizza drop back onto his plate. "As far as the birthday thing, it's what brought us together and why we are friends to this day. I'm sorry that little detail means so little to you."

Sandy warmed her tone. "Okay, a bit harsh perhaps. I just don't want you to jump to conclusions so much. It can get you in trouble. But you can certainly put 'man of science' as one of your positive features in the mental category. And your logic is impeccable, worth at least two of your ten points."

Mark took a swig from his Mello Yello, not flattered by Sandy's positive words. "I am well aware of the *Birthday Paradox*, *Monty Hall Problem*, and the *Benford's Law* for that matter. Or *confirmation bias*, apophenia, or the *Barnum Effect*. You don't need to school me on probability or causality. But I have also studied license plate synchronicity and heart math. And that gets a little bit more complicated. I'm not an idiot, you know. I am just open-minded; that's all like any real scientist should be."

"License plate synchronicity?" echoed Gavin, as he wrote "Ladies Man" with two exclamation points as one of his positive features. "That one is new to me. I'm all ears."

Mark took a bite of pizza. "I am okay chatting about it, but the minute you start doubting me, this convo is over, got it?"

"Fair enough, fair enough," said Sandy, putting up her hands like a traffic cop stopping traffic.

"Synchronicity is the idea that events are connected, and things don't always just happen randomly. It's the idea that there are forces in the universe larger than ourselves. Even Carl Jung has entertained such notions. And William James has been said to have taken an interest in things like ESP. So don't play me for a fool."

"Hey, I didn't say anything," said Sandy, putting her palms up.

"You are thinking it, though," said Mark. "And no, I am not referring to ESP."

Gavin put "good with numbers" on his character sheet as a strength, given that he was a certified public accountant. "So Mark, are you referring to like, spirituality or religion?"

Mark rubbed his eyes. "I think it may have an element of pantheism, the spiritual workings of nature and the universe, and other such ilk."

"What do license plates have to do with it?" asked Sandy as she fidgeted with her ten dice pool in her hands.

"Nothing really, except that numbers are a very easy way to study energy flow, as you can easily detect patterns in numbers, sequences, or strings. Even the very dice you hold in your hands. For example, I may be thinking of a three-digit number, like 497, and you roll three dice, and it pops up. With three six-sided dice, the probability is 216. With three twenty-sided dice, it would be one in eight thousand. The theory goes that in a very heightened and incandescent state of emotion, you will notice, if not cause, odd combinations of numbers to come to the fore, like spotting the same license plate two or three times in a row or a sequential series. Or you designate a certain number as having some significance, and lo and behold, you see a car with that very same number within the next three plates you see. There have been times when I have literally predicted what the next license plate would be. But it only seems to happen when you are in a really anxious or even paranoid sort of mood. It's almost like your unconscious is willing it to happen. In other words, behind the veil of objective reality, there may be an emotional landscape that resembles an ocean, and all the energies people give off make waves, and these waves often clash with each other. Haven't any odd coincidences ever happened to either of you?"

Gavin took a slice of pizza. "I still like to think it was a message from Grandpa when I heard Billy Bragg's 'Tank Park Salute' at a grocery store, of all places, the day before his funeral. Even I like to think maybe it meant something, but who's to say?"

"I guess I never really gave it much thought one way or another," said Sandy. "Maybe some very odd things have happened, and I just didn't stop to notice."

"Lucky you," said Mark, taking Sandy's advice and putting "man of science" on his character sheet as a positive feature. He also put "slow to react" and "indecisive" as two negative features. For trauma, he put "Asperger's tendencies." He continued. "Not just license plate synchronicity. What about the Ganzfeld experiments?"

"Oh yes," said Sandy, looking at Gavin's character sheet. "In fact, didn't you and Mark try to conduct your own double-blind Ganzfeld experiment? If I recall, you guys didn't get the results you had hoped." She looked to the side and mumbled to herself, "I should really be more smug about that!"

"Trust me, you are plenty smug," said Mark. "In fact, I think one of our trials actually produced the opposite of the intended effect. Honestly, I am still not sure we replicated the successful studies correctly. But some respectable academics have purported results higher than what would be expected by chance."

Sandy looked at Gavin. "Knowing Gavin, he would have been hyper-fixated on booze or something, skewing the results in the opposite direction."

"Hey, give me some credit," said Gavin, holding his coffee mug as if it were a champagne flute. "It's like a reverse superpower. Just as impressive, just in the opposite direction."

"Perhaps," said Mark. "But you also gotta have good controls for these experiments, and the white noise has to be set at a perfect level. Also, it's a talent to even know how to channel the psychic energy necessary to send such messages in the first place."

"I think you will lose many scientists when you use words like 'psychic energy,'" said Sandy. "But doesn't it all sound a bit 'pseudo-sciency' to you? I mean, it kinda sounds like confirmation bias or wishful thinking to me. I get this image in my head of a rickety stagecoach proffering wonder tonics to a gullible and fickle public."

"Okay, you are starting to mock me," said Mark.

"Okay, okay, I really am not trying to be condescending here," said Sandy, putting in details of her own character sheet. She put "political savvy" as one of her positive features and "lack of empathy" for one of her weaknesses. She put "fear of heights" as her trauma. "I just wonder if it's all just coincidence, plain and simple, as boring as that may sound."

Mark continued. "At first, I thought so too, but there has always been two schools of thought on these matters. The 'Mulder' camp thinks it could have something to do with existential energy or even the collective unconscious. Mind over matter and all that. And then there are the Scullies, like yourself, who are a bit more hard-nosed about it all. Either way, as they say, absence of proof is not proof of absence."

Sandy rubbed her eyes and groaned.

Mark continued. "I am a rather curious fellow, Sandy, and I'm afraid sometimes my wishful thinking gets the best of me. But rest assured, by the end of the day, I am a scientist, and I try hard to be objective. But I have my hopes, and I have my dreams."

"So are there any experts on these subjects, like license plate synchronicity?" asked Gavin, adding "charming" as a positive feature on his character sheet. For "deficits," he put "scatterbrained" and "always hungry."

Mark downed his entire Mello Yello, grabbed another, and opened it. "Okay, Elliot Benjamin is a name that comes readily to mind. He is a proponent of license plate synchronicity, and he has written on the subject. He is not well-known, mind. His stance is that such coincidences are related to quantum physics, and they are not just random. It appears paranoid mind states might play a part or fear-laden intrusive thoughts of impending doom. Now the 'Scully' camp, on the other hand, including folks like David and Andrea Lane, take a more conservative stance. They chalk it up to basic statistics, like the birthday paradox or confirmation bias we just discussed."

Sandy put "fast runner" as one of her positive features on her character sheet. "So what do you hope to prove with your current experiments, the ones about doing truly random things to disrupt the cosmos?" She laid her hands on the table, palms down, and spoke very slowly. "Again, not being patronizing."

"It's patronizing how you keep saying that," said Mark."

"Apologies," said Sandy. "Hey, I am trying here! Give me some credit!"

"Not with your credit score, I won't!" said Mark. "It's okay. Anyhoo, issues like license plate synchronicity, Heart Math, or even the Ganzfeld experiments are not just about coincidences. It can also be about your mind state when these coincidences occur. And people like Elliot Benjamin incorporate quantum mechanics into the picture. My current experiments regarding doing odd things to disrupt the cosmos are akin to throwing stones into a pond—like talking to the universe in a manner of speaking. Tossing a message in a bottle out to sea. Or sending off a note in a helium balloon. Or dispersing messages via SETI. It's all about catching the attention of the universe in some way, shape, or form."

Sandy rubbed the tiredness from her eyes. "And once again, there's that confounded existential need of yours to see beyond the tapestry of the world. Most people could care less."

"You being sarcastic or serious?" asked Mark as he downed about half of his second can.

"A little of each, I suppose," said Sandy. "But I am not making fun of you, rest assured. All that research you have been doing, you are no dullard. Maybe a little gullible, perhaps, but you are far from stupid."

Gavin finished allocating his ten additional points around the six subcategories of attributes, as well as adding all his positive and negative features in each of the three main categories. For trauma, he put "fear of spiders and snakes."

Mark cracked his knuckles several times. "My theory is that if you do something out of the ordinary—something nobody has ever done, something so random and off the wall—it will disrupt or 'shake' the universe and the very fabric of the space-time continuum. Like shaking a dirty rug in the wind. Strange things can happen to you as a result. Unexpected things. Things that normally wouldn't happen. Things that normally couldn't happen."

Sandy took a can of pop and positioned her fingernail like a wedge to get the tab open without making too much of a racket. "So, did anything odd actually happen in return?"

Mark paused and thought a moment. "Well, one time, I kissed a ball-peen hammer exactly 131 times while holding an ostrich feather between my toes."

Gavin laughed. "What can I say? I am confident that has never been done before in the history of the world. I might actually pay good money to see that."

"You make jest," said Mark, smiling at Gavin. "And I take cash or check."

"Hey, I was being perfectly serious that time," said Gavin.

Sandy nodded her head. "So I guess you not only suck at detecting sarcasm, but you also assume sarcasm where none exists."

"What can I say, type one and type two errors," said Mark, filling in more details of his character sheet. He used a fairly even allocation of his ten points around the six sub-categories, roughly two in each, give or take. He compromised and put "open-minded" as one of his positive features and also put "can sometimes be too superstitious" as a negative feature, just to humor Sandy, if anything.

"Okay, just don't mention type 1 or type 2 errors on any of your dates," said Sandy. "Or mate selection theory, for that matter."

"The last date I had was in my morning muffin," said Mark. "But anyhoo, the very next day, I saw a commercial where an ostrich was burying its head in the sand while all this activity and commotion was going on around him. And when he pulled his head out, do you know what he found he'd missed out on?"

Sandy slapped her palms on her knees and leaned ahead. "What?"

"Well, the house behind him was demolished by high winds."

"So?" asked Sandy.

"I hate it when people say 'so' like that. It's unbecoming."

"Oh, it's unbecoming, says the posh aristocrat," mocked Gavin.

Mark fiddled with his character sheet. "Anyway, the point is that the commercial was about selling hammers. I mean, not ball peen hammers per se, but hammers nonetheless. Now I understand that this example was perhaps more auspicious and fruitful than most. My suspicion is that disrupting the space-time continuum with complete randomness might more often than not produce outcomes that are just as connected, just as real, but far more subtle. And while it might be difficult to spot the connections between events, the connections are there. I am sure of it."

Sandy leaned ahead. "Or a blind coincidence, plain and simple."

"Perhaps," said Mark. "But perhaps not. Speaking of ostriches, far too many people put their heads in the sand when it comes to existential matters of the human condition. Existence by its very nature is a miracle and a mystery. There could be aliens somewhere equally impressed by our existence here on Earth. Even a simple coin toss is not technically random," said Mark as he avoided Sandy's inquisition. "We only call it that because we don't know how it will land. But fate knows. The universe knows. Our very fingers know. The laws of the universe will predict it every time."

"So, are we gonna play here?" asked Gavin. "I don't think most apocalypses wait until we are ready for them. Let's kill some robots. Or run from them. Whichever comes first."

"Do you wanna be the GM?" asked Sandy.

"You being sarcastic?" asked Mark.

"Nope, not that time," said Sandy. "What can I say? You have a knack for it."

Mark smiled. "So you are capable of compliments after all."

· —

CHAPTER 6
A BEDTIME STORY (PART 1)

Main Characters: Faith and Hope
Date: November 5, 2032, Friday, 9:00 p.m.
Setting: Augusta, Maine

"Hey, please don't leave, Hope!" shrieked the twenty-eight-year-old Faith, as her hospice worker Hope tried to slip out the creaky door of her designated room unnoticed. This particular building was its own facility, and it housed between forty to fifty patients at any given time. There were five floors, with ten bedrooms per floor. Each room had two rooms, a bedroom and a bathroom. Food was delivered to each room by hospice staff. Faith had been working at this same location for the last eight years.

Hope returned and closed the door, and this time it didn't make a sound at all. "Funny how this door only creaks when you try to leave. It seems to be just fine when you come in." She hobbled back to Faith's trundle bed and took a seat at Faith's college-style desk that she'd received from her friend Marcy last Christmas.

Hope was dressed in a high-pile beige fleece sherpa jacket and black denim jeans. Faith was in her chamois pajamas, what she liked to call "Chamois Jammies," with an argyle pattern. She was also clutching her stuffed penguin, Sally.

"Are you mad at me?" asked Faith. "You don't have to stay if you don't want to."

"Of course not," returned Hope. "I apologize if I seemed that way. I actually thought you were asleep. And I must admit I was feeling a bit hungry and was gonna take a snack break in the ground-floor lobby."

Faith's trundle bed was in the center of the room and had a second pull-out bed where her Shetland sheepdog Menace was sound asleep. The bed itself was like the eye of a hurricane, a diminutive sanctuary of organized security, as a deathbed should be, sitting in the blast-zone of toy chests, scattered clothing, Christmas and Thank You cards, wrapping paper, and shelves of porcelain dolls adorning the walls. Even the air itself was filled with intensity, as Faith was using her smart-diffuser to disperse multiple essential oils at once, this time combining "Calm," "Stress Relief," and "A Restful Night" as if the combination would somehow augment the properties of the others, a veritable whole greater than the sum of its parts. The actual scents behind their marketing epithets were a blend of things like lavender, lemongrass, and chamomile. But Faith was a creature of habit, and she chose her scents carefully, like a golfer choosing just the right club for just the right situation.

The manner of Faith's environment was in stark contrast to her parents' domestic sensibilities and had been cause for alarm on more than one occasion when they came to visit. Faith's home of origin virtually ensured that all manner of figurines, collectible silent-film star plates, 2050s appliances (GPS vacuums, smart toothbrushes, and the like), dusted furniture, and even bills were arranged with a steadfast and symmetrical alacrity. And regarding the matter of Christmas cards, her parents had a spare room containing nothing but boxes, ribbons, bows, and wrapping paper, giving them the peace of mind of never having to purchase such sundries for Christmas ever again. The very idea of actually using many of their possessions sent a shiver down their spines, as this meant they would have to worry about putting them back in their proper places again. Even their prized record collection was a decorative landscape, as they had their compact discs neatly placed on wire book easels as if they were little pictures and feasts for the eyes, as opposed to a more visceral auditory medium. But Faith was resigned to die with dignity, and in her case, that meant being as messy as she cared to be.

"You have quite the aroma in here," said Hope. "What is that, perchance?"

Faith smiled. "Just a hodge-podge of different things I programmed my smart diffuser to mix, and in a specific ratio. Do you not like it?"

Hope tussled Faith's hair. "On the contrary, you might make a good alchemist or witch."

Faith laughed. "I will take that as a compliment, Miss Hope. I know I am considered a bit old for bedtime stories, but could you read me one? I figure since I only have about a month to live, I can throw social expectations to the wind."

"Well said, Miss Faith! Even without death hanging over one's head, social expectations are the shackles to which fools bow. Speaking of witch, again with the 'T' spelling, do you want to hear a story about a certain type of magic?"

"Like black magic or white magic?" asked Faith.

"Not exactly," said Hope, turning her head but maintaining her gaze at Faith. "I am thinking more of a type of magic that can be painful or pleasant. Perhaps something more like gray magic."

"I have never heard of gray magic," said Faith. "What's this special kind of magic like?" She pulled the fleece blanket and heavy comforter up to her chin as if she were a child in earnest anticipation.

"It's what is commonly called karma," said Hope, leaning forward at the desk. "Do you want to hear about it?"

Faith smiled, keeping up the child-like persona. "Of course. Is the story nice and scary? Just as long as it's nice and scary."

Hope kept her gaze on Faith while turning her head to the side. "Can a story be both nice and scary?"

"Sure it can! Is there any other kind?"

Hope smiled. "Well, it doesn't have monsters or goblins, if that is what you mean."

"Well then, how can it possibly be scary?"

"Because my story isn't make-believe," said Hope. "And that's what makes it scary. Monsters and goblins? They are not real, so how can they possibly be scary?"

"I guess you got me there," said Faith. "I'm all ears. Why don't you tell me?"

"All right then," said Hope. "But before we get to the karma police, we gotta talk a little bit about the setting. A bit of back-story, if you will."

"I'm ready," returned Faith. "Just don't waste too much time on that part."

And so Hope reached for a random book from Faith's bookshelf, a certain *Wuthering Heights*, not to read from, but to have something to fidget, like a public speaker holding note-cards without any actual desire to use them.

"It's a bit warm in here. You sure you need all those blankets?" asked Hope.

"Not really, but they help me feel safe," returned Faith.

Hope smiled. "I see, so they are more like 'Linus Blankets.' I know the feeling."

Faith took a deep breath, closed her large brown eyes, and smiled, clutching her blankets.

Hope licked her finger, and with a swoosh sound, flipped to page one of her book.

***

Once upon a time, when Earth was new, there was a war on. This was not a war of bloodshed, gangrene, amputation, or casualty. Nor was it a war against good and evil. This was an invisible war between two equally truculent and competing energies from behind the veil of the world's great curtain. A war between the very nature of pain and pleasure, each vying for dominance. But like equal amounts of fire and water, every battle seemed to end in a stalemate or some sort of armistice.

"Why is this happening?" Pleasure would ask, not knowing anything other than hedonistic felicity and rapture.

"I must admit I do not know," Pain would say in reply, a glutton for punishment.

Each side of this war failed to see that they needed the other side. After all, you can't have pain without pleasure. And you can't have pleasure without pain. You can only understand one if you have felt the other. Or so the theory goes. After all, if any war or game were truly fought on a level playing field, all things being truly equal, in all sense and manner of the word, it would surely end in a tie or stalemate each and every time. To be a victor is to have an advantage of some shape or form — fair, unfair, anticipated or unanticipated, or otherwise. And that was the sad truth. Or happy truth, as the case may be, depending on whose side you were on. And to the victor go the spoils. But who decides what is truly fair? That would be the province of who would later be dubbed the "karma lords," or what we mere humans sometimes like to call the "karma police."

Even in our current zeitgeist, the platitudes in our world that allude to karma are many. They all convey the dictum that people get what they deserve and deserve what they get — although these expressions usually place far too much emphasis on the punitive, without also acknowledging the fruitful rewards that can be gleaned from acts of virtue. The indelible reputation, then, of karma lords more often than not emphasizes sweet revenge, which does a great disservice to the benevolent ambitions karma lords may also hold.

All is fair in love and war
No pain, no gain
Don't judge lest ye be judged
You reap what you sow
What goes around comes around
You made your bed now you must sleep in it
The buck stops here
Eye for an eye and a tooth for a tooth
Karma's a bitch
Just desserts
Comeuppance
Now the shoe is on the other foot
Getting a taste of one's own medicine
You do the crime you do the time

What goes up must come down
You give as good as you get.

To be a karma lord is to feel every emotion and to think
every thought. Every pain, prick, stick, smirk, scrape, scratch,
insight, envy, sardonic sarcasm, boisterous guffaw, coveted
promotion, success, blemish, pleasure of the flesh, melancholic
moan, premature birth, expedited or slow death, ecstasy, hanging
by the neck until dead, steadfast delusion, hallucination, shame,
jovial grin, guilt, slight, mishap, misstep, unrequited love,
rejection, torture, elation, asphyxiation, sanguine sigh, drop,
aberration, infirmity, pathology, death by firing squad, wistful
regret, compunction, consumption, contention, infection, slice,
dice, stab, bludgeon, intractable ailment, burn, joyous revelry,
nick, Iron Maiden, crestfallen gaze, wistful stare, lovesick sigh,
infatuation, oblivion, rising of the lights, murder, the grieving of
billions of dead dogs, and crib death, just to name a few. And
to the extent that the aggregate sum total of joy is equal to the
absolute value of all the world's pain, it is all most agreeable, and
all remains right in the world.

Karma lords waste little time on the laws of the land.
They are much more concerned with the abstruse laws of nature.
Contrary to Earth lawmakers and their enforcers, the investiture
of karma lords lies with the stars and the moon, the sun and the
planets, the galaxies and the heavens. Theirs is not a hegemony
based on birth order, nepotism, bloodline, pecking order,
hierarchy, or class affiliation. In all of truths, their mere existence
remains unknown, and questions concerning their existence
are relegated to the nether-regions of that which is considered
legend, folklore, and pseudoscience. Even those that claim belief
are speaking mostly out of turn, as they have no more reason
to believe than any other persons of the world. After all, the
credulity of karma police is hinged on little more than wishful
thinking.

This is not to say that the entirety of their work goes
unnoticed. Much to the contrary, they are like stagehands, toiling

behind the scenes to ensure the show goes on. Standing outside the spotlight, they are luminaries without illumination. Theirs is a province devoid of accolade and approbation. But with these stagehands, their pervasive labor is mostly a pragmatic affair, as they busy themselves with the details so that everything goes smoothly behind the veil of the world's great curtain. As they say, the show must go on.

But without giving credit where credit was due, humans tended to steal the spotlight by merely "discovering" the laws of science, with little regard for who "passed" these strictures in the first place. Humans would have us believe that the mere "stumbling over stones" and the turning over of evidence somehow equates with the stuff of creating the very concept of science that allows such discoveries to be made in the first place. Nonetheless, lurking behind the shadows of the world, karma lords are the truly unsung spartan heroes. They shed tears for the world and receive none in return. They carry the weight of the world on their shoulders, and they also shoulder the blame.

Karmatic functionaries did not take their place among the stars through fleeting fancy, sudden whim, or arbitrary appointment. The populace can rest assured there is a method to their madness and a madness to their method. And contrary to how victimized a person might claim to be, only the karma police can know for certain just how much pain and suffering a person is actually going through, with an accuracy of twenty decimal places.

But the question remains — if karma lords were not elected, how were they granted holy or divine investiture? How did they take their position among the stars and moon? Being hum-gods, karma lords take their place between humans and gods on the existential pecking order. And while they may enjoy a semblance of divine knowledge, they do not have all the secrets of the universe in their keeping. To this end, they are just as much in the dark as humans are. And while they may have some of the secrets of the universe in their grasp, they cannot see into the heavens and that which lies in the sixth dimension.

Karma lords do not dabble in alchemy, cauldrons, bubbling potions, talismans, or any manner of witchcraft. But this is not to say karma is devoid of magic or divine providence. And just as is so common with the ways of the world, with power comes great responsibility. As such, if a karma lord were to dole out any punishment of a highly draconian nature, with intent to hurt, harm, impugn, or otherwise impose suffering of any kind, physical, psychological or spiritual, it would only seem prudent that this particular karma lord likewise subject himself or herself to the very same in return. Only by suffering the difference will the karma of the universe be reconciled and brought back into balance. In the event, the punishment that befalls any living creature does not fit the crime, or the reward does not fit the noble gesture, the karma lord can expect to expurgate this disparity and make up the difference accordingly, either through their own pain and suffering (like positive punishment) or the withholding of pleasure (like negative reinforcement). As it stands, karma lords are held to the very same standard as the populace they oversee and govern. As such, checks and balances are woven into the very fabric of the system. It cannot be emphasized enough that, appearances notwithstanding, a guillotine should never be confused with the stocks, even if they both happen to fall over the neck.

But what about appearances? As with the pitfalls of anthropomorphism, god-heads often resemble the incarnate caricatures of human folk told in the tales of old, with limbs, beards, furrowed brows, and irascible temperaments. And karma police are no different in this regard, as legends and lore can attest. But this motif does not stop at appearances. There is also often an assumption that god-heads indulge in complete divine knowledge accompanied by a strict and stoic rectitude. But with assumptions come many questions. What if the gods are equally in the dark as humans, as they blindly wander in darkened caves, unable to notice the shadows within the shade, stumbling in the dark corners of the world, searching for an existential reprieve from the mysteries of the plane, much like their human brethren?

This is especially true for the karma police, as they sit below even the very gods on the existential pecking order.

Mortal men and undying gods are not as disparate as one might assume. The world of hum-gods, a purview of which the karma lords are privy, proffers examples and cases in point. These patrons of the heavens are part human and part god, a waxwork and patchwork of flesh and spirit. So what is the tentative tenure of their mortal yet immortal existence? The answer is rather obvious. Some may exist for five days less than infinity, while others may have a half-life of a thousand years less than forever. This simple truth might seem quite delphic for humans to discern, but in the fourth, fifth, and sixth dimensions, it makes increasingly more logical sense. Sadly, every myopic Earth theory that has attempted to make sense of this has been tenuous at best and met with more questions than answers.

Karma lords are charged with the task to "serve and protect" the human race as well as the animal kingdom. Their mandate is to create law and order in a universe fraught with chaos and disarray. Where politicians and police pass and enforce the laws of the land, the karma lords pass and enforce the laws of nature and beyond. Contrary to what humans may think, the systems of law and order that permeate the continents, countries, and provinces of the land are highly primitive and based on the very basic Carrot and Stick Principle. They are at their core, at least ostensibly, based on Behavior Modification or Motivation principles.

And despite having access to five of the six sides of the Krystal Kube, the karma police do not know who or what the "true God" is any more than human folk. They, too, are resigned to trust in the faith. Some ascribe to the religions of the land. Others dream up their own interpretations. And while some karma lords believe in a more pantheistic Mother Earth or Mother Nature, others believe that existence is merely a stroke of luck (good or ill), a brush with happenstance, or the simple aftermath of a fortuitous serendipity. But just as with the police of human-folk, the karma police hope to create order among the populace, regardless of the origins of the world.

The Krystal Kube can see into six dimensions. The first three dimensions, of course, are spatial and include the X, Y, and Z axes. The fourth dimension is time. The fifth dimension is where things occur "behind the scenes." And this is where the karma lords do the bulk of their work, toiling behind the scenes of the world like stagehands to a play, breaking the fourth wall. The karma police do not have access to the final side of the Krystal Kube, the sixth dimension. To see into the sixth dimension is to attain all the secrets of the earth, stars, and planets, the wherefore and why, and also the afterlife. It is believed, however, that only the very gods themselves can gaze into the sixth and final dimension.

So while karma lords may have access to a few more of the world's best-kept secrets, in many ways, they are still the blind leading the blind. This is not to say they lack vision. But their vision is not tied to the literal anatomy of cellular rods and cones. What they do harness is a vision that is even more directive. Such vision might be more akin to traffic cones and lightning rods, used by human folk to guide traffic and channel electricity.

***

"These karma police sound bigger than life," said Faith. "Is this a tall tale?"

Hope smirked. "A tell-tale tall-tale? Most certainly not! A wide tale? Perhaps. As in, wide in vision."

Faith smiled. "Please keep going, Miss Hope. I want to hear more."

"I was just getting there," said Hope. "Hold your four horsemen."

Faith clutched her blankets. "Can you tell me more about ancient Earth? What's it like? Is it just like modern Earth?"

"We will find out soon enough," Hope said as she licked her finger and opened her "placebo" *Wuthering Heights* book. And with that, she continued with her story.

***

The twelve elegant and aged "statues," as they could

be called, stood proudly around the perimeter of the square Colosseum within the interior of the grand Pantheon. But they were not just statues, per se. Nor were they wax figures. They were actual statesmen, in the flesh, preserved by taxidermy. The men were wearing regalia reminiscent of ancient Assyrian court officials. The women's appearances were more akin to ancient Etruscan. There were three such figures surrounding each corner, comprising a total of eight men and four women. These incarnates reprized the various governors that had come and gone throughout the relatively short dystopian history of Ancient Earth, governed by the island civilization called "Goldilocks's Dilemma." It was said that the entire island was a city devoid of any vestiges of rural areas, a veritable Babylonian sin-city of ill-fated and insatiable peoples. It had been hypothesized that Goldilocks's Dilemma was governing Ancient Earth even before the rise and fall of all of the subsequent civilizations, including the Roman Empire, Babylon, and Atlantis, and was rumored to have had access to iron, copper, bronze, and other resources of the world that were said to have come much later. It is not known where Goldilocks's Dilemma was located. Some say it still exists. Some claim it rests in the deepest parts of the oceans. Others think it was where Atlantis was located before it was called Atlantis.

In this particular dystopian zeitgeist, each governor held their seat for ten years. The manner of dress of these illustrious dignitaries was representative of how these particular emissaries were adorned during the period of their highest stately influence. Most of these statesmen had their standard-issue military frock coats, some with shoulder brushes. The crest on the left side of the jackets all showed the inside view of a bristlecone pine tree. Each ring represented a year in the service.

Before the karma lords held their positions, it was within these very walls that all the important decisions were made from all manner of man-made governing assemblies throughout Goldilocks's Dilemma.

In this mysterious world, taxidermy of humans was "standard operating procedure." Such "preservation of the flesh" was a custom not out of place in this ancient zeitgeist. The only certainties in this world, it was also said, were "death and taxidermy." And the two were certainly not mutually exclusive. The so-called "lower" animals, of course, were not required to be preserved like humans, but the option was still open at the behest of hunters, museum curators, and other proprietors of such decedents. Naturally, most animals were relegated to the systems of rot and spoil endemic to the "animal condition." The places that housed the cadavers of the dead were called "mausoleum museums."

In Ancient Earth, the Church had more authority than the Crown. And nearly every religion of the inner sanctum subscribed to the practice of applying taxidermy to humans as a token of respect, regardless of the decedent's level of moral rectitude displayed during life. The very idea of allowing flesh to rot or be consumed by maggots was considered a highly sordid state of affairs and tantamount to blasphemy, as it was considered a desecration of the holy and bodily temple. Even a great many atheists and agnostics considered the practice of burial, decomposition, or cremation to be an archaic practice. Still, there were those dyed in the wool scientists who didn't much have an opinion either way. Sanctimonious or blasphemous, it was all the same. Empty vessels are empty vessels. Que sera sera.

The mausoleums that replaced the graveyards were much like wax museums. The main difference, of course, was that these patrons of the dead were not made of wax at all, but statues of stature, and quite literally, "in the flesh." Abasement and vandalism of these mounted cadavers was strictly prohibited and punishable to the fullest extent of the laws of the Church or the Crown.

Most of these "wax museum mausoleums" that housed the cadavers of the patrons of the lower echelons were less-than-ornate and lacked the sheen and shine of the more opulent structures that housed the incarnates of fame, fortune, status, achievement, or philanthropy. These lesser buildings of the former had the tile floor, brick and mortar walls, and sterile ambiances of a run-of-the-mill city library. And what they lacked in panache, they made up for in practicality, with wooden commoner's furnishings, a copper chandelier, or the odd portrait on the wall of its modest benefactors or contributors.

On the contrary, the more lavish of these resplendent wax museums that housed, the more illustrious elite resembled city capitol buildings, with the usual ornate graces of a more regal beauty and bounty sprinkled throughout. This was visible in the details, from the luster of golden chandeliers, flying buttresses, or the carefully placed oaken grandfather clocks set to Greenwich time, or the various hand-painted and commissioned portraits adorning the polished stone walls with their pink ivory wood frames. These latter buildings were the bastions of opulence that housed the aforementioned nobility of regal statesmen, high-ranking military officials, venerable philanthropists, martyrs, high caliber artists, esteemed luminaries of the medical community, noble benefactors, and stalwarts of the arts or master crafts. Those of the living were accustomed to spending ample amounts of time and coin to bear witness to these towering giants of yesteryear. Through the humility and humbling effect that death oft-brings, for better or worse, the occasional faux pas or random act of indiscretion posed by these statesmen during their course of life was for the most part forgiven or ignored, save for the largest of vices.

Still, there were also the dark halls and corridors that housed those that were considered the well-known but ill-fated reprobates of the Crown and the iconoclasts of the Church. These were considered the "infamous" at best and the "heathen" at worst. These were the cadavers that in another time and place may have been burned or cast aside in paupers' graves. These gloomier halls were often underground mazes, like the tunnel systems that sometimes marked the old Victorian asylums. Such mausoleums required a tour guide, and there were many tales of people who wandered off, never to be seen again. These facilities were often unkempt and dingy, with the acrid smells of old underground air mixed with the scents of poorly embalmed and slightly rotting corpses.

Yet some of these less-than-dignified statesmen often attracted larger audiences than the more respected variety of cadavers. These "tourist traps," as they could be called, were where the pathologically curious could find repose and guilty pleasure in gazing upon the serial murderers and despots of the old world, positioned in less-than-dignified poses — for a nominal fee, of course. Particularly popular were the low-brow dioramas depicting a myriad of bellicose warmongers, creatively shown in over-the-top poses or lurid displays of affection.

Needless to say, these approximations of "wax museums" were natural catalysts for "waxing nostalgic." And in accordance with terror management theory, the preservation of these cadavers proffered, at the very least, the illusion of immortality. This sentiment was to the chagrin of "The Lesser Men," who advocated for the more natural processes of leaving flesh to rot and spoil.

As chaotic as this world might still seem now before the karma lords seized control of Ancient Earth and Goldilocks's Dilemma, existence was all the more terrifying. There was no law and order whatsoever. No checks and balances. Not even a term, let alone a synonym, for this idea we now call "fairness." It was all manner of revenge, tit for tat, and dog eat dog hooliganism. Murder was normalized. Stealing was encouraged. The ends always justified the means. And while the human race did not use the actual colloquialism, they wielded the marquee "all is fair in love and war" to a ridiculous extreme in fighting spirit. So while the world arguably always had a streak of dystopian fervor, it could also be said that this new world was at least a kinder and gentler place to hang one's hat, a more comfortable form of captivity, as it were. And thankfully, for the sake of mankind, there also existed a prescient dreamer who was ranked above the karma police but below the gods. This mysterious figure went by the epithet of "Docent Randii." He elected a very special karma lord to watch over our world, a karma police who was tough but fair. And it was at the aforementioned Grand Pantheon that they chose to do their grand work. But not on Earth. The Docent Randii removed the holy structure from the ground with the ever so slightest twitch of his finger, and he relocated the entire place somewhere among the stars, in a different dimension and timeline of Earth. Nobody knew for sure exactly where. But it was somewhere. Someplace. Sometime.

***

And with that, Hope slowly closed her book, as if she were a preacher closing a holy tome.

"But I am not ready for sleep!" shrieked Faith in a loud whisper.

"Well, that makes one of us," said Hope.

Faith sat up. "I'm not even scared yet."

"Scared?" huffed Hope, reeling her head back in disbelief. "Well, are you scared of Santa Claus?"

"No, of course not," said Faith. "Should I be?"

Hope put *Wuthering Heights* back into its rightful slot. "He's a karma police, you know. Does he not reward good children with presents and punish bad children with coal? He's not always so jolly. You don't want to get on his bad side either."

"So when did you stop believing in Santa?" asked Faith.

"Who said I stopped believing?" asked Hope.

Faith pulled her covers down to her waist and stared at her feet under the covers. "When I was eight years old, my friends at school told me that parents made him up to get kids to be good little boys and girls. Almost like a bribe."

Hope continued. "Ironic that—some people say the same thing about religion."

Faith's expression appeared bewildered. "So is religion the adult version of Santa Claus?"

"Well, that depends on who you ask," returned Hope, followed by a smile. "Still, you might wanna be careful who you ask. You never know who you might offend. Or how biased the source is."

"Offend? By asking a question? My teacher—well, my old teacher when I was well enough to go to school, anyways—said there was no such thing as a bad question."

"I'm afraid not all have such an open or humble mind," said Hope. "But children ask the best questions, the big ones adults are too afraid to ask."

Faith sat up. "But I want to hear more about the karma police. You were just about to talk about them!"

Hope stood up from the desk. "Yes, you can hear the entirety of the story up to the bitter end. But this karma police in front of you needs her sleep so she can spin a good tale next time. Sleepy storytellers forget details, you know. But you may need to remind me where we are at. I don't always remember everything, either from getting older or from simply wanting to forget. Either way, my mind is about as sharp as mild cheddar these days."

"Hmm," said Faith as she tapped her chin with her pinkie finger. "What we need is a mental bookmark, a word that will jostle your memory to remember where we are."

"Fair enough," said Hope. "How about we make 'Taneur' our secret password, like a tanner of hides. And when you mention the word, I will remember exactly where we are."

"Tanner," Faith repeated as she clutched her battered teddy bear with the two hand-sewn buttons for eyes. She then snuggled into a resting position. "Maybe we can end all our stories with a secret password. It makes me feel like I am not dying that way, as I have something to live for."

"Sounds like a plan to me," laughed Hope as she left the room and slowly closed the large wooden door behind her.

This time the door didn't creak at all.

· —

CHAPTER 7
A BROTHER'S DRUTHERS

Date: July 01, 2019, Thursday, 2:00 P.M.
Setting: Veranda Flats
Main characters: Mark, Sandy, and Gavin

A Police Sting Desperately Needed for the Masked Beekeeper

It appears Amrak has found cause to reprise his role of killing people on Valentine's Day. At the very least, there were only two deaths this time as opposed to the seven he killed in 2017, back when he recreated the 1929 St. Valentine's Day Massacre.

Fred Nicks, a homeless man from Boston, was killed by Amrak while dumpster diving to fetch an office chair and some random bedding. When he was completely inside, Amrak shot him in the knee with a .22 rifle to immobilize him before he jettisoned his killer bees into the confines of the container. Nicks was found later that day, the lid of the dumpster held steadfast by a menagerie of concrete blocks. He was released from prison two weeks ago for killing his best friend in a bar brawl thirty-two years prior.

The other casualty on February 14 belonged to Kimberly Rice in Eugene, Oregon—his second victim in the state since 2017. She was released from prison a week ago for pushing her elderly grandfather down the stairs twenty-seven years ago.

He did not reserve his murders to just Valentine's Day, however. Another occurred on February 6 and belongs to Jacob Swanson from Arizona. He was minding his own business, quite literally, as he was readying his small bait shop in Apache

Junction for the day's anglers heading to Canyon Lake. Amrak, likewise minding his own beeswax, tossed in an entire hive of Africanized honey bees, also known as "killer bees," into the aptly named bait shop. But this time, the shop-owner was the bait. By the time his first customer of the day arrived for night-crawlers, Jacob was already dead, and the ex-con was now truly an ex-con. In all of these cases, police confirmed that Amrak also left his signature MO, a garden flagpole shoved into their bodies. And pinned between their bodies and the flagpoles were identical notes, which read, "Let this death be a lesson to you all. What goes around comes around. I am blessed and cursed with karma. And sometimes, it's not the hand that guides the pen, but the pen that guides the hand. But either way, the pen is always mightier than the sword."

-------from *Vigilante Vignettes* magazine, March issue, 2019

"Okay, Gavin," said Mark as he came into the living room and plopped into the Lazy Boy, holding a small notepad. "You ready?"

"As ready as I will ever be," said Gavin with zest and zeal, as if he were on a game show. He was laying stiff as a board on the sectional in the living room, with half a ping-pong ball over each eye.

Mark removed his pencil from above his ear and flipped to his script. "Which image was the most salient during the last thirty minutes of ESP transfer: dairy group, meat group, fruits and vegetables, or grains?"

"Grains, definitely grains," said Gavin with a booming voice. "Most definitely grains. I see bread products. Pita bread. Pumpernickel. Crumpets."

"Damn it," said Mark, followed by a frustrated sigh. "You suck at this."

Gavin yanked the ping-pong balls out of his eyes and sat up. "You are the sender—you are the one that is supposed to transfer the correct images into my brain! My job is to kick back and listen. You know, 'message delivered' and all that."

Mark huffed. "Well, maybe if you had better ESP, I wouldn't have to work so hard!"

Gavin rubbed his eyes. "As long as you can't tell what I am calling you in my head right now, we are all good."

"Real funny," continued Mark, flipping to a new page in his notepad. "Maybe I was too distracted. Should we try again?"

"What are you guys doing?" asked Sandy as she appeared from the kitchen and stood in the doorway. "Last time I checked, it was starting to look like *Clockwork Orange* in there!"

"We were conducting another Ganzfeld experiment," said Gavin. "Want to join us?"

"Ah, no thanks," said Sandy. "I got less childish things to do, as it's my turn to clean the Keurig and do the dishes. You know, adulting."

"Where is your creative spirit?" asked Gavin. "Your scientific curiosity? 'One giant leap for mankind' and all that?"

"I will take a rain check," said Sandy. "That's junk science anyway."

"Ye of little faith," said Mark. "What can I say? One man's junk is another man's treasure."

Gavin resumed his position on the couch and placed the ping pong halves back in his eyes. "We are doing some very dignified and noble work in here."

"Said the guy with ping-pong balls in his eyes!" said Sandy. "You guys have fun with that. What's your hit/miss ratio, anyway?"

"Less than twenty-five percent, which is actually fewer hits than expected by chance alone," said Gavin. "Don't ask me. I have decided to call it anti-ESP. It's a gift."

"Wow, some gift," laughed Sandy. "A superpower where you perform under chance levels. Not sure if you are gonna save the world with that one."

"Hey, don't mock," said Gavin. "Instead of putting thoughts into someone's head, you can drive them out. There could be a use for that."

Mark smirked. "Like make someone forget everything they studied for an exam?"

"Precisely," said Gavin, snapping his fingers. "I think I could actually work with that!"

"Okay, should we switch roles?" asked Mark. "Let me be the receiver, and you can be the sender."

"Fine by me. Maybe my ESP sensibilities will be better than yours." Gavin sat up and took the ping-pong ball halves out of his eyes.

Sandy sighed, shook her head, and returned to the kitchen. She fired up the Keurig, and soon the aroma of Starbucks Pike's Place permeated the air. Since Mark and Gavin were busy, she seized the opportunity to do some reading in her room. With her coffee in tow, she meandered down the hallway towards her room. The smell of Mark's favorite incense, "Dragon's Blood," emanating from his room distracted her. She popped her head into his room to see if it was still burning unattended, and sure enough, it was.

Damn that guy, lucky he hasn't burned the house down yet, she thought to herself. She dumped some of her coffee atop the incense cone, which was sitting in a metal ashtray. But something else caught her eye. Mark's computer was left unlocked, and his desktop wallpaper showed the famous — or infamous — depiction of Sylvia Plath with her head in the oven.

What the hell? Sandy thought to herself. She looked out into the hallway, heard Mark and Gavin still fussing with their Ganzfeld experiment and trash-talking down the hall in the living room, and quietly closed the door. She waddled to the Herman Miller Ambi office chair in front of the computer and hunkered down. She noticed a folder named "Death Hag." *Probably just some shock value,* she thought to herself. As her curiosity took over, she clicked into the folder. There were hundreds of photos, all of dead bodies. Some of the photos were old, some new. Some were black and white, while others were in full color. Some of the dead people were male, others female. While some of the people were dismembered, many of them were also simple run of the mill coffin pictures taken at a funeral. She spent some time perusing the thumbnails without feeling a need to go into any of them in any more detail.

"Snoop much?" asked Mark in a loud and angry tone from the doorway as he stood there with the door half-cracked open.

"Wow! You scared me!" returned Sandy with a jump as she popped up from the chair, knocking the computer mouse off the desk. She retrieved the mouse and set it back on the desk. "I thought you were hanging out with Gavin."

Mark shook his head. "Yes, well, I thought I would bring my Dragon's Blood out here for some muse."

"What's a death hag?" asked Sandy, like an overzealous news reporter.

"Why are you in my room?" countered Mark as he marched in and turned off the screen.

"I get to ask the questions," shouted Sandy. "After all, you're the one that got busted. And you can turn off the computer all you want. I still saw what I saw."

Mark thumped his chest with his index finger. "Me? I just busted you in my own room!"

Sandy raised her voice. "And I just busted your little funeral procession!"

"Either way, your trustworthiness rating just dropped fifty points," Mark shot back.

Sandy switched the screen back on. "Well, sometimes people have a right to snoop, especially if there is a valid reason. Frankly, you just made my worry meter raise fifty points."

Mark yanked the monitor plug from the wall. "Just chill, okay? It's not as weird as you think."

Sandy sat back on the chair in front of the computer and rested her foot on the armrest. "Then answer my question, what is a death hag?"

"Timber," said Mark as he fell on his bed like a tree and sprawled out over the covers, as if oblivious to her question.

Sandy turned around in the chair and faced him. "That's real mature."

"Thanks," said Mark.

Sandy asked her question again, in the exact same manner and decibel level as before. "What's a death hag?"

Mark sighed as he fluffed his pillow and placed it under his head. "A death hag is just a slang term for someone that is fascinated by death. That's all. Nothing more, nothing less. Now stop worrying already."

Sandy leaned ahead. "Well, excuse me for thinking the term sounds rather frightening. It makes me think of a character from one of your fantasy role-playing games—you know, not like the one we were just playing. But what about those creepy pictures in your computer? That somehow doesn't seem all that innocuous to me."

"Death hags just take scientific curiosity to a higher level," said Mark, as he turned his head to face her. "Relax, lady."

"Lady?" asked Sandy. "I think I resent that. But what's the point in it? Shock value? Are you people crying out for help?"

"'You people'?" said Mark. "I think I resent that. I thought 'you people' were above using the phrase 'you people.'"

"Smartass much? Besides, you called me 'lady' in a similar manner."

Mark turned his head towards the ceiling. "Remember in our university psych class when we were reading about terror management theory? Earnest Becker's Denial of Death and the like?"

"Somewhat, but it's all a bit hazy," said Sandy, letting her guard down a bit. "Maybe I was recovering from a hangover at the time. Although I must admit that most of that stuff fell right out of my brain the second after I finished the exams. Use it or lose it, I guess. We remember what we want or need to remember."

Mark stared back at the ceiling and continued, speaking as if his very bed were a Freudian couch and Sandy were a psychoanalyst. "It all goes back to the fear of the unknown. What lies beyond life and death. Most things in life are nothing short of illusions, fallacies, or *Linus Blankets* that give us a false sense of security. Politics, religion, or any other belief system. The truth is, nobody knows where we came from or where we are going as a human race." With a swoosh sound, he turned his head to Sandy without lifting his head from the pillow. "And that, m'lady, is the crux of terror management theory."

"M'lady?" asked Sandy. "That sounds a little bit better. But this fascination of yours just seems wrong, somehow."

Mark looked towards her. "These questions are big, and people treat them like they are small."

"I guess I don't really care," said Sandy. "I am too busy trying to survive, eat, and keep a roof over our heads. You can keep your razors. I will save mine for shaving my legs."

"Passive aggressive much?" said Mark, before returning his gaze back to the ceiling. "You frame my existence as if I am quite the layabout. It wasn't all that long ago I was working. Besides, I am trying. I just interviewed at Anodyne a little over a month ago."

Sandy spun herself around in the office chair as she spoke. "Well, trying doesn't pay the bills. I'm afraid I am too busy with all the 'little pictures' to give the 'big picture' too much thought."

"But seriously, haven't you ever wanted to gaze into the very wells of a dying man's eyes and try to grasp the secrets of the universe?"

"I haven't put that one on my bucket list," she said. "I might consider putting it on my fuck-it list, though, the stuff I never want to try as long as I live."

Mark smiled. "I never heard that one." He grabbed Gavin's badminton birdie from the floor, just near his bed. He proceeded to toss it in the air and catch it. "Besides, none of this is any different than when I worked my Capstone experience at the mortuary in Vancouver. I saw dead people there all the time. And those were real cadavers, not just pictures."

Sandy stopped revolving in her chair. "Yes, but isn't saving videos and pictures of dead people a little bit different?"

Mark caught the birdie and held it to his chest. He glared at Sandy. "How so?"

"I mean, it's definitely not normal, right?"

"Those are your insecurities talking. Besides, there is no such thing as normal unless you are referring to the normal curve in statistics. Many of those pictures in the death hag folder are well-known in the death hag community. People like Bud Dwyer, Evelyn McHale, Christina Lubbock, Jordan Romero, and Michael Marin." Mark kept mum about his other folder that Sandy didn't seem to notice, the one called "Stunts and Parkour" containing dozens of Mark's death-defying exploits, each incident containing fear measurements from his Madcap helmet. Not only did he not want Sandy to know that he was into a modest version of free running, roof jumping, parkour, and stunts in general, but he also saved pics of people who had died doing such various stunts, including the likes of Jim Bailey, Wu Yongning, Pavel Kashin, and Jane Wicker. His fascination with stunts and parkour were partly for research purposes and also arguably due to his increasing suicide ideation and risk-taking behaviors. He spoke up to rally Sandy's attention elsewhere. "I also have a folder called 'near-death.'"

Sandy's eyebrows raised. "Near-death?"

Mark nodded. "Death hags also like to look at pictures of people just before they died. There is something properly existential about that."

Sandy sighed. "With all due respect, you are a bit of a psycho. And I mean that in the most pleasant sense of the word. No offense."

"No offense? Well good, because I got no defense!" said Mark. "And 'with all due respect?' Now that's rich, and I mean that in the most unpleasant sense of the words."

Sandy smiled from ear to ear as she pushed Mark's buttons like a child with a speak and spell. "I still love you, even if you are a psycho."

"Glad to have your vote of confidence. People fear what they don't understand and all that. We are after the truth of truths and waste no time with insecure or ignorant people. Do you remember the movie *Flat Liners*?"

"Sure I do," said Sandy. "How can I forget?"

"Death hags are kinda like those guys, but without having the need to risk their own necks in the process," said Mark, realizing full well that his own penchant for parkour and dancing with death made him an exception to this rule. "We are equally curious, however, to ascertain the truth of truths. I really don't get why nobody seems to care about this shit. It's like the most important thing in the world, and people treat it as less important than what brand of toothpaste to buy."

Sandy spun around again in her chair. "Some things are just so big that you can't see them when they are right in front of you."

Mark laughed. "You make it sound like the Nazca lines of Peru."

Sandy stopped spinning. "I suppose it's like the old elephant in the room that people tiptoe around. Besides, you are the one with the degree in mortuary science. You naturally would care about this stuff more than your average Jane or Joe."

Mark paused before continuing to toss his birdie up and down. "Indeed, but there is a third side to every story, no?"

"And what is the third side?"

"The first side is person A's perception of what happened. The second side is person B's perception of what happened."

"And person C?"

The shuttlecock made a thud against the wall as Mark whacked it with his hand by accident. "There is no person C. The third side of the story is what actually happened. The objective truth transcends subjective perceptions. Unfiltered raw data."

"I see," said Sandy. "Makes enough sense, I suppose."

"But it's not just about death," continued Mark as he sat up. "It's also about life. Not just about why and how people die, but also about why and how people live. They are two sides of the same coin, eh?"

"I guess so," said Sandy. "I just worry about you sometimes, that's all. Underneath my brazen and cavalier demeanor. Can't hate me for that."

Mark leaned in towards Sandy. "Well, thanks for the

sentiment. It's appreciated, if not altogether warranted. But it's my curiosity that gets me into trouble. I just have this need to know what happens when people die."

"It just all seems so creepy, I guess." She spun herself in the chair a few more times, this time much faster than before.

"Shit, I hate that word," said Mark. "Honestly, I find it 'creepy' that you are not into it. Anyway, I am just your everyday boilerplate and garden variety death hag."

"Garden variety, death hag?" said Sandy with glee as she spun faster and faster. "Do you hear yourself? I think that is what you might call an oxymoron!"

"I might call you an oxymoron," said Mark.

Sandy stopped dead in her tracks and faced Mark. "Is that supposed to be witty?"

Mark chuckled. "It scores about a fifty percent on the witty continuum."

"Lovely," said Sandy. "'Tis a shame you feel the need to laugh at your own jokes."

"It's the eyes, Sandy," said Mark in a whispered voice. "I can't help but stare into their sad and dejected eyes. It's as if I can almost see something. Something deeper. Something more poignant, mysterious, and meaningful than yesterday's weather report. That's the only point of our humble little community. Nothing nefarious, rest assured."

Sandy raised her eyebrows. "Humble little community?"

Mark stood up and wandered towards the computer next to Sandy. She put her left arm around his waist and tugged at his belt loop with her right hand as she guided him onto her lap.

"Careful you, this is an expensive set-up I have here," returned Mark as he continued to pull up the home page for "WHY," the name of his favorite death hag online community. He pointed at the screen to the "about" section. "See for yourself. We are just fascinated by existence and the human condition. Why we are here and the like. Life is one side of the coin. And on the other side is death."

She leaned over and looked at the screen. "I see, literally if not figuratively."

"Well, thanks, I think," said Mark. "Life as we know it is a real-life *Twilight Zone* episode, maybe something like the 'Five Characters in Search of an Exit' episode. Or something from the 60s version of *Outer Limits, which you had playing on the TV a while ago*. The moment we are born, it's like 'Zap!' here we are, not knowing where we came from or where we are going. How are we really supposed to know what to believe, or what is real, or what separates fantasy from illusion? I want to transcend the need for terror management. I don't want to settle for making my own meaning from meaninglessness. I want to know the truth of truths, the objective center of the subjective layers. Terror management implies making sense of limited information. I want all the information I can get my hands on until there is no longer a need for managing one's own terror."

Sandy pointed at the picture of the grim reaper with fire in his eyes. "I like that image, though."

Mark stood up and went near the door. "But this is 2019. Hasn't the human race been in the dark long enough? Why are we here? What is the meaning of this place?"

Sandy stood up from the chair. "Some questions are just too big to care about. It's like an ant wandering too far from the anthill or a bee flying too far from the hive."

"Those creatures don't care about mortality and existence," reminded Mark. "I'm afraid that curse belongs to the human race. Haven't you ever watched the sequel to *Ghost in the Shell*?"

"What's going on?" asked Gavin in a tired voice, yawning and rubbing his eyes, suddenly appearing in the door wrapped up in a fuzzy fleece blanket.

"You don't want to know," said Sandy. "Trust me."

Mark went through the door and put his hand on Gavin's shoulder. "Let's just say it's time to pull Schrodinger's cat out of the bag."

--

CHAPTER 8
RAIN CHECKS AND
"THE MAN THAT CRIED FOUL"

Date: March 9, 2017, Thursday, 1:00 P.M.
Main character: Madeline Fischer
Setting: South Dakota State Hospital in Sioux Falls

Day of love or day of hate? Evil Vigilante Recreates the 1929 St. Valentine's Day Massacre, Leaving Seven Dead.

Seven people were killed in Portland and Seattle on Valentine's Day, all of them ex-felons with murder charges. All seven died from severe stings from killer bees. There have also been confirmed sightings of a mystery man in beekeeper's garb around the crime scenes. In all seven cases, there was a note pinned to the bodies which stated, "Karma's a bitch. Just because the criminal justice system has become a joke, this does not mean karma will smile just as kindly. People will get what they deserve. Even on St. Valentine's Day. Bee Warned!---Amrak."

The one casualty in our Portland was Tessa Fischer. Not three days after she was released from imprisonment for killing her landlord, the mysterious man in beekeeper's garb waited outside her Portland, Oregon home until seeing her get into her pickup truck for work. Managing to trap her inside, he released swarms of the importunate killer bees into the vehicle. She was found less than a day later. She is survived by her two daughters.

--------*The Multnomah Contribution, February 16, 2017*

"Can you please come back to the group?" said the lanky forty-five-year-old counselor, a certain Tamara Mullen, to

Madeline, with a soft but resolute tone.

Madeline stared at the window for a brief moment before turning around. The other six group members stared at her as if she were about to walk the plank, at least until she made eye contact with them, at which point they stared either at the floor or ceiling in an attempt to save face. One of the hospital orderlies, a fifty-two-year-old and burly Herman Wentz, was sitting on Tamara's left, keeping watch over the group and taking down notes in shorthand as Tamara spoke.

"I am sorry, but the quality of my auditory reflections will be all the better if you allow me to see my visual reflection in this here window," said Madeline softly as she tapped on the pane with her long fingernails. "I look almost transparent. As such, perhaps my reflections to you will likewise be all the more transparent as if this is a window into my very soul. Besides, the rain always puts me in a pensive and wistful mood." She looked at Tamara over her shoulder. "I would like to stay here if it's all the same. Just sayin'."

"Fine," said Tamara. "Since you are so melodramatic about it. But you gotta start challenging yourself to leave your comfort zone once in a while. I know being in groups is a trigger for you, but we also need to practice sitting with discomfort to overcome our anxieties and fears. And you have to pay attention and listen to the other group members. This group isn't all about you, Madeline."

Madeline stuck her tongue out in the window, where Tamara couldn't see her. She giggled when she saw her tongue in the reflection as if she was sticking out her tongue at herself.

The compulsive liars' group became immersed in their own conversations about all manner of lies—white lies, lies of omission, or that first time when someone caught you in the act of lying. And all the while, Madeline just kept staring out the window, lost in her own world. Thoughts of her parents, and all the events that had brought her here, tugged at her tear ducts. She noticed her own tears falling in her reflection, and they seemed to intermingle with the falling rain outside—it was difficult to distinguish one from the other. The drops were thick and heavy, and they reminded her of the misty morning dew that she used to admire from her garden flowers at early dawn back in Oregon.

Her thoughts of the present group drifted away as she reminisced and recollected what it had been like living in Portland with her parents. She recalled how it wasn't a big happy family per se, but a family nonetheless, with the ebb, flow, and day by day drama, distractions, and doldrums of people who have a place to hang their hat and call home. She started to wonder if the reflection in the window was not a reflection at all but rather the semi-transparent ghostly image of some sort of phantom. The image somehow seemed younger than how she actually looked, and she wondered if she was seeing a version of herself from the past. She was surprised at how sullen she looked during this bout of wistful melancholy. It was as if all the regrets of what brought her to this awful place had somehow come to the fore, flashing before her eyes like a movie playing in "fast rewind."

***

Madeline was committed, legally if not mentally, to the Sioux Falls Mental Hospital on February 22. Madeline was given an initial commitment of at least three years, a tenure that was quite rare in this day and age of deinstitutionalization and community-based treatment. In addition to a strict medication regimen, she had various groups to attend during the day: Dialectical behavior therapy (for emotion regulation), grief group, eating disorders, and another that combined the struggles associated with anxiety and/or dolor. However, it was Madeline's first day in her new compulsive liars' group, which was composed of three males, three females including herself, and the two staff, Tamara Mullen and Herman Wentz. Today the group was talking about the costs and benefits of compulsive lying by putting together a payoff matrix.

As of March 9, 2017, Madeline was a thirty-eight-year-old Portland, Oregon native, impetuous to a fault, who moved to Sioux Falls in the winter of 2009 to work as a research assistant at the University of Sioux Falls. With a European pedigree, she was a virtual mish-mash of German, Polish, and Czech descents. Being a fourth-generation person from the States, she was acclimated to the mixing of cultures endemic to the hustle-bustle, hullabaloo, and hoi-polloi of her modern world.

Our Madeline struggled with various mental health aberrations and an assortment of addictions and compulsive behaviors, including lying, thieving, and spending. Her treatment plan included working on impulse control and learning to delay gratification by focusing on the "window of opportunity" that exists between the "S" (stimulus) and "R" (response) in stimulus response chains.

Due to her mother's death, she had a sizable next egg of just over three-hundred-thousand dollars, although she also had unpaid debts in the thousands, which diminished this stockpile by about sixty percent.

From a purely academic purview, our Madeline was one year short of her B.S. degree in sociology, which proved to be both a blessing and a curse. Madeline herself later concurred with those cynics that a "B.S." degree in sociology was both literal and figurative. But the ambit of philosophy, including sociology and matters of crime and punishment, was her passion, wheelhouse, and raison d'être, for better or worse. She often wondered if the more you knew, the more miserable you became. In fact, it was said that her mother once proclaimed that she cried for a full hour the moment she was born as if wanting to claw her way back into the safety of her mother's uterus, never to leave again.

***

"So Madeline, can you answer the question?" asked Tamara, speaking in a loud voice.

Madeline turned from the window. "What question?"

Tamara sighed with disapproval. A couple of snickers were heard from members of the group, and Madeline glared at each of them.

Tamara continued. "The question we were just talking about for the last fifteen minutes?"

"I'm sorry, Tamara," said Madeline. "I wasn't paying attention. But these stools are super hard. Do you happen to have a stool softener?"

The group burst into peals of laughter. Tamara made hand motions to silence the group.

Madeline smiled at the ruckus she had just created. "Just

sayin'."

"Well, thanks for at least being honest about not paying attention. Now let's talk about yesterday's easy assignment, to analyze 'The Boy that Cried Wolf.' So what do you think is the moral?'"

"Well, I suppose I know the answer you are fishing for," said Madeline as she tapped her finger on her chin. "This is a compulsive liars group, after all. And I know that answering a question with a question is generally your purview. But if I may risk a question of my own, did you know that there is actually a second moral to 'The Boy that Cried Wolf?'"

"You are a compulsive liar, Madeline, and I worry that your so-called reflection is actually a deflection, a red herring to circumvent what the real lesson is." The other five members of the group stared awkwardly at the floor.

"Well, okay then," said Madeline. "So much for person-centered treatment."

"Now you are being defensive," said Tamara. "And avoiding your feelings."

"The only reason I am here is because I fibbed about my suicide attempt," said Madeline. "Just sayin'."

"Yes, Madeline, but that's a pretty serious thing to lie about, isn't it? You shouldn't say you didn't make that attempt when you know you really did. You might not realize it, but we care about you."

"Yeah, sure," blurted Madeline. "As if you would be sitting there talking to me right now if you weren't getting paid for it."

The same two members snickered in response, and she couldn't tell if they were laughing with her or at her.

"Madeline," continued Tamara. "I am asking you to show some respect, not just for me, but for your fellow group members."

"But I don't want to be the center of attention right now like I clearly am, so I will answer your stupid question regarding 'The Boy that Cried Wolf.' I do not deny your stupid and obvious lesson. The truth of the matter is, you have denied mine. Perhaps you are the one being flippant and resistant. Isn't that almost just as bad as lying? A lie by omission?"

Tamara's voice became louder and more assertive. "With all due respect, Madeline, you are here as the patient. You are here for a reason. This is a group for compulsive liars. This is not about me. However, as long as you find genuine insight in the first moral, I will entertain yours. Do you, at the very least, see a modicum of merit in the first moral?"

Madeline stood up and faced the group as if she were a lecturer in a university. "The first lesson is for the child. Everyone knows that. If people know that you have a running history of lying, they might not believe you when you are finally telling the truth. After a while, people stop believing you because you have burned too many bridges. Still, this group isn't entirely meant for me, as you said. In fact, some of the others here are far bigger liars than I am, like John here." She slapped him on the shoulder.

"Hey, what?" asked John, a fifty-year-old plumber who'd had many affairs and had no reservations about lying to cover any of them up.

"It's okay, John," said Tamara as she smiled at him. "Remember, we can't control what other people do, only how we respond to what others say or do. People can't make you do anything or feel anything. Only by allowing others that power do they continue to have power over us."

The group members nodded in agreement, except Madeline and John.

"Okay, whatever," said John. "Or maybe Madeline is just a bitch!"

"Shut up, John!" shouted Madeline, putting her finger so close to his nose it almost made contact. "Maybe you are a bastard! And bastards are worse than bitches!"

"Madeline, stop," said Tamara. "Or I will have to ask you to leave."

"Me?" shouted Madeline as she pointed at herself and then pressed her thumb into John's abdomen. "What about him?"

Tamara continued with a softer voice. "Before you snapped at John, you actually did a good job there. You displayed excellent insight regarding the lesson of 'The Boy That Cried Wolf.' And I think I even heard a little bit of change talk.

"Oh, stop with that phony validation," shouted Madeline. "That fable is meant for school children. You don't need to feign enthusiasm for my less-than astute observations that a toddler could have made in preschool. How fucking patronizing."

"It's always a big deal when a compulsive liar can display insight," said Tamara. "Don't underestimate yourself and sell yourself short. And since you were able to listen to me with respect, I would now like to hear your perspective about the second lesson of the story. Go ahead, I am giving you the floor."

"How generous of you." Madeline sighed, hoisted her chair above her head, and took her seat in the circle of chairs, somewhat enthralled to have found a captive audience, if not showing it too overtly. She continued but while staring at the tile floor. "The second lesson is meant for the adult. Just because a person has a history of lying, this does not necessarily mean that what comes next will be a lie. This is a mistake on the adult's part. It reveals the pitfalls of making assumptions and relying too much on past experiences. After all, if the adult believed the boy that cried wolf, everything would have been fine. The adult was an idiot for not considering that possibility. Just sayin'."

"True, but the child should not have lied," said Tamara.

"Hey, you said you would give me the floor, this tile one right here," snapped Madeline. "The adult should not have made assumptions. The problem is we tend to moralize such fables, failing to see the many strings that pull the puppet. And far too often, the child gets the brunt of the blame while the adult gets let off the hook. The adult and the child both made assumptions. It was more of a misunderstanding than anything." Tamara let Madeline continue. "'The Boy that Cried Wolf' is just as much about pragmatism as it is about morality. If one of them had been able to spot their own bias, the story would have ended differently. Not all of us are idiots in these groups, you know."

Herman was busy with his notepad taking down Madeline's comments, flipping a page in the process.

"I suppose you have a point in there somewhere," said Tamara. "As much as I am loathe to admit it."

"Thanks," said Madeline, donning her most smug impression.

"But you forget, Miss Fischer, we counselors are people with feelings too. Clients like to assume our lives are so much more glamorous than theirs. And that is also a bias you need to consider and own up to."

"I'm sorry, Tamara," said Madeline. "But my many other lies notwithstanding, rest assured I am telling the truth when I say once again that the karma police killed my parents."

"Rest assured?" said Tamara. "That's hardly very reassuring news, Miss Madeline. I think I would be more assured if you were actually lying about that. But all manner of kidding aside, don't you think it's possible that maybe, just maybe, your ideas about karma police are a defense mechanism? A way you protect yourself from what happened with your mother? Sometimes we believe our own lies."

Madeline's mouth was agape. "Why would I make up something like that?"

"I don't know, Madeline, you tell me," said Tamara. "I am not trying to minimize your reality. But could your stories about the karma police possibly be a fantasy you are nursing? A way to place distance between yourself and your emotions? It's just a theory, mind you. I'm just asking you to consider its plausibility."

"The sad reality is that psychiatry is aligned with the world," said Madeline. "Your kind will never give the time of day to anything that has to do with the paranormal. And yet, anything remotely touching that territory will get you branded as a delusional psychopath worthy of asylum. And not the good kind of asylum, like the safety granted to a political refugee. But rather, the kind I am sitting in right now."

Tamara smiled. "Well, Madeline, people here struggle with delusions, and I can't have you going on about such things.

We can talk about it in private later."

"Well, maybe religions are just socially acceptable delusions," said Madeline.

"Enough," said Tamara. She looked around at the other group members. "Does anyone remember what the keyword is that separates a harmful behavior from a harmless behavior?"

"Impact!" called Dennis as he raised his hand.

"That's right," said Tamara, nodding in agreement.

Dennis smiled from ear to ear as he looked from one side of the group to the other.

"But you should let me call on you before you blurt something out," said Tamara. She looked around the room. "What makes something a problem or disorder is the degree to which it negatively impacts one's relationships, work, finances, marriage, housing status, time management, or mental or physical health. There is a big difference between healthy caution vs. unhealthy paranoia. While it's good to keep a winter survival kit in the car, it's a bit excessive to dig a bomb shelter in your backyard at the slightest dip in the stock market."

"Whatever," said Madeline.

"What was that, Madeline?" asked Tamara, knowing full well what she'd said.

"Whatever!" shouted Madeline, more loudly than before.

"I'm sorry, Madeline, but the 'whatever' defense doesn't stand in a formal debate or a court of law. Or this room, for that matter. Some excuses don't hold up. Kinda like the other day when you said that leeches and parasites steal from others to survive in the wild, so that makes it sometimes okay for people to do the same. You have to know the difference between a valid reason vs. a rationalization, Madeline."

"How is this for winning a debate?!" shouted Madeline as she put her fingers in her ears and stuck out her tongue at Tamara like a child. About half of the group members laughed, while the others just stared at the floor in awkward silence.

"Madeline, I think you should go to your room for a little while," said Tamara, pointing at the door. "I think you need a little break."

"I must say I am inclined to agree," said Madeline as she stood up, grabbed her folding chair, closed it, and slowly made her egress towards the main exit. Tamara let her go, as her calm gait appeared innocuous enough. However, just as she was about to place her chair on the wall rack, she kept it and made a mad dash towards the same window she was looking out before. She hoisted the chair above her head.

"Madeline, you put that chair down!" shouted Tamara as she snapped her fingers at Herman to rush to her. The rest of the group turned to face the impending drama that ensued.

"Don't you dare break that window!" shouted Herman as he got up and rushed to the scene.

Madeline swung the chair like a baseball bat against the glass. It was a thick pane, and it didn't break from the first attempt. She took two more swings at the window before Herman could get to her. Just as the window shattered, she dropped her chair to the floor and began to climb out, ready to jump from the second-story window. But not before Herman grabbed her scrubs and yanked her back inside. She fell hard onto the tile floor, dropping the chair with a loud thud.

As they were grappling, Tamara motioned to the rest of the six group members to get up and leave the room. They acquiesced, although they wanted to watch the drama ensue. Tamara stood near the door and guided them out, one by one, placing her hand on each of their backs in the process. After they left, Tamara dashed to Herman to give him a hand.

"Get off me!" exclaimed Madeline as she continued to squirm around with unpredictable flailing movements on the tile floor. "I didn't kill my parents! It was the karma police! I am telling the truth! I am telling the truth! It's not a delusion! You have the delusion!"

"That's enough, Madeline," said Tamara as Herman fought to hold her still. She was thrashing and flailing on the floor with such reckless abandon Herman had to try multiple times just to get a firm hold of her by snagging her left arm with his right hand.

"It's not a delusion!" shouted Madeline as she continued to squirm. "Stop treating me like a petulant child! I'm a reformer! I seek a better world!"

Tamara grimaced. "Well then, stop acting like one!"

As they were grappling and vying for dominance, Madeline kicked Herman off her and jumped to her feet. She hobbled to the door with a fresh limp. Just as she reached for the handle of the door, Herman went for plan B. Handing Tamara his syringe, he made another mad dash at Madeline. Tamara followed suit. Herman took hold of the scruff of her scrubs with one hand and snatched the syringe from Tamara with the other. Just as she felt him jab it in, she surrendered and flopped to the floor and started sobbing, well before the antidote took any effect. After all, it wasn't the first time she'd gotten the syringe. She knew full well that willpower alone wouldn't and couldn't overcome the strength of that tranquilizer. Nonetheless, he strong-armed her back to the closest chair and sat her down with a loud thud. Tamara helped hold her still with a reassuring but firm grasp.

"You don't have to be so rough—it's not as if I am even resisting arrest," said Madeline.

"Arrest?" asked Tamara. "Isn't that a bit dramatic?"

"It's either that or you are putting me down like a dog at the vet."

"Now that's even more dramatic than what you said before," said Tamara. Herman nodded in agreement.

Madeline didn't say a word. She just sat still and quiet, save for the slow and deliberate heavy breaths she was taking.

"It's just a scary delusion," whispered Tamara into her ear. The latter was close enough that Madeline could feel her breath against her cheek, and she closed her eyes.

Tamara continued. "Now would actually be a perfect time to practice your positive self-talk, emotion regulation, and thought-stopping skills. You can prove to us that you are getting better." She looked towards Herman. "Isn't that right, Herman?"

Herman nodded multiple times in rapid succession. "Yes,

absolutely right."

Tamara smiled and settled her gaze back on Madeline. "See? Now please repeat after me. 'This is just a delusion. It's not real. This is just a delusion. It's not real."

"It's just a delusion. It's not real," said Madeline with a deflated and tearful voice, as if the wind was taken from her sails.

"I don't want you to simply say it. I want you to mean it," said Herman.

"He's right," said Tamara. "You sound very disingenuous in your tone."

"It's just a delusion. It's not real," said Madeline with a louder and slightly more confident conviction.

Tamara looked around the hazy room and noticed several of the group members staring through the window of the door, getting an eyeful of the impending scene.

"It's okay, Madeline, settle down," said Tamara, rubbing Madeline's shoulder. "You are okay. You are safe. Relax, and breathe. Herman here is just trying to help. You are safe here. I know you have been through a lot. I would be more surprised if you hadn't ended up with all these problems after what you have been through. But even still, if you ever break another window like that again, you will have to pay for it yourself." She nodded to Herman to get some tissues. He fetched them from Tamara's office down the hall and returned about two minutes later.

Madeline yanked out five tissues in rapid succession and patted the wad against her eyes. By now, Madeline was feeling very languid, and her demeanor had become very calm, partly due to the sedative and partly due to her own loss of will. Her eyes were closing. Tamara nodded once again towards Herman, and they each took an arm to help guide her back to her room about five rooms down the hall, just across from Tamara's office. Everything was a blur to Madeline as she hobbled along between the two staff as they marched her to her quarters to the tune of the jingle and jangle of Herman's many keys, even as he unlocked the door. She was placed down on the bed. They also helped ease her down on top of the covers, so she was lying on her back. Herman stood by the door as Tamara sat on the edge of Madeline's bed.

"Now, I want you to lie there and think about your actions," said Tamara. "We believe in you. But you need to believe in us. And yourself, for that matter. I know from group that you practically have your DBT skills memorized. You just gotta learn how to use them in real-life 'in vivo' situations. Where you need them the most, right? It's all about impulse control, Madeline. Gone are the days where your tantrums get rewarded. Not on my watch. I know that sounds rather mean and nasty. But there is still a place in psychology for tough love, don'tcha think, Herman?"

"Hmm?" asked Herman, trying to remember what he'd just heard. "Oh yes, that's true."

Madeline wiped her eyes with the corner of her pillow.

"And enough with the lies," continued Tamara, patting her thigh. "There is no need for it. There is nobody left to charm, impress, woo, or otherwise manipulate." She leaned in and faced her. "This behavior may have served you well at one time, but not anymore. You can start telling the truth now. Who knows? Maybe they will let you out of here in five or seven years. Stranger things have happened. But we really have to work on your transference issues. Now chin up, right?"

"Thank you," mumbled Madeline, still wiping her eyes with the same now wet tissues Herman had brought to her before. She wondered if it counted as a lie if you thanked someone for something but didn't quite mean it. As far as she was concerned, she'd just added another five years to her stay. At this point, she didn't think anything really mattered.

Tamara gave Herman another of her trademark nods, as Herman had by now become quite adept at deciphering them. "But don't leave out Herman here. He is trying to keep you and others safe, ya know? I know it might not seem like it to you, but our Herman here is quite the unsung hero. He is our gentle giant."

"That's why they call me an orderly," said Herman with a haughty laugh. "I just try to keep some law and order around here. And there is nothing mean or cruel about keeping people safe. I'm like the good guy that nobody likes."

Tamara got up and walked towards the door. They left and closed the door behind them, and Herman locked it. Madeline closed her ears so she wouldn't hear the sound of the deadbolt. She uncovered her ears again and caught the tail end of their conversation.

"Don't you just hate the clients with psychology or sociology degrees?" asked Tamara as she and Herman made their way towards the hospital cafeteria group room to finish cleaning it up and closing it for the night. Madeline felt sad at how two-faced they now seemed.

"And they say doctors and nurses make the worst patients," said Herman. "Counselors are the worst. Remember Sarah?"

"How can I forget?" said Tamara, thinking they were out of earshot.

As for Madeline, she just stared at the ceiling. She began counting the little bumps on what she always liked to call a "cottage cheese" ceiling. She began seeing patterns, much like seeing faces in clouds or symbols from the Rorschach inkblot assessments she had taken. There was one especially large bump. "I think I will call you Peter," she mumbled aloud.

Madeline continued to muse. Some chose between "truth" or "dare." And yet others "dare to tell the truth." And even then, human memory could be deceptive. After all, if you believe your own lie, is it really a lie? She knew she did not kill her parents. Was it really such a sin to have a corpse in your house? And why did the moose head fall just in the nick of time to save her life? Surely there were no such things as accidents. Was karma, like, really a "thing"? It had to be. Every thing was a thing. But then she had an idea. Maybe she could find a way to study karma for herself. And find out if the karma police were real, and if so, whose side they were on. But how would she leave the hospital to conduct her studies? And how could she elicit help from others in the interim?

Several tears fell from Madeline's eyes, like the initial droplets that precede a deluge of rain. But the storm never came, as her thoughts instead turned towards the aloof and cold stare of philosophy. Why did people cry? Emotional catharsis? A manipulation to get others to rush to their aid? A mad-cap symptom of mental illness? A learned behavior? Gender role conformity? It didn't matter. She had bigger fish to fry. These thoughts, schemas, and concepts started to jumble into each other, like when you push your thumb over freshly inked letters until they smudge into each other.

And then she drifted off to sleep, finding temporary sojourn in surreal nocturnal landscapes. And as sweet dreams and nightmares vied for dominance, the dreams came out ahead, and she dreamed about sweeter times to come. Blissful ignorance, perhaps, but bliss nonetheless. But despite her repose in dreamscape, our Madeline had a choice to make. Either she could believe what could be a lie, or she could deny what could be the truth. Or deny the lie and accept the truth. But in the end, molehills are molehills, and mountains are mountains, notwithstanding our subjective interpretations.

And all the while, there was a fly on the wall, of the most figurative variety. Taped to the wall, as pushpins were not allowed, was a copy of the story she'd written the very night her mom died. It was also the very beginning of a strain of "delusions," depending on who you asked, that all played a role in landing her in this very asylum. But if one were to ask Madeline herself, she would not have used the term "delusion" at all. It was rather the stuff of melancholy and wistful nostalgia, a dreamer with longings to reform our brutal and cold world. In either case, the story was there, staring at her as she drifted off to sleep, like a dream catcher or shepherd watching his flock.

And this is what it said.

***

Jack of All Trades by Madeline Fischer, February 14, 2017

Once upon a time, there were massive balls called planets,

encircling an even more massive ball of fire called the sun. And there were also moons and stars. And one planet, eventually named Earth, was a home to organic robots, eventually called "people" and "animals." The former were beings with two arms, two legs, and a head attached to a body. And on this head were tools in which to experience the world; cameras for vision, later called eyes; recording devices, called ears by some, for auditory purposes; a tongue for gustatory experiences; a nose for olfactory ones; and tiny sensors placed on the skin for tactile purposes. Some even asserted a sixth sense, not a penchant for seeing dead people, but vestibular sensibilities for balance and spatial awareness. These beings were eventually, and arbitrarily for that matter, emblazoned as "humans" by people called "linguists." And among these creatures were other creatures, many of them also with limbs, appendages, and sensory tools, but often these appendages were in different places. Some of these creatures swam in the sea, and others walked or crawled on land. And there were even some that took to the skies. And these latter kind were called animals.

But humans, in particular, had a penchant for asking far too many questions. Over time, these organic robots emblazoned as "humans" invented language in order to share ideas and give meaning to this world of mysterious origin and unforeseeable future. And while the complexities and nuances of language proffered common nomenclature to what people saw and witnessed, it also offered the ability to share thoughts and ideas. Language became a vehicle for emotion and logic alike, and it didn't take long for religion, philosophy, and science to become born. Or even sophistry, for that matter. These also gave the illusion of order in a chaotic world.

But where did these flesh robots come from? And is there life on other planets as well? Why was life like a science fiction movie without the fiction?

Where am I? thought the naked man in the middle of this mysterious world, wearing only an old-fashioned dunce cap as he shot cursory glances around the empty abyss that surrounded him. It appeared to be an ancient Roman amphitheater. It did not appear to be a relic of the past, however. It was as if the Roman Colosseum were just built, and thanks to surreal magic, built in less than a second. It did not appear worn and weathered from time or elements. Around the large space of the amphitheater were marble statues of all manner of arachnids, spiders, centipedes, and many others.

Then seemingly out of nowhere, a massive box started to appear in the center of the amphitheater, first transparent and then more and more opaque. "I am Karma Incarnate," said an ominous and muffled voice emanating from the box. The front of the box depicted a strange symbol, two overlapping snakes, that formed the image of a dollar sign. The snake forming the "S" had a head on each end. And the vertical "I" snake juxtaposed over the "S" had a tail on each end.

"You will find that irony, symbolism, and allegory are not reserved for literature or even dream analyses. These concepts are endemic to life and can be found anywhere and everywhere. Life is a work of art. There is meaning to be found in the most trivial of crevices. You just have to look for it. Everything happens for a reason!"

The naked man paid little attention to the arbiter's rhetoric, as he was afraid. And fear can have a profound way of affecting one's faculties. All he could do was gaze at the arachnid statues encircling the massive box, one at a time, in a clockwise fashion. He was starting to get anxious, as evidenced by his trembling demeanor, sweaty palms, and knots in his stomach. "Please don't hurt me!"

"Make no mistake, I can sense your trepidation, the Honorable Judge Maxim Damp," said the muffled voice of this dark figure, already knowing the naked man's name. "And for your fear, I apologize. However, the truth is you are not nearly as fearful as you should be. Towards your kind, I am not propitious. You would rather 'jerk the knee' than 'scratch the chin.' Ye of too much faith! Instead of poring over your dusty tomes with a fastidious fervor, you would rather mock and impugn works of art like The Thinker, in all your emotion-laden and knee-jerk employs as if an open mind or critical thought were the stuff of dissolute fools and false idols!"

"No, that's not it!" Maxim looked around as if waiting for a candid camera, in this moment the equivalent of a veritable guardian angel.

The voice from inside the box let out a maniacal laugh, and it was strangely not even muffled.

"Am I dead?" asked Maxim as he shot glances from one preserved cadaver to the other. All the eyes of the "statues" glowed a crimson fire red, now all staring directly at him.

"Do the dead beg for life?" returned the mysterious voice. "How dare you tempt my irascible nature! The good news is that you are not dead. But the bad news? You may soon very well wish you were!"

And with that, Jack popped out of the box. The jump-scare made Maxim fall to his knees, and he didn't even notice that he had urinated until he felt the warm and wet sensations in his groin and on his bare toes.

But then the winds picked up. A dust storm was swirling around the area, making the landscape almost invisible. The fine particles were now aloft and left a gritty texture in Maxim's mouth. Maxim clutched his dunce cap in the face of the wind as if it were actually functional headgear. As the dust settled, columns of iridescent light shot from the ground to the sky, or possibly from the sky to the ground, as it was difficult even for semi-omniscient narrators to know for certain. Either way, the light became blinding. After the illumination died down, the large interior of the Colosseum constructed itself into a second anachronism, an old-fashioned 1930s era carnival fairgrounds. There were Ferris wheels, carnival games, and carousels. There were transparent ghosts of patrons from the bygone era walking, laughing, and buying cotton candy as they mingled among the carnival barkers and groundskeepers. All the clothing and regalia adorning patron and staff were from a bygone zeitgeist. Their colloquial conversations were also from the past, as evidenced by the people discussing current events and presidential matters of the 1930s.

"When you attend an event called an 'amusement park,' always make sure you know ahead of time who's amusement is being provided for!" shouted Jack with a now clear and booming voice, free from the acoustical confines of the box. "And when you enter the gates of a fairground, always make sure you know ahead of time what the meaning is behind those words."

"What is this infernal place? Damn your Pandora's Box!"

The honorable judge's glances shot in all directions, every which way, top to bottom and side to side. None of the ghosts of the past seemed to notice him or the Jack in the Box. The diorama was somehow superimposed over them as if the box and impending scenery were the stuff of the ghost of Christmas past. Maxim looked at Jack as tears started to cloud his vision, like trying to watch a film using a wet camera lens. Or late-stage cataract. These were certainly not the tears of despondent melancholy, elated ecstasy, or wistful nostalgia. They were fear tears.

"What is the purpose of these confounded fairgrounds?" asked the man, shooting his gaze around the amusement park like laser beams.

The voice thundered. "You have your grounds for fairness, and I have mine!"

Jack climbed out of the box, revealing spindly legs and a segmented body, like the body of an arachnid. He held a king's scepter in his right hand. It had a long gold handle, and on the tip appeared to be a bust of a black gargoyle of sorts, like the mascot from a bottle of "The Culprit" wine.

"Am I the first to see the entire body of a Jack in the Box?"

"You should consider yourself lucky," said Jack, approaching Mr. Damp. Jack pointed to the carousel with his scepter. "Consider this your censure. Now please enter the paddock."

Maxim and Jack mounted two of the side-by-side horses,

ones that were unoccupied by specter patrons. Jack's eight spindly legs surrounded the horse like a spider poised over a fly.

"What is the meaning of all this?" asked Maxim as he looked this way and that, to and fro, before settling his gaze on Jack. "Why are we in this amusement park?"

"What, are you not amused?" asked Jack, lifting his eyebrows. "That's a shame. Then again, your equestrian ride on this carousel is not for your own amusement. It is for mine!"

Maxim tried to dismount, but he was affixed to the horse as if by indomitable animal magnetism. He struggled and squirmed to break free, but to no avail. Jack was as free as a wild horse and could come and go as he pleased, unlike the horses fixed to the carousel. But he, too, mounted a horse purely from the will of his own volition. With a creak and crack, the carousel began turning—not counterclockwise as typically done in the United States, but rather clockwise. But it also did not turn in a continuous fashion. Instead, it jerked ahead, 1/60 a rotation per second, as if the carousel were transfixed to the hands of a clock.

"Do you recall, Your Honor, when you sent that poor kid to the electric chair some seventeen years ago?"

Maxim appeared taken aback by the flippant question. "Of course I do. He was guilty of murder. How dare you disrespect my judgment."

"So you say, but the truth is he was not guilty of anything but being at the wrong place at the wrong time."

"That is not what the courts decided," said Mr. Damp.

"How dare you question me, the one who holds all the secrets of the universe?! He sat on death row for all of ten years, innocent all the while, anticipating his death every day of that time. He not only suffered the agony of death itself but the anticipation anxiety of waiting it out."

Jack dismounted the horse and stood in front of the carousel. By the time Maxim made a full rotation to meet him once again, Jack was now dressed as a judge, wearing a powdered peruke with a ribbon, and holding a book of law. But the carousel kept turning with the pinpoint precision and accuracy of Greenwich time. And with a voice of thunder, fire, and brimstone, Jack shouted loud enough that Maxim could hear him at a constant decibel regardless of what location he was at during the rotation of the carousel as if the Doppler effect didn't even exist.

"I sentence you to ride this carousel for no less than ten years," said the voice of thunder. "You will not feel any hunger, fatigue, or thirst. All your drives will be satiated and otherwise staved off, save for the pangs of loneliness, boredom, and fear of anticipating your painful death ten years later. And yes, when that time comes, you will also know what it's like to die in an electric chair. Does this shock you?"

"You can't do this!" shouted the judge, careening his neck this way and that, looking for any hint of egress. And at that moment, the horse was burning with rage, with fire in his eyes and flames in his mouth. And it made a guttural noise as if it were a lion.

"As they say, Your Honor, you should not have judged, or ye be judged."

"But I didn't even know! You can't do this! Please! I beg of you!" He kept glancing to and fro, looking for any vestige of egress he could find.

"Then you should have erred on the side of caution, benefit of the doubt, innocent until proven guilty, and all the other maxims of your ignoble profession. Do you even remember that child's name? If you remember, I might reduce your sentence by a full year."

"But I don't remember! That was seventeen years ago!"

Jack raised his scepter. "What a shame. Think, you fool!"

And at that moment, the judge vomited all over the wooden floor of the carousel, his dunce cap falling off.

Jack grinned. "And yet, he undoubtedly remembered your name. And he probably still would — if our Jacob Swanson was still alive, anyway. Still, I think you will find that my judgment is more than fair. Have you perchance heard of the Pilgrim's Purgatory?"

"Please, I don't want to know!" Mr. Damp clutched the

pole as high as his hands could go, his head hanging low, sobbing as he went up and down, to the tune of "Sidewalks of New York" playing on the calliope.

And in less than a second, the horse the judge was riding turned into a wyvern, and it turned its long neck around towards Mr. Damp. The latter could see his reflection in its hideous eye. The creature let out a shriek as if sharing the karma lord Jack's sentiments and disdain towards the "honorable" judge.

Jack closed his eyes and continued as if the details of the visual landscape he himself created would deter his ability to paint the story's picture with full uninterrupted impact. "A pilgrim had premarital coitus and was sentenced to sit in a special purgatory. It was an empty bowling alley. No people. No creature comforts of any kind. After a thousand years, he was given a chance to bowl a perfect three-hundred-point game. If he failed, he had to wait another one-thousand years for another chance. So far, he has tried ninety-seven times. His highest score so far was 287. He has been sitting there now for over ninety-seven thousand years. He gets another chance in about 237."

Mr. Damp screamed and cried at the same time. "That's not even fair! That sounds horrifying!"

"And yet, humanity's version of an all-eternal 'place of punishment' is not much different, eh? Far worse even, when you stop and do the math."

Mr. Damp shook the tears from his eyes as he couldn't even remove his hands from the pole. "But what does that have to do with my dire situation?"

"I think even you will come to realize that my sentence is more than fair when you think about what happened to poor Jacob. Just think of the Pilgrim's Purgatory, and it won't seem so bad. One must be positive in these matters."

And at that moment, Maxim awoke from his slumber, in the cozy bed of his mansion, next to his beautiful wife, in a profuse and cold sweat. And like a bashful phantom, the sun peeked its head above the horizon as if to ascertain the safety of its surroundings before coming out any further to dispel the dark and vengeful night.

In similar accord, Maxim's eyes creaked open like a slow sunrise, and the realities of the world crept into focus, including the peripheral and diminutive echos of joys and regrets amassed over the ebb and flow of his lifetime as a judge. In a rare moment of nostalgia, he reminisced about each career milestone he could recall, each joy, each misfortune, previously tucked away, lost or misplaced, in the catacombs and recesses of his brain. But they were not all pleasant memories. He also thought about all the people he had sent to death, the memories coalescing together like shards of glass, juxtaposing and assembling until all the bits of detritus formed a mirror. But as they say, to recall such memory would invariably require but a lifetime, to approximate the emotional landscape of the original events in their full richness of visceral detail and flavor. Memories, after all, are merely "semblances of remembrances," a snapshot summary, a recapitulation, a rundown, an expedited mock-up, a sub-par replica, a hollow shell or husk, all devoid of any subtlety or nuance of detail, imagery, and sensory stimulation of the original. But in the grander scheme of things, at least for Judge Maxim Damp, it was for the best. After all, some things are probably best forgotten, or at least simply alluded to in passing.

Maxim slept almost an hour later than usual. *Was this a dream?* he thought. And all the while, his wife appeared lifeless, in the land of sweeter dreams. He used the corner of his blanket to wipe the cold sweat off his face and head. He crept out of the bed sideways so as to not wake her and hobbled to his computer in his red-carpeted living room, near the bearskin rug. He googled the name of the kid he'd put on death row all those years ago. The name "Jacob Swanson" came up. He wondered, how can someone in a dream tell you something you normally couldn't remember in real life? He wondered if a man's guilty conscience could dredge up such details when your conscious — or conscience, for that matter — would normally opt to forget.

Our honorable judge was a "by the book" and "paint by numbers" sort of fellow, but even he felt uncomfortable about such a lucid dream. Did he really allow an innocent man to die? Although he was already an hour late for his legal appointment, he just lay there in bed and wracked his brain. Usually, such shirking of responsibility would have provoked his ire all the more, but today was different and for reasons that only he could fully understand. And as of now, such so-called irresponsibility was all the more justified.

This is ridiculous, Maxim eventually thought to himself. He got up and decided to go along with his morning routine as usual, with the same pace and astute resolution to which he had been accustomed, preparing for yet another day at the salt mines, to the old familiar beat-tunes and dockets of lawyers, juries, courtrooms, gavels, egos, probity, rhetoric, suppositions, conjecture, cognitive fallacy, hearsay, non-sequitor, crocodile tears, compunction, Latin platitudes, and black robes.

But for Jack, the day was not quite so pedestrian. On the very day that our honorable judge got up to go back to his employments and pursuits, Jack's eyes grew black as shadows as he assessed the virtues and vices of our poor and pitiful judge. And for a fraction of time, he felt and experienced all the pain that Jacob Swanson had felt during all of his seventeen years. All the existential pangs and pains of anticipating humanity's most compelling and frightening mystery of the great abyss. All manner of it, be it psychological, physical, and otherwise, were felt as if they were a lucid dream, and yet, not a dream at all. But that was just the beginning. For all of five seconds, Jack felt every nuance of painful emotion ever suffered on the planet. And not just by the judge, but many others. And animals too. Billions of them. As many as fish in the sea. Every fish. Every sea. Down to the very bottom-lickers and bottom feeders of swamps and mud.

But all was not for naught, as the next five seconds were a time of convalescence. If observers had happened to be present, in a purely hypothetical fashion, they would have surely noticed the pain leaving his body like lava from a volcano. By the end of that five-second epoch, Jack's expression was one of relief, a look that was so flat and so placid it appeared as if it were a threadbare carpet, revealing the weathered erosion of long years, equable wisdom, and the quiet dignity that can only come from well-worn experiences. If Jack was a Douglas fir, he would have grown billions of rings on this one solitary day. And yet, the rules of dendrochronology did not apply. But to the extent that billions of voices were screaming in agony, or dancing in delight, or waxing nostalgic, or suffering in silence, our Existential Arbiter of Justice, a certain Jack in the Box was there, taking it all in, with a quiet dignity, caring nothing for revenge nor superfluous hedonism, but rather the proffering of well-deserved and well-intentioned empathy and justice for all. At least in theory.

-- --

CHAPTER 9
COLLECTIONS OF RECOLLECTIONS

Date: February 28, 2017, Tuesday, 1:00 P.M.
Main characters: Madeline Fischer and Dr. Zeck
Setting: From the office of Dr. Simon Zeck (less than a week after her commitment)

Sprawled out on the aniline leather Freudian couch, Madeline was just staring at the ceiling with her head on the raised headrest. Dr. Zeck was seated in his Wells Leather Swivel Desk Chair. While her psychiatrist Dr. Zeck was certainly no psychoanalyst, he did find a certain utility in how conducive such a couch was for free association and unbridled self-disclosure. His office was the most lavish room in the asylum, with a walnut desk and bronze busts of some of his favorite heroes of psychological intelligentsia: William James, John Watson, and Carl Rogers. He also had framed prints of the likes of Albert Ellis, Clark Hull, Mary Dinsmore Ainsworth, and Fritz Perls. The room also had a hardwood floor, which clashed with the sterile and pedestrian linoleum that graced the patron corridors of the asylum. Dr. Zeck was wearing his belted suit from Dolce & Gabbana. Madeline was in her light blue scrubs. And the scents of "Bamboo & Waterlilly Bliss" were permeating the air from the Glade Plug-In.

"So what's it say in that cute leather-cover book of yours?" asked Madeline, peering around the couch to get a closer look, prompting Dr. Zeck to close it. "Must be important. Either stuff about me or your love letters."

Dr. Zeck laughed. "I assure you it's the former. Make no mistake."

"I hope there are good things in there about me alongside

the bad," said Madeline as she returned to her original position. "You people always focus on the bad. And then you dare say that we are the ones that focus on the negative."

"Well, this is just a little note from Tamara," continued Dr. Zeck as he kept skimming the document. "It says 'Madeline was caught in a lie today, as evidenced by several of her stories not matching up. She would be a great candidate for our upcoming compulsive liar group.'" Zeck glanced up at her from above his glasses. "It also says here that 'Madeline presented as melancholy, as evidenced by her soft-spoken voice, subdued effect, and teary eyes.'"

"Tamara presented as a bitch, as evidenced by her big stupid face," said Madeline, smiling to herself.

Zeck removed his glasses completely and put them in his coat pocket. "Come come, Madeline, that sort of talk might work with your schoolyard rebels, but it won't win you any favors in a place like this." He looked at her on the couch. "Besides, she's a colleague of mine. You need to show some respect, please. We don't talk like that about you."

Madeline glared at the ceiling. "Yes, well, I am sure behind our backs you all let your guards down. I wish I could get some respect."

"Respect is earned — you of all people know that."

Madeline scanned the office. "But look around this place. Isn't it all just so pretentious?"

"A blunt question," said Dr. Zeck. "I always have this hope that the patients won't see things that way, but alas, that is not the case. Did you ask that question out of depression masked by envy?"

"Maybe," continued Madeline. "I mean, it's just a reminder that many of us in here don't even have high school diplomas. Wouldn't reminders of other people's success make anyone feel sad?"

"I suppose it would," said Dr. Zeck as he scanned the room. "But it could also be an incentive for you folks to go out there and get your education. I guess for me, I like to think of all this as being surrounded by my academic heroes. Besides, you almost completed your sociology degree. That's more than lots of the folks in here. You should feel proud. But you do have that pesky envy streak. You can do one of two things with envy, you know, Miss Fischer."

Madeline stared at the ceiling, looking at the cottage cheese bumps. "And what is that?"

"Use it as a motivator," continued Dr. Zeck. "The unhealthy method is to bring others down to your level. The healthy way is to bring yourself up to theirs."

Madeline careened her head towards Dr. Zeck. "So the bad kind is like what Tonya Harding did to Nancy Kerrigan?"

"That's a perfect example," said Dr. Zeck with a guilty chuckle. "Great insight. That's the worst way of handling it, but perhaps the most immediately gratifying."

"What do you think she could have done differently?" asked Madeline with a soft-spoken voice, returning her gaze to the ceiling.

"Why don't you tell me?" asked Dr. Zeck as he put his glasses back on and poised his pencil over his notepad.

Madeline proceeded to pull at a thread from the side of the couch. "Well, I suppose she should have channeled that energy into something positive. But do humans always have the capacity to do what they should do? Maybe she didn't have a choice."

"We always have a choice," said Dr. Zeck. "Could you please not pull at that thread? That sofa isn't a Walmart special."

"I am a fidgeter," said Madeline.

Dr. Zeck got up from his leather chair and took the basket of fidgets from his desk, and handed them to Madeline. "Okay, just fidget with something else."

Madeline took the basket and was torn between the fidget spinner and the six-sided cube with different stimuli on each side. She took a moment but decided on the latter and handed the basket back to Dr. Zeck. Dr. Zeck smoothed over the thread with his hand and returned the fidgets to his desk. He then resumed his position on his chair and crossed his legs.

Madeline proceeded to play around with her fidget cube, her favorite side being the one with the roller ball. "Yes, but if she knew there was a better way, wouldn't she have done that option instead? I mean, hindsight is always 20-20, right? How much control do people really have over crimes of passion?"

"Again, why don't you tell me?" continued Zeck as he scribbled as fast as he could what Madeline had already said. "Besides, don't you have some academic background in crime and punishment as part of your sociology degree?"

"I guess so," said Madeline. "Unless we shared Tonya's disposition and her personality, and her experiences, how can we say with confidence that we would have, or could have, done anything differently? It's easy for people to make assumptions when you weren't even there to begin with. It's just armchair quarterbacking, kind of like what you are doing right now."

"Come now, Madeline," said Dr. Zeck. "You don't need to hurl insults at me. I am on your side. The fundamental attribution error and restraint bias are very real things. This is true."

Madeline disclosed. "Okay, so I didn't get the best grades in statistics, but I do remember this thing they called 'degrees of freedom.' The definition was fairly technical, but I thought about it in more sociology terms and about how it applies to people and the world."

Dr. Zeck pointed his pen at her. "You have the floor, Miss Madeline. Please continue."

Madeline fixed her gaze towards the snow falling against the large window. The large snowflakes melted soon after they made contact with the glass, basking in the residual warmth of Dr. Zeck's cozy room. "So when people are faced with environmental barriers, I feel like we have a limited number of options, in the heat of the moment, like. In sociology classes, they called it 'social determinants of behavior.' We have limited control, given the parameters and constraints we are in."

"You are correct," said Dr. Zeck, pointing his pen towards her. "Up to a point. But you also gotta remember that sometimes we have more control over life situations than we think we have.

This is called having a healthy 'locus of control.' Do you feel you ended up here due to having limited options?"

Madeline coughed to buy a moment of time. "Well, sure. I mean, it's not just alcohol or drugs that make people act under the influence. I was at the mercy of my genetic makeup, my life history, my personality, trauma history, mental illnesses, and the current mood I was in. I had limited degrees of freedom. A person getting out of bed despite the deepest melancholy is a much larger achievement than a die-hard optimist with rose-colored glasses. It's about context."

"I concur, Madeline!" said Dr. Zeck, clapping his hands together. "I am well-versed in the 'Power of One.' Going from 0 to 1 is infinite, and going from 19 to 20 is marginal, expected, and otherwise inconsequential. I would be honored to hear your story, Miss Madeline. Will you tell it to me?"

"I don't see that I have much choice in the matter, but I will humor you just the same," said Madeline. "I like stories, so I hope you don't mind the occasional hyperbole or dramatic license."

Dr. Zeck leaned back in his chair, cherishing the moment. "You do seem to have a penchant for drama, Miss Madeline, but please tell the story as you see fit."

Madeline squirmed this way and that on the couch until she found a comfortable position and put the pillow alongside the headrest as she stared at the ceiling. She let the light sounds of snow beating against the window be her muse. And then she began to free-associate.

"Okay, so I am a native to Portland, Oregon, living with my mother and my twin sister Nova. You see, my dad died when my sister and I were like four or five, apparently in some freak car crash in Canada. At least, that is what my mom told me. And every time I tried to ask her about it, she just sort of changed the subject 'for my own good.' So that was my first abandonment issue. My second abandonment issue happened when I was seven, and my mother was served a life sentence for killing our landlord in a meth rage. I didn't know it at the time, but it was her way of grieving my dad's death. My aunt Emily Fischer took care of Nova and me if you could call it that. Who knows, maybe some of these early experiences are where I picked up some of my transference issues. Then again, Nova seemed to have turned out just fine."

"Why don't you let me use the fancy words?" said Dr. Zeck. "You just tell me your story in some modest detail."

"Fuck you," said Madeline, clamming up her body into a small ball. "I won't tell my story if you are going to get all know-it-all on me. I basically have a sociology degree. At least let me use it for something. You are the one that actually gets paid to use yours. Besides, my parents were fucking killed, for crying out loud. And who knows, maybe you have some counter-transference issues to work on."

"Fine and good, have it your way," said Dr. Zeck, raising his palms towards her. "I don't mean to condescend. It's just that some clients deflect their problems through obfuscation and by playing psychiatrist."

Madeline "unclammed" her body and straightened her legs back out on the couch.

"I was pretty young to remember my dad, but I remember he was kind enough and took care of our basic needs. At least, that is what my mom told me. Of course, the surviving parent always has a way of making the deceased seem bigger than life. It was weird, though. When he died, I remember asking my mom where he was. And when she said 'he is in a better place,' for some reason, I called bullshit. Even at that age. I asked her, 'Well, how do you know this?' She just said, 'I just know.' I remember then asking, 'Well, how do you know?' and at that point, she told me to go and play outside with Nova, as if I was somehow digging too deep. And from then on, I knew I was a natural-born philosopher and reformer. It wasn't until many years later that I read an article called 'The Subjectivity of Reality,' and it resonated with me and my inability to simply accept things as they are or should be. It was as if I was meant to read it. And even though I never really knew my dad, I could feel a void ever since, as if something was missing in my life. I never really felt completely safe, as if always waiting for the shoe to drop as if the world were somehow more dangerous than it really was. But then I thought of how humans are essentially animals, whether we want to admit it or not, and the world really is dangerous, and whether we are talking about polar bears or people, it all boils down to a basic quest for survival. So in some ways, I think the death of my father was a big factor in my decision to go into sociology. Nova went into veterinary science. I am not sure how much any of this really affected her. The lucky bitch."

"You resent your sister?" asked Dr. Zeck.

Madeline careened her head around and saw Zeck scribbling away. She resumed her gaze and continued. "I guess so. And why shouldn't I? I'm jealous of her. She got all the breaks and is living the good life with her fancy job, nice house, and wonderful life out in Fargo."

"Be careful. You can't always judge a person's happiness based on appearances," said Dr. Zeck. "We had a gentleman in here once who seemingly had everything. Other clients here would even ask him, 'what do you have to be depressed about?' Some of them thought they were helping by saying such things, but they just made him all the more depressed."

"The grass isn't always greener on the other side of the picket fence," said Madeline. "But trust me, Nova is different. She loves thinking about me suffering in my sordid little existence."

"Just think about what I said," said Dr. Zeck. "Before getting so defensive. If she really is gleaning joy from your jealousy, then don't let her win. Happiness is the best revenge. Anyway, this isn't a counseling session. Please continue with your story."

Madeline let out a heavy sigh. "So two years came and went. I remember my mom sitting in the basement messing with all manner of weird chemicals. Beakers, flasks, you name it. I asked her if it was a chemistry set and if I could help her. She yelled at me to go to my room. But over time, I came to understand more of the big picture. I remember her complaining about this landlord all the time, and she didn't call him by name.

Just 'landlord.' And by how she carried on about him, I assumed that this landlord must have been someone very important or regal. I mean, come on, anyone with the name 'lord' in his title must have some sort of authority — either that or have the ability to walk on water. This aversion to him was only compounded by Mom's incessant screaming at him on the phone all the time. But some time later, some big cop guy with a weird hat and sunglasses and two guns on his hips came to the door, and there was a lady with him, a lady I would later find out was from child protection services. Seven-year-olds don't always understand the ins and outs of the criminal justice system. But right then and there, my mom, Nova, and I had to go with the lady. And later in the same day, we went to live with my aunt Emily Fischer on the other side of Portland. It didn't take long for me to realize that my mom was taken from me. In all honesty, I thought the police had kidnapped my mother. My mom wasn't the bad guy. That scary policeman was. And I know you are probably already thinking that's where my aversion to authority came from. But you would be wrong."

"You don't worry about me," said Dr. Zeck, scribbling away. "You just go on and tell that story. You are doing a great job."

"Well, I remember Nova and I visiting her in jail or prison from time to time or whatever, which at the time I simply called a 'cage,' because quite frankly, that's what it was. And still is, as far as I am concerned. I was like ten before I started to get the idea that my mother had done some pretty nasty things when she was on meth. I never stopped loving her, though. Even when others seemed to hate her, including Nova. I just saw that as I needed to love her all the more to make up for all the hate others had for her or the hate she had for herself.

"I guess around middle school, I was what you could call a problem child, stealing and lying and all that run of the mill shit that comes with it. The ol' rebellious teenager trope, more or less, although in truth that angst has never really left me. But I guess you would probably say I hated everyone and everything because

I hated myself. Like mother like daughter. I guess I can't really argue with that. I still don't know why Nova just went about her business as if nothing was wrong. She got good grades, smiled at all the right moments, and enjoying her hobbies like scratch art and going with Emily horseback riding. I didn't get along with Emily all that well, and she was bordering on abusive at times, verbally and physically. I tried diligently to make sense out of everything and find a logical reason for why things happened the way they did. Emily would always tell me how my bad behavior would catch up with me and that I should just act more like Nova and good things would happen. I didn't even know at the time that she was alluding to this idea of karma, even back then. One time she told me that she learned all about karma from my dad and how they would spend hours and hours talking about it. I didn't know much about my dad, so naturally, I wanted to know more. But just as with Mom, she kind of shushed me whenever I brought him up."

"I see," said Dr. Zeck. "Just trying to spare your feelings, perhaps. Please, go on."

"So basically, the only knowledge I have of my dad was that he worked as an air traffic controller at the Portland International Airport, and he was heavy into the idea of karma."

"That's not very much information," said Dr. Zeck. "And I can't help but try and see the parallels between the two."

"So naturally, I wanted to cling to anything about my dad that I could, so I sort of clung to this idea of karma for a sense of security and order in the world. Even if I didn't really understand it. But in a weird way, it felt like my dad was with me. Like I was carrying on his legacy. But some things didn't make much sense. For example, if there is this life force called karma, then why did my dad die in a car accident in Canada? At any rate, I held on to this notion that things happened for a reason, and there was a method to the madness. And all the people that hurt me, including Emily, would eventually get their just desserts. I tried to cling to this idea, even if my own life didn't seem rewarded by these karma police in the slightest. I guess it just reinforced the hatred I had for myself or at least gave credence to it. I just chalked it up to I somehow deserved all the turmoil and chaos in my life. At any rate, karma gave me something to believe in."

"I see," said Dr. Zeck with a nod, tapping his pencil to his notepad. "Please continue."

"Growing up like this during high school, I most looked forward to our monthly visits with my mom at the Portland Penitentiary. I really got to know her, you know? She was always so caring and genteel that for several years I didn't even believe she'd killed anybody, and I told myself she must have been falsely accused. I still find it hard to accept. But after high school, Nova went off to college, and that's when we pretty much broke ties, save for the very occasional phone call. I think she was just as happy with the arrangement as I was, especially that time I pretended I was her and slept with her boyfriend."

"You got some of your education from the School of Hard Knocks," said Zeck.

"You could say that. I stayed in Portland for my schooling. But the distraction was good for me, and I somehow managed to get a 3.0 GPA, despite all the mental health issues. I went into sociology and took some courses on crime and punishment. I think my fascination with karma was responsible for that academic focus. Although my mental health got the best of me, and I had to quit school with just a semester left."

"I can see that," said Zeck. "Seems to mesh with your sensibilities."

"Yes, but it's weird. I learned about deterrence theory and how a person's behavior is more likely to be curtailed if the consequence is delivered immediately, consistently, and with sufficient intensity. But karma most certainly doesn't follow those rules. A person might not get punished for something until years later."

Zeck nodded and scribbled away.

"Anyway, I was practically still in my college graduation garb when I high-tailed it out of Portland. I wanted to get away from Emily, and Nova, for that matter, so I found an opportunity to move to Sioux Falls in 2009 so I could work as a research assistant for Decree Sciences, a place that tests generic versions of name brand medications. Pretty boring stuff, I must admit, but at least I felt like I was doing something sciency, even if I was just painting by number. They wanted any bachelor's degree, so at least I kinda felt like I was using my degree, even if only ostensibly. Besides, they didn't mind that I was just a few credits shy of graduation and only had a 3.0 GPA. I guess they were hard up! But the void from my deceased father still weighed on me." Madeline paused and looked at Dr. Zeck. "You didn't fall asleep, did you?"

Zeck laughed. "Not a chance. You have quite the story, Miss Madeline. Besides, I care about my patients."

Madeline rolled her eyes. "I highly doubt that. When you go home, you will forget I even said anything about it, as you leave your workday behind you and call such dismissal and denial 'self care.'"

"One should never take their work home with them. That goes for you too, Miss Madeline Fischer."

"How convenient. I wouldn't want to rain on your parade and your cozy little life outside of here. Your suburban wife might be right disappointed when you sleep together."

"Hey now," said Zeck. "Don't cross any lines."

"I didn't mean sex," said Madeline. "How can people have sex while they are asleep anyway?"

"It's a figure of speech," said Zeck. "Surely you knew that."

"I guess," said Madeline. "But it's a stupid expression. Sleeping should mean sleeping."

Zeck guffawed. "I can't argue with you there, Miss Madeline! A true pedantic. I am in good company. Please, please go on and continue your story. And your mother?"

Madeline continued. "So when she was finally pardoned on January 1st, I was so excited. I even thanked the karma police for granting her such clemency and giving her a new lease on life, as opposed to her old 'leash on life,' as I liked to call it."

"What about your aunt?" asked Dr. Zeck, peering up at her while scribbling in his notepad.

"Emily? I talk with her maybe once or twice a year. I actually prefer her divorced husband, my uncle Marvin Brix, who now lives in Colorado."

"Tell me more about what brought you here," said Dr. Zeck with a calm voice.

Madeline continued again. "I guess my really aberrant behavior started when my mom died at the hands of Amrak, just two weeks ago now on Valentine's Day. That's when I changed my beliefs on karma. I still believed the karma police exist all right, but they were most certainly not concerned about fairness. They were out to get me, plain and simple. And that is what I believe most of the time, even now as I am talking to you. Do I believe Amrak is a karma police? Sure I do. But do I think he is right? Absolutely not. He took my mom from me." Madeline sobbed. Dr. Zeck brought her an almost empty box of tissues, where the top tissue wasn't protruding from the box. Madeline fished around in the box and pulled one out. "Tissues are for issues," she said as she set the box on the floor.

Dr. Zeck gave her a moment before continuing. "I am well aware of Amrak; make no mistake. I was fascinated by him well before the incident with your mother. And there is no excuse for what he did. You know, Madeline, even psychologists and mental health folk consider the expectation of fairness a cognitive distortion, as cynical as that might sound."

Madeline wiped her eyes on her scrubs, turning the light blue a darker shade, then sat up on the couch and burped. "Do you mind if I get up? I feel like my stomach is acting funny."

"You go right ahead. The purpose of a Freudian couch is to allow free association and unbridled self-disclosure. If you do better standing up, be my guest."

Madeline sat on the edge of the couch and removed her lace-less Crocs and socks. She stood on Dr. Zeck's bearskin rug and scrunched her toes into the fur. After a brief moment, she walked towards the large globe just to the right of the large window, the snow still falling outside thick and heavy. With a hard whoosh, she spun the globe like a child spinning a top.

"Hey, careful with that," asserted Dr. Zeck. "I got that globe when I was on sabbatical in Madagascar."

"Lucky you," said Madeline. "That's gotta be like the most elitist statement ever uttered."

"I'm just telling you the truth," said Zeck. "That globe is dear to me. Please don't touch it."

Madeline closed her eyes and poised her finger over the globe. The globe settled to a halt, and Madeline's finger landed on Spain. She opened her eyes. "That's where I wanna take my sabbatical."

"With all due respect, Miss Madeline, you need to hold a special position to take a sabbatical."

"With all due respect, you are a pretentious class-hole," said Madeline. "I just want to go to Spain. I don't need any damn sabbatical to do that."

Dr. Zeck took a deep breath. "Class-hole? Easy Madeline, don't get yourself worked up into a frenzy. And please don't be so cavalier."

"Apologies," said Madeline using a disingenuous tone.

"So you would leave fate to decide your vacation destiny?"

"If there is such a thing as karma, why not leave it up to them to decide? My life is screwed either way."

Dr. Zeck flipped a page in his notebook. "Please, tell me about what happened after your mother died. And please leave that globe alone."

Madeline sighed. She stared out the window and smiled at the five or so residents below, making snowmen and snow angels like children. Looking out the window somehow made her feel as if she was alone in the room, even more so than when she was on the couch. She felt an aura of psychological safety and, for some reason, did not feel ill at ease to allow herself to be vulnerable in her moment of self-disclosure.

"So when my mom died, Emily called me from Portland, just a day after Valentine's Day. She was so aloof about the funeral details she didn't even stop to think that maybe it would all be tough on me. She said I was being selfish because I initially left all the details to her. I guess I just couldn't deal with it, you know? But then I sort of lost my mind, as you would say, and had a better idea. I called Emily and told her I would take over the funeral arrangements from there, like all by my lonesome. She was ecstatic and told me she didn't think an irresponsible and labile person like me was capable of adulting like that. So I booked a flight to Portland and got there two days later, about five in the afternoon, and she let me in—not so much with open arms, but she let me in nonetheless, me and my travel belongings and a meth pipe. And that was that.

"Emily wanted a proper burial, but I convinced her that incineration was more practical, and it was much cheaper also. But then things got weird, at least according to other, more 'normal' folks. They said I could go there at the 'Bridges of Portland' funeral home and look at the body one last time before it was incinerated. I seized the opportunity. Strike when the iron is hot, so to speak. Or before it is hot, in this case. So I took the quilt my mother made for me and brought it with me. I told the folks there that I wanted to put the quilt over her as a sort of sign of loyalty and respect and that I wanted the quilt to stay draped over her as they burned the body. At first, they kind of hesitated, but I said it's part of my religion. And with that, they acquiesced. I also told them I wanted to be left alone with her, for a moment of silence, before they burned her like a marshmallow."

Madeline paused. One of the snowmen outside was so large it took three people to hoist the midsection onto the bottom ball. She looked at the headless snowman and couldn't help but smile at the irony.

"So what happened then?" asked Dr. Zeck, watching her stare out the window.

Madeline returned to the couch and sat on it. She gazed at the floor as she continued. "Well, what they didn't know was that I also brought a laundry bag containing the quilt, plastic wrap, wet wipes, and a fully charged electric turkey knife. When they left me alone with Mom, I proceeded to cut off her head."

At that point, Dr. Zeck's eyebrows raised, and he moved his hand even faster to keep up.

"I took off my coat beforehand so that any blood spatter would get on my red flannel shirt instead, which I could cover up with my jacket afterwards. This was the toughest part, and I was very careful to clean up any mess. When I got the head, I covered it in plastic wrap and put it all in the laundry bag. I put some plastic wrap around her neck area, too, not just to stop the blood but to also prop up a sort of make-shift fake head, and covered the entirety of the body with the quilt. After cleaning up with my can of wet wipes, I put my coat on and went back out into the main lobby and told the nice lady that I was done. I didn't even have to fake any tears to make it look more believable, as I was crying in sorrow the way it was. When Thomas came back to me, I reminded him not to remove the shroud for holy reasons and to burn the body forthwith. And that must have been what happened because they never discovered the missing head, and nobody ever said a peep about it. My father was a big game hunter—I'm talking African safari kind of shit. And thankfully for me, the taxidermist he used was a sketchy sort of fellow, a real tough customer. I didn't waste any time. I called him later that day and asked how much he would charge to mount a human head. And to think he actually hung up on me!"

"Heaven forbid," said Dr. Zeck. "How dare he."

"What's that supposed to mean?" asked Madeline. "You being sarcastic on me?"

"Well, did you actually expect him to honor such a request?"

"I guess so," said Madeline. "But it's not like I was asking him to kill anyone as if I was asking him to be a hitman or anything. My mom was already dead. So I don't see the big deal. You can't murder someone that's already dead, no matter how gruesome it looks."

"Most people would see what you did as a big deal, make no mistake," said Dr. Zeck, taking notes with reckless abandon.

"Murder or no murder. It's still not altogether another day at the office, now, is it? But please, keep going. I am not judging you."

Madeline continued, sometimes using flamboyant body language and occasionally making eye contact with Dr. Zeck. "Being as industrious and obstinate as a spider spinning a web, I went ahead with plan B. I called back, and naturally, he didn't even pick up. But I left him a message. So the typical cost of mounting an animal head is like around one thousand dollars or so. But since this was such an odd request, I initially offered ten thousand. About three hours went by, and I never heard back from him. I was just about to give up and toss the head into my aunt's fireplace, but I realized I had set my phone to silent. It turns out that only an hour after I called him, he left me a message of his own. After some half-hearted condolences, he said he would do the job for twenty-five thousand, as long as I gave him documentation proving I did not kill my mother myself. The nerve of that guy!"

"Yes, the nerve."

Madeline glared at him and continued. "Anyway, this was easy, as I still had the paperwork from 'Bridges of Portland' to show him that the body was incinerated. And since he knew that what I was asking of him was illegal, he gave me further instructions to keep the head hidden in my home and never let anyone see it. And if anyone did see it, he told me to simply tell them it was an expensive movie prop to satiate my alternative lifestyle, eccentric sensibilities, and love of old silent film. So I was able to get the head to him before I returned home to Emily's. The following day they held the formal funeral, with the urn sitting at the front, missing a few of its ashes, of course. The day after that, I was able to borrow Emily's Plymouth to retrieve the head from the taxidermist. Since there was no smell to worry about, I was easily able to take it with me in a red gym bag on the carry-on rack of the plane. So when I got back to Sioux Falls, I kind of went against the taxidermist's protocols, as I put the head right next to my dad's large game moose head with the large antlers. My only regret is that I never even thought to have my pet cats and dogs taxidermised over the years. As if Tessa would have let me anyway!"

"Taxidermised?" asked Zeck. "Is that a word, Miss Madeline?"

"If it isn't, it should be!"

Dr. Zeck smiled. "Well, somebody gets to invent words. Might as well be us. Sounds like quite the morbid diorama."

Madeline sat on the Freudian couch and looked at Zeck until the silence became uncomfortable. "I found it oddly reassuring as if my mother had never died. I saw her as a sort of guardian angel or patron saint, keeping watch over me. Two or three days later, I asked her a question. I asked her to give me a sign to prove she was watching over me. But this did not happen. And I resented her for it. She was never one to miss a beat to check on me. I figured wherever she happened to be, she, of all people, would find a way to check in on me. Even something like death wasn't enough to stop her. And the fact that she didn't, I wondered if she either didn't love me or if she even existed at all, and all the tales of an afterlife were just fairy tales. Or my preferred theory, the karma police were simply keeping her from me. But damn, I missed her. And over the course of the next day, I felt more and more disconsolate until I finally made up my mind."

"Made up your mind to do what, exactly?"

Madeline didn't say a word. She pulled out several more tissues from the box on the floor, wadded them up into a ball, and sobbed into the lot of them. Dr. Zeck afforded her some time to cry. After a minute or two, Madeline continued as Dr. Zeck continued taking notes in shorthand.

"I went to the hardware store and purchased some nails and a sturdy tow rope. In the privacy of my own ambitions, I added extra nails to secure the moose head. I tethered the rope to the antlers. I had no idea how to tie a proper 'moose noose,' so I did the best I could to make a loop."

"Moose noose?" asked Zeck.

"Well, yes," said Madeline. "I'm proud of that one."

"Well, isn't that amusing," said Zeck. "You have a rather macabre sense of humor. Please, go on."

"I dragged in one of my kitchen chairs and made sure I got the height just right. So I got up on the chair and made the plunge. I felt more and more enervated the longer I dangled. And just as I was passing out and the world was turning into oblivion, the mounted head somehow fell off the wall, be it from chance, fate, serendipity, kismet, or some other miracle. Not less than fifteen minutes later, the milkman entered the house and found me prostrated on the floor, unresponsive. He called 911 and did his CPR routine until an entourage of first responders came to the scene—and a scene it was. I was taken to the hospital. And after a short period of convalescence from my neck wounds, I was placed under involuntary commitment under the regulations of SDCL 27A-1-2 under South Dakota law, as I was considered a danger to myself. I was ultimately committed to this very Sioux Falls Mental Hospital, in accordance with statutes in Minnehaha County. The first responders, being mandated reporters of vulnerable adults, contacted the Sioux Falls Social Services and told them everything about the mounted head in the living room. Needless to say, they did not assume it was a gothic novelty item. And in their eyes, it was a red flag."

Madeline was now crying ample tears, perhaps enough to fill a rain gauge up to half an inch.

"Let it out, Madeline," said Dr. Zeck. "You are in the right place.

Madeline donned a tear-laced smile. "Tissues are for issues."

· —

CHAPTER 10
FOLLOW THE MONEY

Main characters: Madeline Fischer
Date: March 14, 2017, Tuesday, 2:45 p.m.

The Man with the Insatiable Itch: A short story by Madeline Fischer

Thrice upon a time, there was a man who was born into a world of organic machines. These "robots," as it were, had organic parts, not much different than machines, save for being softer, and included such things as fur, bone, muscle, organs, and scales. There were also fluids, much like gasoline, oil, or washer fluid, and these included such things as blood, sweat, and tears. There was even a part called the "brain," which served as a sort of computer database and processing center. And like a mish-mash of gears, pistons, or combustion chambers, all these parts served a function, working in tandem, and were no less impressive in their respective complexities than the non-organic juxtapositions of bits of plastic, battery, or metal.

At first, all this man's cohorts wondered in tandem at the wherefore and why. After all, it is a strange thing to be born into a world of machines and not wonder where they actually came from. But over time, they became habituated to these machines' somber omnipresence and acclimated without any further need for hard and well-researched answers. After all, what could they do to unearth such mysteries? Who could they ask and turn to for help? And many satiated any vestige of curiosity through such things as sophistry, sometimes with a blind-faith and sheep-like acquiescence.

But this man was not quite so easily fooled or satiated. He never lost his sense of wonder, curiosity, or humility to have more questions than answers. He was a man with an insatiable itch. Try as he might, he could not reach this itch. No matter what he did, it was always just out of reach. He couldn't hear it, see it, smell it, or taste it, but he could feel it. And it wasn't the sort of feeling like running your fingers over the contours of a pine cone. Nor was it like getting burned or cut. It was somewhere between these two extremes. It wasn't the worst pain in the world, but it was a nagging thorn in his side nonetheless, and one he had tried to rectify any way he could. He tried reaching the itch with all manner of tools and creative methods. He tried topical creams. He used a loofah. He tried distracting himself with pleasing sights and smells, hoping they would take his mind off the itch. But no matter what he did, he just couldn't quite reach it or forget about it. The itch was ever present, begging to be reached.

Over time, however, he learned to live with it in the best way he knew how. He never learned to like it, but he learned to co-exist with it. It was sort of a mutual arrangement, like a parasite to host. If you can't beat it, join it. And in so doing, the man came up with language and all manner of religions, philosophies, and political ideologies, all trying to make sense of this world to reach the insatiable itch. But the question remained. What happens when you die? So he composed a theory. As the body gets older and organs begin to fail, could you theoretically replace the organs one by one and find immortality in this manner? However, a possible caveat: If there is this "soul," does each organ have a "soul piece"? Do sperm and eggs contain "soul matter"? He died before he could find out. On the other hand, perhaps he found out everything he needed to know.

---------------- *Madeline's Journal, December 25, 2015*

It's not what you know. It's who you know, thought Madeline to herself as she was eating her scrambled eggs and charred bacon in the breakfast room of the Sioux Falls hospital. *Still, sometimes what you know about the people you know can be the most important thing of all.*

Madeline thought about her social support network, other than Emily, of course. She figured there were only two family members she really knew all that well—her uncle Marvin in Denver, Colorado, and of course her identical twin sister Nova, who was a veterinarian in Fargo, ND. She wondered further about their usefulness and whether they could be beneficial to her somehow. But she didn't want to take advantage of her friends in any way.

Feeling excited about her newfound revelations, she dumped the other half of her food in the dumpster and went to the main lobby. She took a seat on the large plush couch and stared out the window. It was a warm day, and she noticed that the last of the winter's snow was almost totally melted. She couldn't help but wonder for a moment how the Upper Midwest could get away with calling March 1st as spring, given how winter always had such a way of hanging on for dear life.

She decided that Marvin probably wasn't very helpful all the way out in Colorado, other than for some quick cash. So her thoughts quickly went back to how she could ingratiate herself back into the good graces of her sister Nova. The bottleneck was she hadn't talked to her in over a year now. So how could she regain her trust and help without seeming like she had some sort of hidden agenda? Would she be willing to be complicit in her schemes after she'd burned all those bridges years ago? After all, there was that one little time she pretended to be Nova in high school and slept with her then boyfriend, Thomas Stone. Oh yes, and that time she got her to help pay for that "surgery" so she could spend the money on something else. While Marvin had always had a fondness for "little Madeline," despite her ignoble shortcomings, Nova was a different duck and not quite so magnanimous. After all, she could nurse a grudge for years, with the tenacity of a hungry baby clutching a bottle, with emphasis on baby. Still, a highly tactful and politic strategy was in order. And a tall order it was. But she felt up to the challenge.

Madeline got up and approached her favorite gregarious

receptionist, a certain Jason Mattson. He was a short and middle-aged fellow and had an affinity for wearing cowboy boots and bowler hats, an odd combination that meshed with her eccentric and eclectic sensibilities.

Jason tipped his hat like a cowboy and feigned an exaggerated wild west dialect. "Pleasure to see you, Miss Maddy. I reckon you need some help?"

"Sure, why not," said Madeline, smiling. "Got a pen, perchance?"

"A Bic round stick medium suit your fancy?" posited the gentleman as he held one out to her, keeping up his cowboy facade.

"You make it sound like choosing the right golf club," said Madeline, plucking it out of his hand.

"I am only being facetious," said the man, using his normal voice. "If it were up to me, we would still be using feather quills and inkwells round these here parts."

Madeline smirked. "Well, thanks to Bic — they cater to our shaving, writing, and lighter needs."

"An eclectic company," returned Mr. Mattson. "I wonder if MacGyver could find a use for all three at the same time."

Madeline considered him as she tapped her chin with her index finger. "Reminds me of the farmer's dilemma. Hmmm...I got it! If Mac was in a dark prison, he could use the razor to cut the ropes off his hands, the a lighter to read a message sent from the messenger pigeon, and a pen to write a message back!"

"There you go!" said the man. "Who needs MacGyver when we have Madeline? I'm equally impressed that you even know MacGyver to begin with."

Madeline maintained her smile as she analyzed the pen top to bottom. "Thanks. A Bic round stick medium will be perfect for this job." She began walking towards the main hall to go to her room.

"Where do you think you are going, young lady?" shouted Jason after her.

Madeline went back to the reception desk. "I hope you

didn't think I was going to steal the pen because I wouldn't do that with you. You have earned my trust. Besides, I know full well that pen thieves get sent to the pen."

Jason laughed. "It's nothing to do with stealing, I'm afraid. I really wish I could bend the rules for you, but clients can't take any sharps to their rooms."

Madeline handed it back. "So even pens are considered sharps these days?"

"Well, they are sharp, ain't they?" said Jason as he wrote the word sharp onto his palm. "Not two years ago, a patient stuck a pen right into his very eyeball. They say he went blind and wore an eye patch for a full year."

"Gosh, I guess the pen really is mightier than the sword," scoffed Madeline. "Not only that, but one of these little guys signed my commitment paperwork. Funny how one little cheap-ass Bic can sign the very execution papers to send a man to his death. They should really allow glitter pens for that."

Jason laughed. "I really shouldn't laugh."

"It's okay, permission granted."

Madeline held up the pen from the visitor sign-in book, which was attached to the clipboard by a string, and looked at it up close. "Fine point, it says on the side. Does this mean everything you write will be articulate, as in making a good point like in a political debate?"

The man laughed. "I somehow doubt it."

"Oh yes, I was thinking of magic markers," said Madeline. "My mistake!"

They both laughed.

"This is why I like talking with you, Jason," said Madeline. "We can make a discussion about pens interesting. And you actually make me smile on occasion. You are an amiable fellow, and I like that."

Jason smiled and tipped his hat. He spoke once again like a cowboy. "Thank you kindly. The pleasure is all mine." He took on his usual accent. "You brighten my day as well, Madeline." He pointed towards the waiting room. "You can sit over there in the waiting room while you use your pen. Just bring it back when you are finished."

"Can I write a letter to send, stamps and everything?"

Jason fetched her a sheet of plain white copy paper. "Sure, patients do it all the time." Just as he handed it to her, he shot her an odd stare. "I'm surprised you didn't ask about this earlier, as lonely as folks get around here and with very limited cell phone privileges."

"I guess I don't really care to talk to anybody," said Madeline. "Time flies, whether you are having fun or not. And besides, I actually don't have many friends."

"Apologies, Miss Madeline. That's mighty sad to hear. Sometimes my loquacious demeanor gets the best of me, and I end up shooting my mouth off. And here I am trying to be funny. I should realize that not everyone has a big happy fairy tale family. You just go on over there, and you write that letter. You poor folks need all the support you can muster. Patients just need to be supervised with the pens. But we got the stamps."

"Got any paperweights?" asked Madeline.

"Excuse me?" asked Jason.

"You know, something to keep my stationery stationary?"

Jason laughed as he held up a stapler. "Will this work?"

"Perfect," said Madeline. "I just don't want to press my palms against the page if I can help it, as I always press the pen down so hard my hand sweat gets on the page."

"Ah, hand sweat," said Mr. Mattson. "The scourge of our times."

Madeline nodded and smiled as she took her supplies to the waiting room in eyesight of the receptionist. She was the only one sitting in the ring of nine wooden and cushioned chairs surrounding the two walls. She pushed the magazines to the side of the small coffee table as she set up her writing space. There were several framed pictures of inspirational quotes around the two white walls, such as "Change Your Thoughts, Change Your World," "Embrace the Unexpected," and "Mindset is Everything." One of them showed a person on a mountain top with her hands spread out in the air, and another showed a pile of stacked circular rocks.

Sheesh, thought Madeline. *Are these not the most trite mental health images like ever?* She mused further. *Who's to say that lady isn't contemplating jumping off that cliff?* She giggled to herself at the irreverent thought.

The letter took her no less than two and a half hours to write, and it was now past 5 p.m. She was so lost in thought she scarcely paid attention to the ebb and flow of patrons coming and going into the waiting room during this time. She didn't even notice the coughs and sneezes, which were usually her pet peeves when confronted with a group of strangers.

After she had written the letter, she got up from the chair and walked back towards reception. It was the "changing of the guard," and Jason was just putting on his jacket to leave. Madeline spotted the scrawny twenty-something Penny Schumacher already hard at work in his place—Madeline liked to call her "Money Penny, the power trip receptionist." During the commotion of shift change, Madeline took the liberty to try and sneak back to her room with the pen.

Penny didn't fall for Madeline's scheme and relished in the moment. "Hey miss, you gotta bring that pen back! Jason told me all about it."

"Geez, it's only a stupid pen," Madeline asserted, handing it back after a moment of brief hesitation. "A pen for Penny! A pen for Penny!"

Jason was about to leave the lobby but heard their exchange. He dashed back to reception. "Penny here will make sure that letter gets mailed," said Jason, all smiles. "And don't give Penny here too hard of a time."

"I won't," said Madeline. She glared at Penny. "But only because you told me not to."

Jason laughed to himself and left the building.

"So you got a letter to mail?" asked Penny, reaching for it.

Madeline pulled it back quickly, almost as if she were scared Penny was going to snatch it from her.

"Okay, okay," said Penny. "Just bring it back when you are done, and I can stamp it for you. It's not like I was going to read it or anything."

Madeline bit her lip. "No worries. But could I make a phone call?"

The receptionist opened her lockbox and handed her cell phone to her. "Just bring your phone back when you are done, okay?"

"I will," said Madeline. "I always do."

"No, actually, you don't," reminded Penny with a disapproving scowl.

Madeline grumbled a bit and went to her room, and sat on her bed. She dialed the number to her twin sister Nova. After three rings, Nova picked up the phone.

"Hello?" asked Nova, watching Downton Abbey as she ate her Cornish game hen in her kitchen.

"Three rings as usual," said Madeline.

"Maddy?" asked Nova. The voice was so loud on the phone that it prompted Madeline to hold the phone back an inch from her ear. "I thought it was you. You know me, two rings is too eager, and four rings is too lazy."

"You Goldilocks, you," said Madeline. "So, you married yet? I don't hear any hustle and bustle in the background."

"Nah, 'fraid not," returned Nova with a laugh.

"Is it because you are too cool or not cool enough?" asked Madeline.

Nova laughed as if she felt a bit awkward by this line of questioning. "You can be the judge of that, sis. So how are you? What has it been, like over a year?"

"Things could be better. I am in a mental hospital right now."

"Oh dear," said Nova. "I'm sorry to hear that. I guess Emily never said anything to me about it."

"She probably doesn't know yet," said Madeline, feeling relieved word apparently hadn't gotten out yet, particularly what she had done that landed her in the hospital, to begin with. Even though she knew the mental health system did its very best to keep everything confidential, she also knew that sometimes news had a way of getting out, especially bad news. She continued. "In fact, the newspapers and everyone are being good about keeping everything on the hush-hush and down-low."

"You make it sound like you did something really bad, Mads," said Nova. "You keeping anything from me?"

"No, I didn't kill anyone or anything," said Madeline, wondering if she had already said too much on the matter. "It's just all very embarrassing, I guess." She decided to quit while she was ahead.

Nova strained to pay attention to the plot of her show. "At least a mental hospital has gotta be better than jail, though, huh?"

"I suppose so," returned Madeline begrudgingly. "I know your idea of a silver lining has always been to think about how much worse things could be. 'At least I have my health. At least I have my limbs. At least I am not being skinned alive.'"

"Oh dear, that would be awful," said Nova. "But an attitude of gratitude helps take the edge off, though, doesn't it? Don't they teach that sort of stuff in mental health clinics?"

"I suppose, but it kinda makes me more depressed sometimes, I must say, thinking about the folks that really do have it worse. Besides, it's only been about a month I saw you when Mom died. And that's why I called, actually. How are you holding up?"

"Well, thank you, Madeline, I appreciate that," said Nova, pausing Downton Abbey. "Oh, I am struggling a bit here and there, but at least I haven't cried in a week now. Life goes on and all that, you know? I haven't hit the bottle yet if that is what you mean. But I have been going through the Starbucks line almost every day before work to get my oat milk latte. Not sure if that is related, though."

"Wow, that's hardcore. You gotta get a grip on your vices!"

Nova laughed. "You and your wordplay. So how is it there? Better than the one in Portland?"

Madeline sighed. "Well, being here is every bit as boring.

I mean, we have coloring and scratch art books and art projects, just like in the movies or the occasional walk or community outing. All very pedestrian, though."

Nova considered her. "Pedestrian as in boring, or do you mean you do lots of walking?"

"Both!" shouted Madeline into the mouthpiece.

They both laughed.

"So, how is vet work? You a veteran veterinarian yet?" asked Madeline.

"Oh, you know how it is, not as glamorous as it sounds. Lots of heavy lifting, working with boring farm animals, and spaying cats. It all pays the bills, though."

"With some to spare, I imagine," said Madeline.

Nova paused. "So, is there something I can do? Is there a reason you called me? Or was it just to ask about Mom?"

"Well, sort of," said Madeline. "Since I already have you on the line. And I know what you must be thinking. My M.O. is to call when I need something or some strange favor."

Nova paused once again. "So do you, like, need something?"

"Well, yes and no," said Madeline as she fiddled with her scrubs with her other hand.

"How much is this going to cost me?" asked Nova, followed by a nervous laugh.

Madeline began pacing around her room. "Actually, it won't cost you anything. In fact, I want to pay you back for all that money I borrowed over the years. I did the math in my head, and it turns out that I owe you like three thousand dollars. Truth is, I am prepared to pay it back."

"It's actually closer to seven thousand, Maddy," said Nova in a half-whisper.

"Well, sorry. I mean, I guess—"

"I don't mind it so much as long as you work on yourself and make some changes for the better," said Nova. "I'm not a savage. I just chalk it up to charity. Makes me feel less guilty about my other moral failings. You don't really have to—"

"No, I want to," said Madeline, cutting her off. "I need to. It's part of my therapy. I am supposed to make amends and apologize to the people I have hurt, stolen from, and/or lied to."

"Well, how about that? Good for you, Madeline. I am very proud of you. It seems you have turned a new leaf."

"Yes, and this time it's not a marijuana leaf."

"Funny girl," said Nova.

Madeline began to chew her nails. "But since you brought it up, I do have a tiny and teensy weensy favor to ask. But rest assured, it won't cost you anything."

Nova guffawed. "Okay, now I'm really worried. I'm not killing anyone for you or anything, am I?"

Madeline felt slightly offended. "It's nothing like illegal or expensive. At worst, it's just a little bit time-consuming, maybe. But it's for a noble cause."

Nova's spoke with twice as much volume. "Okay, spill your guts, Madeline. The anticipation is killing me."

Madeline held up her fingers as if taking an oath, despite being on the phone. "I won't do anything under the table, below the belt, under the radar, or otherwise underhanded. It must all be above board and over the counter."

"There sure are lots of bad things that happen underneath things," said Nova. "Now start spilling."

Madeline interrupted her. "I will spill the beans or my guts, whatever comes first. So okay, here's the thing—"

"Stop right there," said Nova. "You know I always get nervous when you preface any sentence with 'here's the thing.'"

"Give me a chance," said Madeline. "There is a chap in my compulsive liar group that used to make counterfeit money, and we have become very good friends. Maybe even more than that. We even kissed a few times. Anyway, he is learning how making such money is a form of lying. I wanted to surprise him with a supportive letter about how much I believe in him and care for him. It's not a marriage proposal or anything."

Nova sighed. "Maddy, can you cut it out and cut to the chase, please?"

"Okay, here's the thing," said Madeline.

Nova let out a sigh, louder than before.

"I am not tech-savvy, and I can't do much in here. I just need you to affix one of those squiggly wiggly QR codes atop a two-dollar bill. It will be a wonderful surprise for him."

"Why a two-dollar bill?" asked Nova.

"They stand out more and beg further inspection," said Madeline. "John will love it."

"John, as in the counterfeit money guy?" asked Nova.

"Yes, that's the one."

"You know, I think you can do better with your choice of men," said Nova. "But I am not here to judge."

"He's actually great, Nova, and he regrets all those money crimes. He is trying to do better like I am. So speaking of cutting, cut me some slack."

"So, how do I know what message to put in the code?" asked Nova.

"I can do that part. Your QR code will simply link to my PDF that I will write and create myself. I already have the letter part written. But it's very important you do not read my message. Not only would that be highly embarrassing for me, but it also goes against the rules of confidentiality we have in our therapy groups here in Sioux Falls."

"Okay, okay, don't worry, I am hardly a Nosy Nellie," said Nova.

"I thought it was 'Nosy Rosy,'" said Madeline.

"People with either name can be nosy," said Nova. "Okay, so will you send me the link to your PDF as soon as you get a chance?"

"Yes, sounds like a plan," said Madeline. "And that brings me to the other reason I called."

"What is it now?"

"Hey, shush," said Madeline. "This is the good part. I want you to visit me more, the first Saturday of every odd-numbered month."

Nova paused to think. "Six visits a year? I think I can

manage that. It's only from Fargo to Sioux Falls, after all. You know, I would like that. We can catch up a bit more — might do us well with Mom being gone."

"Glad you can pencil me in," said Madeline.

"Okay, so when do you want me to bring the two-dollar bill?"

"You can bring it on your first visit, the first Saturday in May. Come about 11:00 A.M., as that's the preferred visiting hour here."

"Sounds like a plan," said Nova. "Oh yeah, and don't forget to turn your clock ahead for daylight saving time. You take care now, Madeline, and thanks for calling."

"Sounds good," said Madeline. "You take care, and thanks for everything."

And with that, Madeline hung up her phone. She gripped the phone in her hand, stared at it for a moment, and began rotating it from one hand to another as if musing about Marvin's perceptions of her. She got up from her bed and went back to the receptionist, Penny, and had her put the phone back in her lockbox. She zombie-walked back to her room, scraping her fingernails on the sterile white wall as she went. Deeper thoughts began to come to the fore. How would she abscond from the mental hospital? How would she get to Split Rock by herself without a car? And what if nobody received her secret embedded message? If there really was such a thing as karma, would it help guide the way?

She trudged into her room. With a loud sigh, she flopped atop her bed and stared at the cottage cheese shapes on the ceiling. She centered her gaze on Peter. She began ruminating about how she could make her egress from the mental hospital. What would it take to get Nova to help her?

"Aha, I got it, Peter!" she said aloud. Her excitement kept her up the remainder of the night as she played out the various schemes and scenarios of how she would make her great egress from the asylum. Her plans became more and more jumbled as she drew near to sleep. "This will be my last lie, Nova," she mumbled. "I promise."

· —

CHAPTER 11
MY INSIGNIFICANT OTHER

Date: July 6, 2019, Saturday, 4:00 P.M.
Main character: Mark Anderson

At around four that afternoon, Mark Anderson shut the door and pulled down the blinds in the living room of his less-than-tidy apartment. The array of bottles, snack packages, and pop cans littering the nooks and crannies of the space hardly stole his attention. As he was alone, he was quite literally left to his devices — or rather device in the singular. He was feeling a nasty urge to strike before his iron was hot. As for Sandy, she was at work running a Saturday errand for her supervisor, and she had dropped Gavin off at the local Starbucks to hang out with his friend Wade in the interim, as their schedules had meshed and Gavin didn't own a car. And since Mark's phone was out of minutes, she had taken care to leave him hers in the event he had to make a call for whatever reason. As such, Mark was alone within the confines or expanses of the home, depending on one's perspective.

Mark went to his oak five-drawer dresser in his bedroom and unlocked the top drawer with the little key he had hidden under the stuffed walrus sitting on his headboard. Without hesitation, he hoisted the 1973 Colt Python out of its hiding place, a revolver willed to him by his late grandfather Charles Anderson. The top drawer was labeled "underwear," and thankfully (for him at least), this was enough of a repellent to keep any snoopers away. He set the gun and bullets on top of the dresser for the time being. He stripped down, tossing his black jeans and long-sleeved Akira tee on the carpeted floor until he was completely naked, as he didn't want to soil his clothing. Last but not least, he fired up his lava lamp on his computer desk.

Mark took the pistol and box of bullets from the bedroom dresser and set them in the bathroom sink, as his bedroom was adjoined to the bathroom, which was also adjoined to Sandy's bedroom. After a second trip, both pillows from his bed were chucked into the bathtub. The third trip was to retrieve his black and hard-cover "Mark's Journal of Existential Musings" from his computer desk and the feather quill and inkwell set that Sandy had given him for Christmas. The side of the tub offered a perfect place upon which to set these items. He installed the second curtain and rod he had purchased a month ago and tucked the outside curtain inside the tub so that both sides of the tub were enclosed and splatter proof. The gun and bullets from the sink were then placed on the side of the tub next to his journal and feather quill set.

Stepping into the tub, he pulled the curtains. The quill plunked into the inkwell, poised to write. "I always wanted to use one of these for existential reasons. I guess it's now or never," he thought to himself. He sat down on the back end and stretched his legs out as far as they could reach in the contained space. But then he realized he'd forgotten what may be the most important item of all, his experimental helmet, *Project Madcap*. This called for a fourth trip to his room, and he put on the headgear as he went back into the bathtub. The pillows were positioned against the wall so he could put his head back. And with that, he dipped his quill into the inkwell. Although he hardly ever used cursive, that was what he used on the note, as he opted for a certain level of formality and panache, especially given that he was using an old-fashioned feather quill for the occasion. After about fifteen minutes and several dips of his quill into the inkwell, he had articulated the following, including a crude sketch of four actual bullet points.

July 6, 2019 (My 5/6 suicide note)

Work

Love
Project Madcap
Existential curiosity

Today I perfected Project Madcap, and now the accuracy and precision of the pain and pleasure readings are impeccable to two decimal places. I expected that this day would occasion excitement and joy. However, and contrary to what I had hoped, I find myself somehow ill at ease. It appears that I must be resigned to a perpetual state of anhedonia. According to the very device I created, it appears that I am indeed a tortured and restless soul. And while the device can't differentiate between psychological and physical pain states, I can only surmise that my pain is of a very psychological nature, as I feel no physical pain whatsoever, save for some minor heartburn and a hangnail. Truth be told, the pain rating of my melancholy, anxiety, and curiosity these days has even approached the very pain ratings I received from my anxiety-invoking parkour experiments. At first, I thought my device was faulty and not giving accurate numbers, but this does not appear to be the case. So what about today? When I stop and think, it becomes apparent to me that it's mostly existential curiosity, the fourth bullet point above, that is guiding my decision. I seem to have an unhealthy need to know what lies beyond the grave. And what about Project Madcap, my third bullet point above? This explains the one missing bullet. It appears that I also have an unhealthy desire to create an even higher fear state in my brain, higher than that induced through any of my parkour experiments, to see if Project Madcap can measure the highest fear states imaginable. And I can think of scarcely anything more terrifying than playing Russian Roulette with five bullets. Three cheers for curiosity. Still, we all know what happened to the cat.

He set the notepad and writing supplies down on the floor outside the tub and began loading the bullets, one at a time, into the Colt Cobra as if it were a Pez dispenser. After putting five bullets into the chamber, he gave the chamber a good spin. He gazed at the ceiling for a moment, lost in thought.

I am quite the bundle of nerves right now, he thought to himself. He took a moment to notice his shortness of breath, stomach pains, sweaty palms, and increased heart rate. While he told himself over and over again that there may not be much pain involved, in the grander scheme of things, he remained feeling somehow unconvinced. The legend of *Scylla and Charybdis went through his head,* as he felt equally terrified of life and death as if stuck in some sort of purgatory limbo. *I wish there were a third option for people that have an aversion for life and death,* he thought. *How painful this is to choose between the lesser of two evils. Oh, how I wish I could escape them both!*

Intrusive thoughts of people getting beheaded in the French Revolution entered his mind, and he thought about an article he had been reading recently where it was claimed some of the heads were still alive and conscious for a short time after the beheading. He further thought about a different article about firing squads, and how some of the guns had "conscience rounds," or blanks, to make the whole ordeal not feel quite so nefarious, antiquated, or ill-mannered to the shooter, as if the mere "possibility" of having a blank were enough to settle unsettled nerves or feelings of lingering compunction.

"What a gruesome world," he muttered. He further wondered why censors seemed more disturbed by sex and swearing on screen than actual acts of violence. *How ironic,* he thought. *And ridiculous!*

He poised the gun to his head and shut his eyes like drapes, like a child mentally preparing for an inoculation at the clinic, as if closing one's eyes can prevent what's coming from happening. Tears began painting his face like watercolors, hardly held back by the dams of his tightly closed lids. He did this several times.

Am I the only person in the world to ever play Russian Roulette with five bullets? he thought to himself. He followed this thought with his best attempt at maniacal laughter as if he were his very own arch-nemesis from one of his favorite graphic novels or animes. He couldn't help but let out a small smile when he recalled that this was about the same odds of winning a free bottle of pop in the nineties by looking under your bottle caps. He took a moment to consider the people in his life. He wondered about those he loved and those that loved him. "What does 'love' even mean?" he asked himself. Thankfully his deceased parents, Randy and Paula, were out of the picture and would be none the wiser for their loss. But he also considered the subtlety of details, like how the funeral arrangements would be handled. And how a lay about like Gavin would even know what to do or who to ask. And what about Sandy? She would probably be pissed, at least at first. Her tears would come much later, to be sure. He could envision her muttering beneath her breath about "how stupid Mark must have been" for even considering something like this. At the very least, cremation would be the only option, considering what state his body would be in.

But despite all the cognitive dissonance and the clashing of values swirling in his brain, the distorted internal dialogue that was victorious were his pathological excuses and rationalizations, such as, "I am just a burden anyway." It was almost as if there were a scale in his brain, with red checkers being life and black checkers being death. But the pros just couldn't keep up with his less than sunny disposition and biased frame of reference, until at last, the scales tipped.

And with that, he spun the chamber, and he couldn't help but be reminded of the big spinning wheel in *The Price is Right*. In the game show, the tiniest twitch of his hand could mean the difference between landing on a perfect $1.00 or $0.75. But in this case, the very tiniest twitch of his hand could mean the difference between life and death. But that wasn't the only caveat of this metaphor. He further mused at the irony of how much different the so-called "prize" was in either case. In one case, you win a boat. In this case, you win your very life. *This sure is a different kind of Showcase Showdown*, he thought.

Like the rising sun, he raised the gun to his head with a slow and steady velocity. He pointed the barrel at his left eye. As before, he squeezed his eyes shut without any chance for light to sneak through to provide the illusion of security. A few intrusive thoughts involving Bud Dwyer and Christina Lubbock popped into his head unannounced.

And with that, he pulled the trigger.

— —

CHAPTER 12
A BEDTIME STORY (PART 2)
"TANEUR AND THE LORD OF NATURE"

Date: November 6, 2032, Saturday, 9:00 P.M.
Main characters: Faith and Hope

Karma Law 1: Punishment must equal the crime

Punishment must never, under any circumstances, exceed the crime. This is the first and most important rule of all. In terms of karma, punishment is defined as pain. Pain can be physical, psychological, or a combination of both. Pain can be experienced in thousands of myriad ways. When pain exceeds the crime, it is considered draconian, and therefore considered revenge.

----*From A Code of Karmatic Jurisprudence, Province of Nature, Tier 1 (see Appendix A).*

***

"Good night, Miss Faith," said Hope as Faith appeared asleep under three layers of blankets. Like a stealthy burglar, Hope hobbled to the door and reached for the knob.

"What about the karma police?" asked Faith, wearing her Sherpa jacket to bed as was her usual.

Hope stopped dead in her tracks, with her hand on the brass knob. "What about them?"

Faith propped herself up, so her back was against the headrest. "You said last night that you would talk about the karma police. Unless I was dreaming."

"So I did, Miss Faith," said Hope, followed by a raspy laugh. "I must apologize forthwith."

Even Faith's dog Menace was panting and staring at her

from the trundle bed.

"'Taneur' was our secret password, so you would know just where we left off. I even put on my 'Cajeput' scent in my Smart diffuser special for the occasion."

"Indeed, you are right," said Hope. "And where would I be without your sharpshooter's memory?"

"I wouldn't hear many stories, that's for sure! But you can go if you are not in the mood."

"Not on your life," said Hope. With a loud screech, she slid a cheap folding chair up to the bed and sat beside her. "This is my treat, I insist." She pulled out the same copy of *Wuthering Heights* from the wooden bookcase. "And what a pleasing scent to set the mood for such an occasion."

"It's okay, really. You don't have to do it just because you feel sorry for me 'cause I am dying."

Hope put her hand on Faith's shoulder, under the heap of blankets. "This will benefit me as well as you. No worries, really, unequivocally and invariably."

Faith smiled.

***

Exactly one hundred years ago, in the center of the Pantheon, was a forty-something humanoid, close to six feet tall. He or she had a visible face but lacked all manner of any defining features. It's not that these details were missing, but they were somehow blurred or blotted out. Surrounding the person were the aforementioned twelve illustrious statesmen, preserved by the fine art of taxidermy.

The mysterious figure was adorned in garments spanning many time periods across Earth's history. In general, he was adorned in what could be considered a semblance of the "imperial regalia" of the Roman Empire, such as that stored in the imperial treasury in Hofburg Palace. But instead of a scepter, he held a Victorian black umbrella, open and poised over his head, although it was not raining.

This figure was tasked to mediate a grand meeting and help our solitary karma lord craft and draft a code of ethics, the rules of fairness and karma that were to govern the dystopian Ancient Earth and Goldilocks's Dilemma. This location was informally called the "mausoleum museum. Speaking of epithets, the mysterious figure went by the name of "Docent Randii." While this illustrious statesman and luminary was not a god per se, he/she was above the karma lords in the existential pecking order. In fact, it was not outside the realms of possibility that the Docent Randii answered directly to the very gods themselves. But even omniscient narrators are not privy to such information, even ones that break forth walls.

This karma lord, under the tutelage of the Docent Randii, was to design and draft not a perfect world, but a better one, a world where things made more sense and what you put in was generally what you got out. A world that was, at the very least, logical. A world that was fair, in a manner of speaking.

The mysterious docent appointed and anointed our one and only karma lord as "Taneur," blessed him with the divine knowledge about all manner of science and nature and tasked him with creating the laws of nature for this new world.

Taneur was a giant among men and a mountain among hills. He was born of the world, with a body of rock and tree and skin covered in patches of sandy beaches or verdant countrysides. And when the suffering of the world would make him cry, rivers of water would come forth from his glint-rock eyes, and water would jettison down his features of bark and bone like tributaries, fjords, and waterfalls, pouring past stony crag and cliff. His face was expressionless, and you could not judge his capricious moods or temperament merely by expression or appearances alone. However, the weather proffered clues to his mercurial and labile temperament. This was evident by one day's turbulent storm or the peaceful calm and serenity the very next day might bring. And while week to week weather patterns were difficult to predict, the four seasons gave some indication of what to expect, be it the autumn colors or the peaceful scenery of large snowflakes dropping from the heavens like feathers into rolling hills of crystal white. But there was nary a single season bereft of turbulent weather that could potentially be a harbinger of bad tidings, as the tales of floods, blizzards, earthquakes, droughts, tornadoes, lightning storms, forest fires, and hurricanes could surely attest.

The Docent Randii gave Taneur exactly one year to complete this grand task. And in one year's time, the two of them were to meet again, in this very location, at noon to draft a very important document, a document so important and so grand that it would govern all aspects of existence. This edict would be called the "Code of Karmatic Jurisprudence." It would not only seek to create and delineate a fair world but also delineate the rubric on how such fairness was to be achieved.

The Docent Randii also granted Taneur shape-shifting abilities so that he could shrink himself down to the size of a human when necessary. In addition, the Docent Randii bestowed upon our karma lord a second very special gift, a gift that was said to be from the very gods themselves. The gift was the "Krystal Kube," a crystal ball of sorts that could see everything in its six sides, past, present, and future. Not only that, but it could also see alternate realities. But Taneur was forbidden from looking into the sixth and final side of the Krystal Kube, as such knowledge was reserved and privy only to the gods themselves. And the Docent Randii explained to Taneur that part of being an ethical karma lord was abstaining from the temptation to gaze into the sixth dimension at all costs.

For a full year and in naked human form, Taneur wandered the world, from ocean to countryside, taking copious notes and observing the way plants, animals, and humans interacted. He kept score of the vice and virtue ratio of many organic lives, using random samples spanning all kinds of humans. The world as it was before was quasi-scientific. Compared to our world as it is now, it didn't have all the laws of nature and systems of the universe we now enjoy. Things didn't necessarily happen for a reason. It was like a half-finished book, film, or other work of art. This was something the gods wanted to remedy and rectify through the work of Docent Randii and Taneur and their moral cleansing of Goldilocks's Dilemma and Ancient Earth.

But Taneur was tasked with an even greater responsibility than being simply relegated as a shepherd of the humans and animals of the world. He was to also overlook the heavens, cosmos, and the very laws of nature. But with power comes great responsibility. And with the divine knowledge that was bestowed upon him by the Docent Randii, he could pass laws of nature, such as the law of gravity, much like a politician passing the laws of man. Taneur knew all about the nature of nature. He created Newton's Third Law of Motion as if he had just established a democratic system of checks and balances. He created the "Conservation of Energy" as if he were a policymaker for "Conservation and Resource Management." He was a lawmaker, to be sure, but instead of vetoes and franking privileges, he dealt with the stuff of worlds, planets, moons, suns, stars, and the very galaxies of the universe. It has been said that he could move galaxies around like stones in a rock garden.

For a full year, he did his very best to create scientific laws that were fair and just, or at least as fair as was scientifically possible. Divine knowledge may be divine, but that was still no guarantee that it was fair or ethical. The two are not necessarily the same. What is divinity, but an act from a god, be it malevolent or benevolent? Divinity, it could be said, is in the eye of the beholder.

Taneur also came to realize during his travels that "fairness" and "learning" were two different things. Fairness, he surmised, was when someone got what they deserved, be it pleasant or painful — something more akin to the abstract concept of "justice." Learning, on the other hand, was a different matter entirely. When you slip on the ice, usually there is some learning that occurs, so you'll take more care in the future. But did you deserve to slip and fall in the first place, in a strictly moral or ethical sense?

Either way, such a pain response could have an adaptive purpose for one's very survival. In such a case, this pain would ironically be most welcome, despite not feeling like it at the time.

Pain as such would be the "lesser of two evils," and ironically, perhaps even a pyrrhic reward, depending on one's perspective. Taneur came to understand that sometimes consequences are there for a reason, for learning purposes. As such, Taneur became very well-versed in the complexities of the "Carrot and Stick Principle," deterrence theory, behavior modification, and the tenets of operant and classical conditioning, going light-years beyond the scope and practice of mere human-folk, on a cosmic and galactic scale.

Since learning was not the main objective of karma, Taneur decided that consequences didn't necessarily need to be immediate (Celerity), consistent (certainty), or intense (seriousness) as per deterrence theory or behavior modification principles. In fact, Taneur wondered and pondered, spending hours upon hours in his study, if it might be better to keep the very idea of karma as a vague principle, something based more on faith than absolute truth. If existential rewards and punishments were doled out with certainty, celerity, or severity, surely people would catch on quickly, and without fail, their thoughts, behaviors, and emotions would be laced with hidden agendas, as they would come to expect rewards and punishments at each and every turn, in accordance to what humans would later call the "Hawthorne Effect." Taneur scoffed at the idea that the gods or watchers of men should rely on this phenomenon to coerce the love and respect of the populace. Most certainly, this would create throngs of "two-faced" people, or fifty-faced people, as patrons of karmatic law are managing their impressions between the "private" and the "public" selves—even the human "Johari window" would eventually acknowledge this.

As such, Taneur created a world where punishment or reward might not come to fruition until years later. For example, if a person cut in front of someone in line at a bazaar or marketplace, someone might cut him or her off in line twenty years later. Or, a totally different fate might befall our culprit, and he or she may experience a totally different repercussion completely unrelated to being cut off in line. He or she might simply trip and fall on a city street, and that would be their comeuppance for cutting in line years ago. As such, it could be almost impossible to trace or track how these behaviors are connected. Taneur decided that it would behoove the karma lords to remain as hidden, covert, and incognito as possible, to hide their very identities from the populace, and to govern from afar, a puppet master without puppets and likewise puppets without strings, as it were.

Taneur realized that in a fair world, the pain you receive should equal the pain you inflict on others. And likewise for pleasure. He tried his best to make sure that pain and pleasure would cancel each other out, like a (-) and (+) charge, of sorts. As one example of the sorts of changes he put in place, the hangover one feels following the overindulgence of alcohol could be said to "make up for" or "cancel out" the over-abundance of pleasure experienced the night before. Taneur also established a system where continued use of this overindulgence might wreak havoc on one's body over time, leading to various health issues, such as cirrhosis of the liver.

Similarly, Taneur created a paradigm where the foodstuffs that tasted more pleasing to the palette would similarly be less healthy in the grander scheme of things. He created hundreds of these tradeoffs, all in the hopes to create a fair world, where what you put in was essentially what you got out. No stone left unturned, no sin left unpunished, no good deed without reward. A well-oiled machine and a tight ship, as things should be. Efficient and logical.

One bottleneck in Taneur's mission, however, was the issue of impulse control. If a person can "hold out" and abstain from the temptation of various hedonistic pleasures of the flesh, would there be an additional reward for such vested patience? It would only seem legitimate. However, Taneur was careful here. He did not consider those with poor impulse control to be any more "selfish," per se, than those who could stave off immediate gratification. In fact, he considered them to be equally selfish, the difference being that the former simply valued immediate but modest gains, where the latter camp valued patience and larger returns on their various investments and laborings. Taneur came to believe that even many of those who proclaimed to be religious, pious, and righteous, and lived an otherwise spartan life, were, in the end, every bit as self-absorbed as the other lot, if not all the more so, as they were motivated by promises of a more auspicious return on their spiritual investments, a promise of salvation, brighter futures, and the opulence that awaits in the welcoming arms of the afterlife. As such, Taneur came to know that even religion wasn't immune from its own version of the "dog eat dog," "survival of the fittest," or "Carrot and Stick" principles of behavior modification. But the question remained. When does a punishment become draconian? When does a reward become superfluous?

Taneur decided that while punishments must befit the crime, the nature of the punishment could change forms as long as the consequence was equal (the concept of "different but equal.") And the same went for rewards. Like conservation of energy.

***

Hope paused and looked at Faith. She noticed Faith's eyes were closed, and there was a wetness about them as if she was just crying. Hope whispered. "Faith, are you asleep?"

Faith slowly opened her eyes. "No, I am not sleeping. I like to close my eyes when I listen to stories, as it allows me to soak in the nuance and detail of every word using all five senses. Please continue. This story is so much bigger-than-life that it makes me forget I am dying. Sometimes I cry a little, but these are happy tears, rest assured."

Hope patted Faith's shoulder and smiled. She continued.

***

A full year came and went, as it always does. Taneur went back to the very same location where he'd met the mystery man a year before. Standing in the middle of the arena, meeting the gaze of all twelve statesmen, was Docent Randii. It was exactly noon.

"Were you able to create a fair world?" stuttered the

Docent Randii with impatience.

"After a fashion," said Taneur. "I did my very best." Taneur handed Docent Randii the thirty karmatic principles he'd established. The docent studied them, looking at them from top to bottom, mumbling all the while. "Well?" asked Taneur, with eyes wide and hands clenched.

Docent Randii paused in thought. "I need some time to look this over and really consider what I am reading. Please meet me here on the morrow, same time, same place. And for God's sake, put some clothes on."

Taneur looked at himself from head to toe. "Clothes?"

The mighty docent raised his umbrella as if it were a king's scepter or wizard's staff. Almost in an instant, Taneur was wearing colonial garb, including a tricorne hat, breeches, and waistcoat.

"Garments to cover the body. They serve a dual purpose — to protect the wearer from the elements and to make impressions on others."

"I see," said Taneur, looking himself over and feeling the garments with his hands. He unclenched his hands, and his wide eyes lost circumference as he gazed at the marble floor with a crestfallen stare.

The docent's parasol made a loud clank as he held the tip with one hand and thumped the handle down onto the shiny marbled floor. "I will see you tomorrow!"

Taneur went to him. "Yes, but—"

And with that, the Docent Randii disappeared. Taneur looked around the arena and noticed something peculiar. All the preserved statesmen now had their eyes closed.

Must be Randii's magic, thought Taneur. *Impressive, if not rude.*

Taneur found a corner of the arena and sprawled himself down on the stone floor. He mused and thought about this, that, and the other thing. Despite the hardness of his bed, his thoughts turned more tranquil, and he eventually entered the surreal landscapes of sleep and dreams. He slept for over twenty hours as if making up for some of the sleep he had lost over the course of the last year, not unlike a bear in hibernation. When he awoke, there were only two hours to go before the docent would reappear. Taneur couldn't help but think about how the very act of sleeping feels like a time machine and can kill time faster than almost anything. He also thought about how humans spend the equivalent of a whole eight-hour workday in bed and wasted a whole third of their lives sleeping.

With a groan and grunt, Taneur rose to the fore and leaned against the wall of the great hall. He mused and daydreamed, this time in anticipation of the docent's grand return. And he wondered what the docent would think of his karmatic principles when given some proper time to go over them. Would he approve? What would happen to him if he didn't? He ruminated for the rest of the time until at noon. on the dot, when the Docent Randii reappeared in a puff of white fog

Taneur stood tall and straight in the Docent's presence.

Randii bowed. "After pouring over the fruits of your academic prowess, I must say I like what you have done. A mighty fine 'well done' is indeed in order."

Taneur glared at Randii. "But I hear a 'but' coming...."

"Hold on, hold on," said Randii, pointing his closed umbrella at Taneur. "You shouldn't be quite so cynical and cavalier about such things, at least not yet." He shook the umbrella at Taneur as if he were chiding a child.

"Apologies for my impertinence," returned Taneur, as he knelt down in front of the docent. "It's just that I was hoping you would be all the more impressed. And I'm afraid I am a rather insecure sort, looking for your full endorsement to justify and uphold my identity as a competent karma lord."

The Docent Randii prodded him with the parasol until Taneur stood back up again. "That display is hardly necessary. Your perseverance of industry has paid off. And in spades, I might add."

Taneur stood up cautiously. "May I ask what the problem is then, my dear Randii?"

"It's not what you wrote so much as what you didn't write," said Randii.

Taneur sighed. "But even I know that acts of omission can be equally egregious."

Randii reassured him. "Do not be taken aback. The laws of nature are now much like clockwork, thanks to your skilled hands. There is much balance in the universe. But even the laws of nature alone cannot guarantee fairness, at least not entirely. Conservation of energy and Newton's 3rd Law of motion are brilliant ideas, to be sure. And it won't take long for humans to take credit for their discovery as if simply locating them were equable to inventing them. But they would be wrong. To their chagrin, that credit belongs to you. And while it may appear to the naked eye that these laws are the stuff of physics, they are equally applicable to the purview of psychology and human behavior more generally."

Taneur nodded. "Physics and psychology are not so different. And just as with physics, in real life, one cannot assume no friction. And this also applies to psychology."

Randii also nodded. "Friction is practically the very definition of what it means to be human."

"Fairness is not an easy science," returned Taneur. "But it is a science, make no mistake."

The docent straightened his imperial crown. "But these are not the only issues here to be cognizant of, Taneur. Even with the myriad ways pain and pleasure can be experienced in this world, there remain lingering threats to our anonymity. It is indeed possible that humans would notice that there is a 'different but equal' measure of stamina in our mysterious human condition."

"What you are saying is that it wouldn't take long for people to figure out that the laws of nature represent the very rubric of fairness or even some sort of divine providence?"

"Indeed," said Docent Randii. "You learn fast, Lord of Nature. But don't let it get to your head."

Taneur paced back and forth in front of the regal docent. He snapped his fingers and looked at Randii.

"What do you propose?"

Taneur faced him. "What we need is a way to create fairness without it appearing fair. But I don't think I can do it alone."

"Meet your cabinet," said Docent Randii, as he stepped to the side like a carnival barker and motioned his arm in a large sweeping motion.

A large hole appeared in the center of the arena, as if by magic. Billowing smoke emanated from the hole, so thick one couldn't even see the raging fire underneath. But Taneur knew it was there, as he could feel the heat on his skin. Soon an entourage of four naked angels appeared, two male and two female. One male and female had a solitary left-wing, and the other male and female had a right-wing. They walked towards Taneur with a slow but deliberate gait, in human form like Taneur, but their skin appeared hard, cracked, and porous like the bark of an oak. They did not appear godlike per se, but like humans with an eagle's wing.

When they got near, Taneur bowed with respect. Taneur didn't say a word as the four figures stood in front of him in a half-circle, with solemn eyes and apathetic blank frowns. The smoke cleared, and the hole they came from had all but disappeared without a trace.

Randii smiled for the first time. "They will be an asset to you and your work. They have varying political philosophies. Let them serve as checks and balances to your own biases. But don't fret. You will always have the final say." Randii's smile dissipated.

Taneur folded his hands as if in prayer. "But I sense there is still a problem?"

"An astute observation," said the docent, his eyes visibly red and saggy from studying karma all night. "Have I become that transparent? The truth is, we need an additional karma lord," said Docent Randii. "This realization is in no way related to any deficiency or incompetence on your part. Some matters are bigger than us."

"You mean more personages than these other four?"

Randii wiped the tired from his eyes. "Let me be more clear, we need a different kind of karma lord. All five of you represent the purview of Tier 1, Nature."

"And where can I find this high-ranking authority? It's not as if I can just get one bestowed from the corner marketplace or have one conjured from the local blacksmith."

"Patience, my dear boy," said Randii. "Patience!"

And with that, the mysterious docent turned around and snapped his finger with the same decibel level as the crack of a bullwhip. Suddenly a ray of light shot from all twelve statesmen and centered on what appeared to be another naked angel hovering about a foot from the floor, this time glowing, but she had no wings at all. When the light beams ceased, she slowly descended and walked toward the group of six twenty yards in the distance with a confident gait. By the time she reached the group, her glow had disappeared, and she looked like a human. She faced Taneur.

"Let me introduce An Incinerator," said Randii. She took a bow and remained silent. "You can call her Incinerator for short."

Taneur wondered as to the meaning of her rather odd epithet, particularly the longer version.

"Let's walk," said Randii, without bothering to see if Taneur was amenable to the request. Incinerator went right along with him to his left in perfect unison. Taneur stood for a moment, trying to make sense of everything that had just transpired. Taneur could hear mumblings of small talk and pleasantries but could not make anything out until he made a mad dash to catch up with him, walking on the docent's right.

The docent led the way, and they walked the perimeter of the arena in a counterclockwise fashion, going from statue to statue. Taneur and Incinerator followed the docent and matched his velocity. The cabinet of four stayed behind and sat on the floor, talking among themselves.

Randii talked without stopping. "There are cases, to be sure, where matters of fairness cannot be achieved through the laws of nature alone and the thirty laws you proposed, as finely crafted as they might be and indeed are."

"Do you always talk in circles?" asked Taneur, as the three of them kept making their circular jaunt.

Randii stopped at the first statue, a Palatio Azwald, and turned to face Taneur. "Don't take this the wrong way, but life as we know it does not have the resources to ensure absolute fairness, no matter how well the laws of nature may hold or are crafted, or how much disruption and intervention we employ. There are moments where fairness can only be settled by giving someone another chance at life—a redo if you will."

"I see," repeated Taneur, although, in actuality, he felt rather confused. "And I suppose if I felt inadequate by this, you would say I am being self-absorbed, for I should not blame myself for being remiss in something I have naught control over."

Randii continued walking, the two following him. "On the mark, precise and/or accurate," said Randii, continuing his walk, as Incinerator's expression remained as fixed, stoic, and steadfast as the bark of a tree. "You can see this with the primitive systems of human law that have come and gone or have yet to come. A person commits a crime, and they receive 847 years in prison. Even a great many people know how asinine this sounds."

"And a person who kills fifty people can only die once," said Taneur. "But of course."

"Precisely," continued Randii. "We need a Tier 2 to create another layer of fairness. Only through reincarnation can a person be reborn and live a worse or better life, depending on their actions from their former life. When matters cannot be resolved in Tier 1, it goes to Tier 2."

Randii led the way past the cadaver of Merryella Quantz, gazing at her quickly without stopping as he continued walking the perimeter.

"Makes some sense, I suppose," said Taneur, as he stole a glance at the female cadaver.

Randii reached the third cadaver, Saint Bertzuffe, and turned around once again to face Incinerator and Taneur. "Karma lords are often an opinionated and idealistic sort, but we are also by the book, unlike Mr. Bertzuffe here. I understand you have your pride, but do we have your blessing to anoint and appoint An Incinerator into our regal hegemony?"

Taneur bent his knee in front of the docent, and An Incinerator couldn't help but track her gaze down to him. "Notwithstanding my initial scholarly reservations, rest assured, you and Incinerator have my blessing. I welcome Tier 2 into our Code of Karmatic Jurisprudence, to accommodate the laws of reincarnation and rebirth."

An Incinerator likewise bent her knee to the Docent Randii, establishing her fealty.

The Docent Randii removed his garish imperial crown like a magician's top hat, and swarms of white doves and bats bellowed forth, intermingling like snow and black smoke. They flew into the heavens, out of sight. The docent reached into the hat and pulled forth a large smoking urn containing steaming water. He stood in front of An Incinerator. "I hereby appoint and anoint you on this day. Your mission, to be completed in one year's time, is to come up with ten additional Laws of Karma, as they apply to the province of reincarnation. And then, and only then, will we have our fair world."

An Incinerator looked up and faced the steaming and boiling water. She did not even close her eyes. She withstood the boiling water without an indication of pain. Taneur winced as he watched, as Incinerator's skin became red and blistered.

After every last drop of boiling water had poured into An Incinerator's eyes, she stood up, bowed, and started walking away, without nary an indication of pain or even where she was going.

Taneur and Randii locked eyes. "Where are you going?" asked Taneur, stepping after her at a jaunt between a walk and a run.

Randii walked to Taneur with a leisurely gait as if not concerned about An Incinerator's leave of absence. He stopped Taneur by placing his hand gently on his shoulder.

Taneur pointed at the woman. "You are just gonna let her leave like that? She's quitting on us?"

"She is not quitting," said Randii. "In fact, she is getting a head start. There is no time to waste. She is starting right here and right now."

And so it was, the mysterious docent appointed and anointed our new emissary of the karma lord as "An Incinerator," blessed her with the divine knowledge about all manner of rebirth, and tasked her with creating the Laws of Reincarnation for this new world. The Docent Randii gave her exactly one year to complete this grand task, just as he had done for Taneur. And in one year's time, the two of them, along with Taneur, were to meet again, in this very location, at 12:00 p.m., to complete Tier 2 of the "Code of Karmatic Jurisprudence."

***

And with that, Hope closed the book.

Faith opened her eyes. "What's our secret password going to be?"

"Last time it was Taneur, so how about we use 'Incinerator,' to represent the karma police of rebirth?"

"Incinerator it is," said Faith with a hard nod. Hope stood up, put the chair back in front of the desk, and slowly left the room. She gave Faith one last look, smiled, and closed the creaky door with a gentle click behind her.

· —

CHAPTER 13
AFTERMATHEMATICS

Date: July 6, 2019, Saturday, 7:15 p.m.
Setting: The apartment of Mark, Gavin, and Sandy
Main characters: Mark Anderson

The bathroom was quiet, save for the hum of the dehumidifier and the "swooshing" of the curtains flapping from the wind coming through the window. Mark was in the bathtub, motionless, his head still against the pillow. *Is this the afterlife?* he thought to himself as his surroundings coalesced into focus. He felt his head, and his hand became wet. "Fuck, is this blood?" He crept his hand back down, and he let out a sigh of relief when he noticed it was just sweat. He next looked at his naked body, wondering if he would see swaths of blood. He was surprised a second time when he saw nothing of the sort. And there was not a drop of blood on the tub or walls either, except for the dry drop of blood still on his arm from when he cut himself shaving.

"Wow," he mumbled to himself, out of surprise. "Wow!" he shouted again, from sheer excitement.

Stepping out of the tub, he hobbled to his bedroom, fighting the very beginnings of a charley horse forming. It was just past seven in the evening, and he figured he must have passed out for several hours from the sheer fear and gravity of the situation. After all, it's not every day you dance with a 5/6 chance of death. He picked up the gun and popped open the chamber. It still had the five bullets from before. *Wow, talk about a near-death experience!* he thought. The lava lamp caught his eye, as it was well-past its warming up period, with globules ebbing and flowing, as if vying for dominance. He checked the pain measurements on his Project

Madcap around the time he pulled the trigger. Lo and behold, the fear measurements were off the charts, further solidifying his faith in his invention. Project Madcap was indeed a resounding success.

Mark flopped onto his bed and stared at the ceiling, with his hands behind his head, taking deep breaths and deep in thought. There was a wide smile across his face. It was strange to think about how events could have been much different with just the slightest twitch of his fingers when he spun the chamber. A fraction of a calorie worth of energy could have spelled the difference between life and death. After all, there was a bullet on each side of the vacant slot in the chamber. In a very general sense, he had survived with only a 1/6 chance of survival. He also acknowledged that it wasn't just about probability. It was also about where the chamber would settle, intensity of the hand motion, velocity of the spin, and friction of the chamber. He entertained the notion that perhaps some of the bullets had a more or less than a 1/6 chance of settling, depending on factors such as these. But even still, without such knowledge, you might as well just chalk it up to simple probability and call it a day. But the question remained. Was it dumb luck that had given him back his life? Or was someone, or something, looking out for him from afar, sparing his life?

After staring at the ceiling in disbelief for a good hour, he rubbed his eyes and stood to his feet. Slipping on the same outfit that was strewn on the floor, a thought raced through his head. *Sorry, Gavin, you're not gonna score my Akira shirt that easily.* After throwing on his black canvas Converse low-tops, he decided to take a leisurely jaunt to the local Shell gas station, a good twenty minute walk. There were a group of gray clouds assembling overhead, which Mark scarcely even noticed. With about a mile of strip malls between him and his destination, it was hardly the scenic route. But with all that had transpired, he was hardly in the mood for any manner of sightseeing, other than his daydreams and psychological landscapes.

About halfway there, near the Carribou Coffee, he was

met with a deluge of rain, the cold variety with thick and heavy drops. And despite being soaked from head to toe, he maintained his leisurely gait with both hands in his pockets and his head down. There were pedestrians around him running for the hills as if being accosted by a rabble of ogres. He couldn't help but smile as he thought about how a week ago, he probably would have been running with them. *But why*? he thought. *Surely a little rain was hardly the stuff of plagues, famines, and locusts unless you happen to be a mogwai.*

But instead of just focusing on almost dying, he instead focused his attentions more on fond evocations, such as playing Dungeons and Dragons, End of the World, or Pathfinder with Sandy and Gavin. And speaking of Sandy, how would she have taken it if she'd found out about this the hard way and saw his lifeless body sprawled out in the tub in a pool of blood, like a chicken thawing out in the kitchen sink?

"Would she be happy I am alive?" he mused. "Or would she be livid that I attempted suicide in the first place? Knowing her, she would beat me up for a few minutes and then hug me so tight I would struggle to breathe!"

The gas station was now packed with people evading the downpour outside. This particular Shell station had about as much floor space as your average Starbucks. It was, more or less, a typical gas station, containing the various odds, ends, magazines, foodstuffs, and other such sundries germane to convenience stores of the Western hemisphere. Junk food, fried food, coffee beverages, and bottles of soda pop adorned the walls like ornaments, beckoning you with their twisted and ragged fingers. Despite the name of a "convenience" store, Mark's day was anything but convenient. But it was, as they say, "the first day of the rest of his life."

The first thing Mark did upon entering the establishment was enter the bathroom, not to use, but to splash some water onto his face. He thought such sensory stimulation might deter his intrusive thoughts regarding Russian Roulette. There were a pair of tall and burly truckers, one on each side of him manning their sinks, and he decided to forego the water idea. When Mark was finished washing his hands, he spotted the filthy hand towel housed in the plastic enclosure. Foregoing plan A, he tried plan B, wiping his hands on his already-soaked jeans. His wet T-shirt didn't offer much better. Using the "Toepener" with his foot, he walked out of the bathroom with wet hands.

Mark spent an inordinate amount of time at the place, meandering around the same areas, looking at the wide selection of snacks with an even more discerning eye than usual. It didn't matter to him that the clerks seemed to be keeping a careful watch over him. All five of his senses seemed to have come alive. Everything on the shelf looked more colorful. The wrappers sounded more distinct. And for the first time in a year or more, he noticed the wonderful smells of machine coffee intermingled with bratwursts turning on their rollers. He found it interesting how the additional markup on items was justified as you were supposedly paying a sort of "convenience fee." But was it really that much more convenient than walking into a proper grocery store and purchasing items there?

Mark settled on a Whatchamacallit and a Mello Yellow, two of his favorite comfort foods since childhood. He walked towards the counter and paid for them with his bank card. With his bag of necessities in tow, he left the building with an upright posture. There was a fresh aroma of rain intermingled with a gentle breeze and a soft bed of fog.

Just as he began walking past the gas pumps, something caught his eye. There was an American two-dollar bill stuck partway into a fresh puddle near pump number four. Though not exactly legal tender in Canada, Mark picked it up anyway, as he knew how rare this type of currency was, thanks largely to his deep-seated knowledge of American television and the handful of trips to see his politically reactionary American uncle Scott Peterson in Wisconsin. Considering that his uncle would be intrigued to see it, he decided to snap a picture of it with his smartphone, knowing full well that this was the kind of clap-trap thing his uncle would most certainly get a kick out of.

Mark picked up the bill with his left hand and spotted the QR code on it. With his right hand, he aimed his smartphone at the bill and clicked the button. It didn't take long before a message popped up on the screen. Mark began reading (and mumbling) it to himself, so lost in thought he forgot about his uncle altogether. He paid no mind to the lingering smell of gas fumes.

As he read, he mumbled all the while, savoring each word as if finding a time capsule or lost treasure. When he finished, he wrapped the two-dollar bill around his phone and placed them both in his pocket.

Mark mused about his dance with both Lady Luck and Lady Death and was beside himself, sleuthing out the wherefore and why of the secret embedded message. Just as with the failed suicide attempt, was this the work of something bigger than himself, or just a flash of whimsy courtesy of his superstitious disposition? Either way, it was an existential experience, to be sure, and his thoughts went to spiritual realms and in lofty proportions. With a newfound pep in his step, he began his journey home. And all the while, he let his imagination run wild, like a child conjuring up visions of adventure, completely giving way to the fantasies endemic to the stuff of wishes, hopes, and forgotten dreams.

"Was this message meant for me?" he entertained. He smiled at the reference to the "pleasure principle" and other esoteric jargon in relation to his own fascination with the behavioral sciences. And while the missive did not use the actual phrase "terror management theory," the fact that it even alluded to it by the mention of Mimento Mori felt almost too close for comfort.

Mark introspected. *Did karma have anything to do with today's events? Was this more than coincidence? Is my invention 'Project Madcap' more than just a pain and pleasure reader? Is karma taking notice of any of my experiments or events delineated in his journal?* He further thought about how things like ESP or license plate synchronicity played into karma. Or how heightened states of emotion played into it all. But even he realized he was getting ahead of himself. Even still, he felt his heart skip a beat when he entertained the fanciful notion that Project Madcap might have more potential than the mere study of pain and pleasure. Could it actually have the potential to measure the very ebb and flow of karma itself? Mark grinned from ear to ear at the very thought.

"Should I risk seeking out the writer of this letter?" Mark wondered. After all, the meeting date was only about two months away. But at the same time, the original letter was penned over two years ago. By any stretch, he figured he had ample time to prepare, at least if Sandy or Gavin didn't commit him to the mental asylum first.

As Mark continued his jaunt by the strip malls and corporate shops, he opened his pop and took a drink, followed by an "ahhhh!" He thought about his newfound sense of purpose, a feeling he had not really felt since his university days. There was also a realization that this was not the typical "sense of purpose" associated with following a tedious routine, going to work, eating, and going to sleep, only to rinse and repeat. This was the other sense of purpose, the kind that makes your heart sing and heels click together as you, sometimes quite literally, jump for joy. With a zest, zeal, and swagger, he made his brisk pace the long way through the very same park where the young woman had chatted with him near the fire hydrant about a month prior. "It's a great day to be bat-shit crazy!" he shouted, followed by his best diabolical laugh. He was in ear-shot of three birdwatchers with binoculars near the swings, and they turned around and stared at him with slack-jawed expressions.

Out of nowhere, his adrenaline was pumping once again, but not in a good way. "What about Sandy? Will she find my suicide note? I never bothered to throw it away! She's gonna kill me! Or worse!"

Mark put the cap on his pop and ran full tilt towards Veranda Flats. Sure enough, he spotted Gavin's maroon Malibu in the parking lot as he approached from several blocks away. *Don't panic*, he thought to himself. *There is still time, at least if I can get upstairs first! Karma has been good to me so far — surely everything will turn out.*

Mark got to the main heavy security door of the lobby and fumbled with the keys as if being assailed by a rabid dog. But it actually took longer than usual, if anything, before he nudged the heavy door open. When he settled into the main hallway, he was out of breath and was coughing and breathing while staring at the dirty floor. Just as he readied himself to make his mad dash up the steps to room 248, he came face to face with the cutting gaze of Sandy Larson herself, standing not ten feet in front of him. She was holding the suicide note in her hands, like a concerned but angry mother wielding a report card with a giant red F on it or a lawyer brandishing an "Exhibit A" piece of evidence in a courtroom.

"Want to explain this shit?" Sandy shouted, disregarding the couple standing some twenty feet down the hall. "Do you know how close I was to calling non-emergency police to do a welfare check on your sorry ass?"

"Looks like some unfinished origami," said Mark, pushing by her. "I would be pissed too."

"Cut the crap, Mark," she said, in fast pursuit. "I said I was gonna call non-emergency police."

"Then why didn't you?" Mark asked at the foot of the steps.

"Why didn't I call? Because Gavin has my phone, you idiot!"

"Fine, whatever," said Mark as he went to their apartment, opened the door, and entered.

She followed closely behind. Just as she entered and closed the door, she thrust the paper in Mark's face. "So, can you explain this?"

"Damn, you almost gave me a paper cut," said Mark, unplugging his lava lamp and next feeding his Siamese fighting fish Fermi in the bowl atop his dresser.

Sandy dropped the note to the floor. "You almost spilled your brains out, and now you are worried about a paper cut? Cut the crap, Mark. And you are into parkour and stunts now?

What's wrong with you? You take better care of that damn fish than you take care of yourself."

Mark pointed at his chest. "I can explain. I can explain everything. It's all good."

"Oh no, you don't," said Sandy, coming in and sitting on the chair in front of Mark's computer, settling in and folding her legs. She glared at him. "It's all good? What the hell is that supposed to mean? A man survives Russian Roulette with five bullets, and 'It's all good' is all you can say? How can any of this be good?"

Mark set down his junk food on the dresser and flopped onto his bed. "I'm alive, aren't I? You should be happy. Sorry I never told you I was a traceur."

"Traceur? What the hell is that?"

Mark sighed and rolled his eyes. "Someone who is into the sport known as parkour."

"Parkour? What the hell is that?" asked Sandy, with the same exact tone and enunciation as her question just before.

"Parkour is a sport, and it's just about getting from point A to point B in the most efficient means possible." He next grabbed an anime magazine from the floor as if this was just another regular day. He flipped it open and began reading as if she wasn't even in the room. "But I am just an amateur and not as young and spry as I used to be. But rest assured, I am quite aware of my abilities and limitations."

Sandy leaned over and ripped the magazine out of his hands. "You better be. You don't always get a second chance. Make no mistake, you are going to get checked into the hospital immediately, and I am taking you there myself to make sure you don't escape! You people have a death wish."

Mark sat up on the bed. "Okay, Sandy, I can tell all this must seem very strange, crazy even, but you gotta listen to me and hear me out."

"That's what they all say," Sandy retorted.

"Who's 'they'?" asked Mark, turning his gaze towards her.

"You know, 'they.' People who get caught or busted. Or

mentally ill people who try to avoid hospitalization. Or people like you!"

"This is way different," Mark said.

"Sure it is," returned Sandy.

Knowing reading his magazine was out of the question, Mark sprang to his feet and paced around the bedroom, not unlike a caged animal, trying desperately to think of something clever enough to say that would placate and appease Sandy's rigid and fixed disposition. After a moment, he thought, *It's now or never. I might as well try the truth.* He pulled out the two-dollar bill from his pocket and handed it to Sandy.

Sandy snatched it. "Okay, a two-dollar bill? These are kind of rare, even in the States, but what's the significance? Are you just trying to distract me or change the subject? I know a red herring or a non-sequitur when I see one. I used to be on a debate team. I would rather talk about this suicide note if you please."

"Take a picture of the money," said Mark, walking towards her.

Sandy's face shriveled up into a look of bewilderment. "What?"

"Take a picture of it," Mark repeated, tapping the bill. "There's a QR code on it."

"I can't. Gavin has my phone, remember?"

"Okay, whatever," said Mark as he handed her his phone. "Go ahead, take a picture. No more excuses."

"Okay, okay," she said, slowly taking his phone as she looked at him with a distrustful glare. "But I smell another red herring."

Sandy set the phone down on the computer desk, straightened out the bill, and laid it down on top of the computer keyboard. She took the phone and aimed it at the QR code. The secret message popped up with little delay.

"Whoa, what is this?" Sandy said, her focus transfixed to this new line of conversation. Her curiosity seemed to replace some of her umbrage.

"There is a hidden smart-label embedded in the bill," said

Mark. He stood next to her and looked at the screen with her.

"So there is," said Sandy as she put the phone down near the computer. She rubbed her eyes and composed herself.

Mark's face drooped. "You are not going to read it?"

Sandy paused, tapping her finger on her lips. "I have a condition. I will read your secret message only if we chat about your suicide note first."

Sandy put the phone down, walked towards him, looked him in the eye, and raised her hand as if to slap him. She held her hand motionless and steadfast above his left cheek. Mark squinted his eyes, waiting to take his medicine. But instead of feeling a forceful slap across the face, he felt himself in a very tight embrace as Sandy sat next to him. Sandy had both arms around him, fingers interlaced across his back. Tears were streaming down her face. Mark wondered if it was the tightest hug he had ever received.

Mark patted her back in a slow and rhythmic fashion, about one pat per second. Sandy relinquished her grasp.

"I must admit," said Mark, "I am not sure if my Project Madcap would record such a tight hug as pleasure or pain!"

"You just make me so mad sometimes," returned Sandy. "But like a weird good kind of mad. Is there such a thing?"

"Why not?" asked Mark with a bit more zest and zeal in his voice. "They say there is a good and bad cry. I don't see why anger can't work the same way. Either way, pain has never felt better."

Mark got up and retrieved the suicide note that had fallen to the floor earlier. He tore it up and let the pieces fall into the garbage can like bits of fish food. He climbed into bed and pulled his blue comfort up to his chin. Sandy climbed into the bed with him, and they were both staring at the ceiling.

"Underneath my front of hatred, finding that note gave me quite the scare," said Sandy. "I mean, I didn't see you or the gun around in your room, and I wondered if you left with the gun to kill yourself somewhere else. I was so scared! You have no idea. Your being a death hag should have been my first red flag.

And I had no idea you were into that dangerous parkour stuff."

"Being fascinated with death is one thing," said Mark. "Being fascinated with dying is quite another. I just took it two steps farther and two steps too far."

Sandy recollected the items from the note. "Two of the bullet points, love and work, were about some form of loss. So while you handled those losses carelessly, I can at least understand your sense of loss there. But the other two were about morbid curiosity of death and doing a reckless experiment with your Project Madcap."

Mark turned to face her. "My first two were also a reference to Sigmund Freud, as he was said to have emphasized these two aspects of human existence as being very important. Still, and as depressing as those losses may have been, it was the other two that pushed me over the edge. I had my Project Madcap helmet on during the incident, and I got the results I was hoping to get. In fact, the only reason I am into parkour is because I test my fear responses during the stunts."

"And yet, if you would have gotten yourself killed, you wouldn't have been alive to know if your invention worked or not. Don't you see the contradiction?"

"Yes, Sandy, I suppose I do, but at the time, it just felt like I was donating my body to science, perhaps a little sooner than expected."

Sandy's voice took on an authoritative resolve. "Okay, no more stunts and no more parkour." She made "no" motions with her arms. "However, I will allow your silly little randomness experiments. The worst that can happen there is you will just look dumb in front of onlookers. What can I say? I am used to it by now."

"Agreed," said Mark with a smile. "Let's just say that I have found my purpose." He pointed at the two-dollar bill sitting on the keyboard. "I am thinking about finding the person that wrote that secret note."

Sandy slugged Mark in the arm.

"Ow!" shouted Mark.

Sandy's voice raised. "Are you crazy? Right when I thought you were starting to make sense. How can we trust this person?"

"You didn't even read it yet," said Mark, rubbing his arm. "Besides, you are talking to the person who just played Russian Roulette with five bullets. Whatever it is, I think I can handle it."

Sandy nodded her head. "I am starting to think that every time you say 'don't worry,' it's my cue to start getting really worried."

Sandy remained silent, staring at the ceiling.

Mark took an audible breath. "Well, regardless of how trustworthy this person is, the way I see it, I shouldn't even be alive right now. As such, I'm not even afraid of this person. Every day is a bonus. I don't expect you to believe this, but I feel as if this person was speaking to me in that memorandum, almost as if he knows me without ever meeting me."

"Perhaps, but aren't you reading a bit too much into this, like you always do? Maybe some wishful thinking on your part?"

"I still think it's an aha moment," said Mark.

"Yeah, aha, as in a crook being caught with his hand in the cookie jar kind of moment."

"Funny girl," said Mark. "There, we talked about my note. Now I want you to read the two-dollar message."

Sandy grumbled a bit and tossed the covers with enough force that they covered Mark's face. She fetched Mark's phone and sat on the edge of the bed. Mark took the covers off of his face, revealing his smile. She read it to the end and got to the last paragraph.

If you can empathize with any of the contents of this rather discursive letter, come join me on the precipice at midnight sharp. Can you stomach the FairGrounds? If so, please consider this humble requisition, and do not be 'dismissive of this missive.'
Sincerely,
XX
March 14, 2017

P.S. I also have a tiny little favor to ask of you. But due to its sensitive nature, I cannot talk about it now. But we will have ample time, should you arrive.

"Wow, that is quite the message," said Sandy, sitting on the edge of the bed in a way she could still face him. "A bona fide Hardy Boys or Nancy Drew mystery. A treasure map and easter egg hunt."

"Isn't it, though?" said Mark with an excited grin.

"Still, I can't help but wonder if you are reading too much into it. It's just that we have had this very same conversation so many times now. I mean, as much knowledge as you have concerning all the various cognitive biases and thinking errors, you yourself sometimes are the first to fall prey to them."

"Wishful thinking? I should say not," said Mark, snatching the phone from her. "Damn your dubious nature. I am just being open minded like all scientists should be. Maybe they are the ones that are biased too far in the other direction. As for me, I try to be objective without losing my sense of wonder."

Sandy spotted the excitement on Mark's face as he perused through the message again. "I know this means a lot to you, though, so I want to help you any way I can. But you gotta do your part. No more parkour. No more stunts. Hell, I don't even care about the death hag pictures so much anymore. That's small potatoes next to the other crap you have been doing."

"Fair enough," returned Mark. "At the end of the memo, he mentioned 'bring your scientific talents.' And that is when it really hit me. What really strikes me is how I have been thinking about Project Madcap all wrong. I mean, it can be so much more than a mere pleasure and pain reader. If that note taught me anything, it's how my invention could also dovetail as a karma reader. All this time, I never even considered how recording pain and pleasure ratings could be used to test karma. I never used to even consider karma all that much until I read about it in that memo."

"Well, karma's a bitch. My friend Erica stood me up for a coffee date once, and she broke her foot that very same day."

"You almost sound happy," said Mark with a wide-eyed grin. "You sure karma's a bitch?"

"Well, for her, it was! I guess it depends on what side you are on. Besides, who am I to judge the sacred decisions of almighty karma?"

Mark laughed. "Teaches me to never cross your path again. Want to know the strangest bit?"

Sandy's eyes widened. "Why not? Could things possibly get any stranger?"

"The whole time I was running home, the word 'karma' was floating around in my head. And then, just as I got close to home, I realized something. My name, Mark A, is an anagram of karma. Now that can't simply be the stuff of coincidence or kismet, can it?"

"Wow, you don't say," said Sandy, considering him. "But still, Mark Anderson is also a fairly common name. "

Mark sighed. "Wow, there is not an open minded bone in your body, is there? You have an answer for everything. When do we stop believing in miracles and birthday wishes?"

"When we realize we don't live forever," said Sandy. "Even still, who am I to stand in your way. What can I say? I admire your newfound passion. It sure beats you trying to kill yourself. I will endorse your little excursion, but only if I come with you."

Mark sighed. "Aren't you blowing this out of proportion?"

Sandy shook her head from side to side. "Nopes. Blowing your head off is blowing it out of proportion. Either you take my offer, or I will offer you a civil commitment to the nearest mental hospital."

Mark ceased his complaining. "Nuff said, fair enough. But isn't it going to get a bit boring and expensive sitting in a dingy hotel for forty days and forty nights?"

"You make this excursion sound like it's of biblical proportions," said Sandy. "And you say I am dramatic. The truth is, I could sit there and watch paint dry if it meant knowing you were safe."

Mark smiled. "Either that or you enjoy all the paint fumes."

"Come now, I am being serious," said Sandy. "But we don't even know who this is. Or where this is. It could be in Japan for all we know."

With the clues in the note coupled with Sandy's searches on the Internet and Mark's searches on his phone, it did not take them long to figure out that the destination was Split Rock Lighthouse. They both stood in front of the fishbowl and watched Fermi.

"And to think, it's only about a nine hour drive from here," said Mark. "How is that not kismet or fate?"

"Well, for one, think about it. The two-dollar bill probably didn't travel very far. It only makes sense that the travel destination wouldn't be all that far from here. I mean, how far can a two-dollar bill possibly travel?"

"And there's that ironclad doubt again, poised and ever-ready to rain on my parade."

Sandy put a few more flakes of fish food into the beta's bowl. "Just don't want to see you get hurt. Chalk it up to tough love if you wish. Even still, I am supporting your little jaunt, so you better take what you can get."

And all the while they had their heartfelt conversation, there was a little replica of sunken treasure at the bottom of the fishbowl. Although it was quite small, the bowl and water acted like a magnifying glass and made it appear magnificent, effulgent, and larger than life, as if the fishbowl itself were some sort of storyteller, poised and ready to spin yarns of adventure through the looking glass of hyperbole and optical illusion. Or, perhaps it was proffering the delusion that real life were more interesting than it really was.

. .

CHAPTER 14
A CRAY-CRAY VAY-CAY

July 10, Wednesday, 2019, around 8:15 p.m.
Setting: Mark, Gavin, and Sandy's apartment

Mark, Sandy, and Gavin were all sitting in the kitchen/ dining area eating margarita pizza and drinking Angry Orchard and "The Culprit" wine out of coffee mugs. Mark and Sandy were nursing their second glasses of wine, and Gavin his fourth bottle of Angry Orchard. The rather loud air conditioner was blazing away, just keeping up with the ferocious hot and humid weather.

By now, Sandy had already filled Gavin in on everything that transpired the day prior, and Gavin decided to trust Sandy's change of heart and humor Mark's wishes, at least for the interim. At first, Gavin wanted to join them on their top-secret James Bond style vacation, but even he understood how prudent it was to stay home and watch over the place. And that's not to mention his mounting debts the way it was and how he couldn't afford a ten-day hotel stay, let alone over thirty. Even still, he always enjoyed a solitary sojourn to play his games without the distraction of quarrels and other such chaotic happenings in the background of life's tumultuous tapestry.

Suddenly Gavin staggered to a standing position, knocking his chair back. "I want to make a toast!"

"A toast with Mike's Lemonade?" said Mark. "Is that a trailer park thing?"

"Just raise your glass!" said Sandy, nudging Mark in the side.

Mark did as he was told, and some sloshed out his mug.

"I want to say how proud I am of my brother," said Gavin

with a slight slur. "For too long have I given him grief about his tinkering around wasting time. Laying around here like a drain on society. A veritable waste of humanity. A junkyard dog—"

"Hey now!" said Mark. "This is supposed to be uplifting!"

"But alas, the joke is on me," continued Gavin. He pointed his bottle towards Mark. "He, my very own flesh and blood older brother, has finished his project. And I will support him right up until he walks up to that stage to accept his Pulitzer!"

"Scientists generally don't get Pulitzers," said Sandy. "I think you mean something else."

"Well, whatever it is that scientists get!" shouted Gavin. "That's the one!"

Sandy stood up and raised her mug. She motioned for Mark to do the same. Mark followed suit. They all clinked their drinking receptacles together.

"Thanks, Gavin," said Mark with a smile. "I really appreciate the sentiment, at least most of it."

Sandy held up her Caribou Coffee mug. "I certainly don't want to inundate our little party with any more toasts, but I want to extend Gavin's warm invitation one step further." She looked directly at Mark's eyes until he looked down again, appearing to be blushing. "You have done amazing work, Mark. I salute you." She made a mock salute gesture with her mug.

Mark shot cursory glances at each of them. "I must say I appreciate this encomium, I really do, even if you are both pouring it on rather thick." He couldn't help but wonder if they were being extra sympathetic on account of his recent suicide attempt.

Sandy finished her wine in several large gulps and slammed the mug down on the table. "Mark, I know we haven't been all that supportive of your industrious endeavors, sometimes even treating you like a fool. The truth is, Gavin and I are the fools."

"Hey!" said Gavin. "Speak for yourself!"

"But we intend to change all that, starting now," continued Sandy. "We would be truly honored if you could extend the courtesy of telling us how Project Madcap works."

"I second that motion," Gavin said, peeling the label off his hard lemonade bottle. "If we could find a way to stick it to the fridge with a magnet, we truly would."

"I must say I admire your change of heart," said Mark, looking at each of them. "But don't be too hard on yourselves. You may have been a bit harsh-harsh, but I have been rather hush-hush. And my own paranoia didn't help matters much. There were times when it was hard to keep mum. But your general lack of interest made it easier for me to keep my secrets to myself. Still, I am flattered you are taking an interest now. Better late than never!"

Gavin and Sandy smiled at each other, appreciating the kind words.

Suddenly Mark dashed out of the room. "Hold on just a split."

"You gonna chuck?" shouted Gavin as Mark left the kitchen.

"No!" returned Mark from the hallway. "I gotta get my invention!"

Sandy and Gavin sat down at the table and engaged in idle chit chat for all of three minutes before Mark returned, standing before them, holding what appeared to be a shiny aluminum cap, appearing much like an upside-down bowl. However, it was speckled with little sensors scattered all around it. He'd also brought some of his "Dragon's Blood" incense to help set the mood for his demonstration. Sandy took the incense from him and got it burning on the far end of the table before returning to her seat.

"It's not pretty to look at, at least right now," said Mark, holding up his Project Madcap helmet and rotating it for everyone to see. "It's just a prototype. Eventually, when I get more of a budget, I plan on creating a helmet-like device, something akin to what is currently being researched and developed in magnetoencephalography, or MEG technology."

"I feel sorry for the kid that gets that word in a spelling bee," said Gavin.

Mark put the device on his own head, and Gavin and Sandy looked at each other and exchanged laughs.

"You look like a million bucks," said Gavin.

"Thanks," said Mark, looking from side to side at each of them.

"I don't think he meant that as a compliment," said Sandy. "I think it looks like a million-dollar version of a tinfoil hat. And given your penchant for conspiracy theory, that assertion might not be too far off the mark."

With the cap on his head, he turned a full circle, like a model on a catwalk. "Given how much all this technology might eventually cost, a million bucks might not be so farfetched." Mark hopped onto the counter. "There is a school of thought that says you can't have pleasure without pain, and you can't have pain without pleasure. They are Yin and Yang, in a manner of speaking. Like good and evil. Or the pleasure principle. Even sci-fi legend Harlan Ellison has made points such as this."

"Well, Mark, you got a captive audience," said Sandy. "We want to hear more, don't we, Gavin?"

Gavin raised his empty bottle in agreement. "And a slightly drunken audience at that. So how does it work?"

"Your curiosity is genuine, I trust?" asked Mark towards them. Gavin and Sandy looked at each other and nodded, almost in tandem.

"You sure you are not just feigning interest because I almost killed myself?" asked Mark.

"Wow, blunt much?" asked Sandy.

"Ye of little faith," said Gavin. "If I was disinterested, I would be asleep by now. And if we do fall asleep, it's probably the liquor talking. So don't take it personally."

"We are all ears, Mark," said Sandy. "Really and truly."

Mark stayed on the counter as he spoke, using hand gestures as appropriate. "Okay, so right now, we are still in the stone age when it comes to being able to detect just how much pain or pleasure someone is actually experiencing when life events happen. Even today, patients in hospitals are still expected to point to a simple picture of an emoticon in various levels of distress to let the nurse know how much pain they are feeling. It's all very elementary, dear Watson."

"I remember doing that for a nurse last year when I had my hernia operation," said Gavin. "And they didn't have a face on the list that depicted how much pain I was in!"

"Right," said Mark. "Well, we all know that covert and implicit constructs like pain, pleasure, or emotions, in general, cannot be observed directly. But my device is different and can measure them like a thermometer measuring temperature. More specifically, I designed my device to record pain and pleasure along four dimensions: duration, frequency, latency, and intensity."

"Even intensity?" asked Sandy. "That's a toughie and a half."

"Reading the intensity of pain and pleasure was the trickiest bit," asserted Mark. "Pain and pleasure are highly subjective mind states, after all. And scientists, as a rule, do not like things you can't see or touch. Hence the need for construct validity in psychology, as psychology is replete with abstract concepts and chicken vs. egg debates. It's paramount that Project Madcap actually measures what it claims to be measuring and is accurate and precise in that mission."

"Just because you can't see something doesn't mean it's not there," emphasized Sandy. "Even kids as young as half a year old can figure that out, according to Piaget's research on object permanence. Even I remember that much."

"Precisely," said Mark. "And don't forget about how scientists predicted atoms before we even had the technology to see them."

"So, how does your little device measure such emotion?" asked Gavin.

"You make it sound like a fifth-grader making a pinhole camera," said Mark. "Still, I suppose I am rather fortunate to have your attention. Make no mistake, my 'little device' can't isolate complex emotions, such as jealousy, anger, wistful longing, or social anxiety. Nor can it tell you where in the body the physical pain is originating. In this sense, you could say my 'little device' is still a bit in the Stone Age in its own right."

"I would say Copper Age," said Gavin. "You shouldn't sell yourself short."

Sandy shook her head. "Ignore Gavin. So did you establish this construct validity of which you speak? Does your device measure what it purports to be measuring?"

Mark continued. "Yes, but it also depends on how constructs like pain and pleasure are operationally defined. Project Madcap's conceptualizations of pain and pleasure are very simple. Pain is anything that feels unpleasant, physically or emotionally, and pleasure is anything that feels good, physically or emotionally. But even such simplicity can be difficult to measure. My little device only has two polarities, negative valence and positive valence. A negative valence shows pain, any kind of pain, emotional or physical. And a positive valence shows pleasure, any kind of pleasure. It is hard to say what the highest levels of pain or pleasure are that can be achieved before thehuman body passes out or loses consciousness. I have reason to believe these high levels have very seldom ever been achieved, save for some of the more—what shall I say—creative forms of torture devices constructed throughout history. And only a very unlucky few have ever felt that level of pain."

"Talk about a Spartan life," said Gavin.

"At first, I thought only having two polarities was simplistic," continued Mark, crossing his legs as he sat on the counter. "But the more I thought about it, you don't really need any more information than that. I mean, people are essentially either in a 'good place' or a 'bad place" and in varying degrees. Pain hurts, and pleasure feels good. It's as simple as it goes, at least in purely existential terms or according to the pleasure principle. And as long as I can break it down into duration, frequency, intensity, and latency, so much the better."

"So I see," said Sandy. "I think I get it so far!"

Mark nodded. "But here is where things get a tad more complex. To fully understand how my device measures pain and pleasure, you need to be acquainted with both the phonautograph and the Frey Effect."

"Wow, the Frey Effect, I think I have actually heard of that somewhere," said Gavin.

Sandy leaned towards Gavin. "Knowing you, it was in the context of some crazy conspiracy theory."

"What can I say? I am a budding academic," said Gavin. "Besides, isn't that the one that got everyone freaked out about Y2K?"

"Close, but Y2K was host to a myriad of different conspiracy theories altogether," said Mark. "I think what you meant to say was 'V2K.'"

"V2K?" asked Sandy. "So Gavin was actually on to something there?"

Mark nodded. "It is slang for 'voice-to-skull.'"

"As in people's brains getting inundated with secret subliminal messages and shit," said Gavin, trying to sound as if he knew more about it than he really did.

Mark toyed around with the toaster as he spoke, pushing the lever up and down. "Well, yes, conspiracy theorists have touted the Frey Effect as being responsible for everything from subliminal advertising and brainwashing to government cover-ups. While I can't say the extent to which this technology has been abused or exploited in our old and cold world, what I can say is that the Frey Effect and the phonautograph have both been instrumental in the creation of my own device."

"But why the Frey Effect?" asked Sandy.

"Yes, and what, pray tell, is a phonautograph?" asked Gavin. "Is that like a phonograph?"

Mark gestured to them to slow down. "The Frey Effect and the phonautograph both suggest that there is a bridge between the objective and subjective worlds. Both of these show how the subjective experience of hearing sound can be either induced or measured via objective means through other sensory pathways.

With the Frey Effect, electromagnetic radiation, coupled with the expansion of the cochlea, can create the sensation of actual sound being heard, without any actual audible sound being present whatsoever."

"Wow," said Gavin. "That definitely does open up the door to a few conspiracy theories or two. I better get started as soon as I sober up."

"Ignore him," said Sandy. "And what about that phonograph-like thing you mentioned?"

Mark stopped fiddling with the toaster and looked directly at her. "Gavin is right, the phonautograph was the precursor to the phonograph, and its use predates the Civil War. It starts with audible sound, measures its tactile vibrations, and transcribes the vibrations into a visual form on a special surface. From there, the visual record can be played back as audible sound. Back when the phonautograph was invented, it could record sound, but we didn't have the technology to actually play it back. But the earliest recorded sounds were captured by this most wonderful device. It's been said that a rudimentary recording of 'Au Clair de la Lune' was recorded as early as 1860. It just couldn't be played back until we had the technology to do it."

"Color me impressed," added Sandy. "And that's not just the liquor talking."

"Ditto on that," said Gavin. "Although it might be partly due to the liquor talking."

Mark continued. "It wasn't too long after this when we had some very early video footage as well, such as the famous 'Roundhay Garden Scene' or 'Man Walking Around a Corner.'"

"Sounds pretty freaking cutting edge for how old it is," said Gavin. "Although nowadays a movie about a man walking around the corner wouldn't turn many heads, lest that corner were a time-warp into a new dimension."

Mark turned to Gavin and nodded. "And you might be inclined to know that it was around 1935 when Lucille Bogan recorded one of the very first F-bombs, if not the first."

Gavin smiled. "Color me a history buff."

Mark continued. "The Frey Effect and the phonautograph show how tactile, auditory, and visual sensory modalities are interconnected. And likewise, how qualitative, quantitative, subjective, and objective pathways are also interconnected."

"Sounds like the very idea of subjectivity is a myth," said Sandy. "I mean when you consider the big picture."

"Ironic how you said 'sounds like' and "big picture" in that very comment," said Mark.

Sandy paused to recall what she had just said and smiled in agreement.

"The whole thing reminds me of hearing colors or seeing music," said Gavin. "Kinda what's happening with me right now."

"Like I said, ignore him," said Sandy, shaking her head.

Mark ignored Gavin and continued. "You are right, Sandy. Subjectivity is a myth. It is simply code-speak for something that can't yet be measured directly. Subjectivity is simply another word for 'A truth that can't yet be measured.' Temperature was considered subjective before the thermometer quantified the subjective experience with actual numbers. And while we do currently have ways of measuring things like stress, pain, and pleasure, these measurement tools are archaic compared to the Project Madcap. So where a thermometer can put a number to 'hot' or 'cold,' or a decibel meter can put a number to the subjective experience of loudness, my device can put a number to 'pain' or 'pleasure.'"

Sandy got up and put out the incense, as it was getting quite strong in the room. She returned to her seat. "Kinda like the classic First Law of Thermodynamics. Energy cannot be created or destroyed, but it can change forms."

"V2K," said Gavin. "Voice to skull."

"Essentially," Mark said as he looked at Sandy. "And sort of," said Mark as he looked at Gavin.

"Hey, what gives?" asked Gavin. "Maybe I shouldn't have had that last drink."

"You're a classy guy, Gavin," said Mark. "I don't care

what people say."

"See, you are getting better at sarcasm," Sandy chimed. "I knew you could do it!"

"Well, perhaps I have more of a proclivity for giving it vs. detecting it," said Mark.

"Maybe your next invention should be a sarcasm detector," said Gavin.

Mark continued. "At any rate, like the phonautograph, thermometer, or decibel meter, my device doesn't measure pain and pleasure directly but accesses a reading via other sensory avenues."

"So, how are constructs like pain and pleasure best measured?" asked Gavin, raising his eyebrows.

"Pain and pleasure can already be measured in myriad ways," continued Mark. "According to research, the subjective feeling of stress can be a function of certain observable bodily functions: neurotransmitter activity, blood pressure, pulse rate, activity of the nervous system, and the activity of stress hormones like adrenaline or cortisol. All of these have at least some predictive merit when it comes to how much stress someone is feeling. But none of these are highly accurate or precise."

"'Reminds me of that book *The Body Keeps the Score*," said Sandy. "My adviser would always bring it up in my health psychology class. He also talked quite a bit about a book with the word zebra in the title. I can't remember what it was."

"*Why Zebras Don't Get Ulcers*," said Mark. "Nice memory. Well, sort of, anyway."

"Yes, that's the one," said Sandy. "And both of these books talked about how damaging stress can be on the human body."

"Sounds like some interesting reads," said Gavin. "But I think I will stick to my manga for the time being."

Mark hesitated. "Yes, but I wanted something even more efficacious and predictive of pain than the body's biological stress response."

"I suppose those things can only take you so far," said Sandy.

"Indeed," said Mark. "As such, my device actually uses MEG technology to measure and record pain and pleasure from the nucleus encumbens region of the brain and predicts how much pain or pleasure you feel with robust accuracy and precision."

"It all makes one wonder if a person can induce the sensation of pain without actually hurting someone," said Gavin. "Just like the Frey Effect. One could call it P2K."

"P2K?" asked Sandy.

"Pain to Skull!" proclaimed Gavin.

"You're the reason universities have institutional review boards, my dear Gavin," said Mark. He risked a smile. "I even used the device on myself while I was experiencing different levels of pain states, including the parkour experiments, or the one that almost got me killed. The pain and pleasure readings increased on par with how much pain or pleasure I was experiencing on a subjective level. Of course, I still had to estimate my subjective experience of pain or pleasure, so some unconscious experimenter effects or biases may be expected. But still, this is very promising, to be sure. Doing the experiments, double-blind would produce even more robust results."

"Layman's terms please?" asked Gavin.

"Hey, Sandy, care to put it in layman's terms for our drunken friend Gavin?" asked Mark.

Sandy glared at Gavin. "The machine can rate your boo-boo better than a nurse holding up a picture card!"

"I said layman, not drooling imbecile," said Gavin. "Still, 'layman' does sound like some sort of obscure sexual innuendo."

"Well, you somehow manage to find a sexual innuendo in just about anything," said Sandy. "You wouldn't hesitate to point out a phallic symbol at a funeral."

"What can I say? It's a gift," said Gavin.

"Yeah, a bad gift, like socks from your uncle," said Sandy.

"It's the thought that counts," Gavin retorted.

"I should kick you out of the classroom, Gavin," said Mark. "But taken together, I call my new unit of measurement meta mass. The absolute value of this positive or negative valence is the overall measure of the psychological affect or subjective experience a person is experiencing, based on the measurable changes in brain activity during the painful or pleasurable experience."

"Meta mass?" asked Gavin, looking up at Mark, raising his eyebrows.

"In a nutshell, I have found the means to quantify the subjective experience. For the first time, emotions have finally become measurable, and therefore, objective. Just like a phonautophraph recording sound and generating a visual output, decibel meters turning sound pressure into decibels, or a thermometer recording expansion and contraction to measure temperature in Celsius, Kalvin, or Fahrenheit. "

"So like, could any of this make us like, rich or anything?" asked Gavin as he looked back and forth between Sandy and Mark.

"Glad to know your heart's in the right place," said Sandy. She looked at Mark and pointed her thumb at Gavin. "If we left this thing in Gavin's hands, we would most certainly have a doomsday device on our hands."

"I second that motion," said Mark.

"Hey, that's my line!" said Gavin.

"So, does meta mass have weight?" asked Sandy. "I mean, in purely subjective terms?"

Mark took a deep breath. "It involves a certain kind of wait, in a manner of speaking. One meta gram with a negative valence is roughly the equivalent sensation of the average person getting an average mosquito bite."

"And what about the flip side?" asked Gavin. "As in, the pleasure equivalent?"

"I would say that one meta gram with a positive valence might feel like the small amount of relief one feels when sneezing," said Mark, imitating a sneeze. "Of course, these are very rough estimates, to be sure, but you get the picture. But remember, the absolute values of these pain and pleasure experiences would be similar, despite being on opposite ends of the pain and pleasure continuum. And the device would recognize their intensities as being fairly equal."

"The absolute value of a mosquito bite is roughly the same as the absolute value of a sneeze," repeated Gavin, squinting his eyes and nodding as if in deep thought. "Sounds about right, I suppose."

Mark nodded. "So that's my didactic explanation."

"I'm impressed," said Gavin. "And that's not just the liquor talking."

"Agreed," said Sandy. "Well done."

"Speaking of which," said Gavin as he left for the bathroom.

"I thought he would never leave," said Sandy.

"I heard that!" shouted Gavin from the bathroom.

Mark hopped off the countertop and started putting the leftover pizza away. "Say, Sandy, do you remember that story we read in high school, called 'The Story of the Widow's Son'?"

"Hmm....not really. I mean, I am sure I read it—I wasn't a truant like Gavin. But still...."

Mark continued. "It was one of those stories with a lesson. In the first half of the story, a boy kills the prized chicken with his bicycle. The mother becomes irate and berates him for such an imbecilic deed of misfortune. In the second half of the story, everything is the same, except instead of killing the family chicken, the son tries to swerve away from the chicken and ends up dying in a freak accident, and the mother blames it all on the son trying to save a stupid chicken. Or something of that ilk, anyway."

Sandy placed her elbow on the table and rested her chin on her palm. "That was an interesting story and all, but what about it?"

"For some reason, that story always stuck with me. I always took it to be about irony and making peace with the lesser of two evils. Like some sort of darker lesson about gratitude and how much worse things could be, or some such ilk. But after reading the secret message on the two-dollar bill, I have just recently come to the conclusion that the story is also about karma and the Butterfly Effect. Every decision we make potentially sends out energy into the world, like planting seeds or tossing a stone in a pond. If we send out positive energy, good things might happen. And the same goes for bad energy. The two parts of the story are essentially like alternate universes or world lines. And while the story isn't really so much science fiction, it still reminds me of the plethora of stories involving the Butterfly Effect or multiple realities. For example, video games like 'Time Hollow' or 'Life is Strange.' Or animes like 'The Melancholy of Haruhi Suzumiya.' Or Steins; Gate and its discussion of Schrodinger's Cat or multiple world lines. And then there's the German program 'DARK'...."

Sandy bit her lip. "I can see how the Butterfly Effect applies, but what about karma?"

Mark got a burst of energy and placed both palms on the table, and leaned towards her. "What if a person's level of karma dictates which reality or tape will play out, based on how many positive or negative karma points you have accumulated in your life? If the woman in 'The Widow's Son' had adequate karma, perhaps the first ending, the lesser of two evils where her chicken dies instead of the son, would be the version that played out. If she had shit karma, though, then maybe the chicken would survive, and her son would get the shaft, as in the second ending."

Sandy rubbed her chin. "But wouldn't it also depend on the son's level of karma whether he deserves to live or die? It can't be just about the mother's karma."

"Absolutely," said Mark, standing up and rubbing his chin. He paced around the room, mumbling a bit. "And that is where things get confusing and complex, right fast. If there is such a thing as karma, it would unequivocally need to be based on the most complex mathematical algorithms known to man to ensure fairness all around and between all parties involved."

Sandy sighed. "The problem is that humans are not given crystal balls to see just how much worse things could actually be. We do not have the luxury of seeing how things might play out in alternate world lines. How can you make an informed decision, or even learn a simple lesson, if you don't know how all the decisions will play out?"

Gavin came back with sweat beading on his face.

"What the hell happened to you?" asked Sandy. "Fall into the toilet?"

"Thanks for the sympathy," Gavin retorted. "If only I could be so lucky. Chalk it up to a case of emesis."

"Emesis?" asked Sandy, staring at him with wide eyes.

"Emesis, as in the fancy word for throwing up," said Mark.

Sandy glared at Gavin. "Well then, why not just say puke, barf, throw-up, or any of its other popular synonyms?"

"Easy," said Gavin. "Emesis sounds more scientific. Almost dignified, even."

Mark laughed. "Either way you slice it, praying to the porcelain god is still praying to the porcelain god. Sometimes a cigar is just a cigar. Nothing dignified about it."

"If it walks like a duck and quacks like a duck...," said Sandy.

"Could be a robot duck," said Gavin, wiping the sweat off his face with his orange fleece hoodie.

"Coming from someone who seldom has his own ducks in a row," said Mark.

"Not true," said Gavin, holding up his index finger. "You might as well hear it from the master. You know what the secret is to having all your ducks in a row?"

"Do tell," said Sandy. "I'm aquiver with anticipation."

"Never have more than one duck!" shouted Gavin. "That way, it will always be in a row."

"Your lofty ambitions shine through every time," said Sandy.

"Well, thank you," said Gavin, making hand motions to straighten a tie. "I, for one, am inclined to agree."

"Okay, enough chit-chat. Who wants to volunteer for my experiment?" asked Mark, standing up and clapping his hands together.

"Now, you sound like a magician," said Gavin. "You sure this isn't pseudoscience?"

"Me, me!" said Sandy, raising her hand and hopping up

and down in her chair. "One time at college, a hypnotist made me jump around like a kangaroo."

"You make it all sound like a cheap parlor trick," said Mark. He walked towards Sandy and set the hat on top of her head. "Okay, put this on."

Sandy straightened out her hair and put the cap securely on her head.

"Now, hold on a sec." Mark made a mad dash out of the room like before. Sandy and Gavin looked at each other, shrugging their shoulders. Mark soon came back with a portable tennis-racket-shaped bug zapper. He approached Sandy with it.

"What the hell are you going to do with that?" asked Sandy, standing up and backing away. "That thing better be for tennis or badminton!"

"I won't be doing anything crazy," said Mark, walking towards her with it. "But I kinda hope you will."

"Are you nuts?" asked Sandy. "And no, you can't call it gas-lighting if it's true!"

"The lady doth protest too much," said Gavin. "

"Okay, plan B," said Mark, digging into his pockets. "I will give you twenty dollars if you do it."

"Resorting to bribes now?" asked Sandy, warming up to the idea. "That's low. Even for you. You're lucky I believe in your research." She acquiesced and walked towards him and snatched the money from his hand. He helped straighten out the hat on her head.

"I will even let you do it," said Mark. "I'm not a total monster."

All the while, Gavin was readying his phone to record the little display.

"And what, pray tell, are you doing?" asked Mark, looking at Gavin.

"Don't worry, it's all in the interests of science," returned Gavin, hitting the record button.

Sandy snatched the bug zapper from Mark with her left hand and sat down at the table. She put her other hand on the net and squeezed her eyes shut. Inching her finger towards the zap button, she pushed it down. "Aaaah!" she screamed.

"Priceless expression, Sandy," said Gavin, catching it all on video. "Wait until this goes viral."

"Okay, now don't look at the meter," said Mark to Sandy. Mark took a small notepad from the top of the fridge and handed it to her. He also handed her a pen from one of the kitchen drawers. "First, I want you to tell me how much it hurt, on a scale from one to a hundred. And write it down on this notepad here."

"Shit, I don't know," said Sandy. She jotted down a twenty-five.

"Think carefully," said Mark, "and try to be as objective as possible."

She crossed out the twenty-five and wrote twenty-seven instead. "What does the meter say?"

"No spoilers yet," said Mark. "I want Gavin to go next."

"Great idea!" said Sandy, readying her cell phone to record Gavin.

"No way, man!" said Gavin. "You are not getting near me with that James Bond spy-grade tennis racket that came from the Q lab!"

Sandy glared and smiled at him at the same time. "Whatever happened to 'in the name of science?'"

"This isn't science. It's a kangaroo court!" said Gavin, standing up and backing away.

Mark smiled and slapped the cap on Gavin's head. "Don't fret too much, dear Gavin. My theory is that since you are quite drunk, you might have a higher pain tolerance than our miss Sandy here."

Gavin un-tightened his muscles a bit. "You mean like *The Legend of Drunken Master?*"

"Precisely," shouted Mark. "Now that's the spirit!"

"I still don't think so," said Gavin. "I think I will plead the fifth."

"Twenty dollars?" asked Mark.

"Fifty!" shouted Gavin.

"Thirty-five?" asked Mark.

"Hey, that's not fair!" shouted Sandy. "I did it for twenty!"

"Take it or leave it," said Gavin. "Chalk it up to supply and demand. What can I say? It's a seller's market."

"Fine," said Mark, reaching into his pocket and pulling out a wad of crumpled bills. He slapped two twenties and a ten in the palm of Gavin's sweaty hand.

"What?!" shouted Sandy. "No way!"

"Take it up with the karma police, Sandy," said Mark.

Gavin snatched the bug zapper from Mark's hand. "I should report you to the IRB board. Even Stanley Milgram himself didn't use actual shocks in his shock experiments, you know!"

"So now you remember some of your homework," said Mark. "It's a sobering feeling, isn't it?"

"Well, I don't know that I would use myself and sober in the same sentence right now," said Gavin.

Sandy readied her phone and aimed it at him with a slow and steady poise. "All right, now this will be good!"

"Okay," said Gavin. "I got this. Let's do it on three. One, two, three!"

On three, Gavin zapped himself. "Ouch!" he shouted, much louder than Sandy had. He even threw the "racket" across the room, hitting the fridge.

"So much for *Legend of Drunken Master!*" said Sandy, hitting "stop recording" on her phone. "This video is priceless!"

"Hey, I wasn't ready!" said Gavin.

"You counted yourself!" said Sandy. "How much more ready can you get?"

Mark tore out Sandy's page from the notepad and handed the pen and pad to Gavin. "How did that feel, one to one hundred?"

Gavin wrote down thirty.

"So what is it?" asked Gavin. "Don't leave us hanging."

"Well, Sandy wrote down twenty-seven, and Gavin wrote down thirty. But this is where the magic happens. The objective pain reading in terms of meta mass for Gavin came out at (-5.84

meta grams). And the objective pain reading for Sandy came out at (-4.34 meta grams). Now, remember, one V with a negative valence feels like the average mosquito bite."

"Wow, that's like amazing," said Sandy. "And to think that I had better pain tolerance than Gavin, even under his higher levels of inebriation."

"Hey, I think I will resent that," said Gavin. "As soon as I process what you just said."

Mark paced back and forth. "That is a bit surprising. But then again, a small part of it could be explained by expectancy effects."

"Expectancy effects?" asked Gavin. "How so?"

Mark continued pacing. "Yes. If Gavin was anticipating more pain than Sandy, he may have felt more pain. Almost like a placebo effect or self-fulfilling prophecy."

"So part of our pain response might be psychological or in our head," said Sandy.

"Indeed so," said Mark, standing still and rubbing his chin. "At any rate, I have done the experiment on myself many times and have gotten similar findings. Not only that, but I was able to bring the pain readings down a bit when I was meditating or doing a relaxation exercise during the administration of the painful stimulus. And I didn't limit myself to the bug zapper. I have pricked myself with diabetic needles, punched myself in the face, cut myself with a razor, you name it. And the more dangerous studies, of course."

"The ones you promised you will never do again, right?" asked Sandy.

Mark rolled his eyes. "Yes, yes, I know. No worries. But needless to say, I plan on taking this research and device with me to Split Rock Lighthouse. The device's utility for studying karma is obvious. I should be able to measure various degrees of pain and pleasure and see how balance might be restored over time. Whoever wrote that letter will no doubt welcome me with open arms."

"I still kinda wish I could come," said Gavin. "Sounds

kinda fun."

"I know, Gavin," said Mark. "But somebody's gotta hold down the fort here."

Sandy pulled up her calendar on her phone and studied it. "I figure we can leave the morning of September 13, which happens to be a Friday."

"Hmm," mumbled Mark as he scratched his head.

"What's wrong?" asked Sandy.

"Friday the 13th? I just hope it's not bad luck."

"You and your superstitions," said Sandy, rolling her eyes.

Mark stood up and stretched and hopped back on the counter. "I still don't think you need to tag along. Your hotel expenses will add up. You are worrying too much."

"I used to hate my grandmother for worrying about me all the time," said Gavin, slumping in his chair with his hands behind his head. "But now, after her passing, I miss it dearly. One should never take it for granted when someone actually cares about you. Too much caring is way better than none at all. I would give my left foot for that kind of love and concern again. Make no mistake."

"Somehow, I don't think that's the liquor talking," said Sandy as she hopped on the counter next to Mark. She looked at Gavin and smiled. "That might be the most sensible thing you have said all day."

――

CHAPTER 15
A BEDTIME STORY (PART 3)
"AN INCINERATOR AND REINCARNATION"

Date: November 7, 2032, Sunday, 9:00 P.M.
Main characters: Hope, Faith, and An Incinerator

Karma Law 31: Karma rule follows a two-tier chain of command

When the laws of nature or the thirty laws of karma alone are not sufficient to create fairness, the matter next moves on to the karma lords delegated as An Incinerator and his or her Cabinet of Four (Tier 2). As the lord of rebirth, An Incinerator can disrupt the natural order of things through the use of reincarnation. In certain cases, a person who accumulates an over-abundance of vice or virtue points may need a restorative justice that is only feasible by being reborn as someone else.
-----*From A Code of Jurisprudence, Province of Reincarnation,*
Tier 2 (see Appendix B).

"Hey, the secret word is Incinerator!" said Faith the moment Hope walked into the bedroom of her favorite hospice patient.

Hope sat down at the college desk next to her with her copy of *Wuthering Heights* as she had been accustomed. "Ah yes, that's the secret word, isn't it?"

Faith smiled. "I wouldn't forget a word like that, even if I don't know how to spell it. Not a very pleasant word either." Faith whispered. "Do you want to know why adults read stories to children?

Hope paused. "Well, I suppose children like being whisked away to other worlds."

Faith pulled the heavy comforter up to her chin and folded her hands on top. "Yes, but it's also a way to help children fall asleep."

Hope laughed. "And yet, you don't seem to be lulled to sleep during my stories."

"I know," Faith added. "I know I am not a child, technically, but I feel like one when I hear your stories. And yet, I can't seem to fall asleep."

Hope picked up the same copy of *Wuthering Heights* and flipped about two-thirds of the way through. "Well, either I am a right good storyteller, or you have a case of insomnia."

"I will opt for the former. So anyway, 'Incinerator' is our bookmark."

"No beating around the bush with you," said Hope. And so she began to "read."

***

The epithet of Incinerator could be considered bittersweet. By its very name, the word resonated with a highly punitive tone, making her a very misunderstood creature of the stars. After all, there were two things being incinerated. On the one hand, a person's current life was being incinerated, and this was certainly not a pleasing thought. But this was not as bleak as one might surmise. As the old life was being incinerated, a new life was being forged from the ashes. Reincarnation was not just about death. It's also about life. And this oft-misunderstood duality was conveyed by Incinerator's very appearance, epithet, and presence.

Like Taneur, An Incinerator was a towering giant. And where Taneur resembled the Earthy nature of the very province he represented, so too did Incinerator resemble the existential themes of rebirth and transcendence. Her ambiance shone forth like a butterfly springing out from a motionless cocoon or a lotus blossom blooming out of the unlikeliest and murkiest waters. While she had the waist of a caterpillar, the top left portion of her body appeared as that of a caterpillar cocooned. On the other side, she had a single butterfly wing. And though she only had the one wing, she could still fly through the heavens with a grace and dignity usually reserved for majestic angels. The wing was painted with the orange and black motif typical of a monarch butterfly, and a monarch she was indeed, in more ways than one. After all, she was the queen of rebirth and death and everything in between. Her arms and legs were comprised of cacti and were covered in thorns. Some had stated that these cacti, like lotus blossoms, were symbols of resilience, as they could endure in the face of adversity, such as the scathing heat and sand-paper dust of the deserted deserts, where few dared to venture forth. Others would tell tales of how Incinerator was a blight, whose thorns were not the symbols of resilience but painful reminders of what happens should one accrue an overabundance of negative karma.

But her ambiance was not just of this world. When she darted across the heavens, she appeared as a shooting star, leaving trails of light, fire, and meteors in her wake. And while it was often said that seeing a falling star is a promise of good luck and good fortune, few knew that this legend originated when an existential traveler spotted Incinerator darting across the heavens. And while afraid, our existential traveler harbored a hope, a fool's hope perhaps, that at that very moment karma would shine upon him and grace his person with all manner of good luck, good fortune, and the promises of good tidings that only karma can bring.

For a full year, Incinerator wandered the world, taking notes and observing the way animals, plants, and humans interacted. She kept a score of the vice and virtue ratio of many lives, using random samples spanning all demographics. She decided that people who lacked empathy would most benefit from reincarnation, as they could be born anew and see the world from another perspective. But since karma did not ascribe to any agenda or place too much focus with "learning lessons," she endeavored to focus more on fairness and the restoration of balance between pain and pleasure in the world. Like the other karma lords, this mission became her modus operandi.

Her goal was simple—to generate ten rules of karma to apply to Tier 2, the province of reincarnation. The Docent Randii made it clear to her that if matters of existential fairness could not be resolved in Tier 1, the matter would go to her and her cabinet of five. So how would Tier 2 be used? She spent an entire year considering this question.

At the very beginning, she envisioned a system where when a person was reborn, they might maintain a small semblance of residual memory from their previous life, but not enough to remember actually existing as a separate being. But the more she thought about it, she realized this would not work because "when you give an inch, you give a mile." Certainly, it would not be prudent to even allow but the tiniest sliver of existential memory to surface. The security and confidentiality of their entire system depended on it. But what about existential wisdom? Could a person retain their life lessons without actually remembering who they were in a previous life? Wisdom without knowledge? Wisdom without memory? Incinerator's heart raced just thinking about these questions.

But when she posed these questions to the Krystal Kube, she had foreseen how some humans had adopted theories such as these. *No*, she thought. *Any existential memory, wisdom, and life lessons learned must be kept separate from the reincarnated organism, compartmentalized and saved in a separate storage device, without any cross-contamination between brains. Their past lives must be incinerated!* This was necessary not just for the sake of confidentiality but also to emphasize the fact that karma was first and foremost an enterprise built on fairness, not of learning life lessons. So when a person was reborn as the type of person they once judged or tyrannized, they would receive their comeuppance. And the same would apply to a person that went "above and beyond" in their acts of selflessness, sacrifice, and favors bestowed onto others.

This is not to say a person would not learn any lessons. But these lessons would only reveal themselves posthumously by the

Krystal Kube's fifth side when the decedent would be granted the opportunity to see beyond the abyss and veil of the world's great curtain. At this time, the person's two memories from both lives would assimilate, and the wisdom would be granted at that time. And unlike learning, which involved the stuff of association and rote memorization, wisdom had a certain dignity about it, perhaps even a sullen cynicism. After all, wisdom is the stuff of "unlearning," more than "learning," the hard lessons born from the school of hard knocks.

A full year came and went, as it always does. Incinerator went back to the very same location where she had met the mystery man one year before. Standing in the middle of the arena, meeting the gaze of all twelve statesmen, was Docent Randii, Taneur and his cabinet, and a new entourage of four angels that would serve as Incinerator's cabinet. Like Taneur's cabinet, these four held the appearances and demeanor of Incinerator, part caterpillar and part butterfly. Like Incinerator, but unlike Taneur's entourage, they each had one solitary wing, although each wing appeared to be from a different kind of butterfly. As with Taneur, they were to ensure Incinerator's objectivity in their employments dealing with matters of reincarnation.

"Were you able to muster a fair world?" asked the Docent Randii, followed by the rest of his hegemony.

"I did my very best," said Incinerator as she handed Randii a scroll containing the ten additional laws of karma she had created regarding the province of reincarnation. Randii took the scroll, opened it, and smelled it deeply, indulging in Incinerator's hard work. Taneur peered over his shoulder, and Randii held it closer to him so he could read it more easily. The subsidiaries held steadfast in their original positions.

"Quite impressive," said Randii, nodding as he quickly rolled up the scroll. "You are a welcome member of our hegemony. You have done a fine job, Incinerator." He paused, almost as if being careful to choose his words carefully. "There is only one thing that worries me."

"I know what it is," said Incinerator. "Say no more. It's the empathy problem."

"Indeed," said Randii, feeling some relief that Incinerator was already one step ahead of him. "And you are modest to boot."

"Reincarnation should ideally only happen once or twice, or maybe three times at the most," said Incinerator. "But reincarnation requires a great deal of energy and disruption. And what if that is still not sufficient to exercise restorative justice and balance? What if the person in question killed ten, twenty, fifty, or a hundred people? Being reborn once or twice would most certainly still not be sufficient."

"Stole the words right out of my mouth," said Randii, pointing the scroll at her. "Like a blight in the night."

"So what do you propose?" asked Taneur, being careful not to press the docent too readily.

Docent Randii walked around the perimeter of twelve statesmen. He paused at the preserved cadaver of a certain "Brocker Smite." Docent sized him up. "Despite his rather self-serving motivations in the matter, Mr. Smite was right in some ways." He turned to the group of eleven that were now following him. "But unlike Brocker's phony religion and his sophistry, we need a very real afterlife, one that can ensure fairness posthumously beyond the grave when decedents have taken their place among the dead. We need one more karma lord, a statesman, to represent the afterlife."

"Yes, but wouldn't that require even more spirit energy?" asked Incinerator. There were murmurs in the group.

While the confusion ensued, the Docent Randii snapped his fingers. Smoke rose from his very fingertips, and a chariot of fire descended from the heavens. Engravings of roses and thorns were etched into the gold on the sides, and they were glowing, making them visible despite the smoke and fire that enrobed the elegant chariot.

A naked man stepped off the chariot and came to the fore, leaving a trail of smoke and fire in his wake. The mysterious godhead took a bow. "Consider me Fate Rifle, caretaker of the afterlife." He was apparently endowed with all manner of existential knowledge, as evidenced by what he already seemed to know apriori. He joined the group of eleven.

Docent Randii turned to the group and spoke as an orator. "When fairness cannot be achieved via Tier 1, Taneur and the laws of nature, the matter moves to Tier 2, Incinerator and reincarnation. And if the matter still cannot be settled by Tier 2, the matter shall be moved to Tier 3." Randii took a bow, moving to the side of the third karma lord. "Meet Fate Rifle of the afterlife." Randii looked at Fate Rifle and considered him from head to toe, bearing witness to the figure he himself helped create. "You have one year to come up with a system of karma as it relates to the ambit of the afterlife. You will meet us here, at this very spot, in exactly one year. Same time. Same place. At that time, we will finally have our fair world."

Taneur and Incinerator looked at each other with apathetic expressions, hiding their doubts of adding yet another tier to their already two-tiered karmatic system.

But so it was, our Docent Randii appointed and anointed our newest emissary of the karma lords, dubbed him Fate Rifle, blessed him with the divine knowledge about all manner of the afterlife, and tasked him with creating the laws of the spirit realms for this new world. The Docent Randii gave him exactly one year to complete this grand task. And in one year's time, the three karma lords, and all cabinets and subsidiaries, were to meet again, in this very location, to complete the "Code of Karmatic Jurisprudence," the very doctrine that would create and shape our fair world, at the behest of the Docent Randii.

***

With that, Hope closed the book.

"You can't stop now!" whispered Faith, her eyes starting to close. "I want to hear about Fate Rifle!"

Hope got up from the writing desk and positioned Faith's blankets over her. She stayed at her bedside until she was fast asleep. Admiring the scent from Faith's smart diffuser, she picked up the "Courage" blend bottle of oil that was sitting near it. She held the bottle, wondering if Faith chose this particular scent based on feeling more fearful than usual. She also noticed that Faith was not wearing her fleece sherpa jacket. Although these did not seem like red flags per se, Hope felt a certain knot form in her stomach. She set the bottle back down.

And with that, Hope stole away to the door. The door decided to squeak as it opened, but Faith did not wake. Hope stared at her for a moment, smiled, and then departed.

--

CHAPTER 16
UNFETTERED LETTERS

Main Characters: Madeline and Nova Fischer
Location: Sioux Falls Mental Hospital, Sioux Falls, South Dakota
Date: September 7, 2019 (Saturday), 11:15 a.m.

Forefathers, foresight, foreman, foursome, cumbersome, cucumber, cool, pickle, in a pickle, not cool, not calm, not cool as a cucumber when I am in a pickle, vegetable, lifeless, bedridden, bedraggled, fruit, fruitless, fruitless labor, powerless, incapacitated, moribund, death and dying, afterlife, afraid, the great unknown, what happens when you die?
----From a free-association session between Madeline and Dr. Zeck on April 7, 2017

Forty-year-old Nova Fischer, Madeline's identical twin sister, pulled into the parking lot of the Sioux Falls Mental Hospital in her green 2015 Volkswagen Beetle. With a "click" of authority, her high heels made contact with the hard-packed pavement. She opened the back door on the driver's side and pulled out a small plastic grocery sack containing various sundries for Madeline's care package, such as Toblerone, crossword puzzles, adult coloring books, a scratch art kit, a silent film (Charlie Chaplan's *Modern Times*), and a pedometer to keep her from becoming too listless and indolent. She also grabbed her black Hammitt Ferris purse, which was also in the back seat.

Nova had chosen to dress up for the occasion, thinking that maybe the class of company Madeline kept might "influence," at least unconsciously, how staff and clients saw Madeline. She decided to wear her Milano silk blue blouse by Ravella, suede high heels, diamond earrings, Wittnauer watch, and black dress slacks for the occasion. As it was chilly, she also had on a long and black Express peacoat, unbuttoned halfway to show off the blouse.

Nova slammed the door of the car with more force than usual. She worried about anyone seeing her, so she seized a swift pace with an erect and confident gait as she found her way to the entrance of the clinic, her purse flopping around over her shoulder. She came in and went to the receptionist, today a certain twenty-nine year old wearing a "Kezia Schilling" name tab and working the seven to three shift.

"Hello, may I help you?" asked the tall and gangly receptionist with a bright smile and perky demeanor, wearing a brown leather jacket. The display was so over-the-top that Nova thought it disingenuous.

"I hope so," said Nova, looking around. "I am here to visit a family member."

"Oh, you must be Madeline's sister!" shouted Kezia. Nova looked around only to see patrons peering up at her from behind their magazines. "I will go fetch her," said Kezia as she handed Nova a "Visitor" sticker to put on her peacoat. "Wow, you two sure look alike. Are you twins?"

"I'm afraid so," said Nova, trying to find a good spot to place the sticker so it wouldn't blemish the fabric of her coat in any way.

"Afraid so? You sound disappointed. I think it's really cool!"

Nova forced a smile. "It's not about being twins per se. Let's just say you don't know Madeline like I do."

Kezia kept on her smiles. "Oh now, that's a shame. She's your sister, you should love her. Blood is thicker than water, right?"

Nova's already faint smile dwindled to a halt. "Well, so is molasses. And you don't see me lapping that up with a spoon."

Kezia kept up her positive and jovial demeanor. "I just love how twins are like real-life clones, like Dolly, the sheep!"

"Thanks, I think," returned Nova. "Um, Madeline?"

Kezia snapped her fingers. "Oh yes, where are my manners?" She walked towards the metal detector and placed her hand on it. "Now, if you could please remove any sharps and walk through here, please."

After setting down her purse and gift bag and removing two rings, a necklace, and her watch, Nova walked through undetected.

"Good job," said Kezia, as if walking through a metal detector were a skill worthy of accolades and approbation.

"Thanks!" said Nova. "Can I take the gift bag to my sister?"

"Just a sec," said Kezia as she rifled through the bag, looking for sharps or mysterious substances.

Wow, she must think I have a grenade and a gun in there, thought Nova, rolling her eyes.

Without putting the items back in their original tidy locations, Kezia handed the bag back. "It's all clear."

"Wow, this place really is like a prison," mumbled Nova under her breath.

"Well, we have to search for contraband — you know, for the patients' safety and the like. But that chocolate sure looks good. I should take that for myself!"

Nova smiled at her.

"Madeline will be happy to get that." Kezia pointed towards the ring of wooden chairs in the corner of the waiting room. "You can have a seat right over there."

Nova took her seat, and not five seconds after she sat down and set her purse in the seat next to her, Madeline came bounding into the room, giving Nova a bear hug. Nova stole a glance at the others in the waiting room, their eyes once again gawking above their magazines to see what the fuss was about. Nova did her best to hide behind her sister, thus relinquishing the center stage and spotlight back over to Madeline. The latter seemed unaffected by the public display of affection, as evidenced by her pale white cheeks, which were in stark contrast with Nova's flushed and rosy red complexion. With the discreetness of a pick-pocket,

Madeline plucked the visitor tag from Nova's jacket during the haphazard embrace.

"Stop that, sis," said Nova. "People are looking at us."

"Good!" said Madeline, loud enough for everyone to hear. She looked at the others in the waiting room and pointed at Nova. "This is my sister, Nova. Isn't she pretty?"

In response to this, one person nodded, two others smiled, and another had cheeks equally flushed as Nova's.

"Can we please go now?" whispered Nova, standing up and bobbing up and down with impatience.

"Okay, okay, you 'normals' are no fun," said Madeline.

"Normals?" asked Nova.

"Yea, you know, people that aren't in mental hospitals. Many of us actually consider you guys to be the freaks, after all."

"Thanks!" said Nova.

They both laughed as Madeline grabbed Nova's hand and tugged her into the visitor's chamber. There were several vending machines in the room, some potted yucca plants, and peace lilies. There were also framed inspirational quotes adorning the walls and a "help is out there" message for those thinking about suicide.

They each took a seat on the cushioned chairs, which were affixed to the floor. But just as soon as Madeline was about to make contact with the seat, she hopped back up and went to one of the vending machines.

"Want a pop?" asked Madeline. "A candy bar? My treat."

"No, that's fine," said Nova, motioning her to pass. "I just had a caramel roll before coming here. Probably two-thousand calories in that one thing alone."

But before Nova could even finish her sentence, she could hear the clinks of quarters falling into the vending machine. "Think fast!" shouted Madeline when she tossed the Whatchamacallit candy bar at Nova.

Nova's instincts kicked in, and she whacked the candy bar against the wall with her flailing hands as she tried to catch it. Nova stood up and retrieved the now smashed bar and dusted it off. The pop machine was her next destination. "Okay, but I am getting us the pop. What kind do you want?"

"Thanks, sis. I want the Mello Yello."

"You're lucky—I hardly ever carry change," said Nova. "Physical money is going the way of the dinosaur." After putting the quarters into the machine with much less noise than Madeline, she came back to the table with two cans of Mello Yello. She slid one across the wooden table towards Madeline.

Madeline stopped it with her palm. "Thanks, Nova."

Nova handed Madeline her gift bag. "Here is your care package, Maddy. This is a rare treat. Don't get too used to it. You know I am more of a 'tough love' kinda gal. So enjoy it while it lasts."

Madeline began rifling through the bag, making all sorts of noise in the process. "Oh yay, don't you just love pressies?!"

As Madeline was exploring the bag, Nova couldn't help but wonder if she may have been showing early stages of her mania. She watched her with a careful eye. "You okay, Mads?"

Madeline paused a moment and looked at her. "Sure I am. Can't you tell how happy I am? You seem somehow disappointed."

"No, nothing like that," returned Nova. "I just don't want you to be 'too happy,' if you know what I mean. You know what happens when you are too happy."

Madeline's smile faded. "How can a person be too happy? What are you getting at?"

Nova put up her hands. "No, it's okay. I don't want to start anything. I'm just worried about you, being in here and all."

Madeline set the bag aside, reprising her wide smile. "So, how are you doing? Like really doing. You know, not just small talk, but the real thing. Like regarding our parents and the like?"

"I still cry sometimes," said Nova. "You know when nobody is looking."

"A toughie like you? That's impressive. Still, you don't have to always worry about keeping up appearances. It's okay to grieve."

Nova smiled. "I know. It's just part of life, you know? I

try to fight my tears, but about half of them come out one way or another. Crying won't bring them back, but I guess it helps a little bit now and then. You know, to soften the blows a little bit."

Madeline paused. "Yea, but does 'inevitability' justify lack of worry?"

Nova looked confused. "What do you mean?"

"I mean, just because death is a part of life, does that somehow negate the pain and suffering it brings? Or make it any less real? People have this lame idea that just because something is outside of your control, that gives you an excuse not to worry. But I feel like things you can't control should make a person worry more, not less. Isn't the very fact that something is outside our control the very reason and essence of why we worry in the first place? Isn't that the very definition of worry?"

"I don't know, Madeline," said Nova as she fidgeted with her purse. "But what else are we supposed to do? It's not as if we can do anything about it. Just live with it. I guess the point is that worrying is pointless in the grand scheme of things. It's kind of like how you always hated the expression 'sticks and stones will break your bones, but words will never hurt me.' I was always fond of it, as it's something you can tell yourself to take the edge off if someone teases you."

"But words do hurt," said Madeline. "That expression is accurate."

"Either way, such an expression can be a great way to reframe the situation or get some perspective should someone hurl nay-says at you."

"How typical," said Madeline with a snarky yet playful tone. "I guess you were always the one to accept the way things are and leave it go at that." She pointed her finger around the room. "I suppose that explains which one of us is sitting in a place like this."

Nova sighed. "Maddy, it doesn't mean you are weaker than me or anything. If anything, it might be to the contrary. Perhaps it's you who are strong enough to question the status quo and ask the big questions most of us are too afraid to ask.

As for me, I just busy myself with my greenhouse when I am not doing my vet work."

"Thanks, Nova," said Madeline, her voice cracking. "I don't remember you saying anything nice about me in quite some time. It means more than you know."

"Well, it's true," said Nova, leaning ahead towards her. "Except the lying. I don't like lying. And I will never understand why you picked up such a nasty habit. It sure wasn't from me, or our parents for that matter."

"I am working on it," said Madeline. "I am learning it's a defense mechanism and a survival skill. It's something I picked up as a little child to get what I needed. We don't look at it as bad behavior. It's part of my disease."

"Here we go," said Nova, rolling her eyes.

"What do you mean?" asked Madeline. "I'm getting better, I really am."

Nova sighed. "Oh, Maddy, you know I am a tough love kinda gal. The idea of some of those counselors excusing lying and stealing just doesn't sit well with me. Your behavior has hurt me more than a few times. But as long as you are working on it, that is the important thing. I won't get too bent out of shape about it."

"It's a work in progress," explained Madeline, getting out of her chair and leaning against the wall near the defaced "Help is Out There" picture, someone having doodled a beard, earrings, and a joint on the depicted actor. "Where a year ago I may have told a few lies every day, now it's probably down to one or two a week. The trick is to actually catch yourself doing it. Here they call it 'Catch it, Check it, and Change it.' A year ago, I would do it so mindlessly, and habitually I was almost oblivious to it. Either that or I believed my own lies. Now I notice myself in the act, and I can do something about it."

"I'm proud of you, Madeline," said Nova as she went to her sister and gave her a tight hug.

Madeline tugged on Nova's hand. "Hey, follow me. I want to show you something."

Nova pulled her hand away.

"Come on!" Madeline started walking towards the stairs that went up to her room.

"Wait, I didn't even finish my junk food!"

"It's okay, bring it with!" echoed Madeline's voice from the top of the stairs.

"Yes, but the sign here says we shouldn't bring food out of this room! Madeline!"

By now, Madeline was already out of earshot. Nova stuffed the rest of the candy bar in her mouth, grabbed her gift bag, and dashed up the stairs after her. Nova reached the top of the stairs and saw Madeline standing in front of the door to her room.

"Geez, Madeline, now you are making me into a delinquent rule-breaker," said Nova. "Sheesh!"

Madeline was breathing heavy from the run. "It's fun, isn't it!?"

"Madeline! Stop it! No, it's not!"

"Just kidding," said Madeline.

"And no, you can't just undo every lie by saying 'just kidding' afterwards! It doesn't work like that!"

Madeline motioned for Nova to enter the room. "After you," said Madeline, sweeping her arm as if introducing a regal dignitary.

They walked in, and Madeline was careful to not let the door close behind her. The room was tidied up ahead of time for Nova's visit. Madeline had spent several hours preparing and had borrowed the vacuum from Jason Mattson for the occasion. She even made her bed. There wasn't much in the room, as any room items were strictly regulated. She did have some coloring books and scratch art on the table, though. And she had a Joy Division and Smashing Pumpkins poster on the wall. There was also a DVD player and a stack of movies, most of them silent. There were no curtains, cords, or sharp objects allowed, as these could ultimately be used for self-harm.

"Let me take your coat," said Madeline as Nova acquiesced to her demand. Madeline laid it down on the recliner across from the bed.

Madeline touched Nova's arm and guided her to a seated position.

"Okay, close your eyes," said Madeline. "They don't allow scarves in here, so I can't use a proper blindfold."

Nova sighed. "Come on, Madeline, I hate surprises."

"Surprises are the spice of life," said Madeline.

"There are good surprises and bad surprises," said Nova. "Could be a birthday party or a surprise gunshot wound!"

"It's okay, Nova. It's only for a minute."

"Fine!" grumbled Nova. "But no more than a minute. Now hurry up!"

With careful stealth and trying to be light on her feet, Madeline took Nova's peacoat and purse from the bed and glided out the door without making a sound. Out of earshot, she opened the purse and slipped a sealed envelope into it containing a check for five-thousand dollars, along with a handwritten note. She also snatched the car keys out of the side pocket before setting the purse back inside the door in plain view. She pitter-pattered down the stairs as she slipped on the long jacket, buttoned it up, and fastened the "Visitor" badge onto the outside of the jacket. Thankfully it was long enough to cover most of her scrubs. She dashed to the receptionist to meet Kezia, and she did her best to hide the small amount of visible blue of her scrubs just above her ankles.

Kezia smiled. "Hey there! You are done visiting already? Madeline is something else, isn't she?"

Madeline tried to adopt Nova's demeanor and mannerisms. "No, I forgot something in the car I wanted to give Madeline. Is it okay if I go out and get it?"

"Absolutely, as long as you show me what it is when you get back. Just like you did before. It's just procedure, you know?"

Madeline nodded without saying a word.

And with that, Madeline went out the door and was a free woman. She wanted to soak up the scenery and enjoy the fresh air, but her minute was probably up by now, so she didn't hesitate for a solitary second. She sprinted to Nova's green Volkswagen like a track runner and plopped herself inside. She went to the bush on the side of the building where she'd placed her special license that morning. The plate was from the "Graham Volkswagen" car lot in South Dakota (as her plan was to make a pit stop in Luverne to quickly change it up to make it look like the car was just purchased and taken off the used car lot). She then left the parking lot of the mental hospital and headed towards Fargo, ND.

After an hour of driving, her adrenaline subsided, and her entire body appeared droopy and languid. Her emotions turned wistful and melancholy. She wondered if there was a way she could have done things differently without lying to Nova like that. But what else could she have done? Madeline thought about how much her compulsive lying really had decreased markedly during the last few months. Did all that progress go up in smoke, as if having a drink after months of sobriety? Surely after this, Nova would never trust her again. She did manage to reassure herself somewhat, though, when she remembered that the old Madeline would have surely taken off with both the keys and the purse and not thought twice about it. At the very least, she gave back her purse, complete with five-thousand dollars. That had to count for something, right?

Even still, Madeline cried for close to thirty minutes before turning on the radio. But it didn't take long for her to realize she had bigger fish to fry. Would she reach the Split Rock Lighthouse while averting detection? Could she continue to use Nova's car, or would it be prudent to ditch it and get another somehow? She alleviated some of her painful thoughts by focusing on the details of her scheme. She decided she could make amends to Nova another time. After all, she had survived her very own suicide attempt, and in comparison, this lie was really just small fries and small potatoes.

"Besides," said Madeline as she fiddled with the radio. She heard "Lightning Crashes" by Live and turned it up. "That will be my last lie. I promise!"

***

Back at the asylum, things were quite different. "Madeline, where are you?" asked Nova after three minutes. "I'm opening my eyes!"

Nova took her hands off her eyes with a dramatic motion and looked around. She wandered around the sterile and bare room. "Madeline?" she asked, at least ten times. When she saw her purse sitting near the door, she snatched it up. She rifled through it, relieved to see her driver's license and cards still there. She seized the note that was visible near the top and chucked the purse on the bed. Without further thought, she began to read.

Dear Nova. As you are reading this, you are no doubt furious at me. You are probably swearing out loud even now. But please hear me out. Sometimes when people do bad things, they get in so deep that it's hard to leave the culture completely, at least at first. And knowing you, you think that's just a cheap excuse. I beg you to listen and trust me one final time. I know I have hurt you one too many times. Probably five too many times. But I want you to know I was working on my problems with an utmost sincerity. Not because the system was mandating me to do so, but because I wanted to change for myself. In my groups, they call this "intrinsic motivation." My counselor Tamara would vouch for me (at least if I had signed an ROI giving her permission to talk to you). And while you are probably thinking even these very words are lies, I want you to consider both lessons inherent in "The Boy That Cried Wolf." One lesson is for the child, and that is the lesson I am learning more often than not these days. When you develop a history of lying, it's harder and harder to dig yourself out of that rut until people believe scarcely a solitary word that is uttered from your forked tongue. And yet, I implore you to consider the second lesson of "The Boy That Cried Wolf." This lesson is for the adult in the story, in this case, you, Nova. The lesson is this: Just because someone has a history of lying, this is no guarantee that everything he or she says will necessarily be a lie. The truth is, Nova, I have been looking forward to your visit, and I have cried happy tears just thinking about it on more than one occasion. And I am probably crying happy tears while you are reading this at this very moment.

I know you have no reason to trust me, but what I am about to say is the truth, for what it is worth. I am not leaving this mental hospital because I don't believe I have any problems. I do have problems. Lots of them. In fact, that's why I am leaving the hospital, as ironic as it may sound. Even the counselors here have been impressed with my insight. They call it "developing discrepancy." Sometimes I wonder if my insight is too keen and adroit, leaving me two steps ahead of them. Still, I know full well how my lying, depression, and anxiety have impacted my life in myriad ways. This much is clear. But you must also understand, Nova, that my failed suicide attempt was a wake-up call of sorts. The good news is that I am alive and well, and I have turned over a new leaf. With that said, my newfound mission is not one of which you would normally approve. In truth, what I am about to say will sound like the stuff of schizophrenic delusion. But it is my staunch belief, my dear beloved sister, that what happened to our parents, while tragic, was also a portent of something rather serendipitous, if not holy. And for the first time in my life, like Joan of Arc, I feel as if I was meant for something greater than myself. As such, I am now trusting destiny to guide the way. Or maybe it's karma. I really don't know.

The crux of the matter is, as I see it that I am lucky to be alive. Every second I breathe, it feels almost as if a bonus breath. And while you are probably writing this off as some sort of manic high or adolescent drama, rest assured that I feel a mental clarity that I have not felt since I was seven. You coming to see me today meant the world to me. Perhaps even many worlds. Please don't see any of this as a mere trick, lure, or any such subterfuge. But it's the only way I could think of to get out of this place. I promise you, Nova, that I will check myself right back in as soon as I finish my mission. And don't worry, Nova, I promise I won't attempt suicide while I am away. I will explain everything when I get back. Please don't fret about my safety, that is, if you even like me enough to care, at this point. I pray we will be BFFs once again. Siblings make the bestest of friends, don't you agree? Please don't leave me. Even if the feeling is no longer mutual, I love you, now and always.

Maddy

P.S. Please don't press charges regarding your car. I will bring it back safe and sound, I promise! You can use my PT Cruiser in the meantime. The keys are under the visor. How's that for collateral? Oh yes, one more thing. I hope you enjoy the $5000 and put it to good use.

— ·

CHAPTER 17
A BEDTIME STORY (PART 4)
"FATE-RIFLE AND THE AFTERLIFE"

Characters: Hope and Faith
Date: November 13, 2032, Saturday, 2:30 P.M.
Setting: Augusta, Maine (Hospice Clinic)

Karma Law 41: Karma rule follows a three-tier chain of command

When the laws of nature, the laws of the land, and the rules of reincarnation are not sufficient for restorative justice, the matter gets passed to Fate Rifle, the Lord of the Spirit Realms and the Cabinet of 4, couched in Tier 3.

----From A Code of Karmatic Jurisprudence, Province of Afterlife, Tier 3 (see Appendix).

"You can come in," asserted the priest, reaching out his hand to Hope. But she just rushed on by, bumping the side of his hand en route. She had Menace on a leash behind her, but she couldn't help but wonder how many decedents had left the world in this very room.

The sixty-something priest saw them together and took his leave. At the door, he turned around. "You don't have much time, Hope — use it wisely. I would give your young friend fifteen minutes, tops." And with that, he tipped his driver's cap and left the room. The room was sterile, with no pictures on the walls and various pieces of medical equipment strewn about the room.

Faith was coughing so hard, her side of her pillow was stained with blood. Hope rushed to her bedside, with Menace in tow in one hand and a gift bag in the other and knelt beside her. She held Faith's hand so tight it almost hurt.

"Can you tell me about 'Fate Rifle'?" asked Faith, some blood trickling down her lip and onto her chin. "Pretty please?" She reached down and petted Menace on the head.

"But of course," said Hope. "I will be with you until the very end. And even then, I won't leave you in spirit. Always and never, in that order." She pulled out Faith's diffuser and plugged it in. "Now, what scent do you want? I grabbed as many as I could find in your bedroom."

"Did you find my 'Peace & Comfort?'" asked Faith with a meek and weak voice.

Hope rifled through the gift bag and pulled it out. She poured the oil, and the scent permeated the room. Faith closed her eyes and smiled when she first noticed the lovely aroma.

"Now, please humor my final moments, and tell me about Fate Rifle, the lord of the spirit realms. I want him to whisk me away as soon as I pass. There I will be waiting for Menace on Rainbow Bridge. You will take care of him until then, won't you?"

"But of course," whispered Hope, patting her shoulder through the thick blankets. "We already talked about that. It was okay then. And it's okay now."

Faith's smile was weak but visible. "So are they real? Your stories?"

Hope squeezed her hand in hers. "For me, it's more than just a story. I believe these stories are real, and I was endowed with existential knowledge from beyond the veil, spoken through visions, dreams, and even through the medium of friends. But that is my belief. This is not to say I always agree with their methods, mind you. Back in 2021, there was an accident in North Dakota where a good samaritan of all people, a certain Elaine Fettig, got killed trying to help a stranded motorist change a flat tire. That hardly sounds fair, now, does it?"

Faith's vestige of a smile dissipated. "No, it doesn't. Makes me mad even."

Hope chuckled and squeezed her hand even tighter. "You

might turn into me if you are not careful. Just remember, there are many who write me off as mentally ill, Miss Faith. And while a great many would not hesitate to write this off as some sort of conspiracy theory, my dear husband and I are very keen on the idea that many of these ideas are very real, be they right or wrong. You can believe what you wish, dear Faith. I will think nothing less of you one way or the other."

"I don't think it's twisted," said Faith, squeezing Hope's hand as well. "I think it's pretty, and I would prefer to think of it as something that might be real and not just a fictional story. But I do wish karma police were nice all the time. It scares me when they hurt people."

Hope smiled and petted her hair like a kitten. "You and I are more alike than you know. Natural-born reformers with a stubborn aversion to reality. And hearing you make that observation, along with seeing Menace and Sally together like that, also reminds me of a good friend I had once. He loved animals too, be they flesh or plush."

Faith clutched Sally tight and pursed her lips. "Speaking of names, you said you changed it. Why?"

Hope laughed. "That same friend I was just talking about once said he dreamed of a world without pain and suffering. Ever since, I wanted people to call me Hope. In his honor."

"Do you believe in hope?" asked Faith. "Is that why you go by that name?"

Hope petted Menace on the head. "Ironically, I go by that name because, more often than not, I don't have much hope. But my name, at the very least, reminds me that 'hope is the thing with feathers.'"

"That sounds like a good friend," said Faith.

Hope smiled. "I am leaving it to him to tell you about a special kind of karma."

Faith scrunched up her face. "Lateral karma?"

"Yes," said Hope. "A simpler and even more loving theory of karma."

"Why can't you tell me?" asked Faith.

Hope looked towards the window and smiled. "Nobody can tell it like he can," said Hope.

Just as she made that comment, an intrusive thought popped into her head of a gravestone. It wasn't just a general schema, but it included the nuance and subtlety of details, such as the sheen of the dark marble and the indentations of the engraved letters themselves. She thought about the tactile sensations of running her fingers over Faith's name and year of death. And the thought that this young lady, in bed at this very moment, would soon be in the ground, left to rot and spoil, and why we call beds "death beds" if you die in them, but we don't call beds "living beds" when you are alive in them. And with that, Hope began sobbing.

Faith scrunched up her face into a puzzled expression. "Are you okay, Miss Hope?"

Hope shook her head as if shaking such intrusive thoughts out of her head like a salt cellar. She wiped the tears away with the sleeve of her fleece hoodie. "I apologize. I guess my mind just sort of trailed off. I was just thinking about how you have nothing to worry about." Hope knew full well that she had just lied through her teeth. And while she never could shake the urge to lie completely, she at the very least knew how to create a better class of lie as a way to make people feel better. Hope took a tissue from the nightstand. "Now close your eyes, Miss Faith, and I will tell you about Fate Rifle."

Faith looked over the side of the bed and noticed Menace sleeping soundly next to the bed. She inhaled a deep breath of her scented oil. And she closed her eyes while clutching Sally against her chest.

Hope got up and walked around the room as she told the rest of the story, using sweeping arm movements and exaggerated facial expressions, almost as if an attorney presenting a case.

***

The very epithet of "Fate Rifle" had a certain melancholy cynicism about it, as if he were shooting sinners into oblivion from the stars, like a hunter from the safety of an inconspicuous tree stand. But this would only be partially correct. Like the other karma lords, any malevolence he had was matched in full by an equal amount of benevolence. Like the others, he was tough but fair. It must be understood that while rifles kill, they can also save lives. However, for him, it was not the bullet that was the crown jewel or crux of this particular metaphor, but rather the scope. After all, it's the scope on a rifle that allows a person to see from afar. And seeing from afar was what Fate Rifle did best, whether he was shooting sinners into oblivion or rationing his bullets for a more pressing matter altogether.

And like his epithet, his appearance was intimidating but also loving. He held an aloof demeanor, neither smiling nor frowning. His entire persona resonated with the images endemic to all manner of folklore, legends, and myths of centuries of religions and cultural depictions of the afterlife. A glowing halo floated above his head, emitting a blinding light, a light so bright it could light up an entire underground tunnel system of caves for scores of miners and spelunkers. Still, this light was just as terrifying as it was a beacon in the night. Based on one's assumptions, it might appear either like doomsday hellfire or a port of call to lonely seafarers. He had a solitary angel wing and a single horn on his head. And while one might suspect he was fully clothed, he was far too bright to know for certain. Staring at him for more than three seconds would all but guarantee certain blindness.

For a full year, Fate Rifle wandered the world, taking notes and observing the way animals, plants, and humans interacted. He marveled at how the stories of people, passed down from generation to generation, spoke of the afterlife and how the nature of the punishments were doled out and castigated upon the masses of sinners, heathens, and usurpers of the world.

Fate Rifle was taken aback by how certain spiritual leaders even appeared to promulgate the idea that a draconian punishment might be bestowed upon you, a more than bold reprisal that far outweighed the nature of the original transgression. Fate Rifle understood that if matters of fairness could not be settled through the laws of nature or the laws of reincarnation, the matter would next get passed to him. As he was the final karma lord left to ensure fairness in Tier 3, he knew he had to make sure the karma laws he brought to the table would be sufficient to ensure fairness. To create a fair world in the spirit realms, Fate Rifle mulled and mused on the problem of multiple murders. Based on this, he was able to craft ten additional karma laws.

A full year came and went, as it always does. Fate Rifle went back to the very same location where he had met the Docent Randii, Taneur, and An Incinerator, and the twelve members of their respective cabinets. Standing in the middle of the arena, meeting the gaze of all twelve preserved statesmen, were the three karma lords, along with their subsidiaries, and the Docent Randii. The group now in total numbered sixteen.

"Were you able to create a fair world?" asked the Docent Randii as Fate Rifle met them.

"I did my very best," said Fate Rifle as he handed Randii a scroll containing the ten additional laws of karma he had created for the new spirit realms.

"Many thanks," said Randii. "Your contribution signifies that our work has finally been consummated by Tier 3."

Randii took the scroll, opened it, and read the words as Taneur and Incinerator peered over his shoulder. As before, the cabinet members stood so steadfast and stiff they looked almost frozen.

Using both hands, Randii rolled up the scroll with haste and alacrity. "Well, ladies and gentlemen, with our third karma lord, I can safely say that we have completed our theocracy. We may not have built an elysium, but at least we have what could be called a semblance of a fair world."

The others looked at each other, nodding, others giving applause.

Randii continued, like an orator boosting the morale of soldiers. "Our three functionaries will ensure that the populace will never again be resigned to a cruel world. Never again will we have to feel pangs of envy regarding what others have or don't have, be it money, wealth, status, or beauty. Life, as we know it, will finally be fair. Taken together, these fifty laws shall be called the 'Code of Karmatic Jurisprudence,' and it shall be promulgated forthwith through all the lands and spirit realms of Goldilocks's Dilemma, Ancient Earth, and beyond!"

***

"The end," said Hope as tears welled in her eyes.

"Why are you crying, Miss Hope?" asked Faith. "Are you sad?"

"Rest assured, Miss Faith, when you are happy, my tears glisten like spring water. And when you are sad, my tears have the haze and hue of bog water. And when you are scared, my tears are like the water from a ravaging waterfall. But rest assured, these are happy tears."

"That makes me happy," said Faith with a bright smile. "Will I get to meet Fate Rifle when I die?"

"Yes," said Hope, nodding approvingly. "I just know it."

Faith pursed her lips. "But how do you know, like, for sure?"

"I can feel it in my very bones," said Hope. "And my gut. And there is nothing other than bones and guts, now is there?"

"I suppose you are right," said Faith. "But is he nice? Will Fate Rifle punish me or reward me?"

Faith knelt down by the bed. "Fate Rifle will know what is right and will bestow you with all the gifts you deserve."

Faith smiled. "Like Santa Claus?"

"Something like that," Hope said with a laugh. She held Faith's hand for a few minutes, neither of them saying a word.

"Hope?" asked Faith.

"Yes, Miss Faith?"

"I'm scared."

Hope stood up and leaned over the bed. She took both corners of the comforter and wrapped them around Faith's shoulders and gave her a hug and a kiss. By now, they were both crying in unison, and their tears mingled and intertwined together in harmony, like two cellos playing a funeral dirge.

"Being scared is a good thing," said Hope as she sat back down in her chair and wiped her tears with her bare hands. Menace was also awake and sitting near Faith's death bed.

Faith wiped her eyes. "A good thing? But what do you mean?"

"Why yes! I would be worried about anyone who is not at least a wee bit worried about death," said Hope. "It shows that you are humble and open-minded, and you try to look at life with an objective eye. You don't make assumptions based on what you want to believe. You have the humble doubts and humility that accompany what is not known or what very well might be."

Faith pointed at the "Get Well Soon" balloon floating on the ceiling. "Do you see that balloon?"

"I saw it the moment I came in here," said Hope. "And I agree with its every word."

"My mom gave it to me this morning. When people are sick, it's not just them that are suffering, is it?"

"No. In fact, there are times when the family might even suffer more."

"Well, I don't want you to be afraid, Hope, so when I die, I am going to pop that balloon for you. And that will be my message to you that I am fine, and you will be fine. And that everyone in the world will be fine. Everyone who has ever walked the earth, in the past, present, and the future. They will all be fine. You will see. And my popping the balloon will prove it for all of mankind."

Hope put her finger on Faith's mouth. "Shhh...."

Faith brushed her finger aside. "I don't want people to be afraid of death anymore. People have been afraid of death since the beginning of time. And we are all just as in the dark as we were thousands of years ago. And I can tell that you are afraid. You are forcing a smile to keep up my morale. But I can tell you are scared too, even if it's not your time."

Hope leaned in closer and cupped her left hand with both of hers. "I want you to know something. I had a friend once that passed to the other side. If he were here, he would say something important at a time like this."

"And what would this special friend have said?" asked Faith.

Hope went from memory. "He and I agreed, that if there is no justice or fairness in the world, then it is up to us to create it ourselves."

Faith smiled. "Do you want to know a little secret?"

"I love hearing secrets," said Hope. "I never outgrew it."

Faith whispered, "As an adult myself, I can say that adults don't know any more about death than children do. They just pretend they do. Adults are really just children in disguise. But they are just as afraid. They just act all high and mighty."

"How can I argue with that?" laughed Hope. "You remind me of myself, that's for sure."

"I love you, Hope," said Faith. "Past, present, and future."

"I love you too," said Hope. "Past, present, and future."

Hope approached her, leaned on her bed until it creaked, and kissed her on the cheek.

And with that, Faith smiled as her eyes closed for the final time, like blinds being turned against the light in a vacant apartment.

Hope draped herself over Faith, questions swirling through her brain. Where did she go? Was there really an afterlife? Did she just fade away into oblivion? What happens when people die? If only adults really knew more than children.

Hope stared at the balloon for a full thirty minutes, not expecting, but certainly hoping, that the "Get Well Soon" balloon would burst. But it never did.

As hospital staff were cleaning out the hospital room, Hope asked to keep the balloon, and she kept it in the bedroom of her trailer home. She kept it aloft for as long as she could, holding out as much hope as possible. It stayed afloat for a full week and slowly dropped closer and closer to the floor until it landed on the carpet, right side up, with the words "Get Well Soon" staring up at her.   _ ·

Look for the story's conclusion coming soon!

APPENDIX A:
A CODE OF KARMATIC JURISPRUDENCE

Tier 1 and the Province of Nature (Taneur and the Cabinet of Four)

Established by:
Taneur (Nature)
An Incinerator (Reincarnation)
Fate Rifle (Afterlife)
Docent Randii (existential foreman and overseer of the Krystal Kube)

Preamble:

We, the karma lords, at the behest of Docent Randii, and with the aid of the Krystal Kube, hereby establish the following capitulation and code of ethics, to be named the Code of Karmatic Jurisprudence. The world we have been given is fair in some ways and unfair in a myriad of others. As such, the world as we know it does not require, or even ask, anything to do with fairness or justice. Ergo, science heretofore has treated the construct of "fairness" as a privilege, and not a right. As existential proprietors of balance, equilibrium, and all that is deemed just, holy, and fair, we solemnly take an oath to establish a highly logical system of fairness and equilibrium in this less than judicious world. This is a fiduciary responsibility as it involves karmatic currency and trust. We choose to abide by this code, as we believe the punishment must always befit the crime, no more, and no less, and without exception. And while we three karma lords strive to seek a mutual understanding, we understand that such concerted agreement is seldom achieved, particularly when discordant viewpoints are proffered. As karma lords, we do our work behind the scenes, and we are tasked with much responsibility. Karma lords, under no circumstance, keep secrets or engage in any conspiracy, nor do we conjoin or ingratiate ourselves with any secret society or godhead, be it transparent, cloak and dagger, or otherwise. If a karma lord is found remiss in duty, and culpable in any such malfeasance, the chief docent ombudsman will resolve the matter in a manner that ascribes as closely as possible to the principles and tenets delineated within the rubric of this very code.

Karma Law 1. Punishment must equal the crime

Punishment must never, under any circumstances, exceed the crime. This is the first and most important rule of all. In terms of karma, punishment is defined as pain. Pain can be physical, psychological, or a combination of both. Pain can be experienced in thousands of myriad ways. When pain exceeds the crime, it is considered draconian, and therefore considered revenge.

Karma Law 2. Reward must equal the virtuous deed

Reward must never, under any circumstances, exceed the virtuous or benevolent deed. In terms of karma, reward is defined as pleasure or relief. Pleasure can be physical, psychological, or a combination of both. Pleasure can be experienced in thousands of myriad ways. When pleasure exceeds the virtuous deed from which it is based, it is considered superfluous, and therefore hedonism.

Karma Law 3. Karma follows Newton's Third Law of Motion and the First Law of Thermodynamics (Conservation of Energy)

Karma follows Newton's Third Law of Motion (every action has equal and opposite reaction). It also follows the first law of thermodynamics (energy cannot be created or destroyed but can change forms). Karma sees to it that if a person inflicts pain on others, he or she will experience the very same amount of pain in return, in one way, shape, or another, at a certain time and place. Similarly, if a person bestows kindness to others, he or she will experience the very same amount of pleasure in return, in one way, shape, or another, at a certain time and place. This much is inexorable. However, a person will never know when or where this consequence will occur. To humans, such foresight is indeterminate. Only karma lords and the Krystal Kube are privy to such information. But no crime is deemed irrevocable. There is always recourse, and ample room for atonement, absolution, and redemption.

The world is energy. Human bodies are merely carriers and vessels of this energy. Behind every human behavior is a motivation, a purpose or intention to help or harm (self or others). Energy with a (+) valence can be called "Pleasure" and energy with a (-) valence can be called "Pain."

Pain and pleasure can come from different sources. Pain could be the result of doing a sacrifice for someone else (as it leaves you in a one down position). Pain can also be the result of being mistreated by someone (or some thing). And thirdly, pain can also be a punishment from the karma lords for a past transgression. It could also be a combination of any of the above. The same can be said for pleasure.

"An eye for an eye and a tooth for a tooth." Karma is consistent with this adage, but only up to a point. While karma is all about "crimes equaling punishments," or "good deeds equaling rewards," the nature of these consequence might take on disparate forms. So while it might seem proper or prudent, to lose an eye as punishment for poking one out, or losing a tooth as punishment for pulling one out, karma might use other avenues of atonement in the spirit of "different but equal."

But the fact remains, the punishment must equal the crime in terms of intensity, duration, or frequency. So there might be some cases where a person loses a tooth for poking out someone's eye, or loses an eye for pulling out someone's tooth. This also illustrates "equal but different."

Clause A: Karma Points

In addition to karma being conceptualized in terms of pain (-) and pleasure (+), karma can also be conceptualized in terms of accruing "karma points" (see appendix D). Accruing positive karma (i.e. karma points) is not the same as accruing positive energy (pleasure) and accruing negative karma (i.e. negative karma points) is not the same as accruing negative energy (pain). In fact, it is often the very opposite. Doing favors for others often involves pain and sacrifice, but it also accrues "positive karma." Similarly, hurting others might have a certain pleasurable payoff, but it also accrues "negative karma." One "karma point" is the equivalent of one meta gram of positive or negative karma.

Clause B: Karmatic Leakage

Karmatic Leackage occurs when a person's actions affect others in a non-symbiotic fashion outside of their closed karmatic system or microcosm. This can occur through the media, global communication, or through the various art forms. This can even happen posthumously, where a certain *piece de resistance* continues to have a long lasting influence on people's minds and beliefs throughout perpetuity, well after the artist has deceased (and yet dispersing energy of pain or pleasure posthumously).

Clause C: Karma buildup

The harboring of resentments is a capstone example of how "karma buildup" works. When a person believes themselves to have been treated unfairly, those resentments build up and are tucked away as potential energy (like a dammed river or a quiver of poison arrows). At a later time, the person may reach a breaking point where all the negative energy is released back into the world as kinetic energy. This happens so as to re-establish balance in the world. Humans often do not treat others the way they want to be treated (i.e. Golden Rule). Instead, they often treat others the way they have been treated in the past. Karma buildup is not limited to a person's lifetime. Karma buildup can be passed from generation to generation as well. The Eighty/ Twenty Principle is a special example of the kinds of conditions that can promote karma buildup, jealousy, and anger.

Karmatic Buildup can also be conceptualized in regards to how many "karma points" a person has accrued. Doing favors or making sacrifices for others accrues a surplus of positive karma and doing acts of vice accrues a surplus of negative karma. The amount of points accrued is contingent on the size of the sacrifice or act of depravity.

Clause D: Karma is often a zero sum game

In many ways, karma is a zero sum game. There can be no pleasure without pain, and there can be no pain without pleasure. Even the "pleasure" one receives from consuming foods on an empty stomach cannot occur without the accompanying uncomfortable or painful pangs of hunger that occur simultaneously. As such, much of what we call "pleasure" might be more accurately described as "relief." In addition, if person A harms person B, person A generally gains while person B generally loses. And if person A helps person B, person A might lose (via sacrifice) while person B gains.

Karma lords have created the laws of nature in such a way that the pain/discomfort (-) spread across the world equals the amount of pleasure/relief (+) across time and space. It might seem prudent that the average person experiences an equal amount of pain and pleasure in their life. However, this is not always the case, depending on the competency of the karma lords, how much positive or negative karma a person accrues, the distribution of pain or pleasure in the microcosm, or other factors). The fact that karma is often a zero sum gain is further illustrated by karmatic differential.

Clause E: Karmatic differential

When person A steals from person B, person A gains (+1) while person B loses (-1). As such, the karmatic differential (absolute value) is actually 2 (not 1). Similarly, when person A does a "good deed" for person B, person A takes a temporary loss (-1) while person B gains (+1) for a karmatic differential of 2. This is similar to the game of Othello or Reversi, when player one captures a disc from player two. Even though player one only technically acquired one disc, it's actually a (+2) gain in because player one not only gained one (+1), but player two also lost one (-1). Not only does this illustrate the concept of how karma is a zero sum game, but it also further illustrates how karma buildup works.

Karma Law 4: Karma adheres to the pleasure principle

Humans are bound by the Pleasure Principle. They seek pleasure, relief, or comfort whilst avoiding pain or discomfort. This pleasure might be intrinsically or extrinsically motivated. Even in cases where humans might believe they are being altruistic, a critical eye can ascertain hidden motivations in such illusions of piety. After all, even acts such as these are yet rife with a great many heavenly (and hedonistic) rewards.

When a person has a goal or trajectory to go from Point A to Point B but their path is obstructed, this is called "blocking." Some of these blocks are external (people, places, or things) and some of these blocks are internal (thoughts, feelings, personality factors, limitations, etc.). Karma police often use "blocking" as a way of punishing or rewarding human behaviors or establishing balance. Humans refer to this as life throwing "curve balls." They are not mere coincidences.

Clause B: Karma and sacrifice (also known as "favors")

Accruing positive karma is marked by "sacrifice" or doing "favors." And this is how positive energy is spread out into the world. When a person makes a symbiotic sacrifice or does a favor for someone else to help them physically or mentally, as evidenced by some sort of pain or discomfort on his or her behalf, the score is tallied and the person is rewarded with positive karma. The larger the sacrifice, the larger the potential karmatic reward at some future place and time (see Appendix D for adjusted "karma points" associated with varying favors or sacrifices). Experiencing pain is a sacrifice and accrues positive karma. Not all sacrifices necessarily benefit others, at least not directly. At any given time, a person may have accrued a surplus of negative energy (pain) or positive karma (via sacrifice).

If this sacrifice happens by accident, however, and it wasn't a person's intent to help another person, the karma reward may be lessened due to the half-hearted motivation of said Samaritan. For example, if a person loses their stash of money and a poverty stricken person finds it, this does not count as an intentional sacrifice or act of charity (but rather an accidental one). It's also possible that losing the money was actually a punishment for one of his or her past transgressions. However, the person still suffered a financial setback, and karma lords will acknowledge it as such, and try their best to level out the playing field.

Clause C: Karma and greed

Accruing negative karma is marked by "greed" or pleasure seeking. Insofar that a sacrifice is "denying something from oneself for the benefit of others," greed can be defined as "acquiring something for yourself at the expense of someone else." This is how negative energy is put out into the world. When a person's behaviors are marked by greed, the person is "cursed" with negative karma. The larger the act of greed, the larger the potential karmatic repercussion at some point in time (see Appendix D for adjusted "karma points" associated with varying acts of greed, violence, or hedonism). Experiencing pleasure accrues negative karma, even if it's not directly at the expense of others. At any given time, a person may have accrued a surplus of positive energy (pleasure) or negative karma (via greed or violence). If this act of greed was by accident, however, and it wasn't a person's intent to hurt someone, the karmatic repercussion may be lessened. For example, if a person was hastily cutting onions and accidentally cut someone with the knife, this does not count as a willful act of greed with intent to hurt (however, karma might punish acts of negligence to a lesser degree, especially in cases where a person is careless or absent-minded).The extent of one's ignoble acts of indiscretion are heavily determined by one's level of greed or intent to injure or impugn.

Clause D: Karma and the appetites

For the purposes of survival, the body has been "gifted" with various natural appetites or drives (such as hunger, sexuality, scratching an itch, urge to sneeze, urination, taking the hand away from a hot pan, etc.). In these cases, karma lords don't have to disrupt or intervene all that much, as voracious persons will naturally seek to satiate these survival-related urges (of course, resources are limited). Often the pain or discomfort associated with the hunger is matched in full by the relief that follows satiation.

Intentionally and purposefully staving off these appetites through self-denial or self-injurious behavior can boost one's own karma (as these are sacrifices), at least temporarily, until these drives once again become satiated. For example, the act of fasting is not only painful for the person doing it, but it can also allow more food or resources to be available for others, boosting one's karma even further. If these self-injurious or self-denying acts have little effect on others, or are done merely for one's own sense of moral rectitude or perceived heavenly gain, their overall or long lasting effects on karma might be more negligible.

Clause E: The miser's misery

Who is more "selfish," the self-denying miser hoarding wealth, or the self-serving hedonist who spends money lavishly? It might be tempting to say the latter, but there are finer details to be considered. On the one hand, the miser is practicing "self-denial" and not partaking in the pleasures of the flesh. However, they are also receiving the peace of mind of knowing that their rainy day fund is plentiful. Not only that, but their wealth is tucked away untouched when it could be used to support the economy (or even feed the poor).

On the other hand, however, the self-indulgent and materialistic hedonist is enjoying the pleasures of the flesh through the modus operandi of "carpe diem." Still, this is further mitigated by the fact that they are also making financial sacrifices, supporting the economy, and contributing to other people's livelihoods (which is laudable). So which of these two kinds of people deserve more or less positive or negative Karma? In the eyes of the karma lords, all things being equal, their karma levels would more or less be considered equal.

Clause F: Multiple pleasure and pain receptors

Pleasure and pain can be felt simultaneously, physically and mentally. To wit, a person might receive a back massage while getting an injection in their arm. But how many emotions can someone actually feel at one time? Humans often assume only one, as in "how are you feeling?," when given an archaic and simple list of "rhyming" emotions to choose from (such as mad, sad, or glad). But again, in truth, things are more complex. Not only are there dozens of synonyms for many emotions, with subtle nuances between them, but there is also the complex matter of augmentation. It is entirely possible to feel "happy" about event A but "sad" about event B, with their additive effects either canceling each other out, or being felt simultaneously (such as a person simultaneously feeling "excited" about their upcoming wedding day but also feeling sad about the funeral they just attended).

Clause G: Self-serving altruism

Even in the dog-eat-dog world of natural selection, it often behooves one to"treat others kindly," as this will increase the chances that they will return the favor in the future. This phenomena can aptly be called "self-serving altruism," although such a term might be construed as an oxymoron. A person choosing to save a family member vs. a stranger from a burning building is further illustration of this phenomena.

Karma Law 5. Karma can take the form of "mirrored consequences"

While the consequence of any behavior must never exceed the crime or virtuous deed, the nature of that consequence can vary. Energy cannot be created or destroyed, but it can change forms (as per conservation of energy). The same holds true for karma and the distribution of pain or pleasure. To wit, suppose a person should violently accost someone in the market square. If the assailant was required to be subjected to an identical punishment (i.e. be likewise unexpectedly accosted in the streets), this would be called a mirrored consequence as it is exact in every possible way. This would constitute the most literal interpretation of "an eye for an eye." If deviation from a "mirrored consequence" is necessary, ethical karma lords "do the math" and see to it that any deviation is mitigated in full, so that the punishments or rewards are "different but equal."

Karma Law 6. Karma can take the form of "different but equal"

Karma recognizes that people can be different but equal, as long as the differences are equal in usefulness, ability, or bartering power. Karma also recognizes that pain and pleasure can be different but equal as well. This is a major aspect of karma.

Pain and pleasure are measured along four dimensions: Frequency, Duration, Latency, and Intensity. The punishment can change forms and still equal the crime (equal but different). However, if one of these variables goes up, another must go down (to maintain conservation of pain/pleasure). This is akin to when humans use a jack to lift a car. While the jack makes the task physically easier, it is mitigated by the fact that it takes much longer to accomplish the task. In terms of crime and punishment, this is akin to being in prison for a long duration of time for a crime that may have only lasted several seconds or minutes.

Note: Matters get more complex when "compounded karma" occurs. This is when a person receives two smaller consequences at two different times to make up for one larger act of virtue or indiscretion that occurred previously (such as slipping on the ice twice on two different days as comeuppance for stealing from the tip jar only once).

Clause A: Tabula rasa and genetic codes

Infants are in many ways blank slates, but they each also have a genetic map which creates disparity in fairness from the onset. Humans each have a different"set of trials" as soon as they leave the womb. Karma lords are careful to ensure that these DNA programs are "different but equal." Like the "character sheets" in a human role-playing game, where characters have pros and cons, people are often different, but equal. Some might have a predisposition to heart disease, and others diabetes. Still others might have a propensity for mental illness. The trials, trifles, and tribulations that befall each person will vary considerably.

Clause B: The Distribution of talents

Many talents are partly genetic. This is why they are often called "gifts" (as a person is quite literally gifted with ability as if a blessing bestowed, or at least the potential of ability, made manifest through further grooming and refinement). With that said, there is often also the component of hard work that is equally necessary, but not sufficient, to channel and refine the potential energy until it becomes kinetic. And in life, talents are treated as if currency, and can be further used to generate revenue, or fame and fortune. Some people's talents remain untapped, due to either lack of discovery or lack of opportunity to groom and refine them. As such, there are times when a person's seemingly effortless talent can unsettle nerves and cause jealousy in others. Karma lords see to it that everyone has at least one talent, and some people more, depending on circumstances.

Those esteemed as "renaissance persons" are particularly apt to raise the ire of irascible underachievers in their midst. However, insofar that the latter must travel a more difficult road, in lieu of having fewer talents with which to impress, this disparity must be mitigated in other ways (the former may have to endure a mental illness, or perhaps experience a more painful death to create a more level playing field).

Clause C: Distribution of attractiveness

Appearances, like talents, often carry a component of genetic endowment. These too may be partly gifted and partly refined through work and grooming. And like talents, appearances can be used as a form of existential currency in which to barter assets in a mate selection milieu. This can bolster resentment with less attractive humans, as evidenced by human sentiments such as: "Don't hate me because I am beautiful." Karma police must also be cognizant of not falling into the trap of what humans call the Halo Effect, and not display favoritism towards people who are more (or less) attractive. Karma police try their best to be fair when doling out bargaining chips and biological assets, and when this is not feasible, make sure this is mitigated through the "different but equal" rule. Humans who are deemed "unattractive" are considered by some to be a "regal sort."

Clause D: Tonics and tinctures

Medicine is a special example of how such energy can change forms. In general, if a medicine enhances pleasure in a certain domain, this boost in pleasure might be mitigated by an equal amount of pain in a different domain. Usually this is done through the medication's side effects. For example, if a soothing anodyne should play a part in reducing one's paranoia, it may be mitigated through a flux of rapid weight gain.

Clause E: The element of risk

If the primitive systems of law and order among humans were perfect, every human crime would be met with a certain punishment. And every act of virtue would be met with an appropriate reward. In the world of humans, this is not always feasible or realistic. To mitigate this "uncertainty of being caught," humans have taken upon themselves to "double down" on the *threat* of punishment, going above and beyond what would normally be appropriate to compensate for the fact that you might not get caught at all. Their logic is as follows: *If you get caught, your punishment will be extreme. However, if you don't get caught, there will be no punishment whatsoever.* Karma lords need not fret about this primitive risk analyses. They know when, where, and to what extent every act of transgression or act of virtue will occur. As such, their systems of law and order are much more robust, consistent, and complex.

Karma Law 7. Karma lords must remain anonymous at all times

Karma lords must maintain anonymity at all times. The purpose of this "subterfuge" is not to engage "behind the scenes" in any clandestine or cloak and dagger skullduggery. The truth is laid bare to rest, that if it should be too transparent for a person to connect the dots between cause and effect, or the very existence of karma or the karma lords, the negative consequences for the world would surely be dire and iatrogenic. The genuineness of human motivation would surly be called into question, as the human race becomes reduced to obsequious sycophants, aiming to please karma lords at each and every turn (a phenomenon they will later call "Hawthorne effect" or "impression management"). A person's belief in karma must remain a courtship based on faith, and faith alone.

Karma Law 8. Karma is more about restorative justice than learning

While karma deals with consequences, a person actually learning a lesson from their acts of vice or virtue may or may not occur. According to human learning and deterrence theory, a consequence must be delivered with *celerity, seriousness,* and *certainty* to effectively modify behavior. But this is not the way karma necessarily works. While the consequences delivered by karma lords are always certain and delivered with appropriate seriousness, celerity is a different matter entirely. Karma may not restore justice for many years after the original act of vice or virtue transpired. As such, karma does not always follow the rules of learning theory. And since karma lords must protect their anonymity and remain incognito, it is prudent that the rules of celerity, seriousness, and certainty need not apply.

Clause A: Sometimes good things happen to "bad people" and bad things happen to "good people"

Suppose that person A harms Person B, and being touched by violence, Person B harms Person C, and being touched by violence, Person C harms Person D. By the time the negative energy comes back full circle and reaches Person A, where it's actually deserved, he or she would scarcely be in a position to connect the "original sin" with such a late-delivered consequence. So naturally, "learning" may not actually occur. When the wrong target (person D) appears to be punished for the sins of person A, this is called karmatic displacement. Ethical karma lords do their best to keep karmatic displacement at a minimum. But there are times when karmatic displacement cannot be avoided, or even when it is intentional.

Karma Law 9. A gory death doesn't necessarily mean a painful one

The actual pain and pleasure of an event can never be assumed based on appearances, availability, or representation alone. A gory death does not necessarily equate to a painful one. In some cases, a gory death may have been less painful than a paper cut. And sometimes watching a gory death is more painful than experiencing it yourself. And the psychological effects that such death may have on family members may be exponentially more palpable than the aggregate physical and psychological pain suffered by the person in the violent and gory death in and of itself. And in similar accord, an agonizing slow natural death from infirmity may indeed be much more painful than criminal acts such as murder, despite the excesses of emotion provoked by the latter. Faceless enemies such as "dying of old age" do not tend to provoke the ire of irascible humans. Karma lords see little difference between the two (outside of how much pain is involved with each).

Karma Law 10. Karma lords can disrupt the natural order of things

While the universe and the laws of nature may appear to be self-operating as if clockwork or a perpetual motion machine, this does not imply that the lords of nature take a passive role. And while the laws of nature may promote fairness in many ways, nature, by its very nature, can be bestial and brutal. The laws of nature, particularly those related to "survival of the fittest," are not based on fairness. Nature selects based on advantage. Those with an advantage win, and those without such an advantage lose. This is why disruption is of paramount importance, and ultimately why karma lords are most necessary in the first place.

In this accord, karma lords oversee and make sure that daily events in people's lives promote balance of pain and pleasure. Good deeds (that promote welfare and pleasure for others) are rewarded (by pleasure) and nefarious deeds (that promote pain in others) are punished (through pain).

When the laws of nature are enough to restore balance of the pain and pleasure continuum, this is called natural karma. When karma lords purposely intervene and manipulate events in a person's life to create order and balance, this is called disruption. Disruption often requires additional energy reserves from karma lord as they must "break natural rules" to intervene.

Clause A: Quid pro quo

In a fair trade, where buyer and seller are satisfied, minimal disruption is necessary, as both parties give and take in equal amounts and balance is maintained (+/-). In situations where one party receives too much or gives too much, karma buildup may occur, and disruption may become necessary to level the playing field and maintain balance.

Karma Law 11. Karma lords operate under a least restrictive environment

Karma lords should only interfere when necessary to restore order, fairness, justice in the pain/pleasure continuum. When a karma lords must interfere and use disruption, it must be used as a last resort. A least restrictive environment is critical.

Karma Law 12. Pain and pleasure have meta mass

Pain and pleasure have meta mass. The standard unit of measurement for pain or pleasure is the "meta gram." A meta gram can have a positive or negative valence (depending on whether it is pleasure or pain, respectively). A meta gram of pleasure equates to the feeling of relief one gets from the average sneeze. A mega gram of pain equates to about the feeling of pain one receives from a mosquito bite. When a person complains about the "weight on my shoulders" they are often referring to meta mass.

Karma Law 13. The Golden Rule is not necessarily altruistic

According to the Golden Rule, one should treat others the way they want to be treated. While this sounds laudable in and of itself, it is also illustrative of natural karma (and an example of paying it forward). If you treat others the way you want to be treated, you also increase the likelihood that they will return the favor in your time of need. The Golden Rule is just as much an "investment" as it is an altruistic gesture.

Karma Law 14. Immediate gratification and delayed gratification as equal but different

Humans have been known to make decisions based on perceived

gains, whether financial, emotional, physical, spiritual, sexual, or otherwise. Every human behavior, without exception, is motivated by pursuit of pleasure or avoidance of pain. Spiritual people believe that their good deeds will gain them the treasures of heaven. People that kill others believe killing will enhance their life in some way. People that don't kill believe not killing will enhance their life in some way. As such, human behaviors are often calculated with strategic personal gain in mind, not unlike the strategic moves in chess or Othello. Sometimes these perceived gains might be immediate, and at other times the perceived gains might come much later. But in either case, the motivation of immediate vs. delayed gratification are considered by Karma lords to be equally self-serving, and merely represent varying value systems. Crimes of passion, of course, lack the calculated strategies of premeditated ones, and tend to be based on immediate gratification. Regardless of whether gain is short term or long term, it's a gain nonetheless, and karma police are well aware of this fact when doling out their consequences.

Clause A: The 51/49 Principle and the illusion of free will

Humans are a prideful pack, and will not hesitate to take all the credit they can while seemingly taking the moral high ground. However, when a person conducts a cost analyses and weighs the pros and cons of two undesirable alternatives, this is akin to choosing between "the lesser of two evils." And while on the surface taking such excessive losses might appear to be the stuff of impulse control, temperance, "will power," or self-denial, closer inspection reveals that this is not necessarily the case.

The fact remains, that if Person A traded places with the very person he or she judges, all things being equal, genetic, environmental, and otherwise, the person would have engaged in the exact same thoughts, feelings, and behaviors and essentially lived out the same life. This is due to the forces of determinism, nature, and nurture. Even humans have acknowledged this bias, and have dubbed it the "Restraint Bias." Karma lords understand that everything happens for a reason.

Karma Law 15. A person's pain and suffering (or pleasure) can be partly self-imposed

If a person learns or "associates" an event as being more aversive than it really is, this needs to be accounted for (as expectations or perceptions, whether accurate or not, can increase or decrease the amount of pain or pleasure experienced. This is also known by humans as the Pygmalion Effect. Pain is pain, whether real or imagined. And karma police take this into account when doling out their punishments and rewards.

Clause A. The Spotlight Metaphor

For those with a heightened passion or nervous disposition, anxiety may be akin to a spotlight, shifting its gaze from one fixation to the next, as if the new worry of the day supplants the previous penultimate concern. And for those who carry such passion or dolorous sorrow, the source of anxiety might not actually come from the glistening objects highlighted by the beam as may seem readily apparent. Instead, the anxiety may come from the spotlight itself (and the strength of the beam). And while such suffering may seem needless, it does not go unnoticed by the karma lords. Pain is pain, and pleasure is pleasure.

Karma Law 16. Quantifying disappointment

Expecting life to be fair or expecting life to turn out in a certain way can set one up for disappointment. And karma lords can "block" one's goals and trajectory at any given moment. The equation for existential disappointment is as follows:

Existential disappointment = Expected outcome/Actual outcome

Karma Law 17. Disruption can occur on a large scale (although seldom ethical)

When a significant number of people are affected by a "major event," this is called "large scale disruption." For example, the Black Plague of the middle ages, WW2, or natural disasters are examples of events that will affect swaths of people. Ethical karma lords understand that humans should never be punished en masse due to the actions of a dissolute few. But there are times when it cannot be avoided. The reasons for using "large scale disruption" might include:

Population Control- Karma police keep an eye on supply and demand of the human race, including allocation of resources. All diseases in general are partly used as a means of population control, be it pneumonia, cancer, or heart disease (or the hundreds of others). Occasionally there might even be a "new disease" introduced to the world. This helps control the population at large. Extreme examples, such as the "Black Plague," usually indicate that a karma lord was remiss in their duties, when a much less heavy-handed approach could have been warranted.

Anonymity- While rare, large scale disruption is also a device to ensure anonymity of karma lords, because when these events happen, people start to question the very idea of a god or even basic fairness in the world. Humans start to ask, "If there is a God, why would he allow such a thing?" Or "Why do bad things happen to good people?" And this kind of questioning is essentially what karma lords want to hear, at least intermittently, as it shows that their existence is not yet known, and is based on a courtship of faith alone. But this can usually be accomplished without using large scale disruption.

Karma buildup- When negative karma buildup accrues over time, a current zeitgeist might have an overabundance of vice points that need to be purged to establish equilibrium again. This could result in mass disruption, such as a typhoon, hurricane, or other natural disaster. Many of the victims that die in these situations may have had nothing to do with the vices or transgressions that led to the karma buildup in the first place (i.e. karma displacement). Even still, balance of energy must be maintained. Ethical karma lords watch for karma buildup and try to prevent it from becoming too extreme so large scale disruption can be avoided.

Revenge- Unethical karma lords could theoretically abuse large scale disruption in a highly unethical manner. When a karma police is discovered to have engaged in large scale disruption for personal reasons, they will be excommunicated forthwith from the congregate of karma lords and punished accordingly at the behest of Docent Randii. Revenge might be endemic to human justice systems, but it is never acceptable for karma lords.

Large scale disruption can also take the form of benevolence, such as creating the conditions for a large scale relief effort of disaster aid, as when a flood, Earthquake, or hurricane takes out a major metropolitan residential landscape. Another example would be the "sudden discovery" of a cure for a disease (in fact, often-times karma lords create both the disease and the cure).

Karma Law 18. Nothing is random

Everything happens for a reason. Nothing is random. Nothing is inconsequential. Anytime something displeasing happens, it is often a punishment for something ignoble you have done in the past. Likewise, anytime something pleasing happens, it is often a reward for something noble you have done in the past. There are no coincidences, and everything has meaning. The sidewalk you tripped over yesterday may be your comeuppance for budding in line at the market seven years ago. The day your name is drawn in a raffle may be your reward for walking an old man across the street last week. And as always, it is preferable that people are not able to "connect the dots" and trace consequences back to their original actions. Skilled karma lords must ensure that the events in people's lives appear random at all times. And while it is laudable that humans believe that all things may happen for a reason, this truth cannot, and must not, be too easy to decipher. The belief in karma lords, order, and connection between events must be a "leap of faith."

Clause A: The economy

The ups and downs of the economy are a prime milieu for the ebb, flow, and equilibrium of karma to manifest. After all, certain aspects of the stock market and karma can often operate as a "zero sum game." While the natural laws of "supply" and "demand" certainly apply, karma lords can also alter these laws to tip the balance in a certain direction (such as whether a stock will go up or down). So while 75% of the variability of the stock market might be explained by "natural karma," the other 25% is attributable to "disruption" and the pull and push of karma lords, as they punish vice and reward virtue.

Clause B: Animals are integral to karma systems

All animals, including humans, are part of the animal kingdom, the food chain, and the ebb and flow of survival, competition, and mate selection. It is also true that animals can experience pain and pleasure (perhaps some more than others, taking into account the tenets of anthropomorphism). As such, karma applies to animals as well as humans (while taking into account an animal's more limited cognitive faculties). When karma does not apply to animals directly, animals can serve as conduits in which to transmit karma to and from humans. For example, if Person A abuses a puppy, leading to karmatic buildup in the canine, the dog might bite the mailman (Person B) years later for to re-establish karmatic balance (even if it was initially Person A's fault for hurting the dog, an example of karma displacement). Humans, like other animals, are part of the food chain and rely on animals for food. However, the pain experienced by animals during this process has everything to do with karma, and humans that inflict pain on animals can expect equal reprisal. And the same can be said for treating animals with benevolence.

Clause C: Plants usually play an auxiliary role when it comes to karma

Humans often rely on vegetation as a source of food for survival. And it is understood that plants don't feel pain or pleasure. Ipso facto, the rules of karma generally don't apply to plants, except in cases where plants are used as vehicles, conduits, or catalysts to ensure pain and pleasure equilibrium in the human or animal conditions. In this sense, plants are similar to the presence (or lack thereof) of inanimate objects or furnishings in the environment. For example, a person's crashing into a tree might be comeuppance for a very serious malfeasance the person caused. Plants also provide livelihood, pleasure, food, and pastime for a great many people.

Clause D: The weather matter

Contrary to appearances, weather is not random. Karma lords control the weather with a true intent and purpose. Every day's weather occurs for a reason. It's one of the myriad ways karma lords balance out the pain vs. pleasure continuum in the world. And while a dreary day may prove troublesome for some, the more astute observers of the heavens will not let a trifle of precipitation to "rain on their parade," even if it does do exactly that.

Karma Law 19. Karmatic law is not the same as human law

The rubric delineated by society's established systems of law and order are "artificially induced" systems of karma. While in theory they may claim to create punishments that befit the crime, these systems are excessively primitive and doctrinaire, and ultimately distractions to the real work of karma lords (and very seldom use rewards in addition to punishments). These primitive codes are by no means a panacea to the ills of the human world. And while they often bandy about terms like "rehabilitation," this does not always occur, and the persons that leave such places may even end in a lesser state than before going in.

When vociferous peoples take karma into their own hands, it affects karma certainly, but karma lords must work around and circumvent their actions to maintain a true balance of pain and pleasure from behind the scenes. And human beings, being emotional and tempestuous creatures, are not highly adept at ensuring that punishments befit the crime. Either humans are lacking in mathematical ability, or they are a vengeful lot indeed, oblivious to their very own biases. And seldom do they take into account the "Who would you rather be dilemma." To their chagrin, the people that create factitious legal systems don't control karma. Karma controls the legal system.

Clause A: The governments of mankind

Governments are only as effective as the people that sustain them. And when humans create an abundance of chaos, death, and disarray, through egregious error, even karma lords have a difficult time putting things right and re-establishing balance in the world. And government and politics are rife with hidden (or quite transparent) agendas. And to complicate matters still further, politics is not always as linear as it is portrayed, using primitive "left" vs. "right" polarities.

Karma Law 20. Victims of suicide are often treated as if victims of murder.

Suicide, the Black Dog's Oblivion, is a most tragic state of affairs. In the eyes of the karma lords, a victim of suicide is usually treated as a victim of murder. Every player who "played a hand" in such oblivion will be held accountable to the extent and ratio of their respective culpability. These negative karma points (with a negative valence) will be discerned and allocated only through the most thorough regression analyses and statistical methods, devoid of any and all emotional reasoning. If five persons played a part in a person's suicide, each of them will receive a partial punishment for their role in the tragedy. Adjustments must also be made to accommodate negligence, as lesser punishments will also depend on the actual level of one's nefarious intent.

Karma Law 21. Karma seeks equilibrium

When conservation of energy occurs naturally on its own accord, due to natural karma, additional disruption by karma lords may not always be necessary. The laws of equilibrium may create balance more naturally. When karma buildup occurs, the excessive karma has to go someplace. For example, when a person has lots of pain (negative energy) built up inside it can be a powder keg and accident waiting to happen, as the person may seek to put the negative energy back out into the world. However, the same can be said when a person has lots of positive energy built up inside. In these latter cases, a person may be looking to "spread the wealth" and put positive energy back into the world or to "pay it forward." In general, karma seeks homogeneity and is attracted to karma of the opposite valence. Negative (-) energy is drawn towards positive (+) energy (such as finding relief or satiating an urge or craving). Another example is the feuding that often exists between the haves and the have-nots.

Karma Law 22. Karma lords utilize statistical methods like regression analyses on a global scale involving thousands and millions of variables

In terms of karma, there are thousands of ways pain and pleasure can be experienced in this world. And there are just as many ways a person can die. Karma lords must understand regression analyses and the role of mediating vs. moderating variables. A person can seldom be sure of the time, manner, or place of their existential demise. While on average a person's age may have some predictive merit, it is also true that even infants lives can be truncated, as evidenced by their diminutive graves marked by marble lambs. And there are indeed many parents that outlive their offspring. And while the mathematical algorithm's of life insurance companies will have predictive value in relation to age of death, the existential algorithms used by karma lords show a level of sophistication that is exponentially greater, and show far more detail than merely one's age of demise, but also: form of death, location of death, and the amount of pain associated with it.

Clause A: Moderating variables

In the purview of "statistics," a moderating variable is one that has predictive value and affects the strength of the relationship between two correlated variables. While moderating variables have predictive value, they do not explain why two variables are related, and cannot be said to be "causal factors." For example, suppose it was found that having green eyes was a predictor for higher crime rates for certain crimes. While green eyes and crime may be correlated, it still doesn't explain *why* green eyes are predictive of crime. Ethical karma police are aware of this distinction, and fully understand that "correlation does not mean causation."

Clause B: Mediating variables

In the purview of "statistics," a mediating variable helps explain why two variables are related. Mediating variables are the processes and mechanisms that explain why certain relationships hold true. As such, mediating variables could be said to be "causal factors." Going back to the hypothetical example, having green eyes would be a predictor, but not a causal factor, for crime. However, the causal factor might be something else, such as an increased likelihood of people with green eyes to be in abject poverty (for whatever reason that might be). In this case, it is not having green eyes that causes crime, but rather poverty (as people tend to become more desperate and willing to commit crimes when survival is at stake).

Karma Law 23. Karma is a numbers game

Karma is, in part, a "numbers game." Sometimes humans don't see much difference between a killer who kills one person compared to one that kills two (and writes them both off as "murderers"). And some killers claim "it gets easier" after your first kill. But according to karma, two murders constitute twice as many "vice points" as a single murder. And ten murders are twice as many "vice points" as five. Similarly, saving ten people from a burning building constitutes twice as many "virtue points" as saving five. This is akin to how ten degrees Kelvin is exactly twice as "warm" as five degrees Kelvin (due to absolute zero).

Ethical karma police are sure to "do the math" when doling out their rewards and punishments.

Karma Law 24. Hard work is necessary, but seldom sufficient, to a person's success

One's ability to navigate the constraints of this world and find success (however defined) depends on one's degrees of freedom. There are many factors that can influence success: availability of resources, assets, psychological factors, genetic predisposition, milieu, learning history, peer influence, aberration, socioeconomic factors, personality factors, blind luck, nepotism, social determinants of behavior, classification systems, and biological disparities. For all practical purposes, "free will" is an illusion, as thoughts, feelings, and behaviors do not occur in a vacuum. There are choices, to be sure, but these "choices" are influenced by myriad forces. Ergo, a "choice" is just as much an "effect" as it is a "cause." All things happen for a reason. Even a puppet can make a decision. But who pulls the strings?

Karma Law 25. There are no "accidents"

"Accidents" can lead to the same disastrous consequences (or happy returns) as intentional acts of vice or virtue. This can apply to negligent acts as well as unanticipated charity. With karma, there are no "accidents" per se. Everything happens for a reason. And sometimes these "accidents" are blessings in disguise (or curses in disguise). Accidents can send unintended ripples of negative (or positive) energy out into the world. Karma police may not punish or reward accidental acts as heavily as the intentional variety (and balance may be restored through natural karma or disruption). Karma lords may also show less flexibility for accidents that are more careless, reckless, or irresponsible in nature. However, if a person is negligent or accident-prone towards others, they can also expect others to act in kind (if others are involved in your accidents, you may be involved in theirs). Often-times those who commit negligent acts feel guilty about what they have done, and these misgivings alone will often atone for what they have done. Just as with crime, punishment must never exceed the accident (and the same goes for reward).

Karma Law 26: Karma acknowledges subjective and objective phenomena

Karma has an objective element. In general, all people have the same *categories* of needs (as per Maslow's Hierarchy of Needs). However, there may be individual differences as to how these categories of needs will be met. So while food is a human need, the type of food enjoyed can vary widely in various various peoples (or across animal species). And this is where objectivity ends and subjectivity begins.

Pain and pleasure are, at least in part, subjective. One person's mountain might be another person's mole hill. Measuring a person's happiness with objective or external measures alone is tantamount to sophistry and tunnel vision (for example, using a financial yardstick to measure happiness). It is said that humans start out as Tabula Rasas, and as experiences become etched onto these "blank slates," divergence inevitably occurs as people live out different pathways of existence. Personality, then, is the reflection of one's aggregate sum of all of life's experiences.

A dollar may have an objective value of 100 cents. However, the value of a dollar varies depending on how wealthy a person is. A destitute person donating a dollar to a charity is making a larger sacrifice than if a wealthy person did the same. Even humans have tried to acknowledge the subjective element in certain cases, such as by proffering stiffer traffic fines to wealthier persons (so the punishment is more fair across class lines).

Some spiritual humans claim that a person will not be given more stress than they can handle. So why do some people seem to have a harder life than others? And why do some have more stress or hardship than others (objectively) but on a subjective level are just as contented? Karma acknowledges the resiliency factor. Those that suffer more hardships than others are often "better equipped" to do so (physically or psychologically). For these resolute, sanguine, and stoic Spartans, their hardships are evidence that they are in some ways a regal sort and high ranking in the eyes of karma (and well on their way to becoming a karma lord themselves). A major loss to a regal sort, such as losing a house in a fire, might bring about a similar level of discomfort as the average person going through a more moderate trifle (like having their vehicle stolen). But because the actual level of pain (meta mass) is similar for these two people, karma lords consider it fair, and the claim above would still hold true.

Karma Law 27. Karma relies on the butterfly effect

All karma lords, in the spirit of ethical practice and scope, must become well-versed in the Butterfly Effect. All karma lords must understand how the simplest decision can affect the future in a grandiose manner. All actions have consequences. And all non-actions as well. Complacency is a decision, and the covert act of omission is just as much an action as overt behavior. As such, innocent bystanders are far from innocent, and indeed guilty of complacency. Human beings make millions of decisions every day, not just by what they do, but also by what they do not do. Inaction is not inconsequential. As such, all people are connected. As has been said, "if you are not part of the solution, you are part of the problem."

Clause A. Ironic tragic factors and ironic lucrative factors

The world is not always predictable. As such, it is not just "criminal behaviors" that lead to dire consequences, as might seem logical or assumed. One cannot always predict how an event, no matter how benign, can lead to unexpected consequences. The most innocent of behaviors can still set the stage and the framework for perfect storms or very tragic outcomes. For example, suppose that the owner of the corner market chose to remain open during inclement weather. Further suppose that a patron of that market called in advance to verify that it was indeed open. When learning that they would keep their doors open, he opted to brave the blustery conditions and icy roads to pick up his favorite tea. En route, suppose further that the driver skidded on an ice patch, and was killed. And while the decision to keep the shop open may be far from criminal, it still played a direct and pivotal role in the tragic outcome nonetheless. When an unpredictable and drastic outcome is hinged on a non-criminal or routine behavior, karma lords call this an "ironic tragic factor." Likewise, a seemingly "negative" event could be a blessing in disguise. This would be an "ironic lucrative factor." Ironic tragic or lucrative factors are sometimes arranged by karma police as a means to manipulate rewards and punishments via the butterfly effect.

Karma Law 28. Karma lords rely on the rules of causality

It is considered unethical for karma lords to conduct their experiments on the "Butterfly Effect" on real people, as this would take many lives. Instead, they must make their experiments using the Krystal Kube. This device is capable of producing actual experiments with actual independent variables, actual control vs. treatment groups, random assignment, without the need for quasi experiments. As such, karma lords must be well-versed in the laws of causality and the three conditions that must be met before causality can be established (A and B must co-vary, A must precede B in space and time, and all possible alternate causal factors must be ruled out). Every present effect of a past cause is also the past cause to a future effect.

Karma law 29. Karma generally follows the Law of Large Numbers (or Regression to the Mean)

While nothing is random when it comes to karma, karma lords aim to make it appear that way (most of the time) so that humans will not catch on to their existence. As such, karma lords generally follow the Law of Large Numbers (although in the eyes of karma there is nothing random about it). And while humans consider the "gambler's fallacy" and the "law of averages" to be fallacious, this is not necessarily the case, as karma lords have the capacity to reward or punish gamblers through winning or losing streaks (while still maintaining the illusion of randomness). According to karma, getting heads or tails is not necessarily 50% on a fair coin (as it also depends on a person's accrued positive or negative karma and other factors). Karma lords opt for anonymity, and being too brazen or cavalier with one's disruption and posturings can only draw unnecessary attention to oneself and one's existence. Appearing random and being random are two different things.

Karma Law 30. Fairness is ultimately measured by outcomes, not opportunity

The illustrious human Ben Franklin once said something to the effect: "The U. S. Constitution doesn't guarantee happiness, only the pursuit of it. You have to catch up with it yourself." Karma takes the opposite stance: Karma does not promote equal opportunity, but equal outcomes.

Karma is about pain and pleasure. Therefore, the human experience of "happiness" is more relevant than any situational factors, including any "pursuit." If a wealthy person and a poor person are equally happy, karma views their lives as equally fair, generally speaking.

— —

APPENDIX B
A CODE OF KARMATIC JURISPRUDENCE

Tier 2 and the Province of Reincarnation (An Incinerator and the Cabinet of Four)

Karma Law 31. Karma rule follows a two-tier chain of command

When the laws of nature or the thirty laws of karma alone are not sufficient to create fairness, the matter next moves on to the karma lords delegated as An Incinerator and his or her Cabinet of Four (Tier 2). As the lord of rebirth, An Incinerator can disrupt the natural order of things through the use of reincarnation. In certain cases, a person who accumulates an over-abundance of vice or virtue points may need a restorative justice that is only feasible by being reborn as someone else.

Karma Law 32. Scrubbing can be used to erase past memories

When humans (or occasionally animals) are reborn, they maintain no memory of their previous lives. The erasing of memories is called "scrubbing." All erased memories must be saved and stored in the Krystal Kube for future reference (where they can be retrieved by the deceased at a later time). By living life as two people, preferably male and female, one should have enough existential wisdom to tease out the role that nature, nurture, free will, and determinism have had on the psyche. One personality is context to the other. Scrubbing is no small feat. Karma lords must be careful to "move the memory" to the memory banks of the Krystal Kube, without erasing it or leaving any remnants. If they are haphazard in their scrubbing, the memories may be lost altogether. However, if they don't scrub quite enough, some residual memories of the past self may be left intact (leaving a threat to anonymity). Ethical and competent karma lords know just how to strike the perfect balance between the two extremes.

Karma Law 33. Reincarnation is reserved for special circumstances

Clause A: Habeaus Corpus

False accusation or false imprisonment are prime examples of situations where reincarnation may be deemed appropriate. If a person spends thirty years in prison, and is eventually exculpated, the person(s) who put him or her there must face the very same consequence, in a reincarnated afterlife. This will atone for their egregious ways, even if they have no memory of their previous life.

Clause B: Philanthropy

There are also cases where a person might go "above and beyond" the call of duty when it comes to helping others through their acts of charity or favors. In these cases, a person may be granted a "new lease on life" to compensate for the extent of their sacrifice.

Karma Law 34. Reincarnation is not temporally contiguous

When a person is reborn, it doesn't necessarily happen the very second a person dies. If this were to be the case, it would almost certainly blow the cover of karma lords. This rebirth may happen a day later, a year later, or even a hundred. Between the death of life 1 and life 2 the person is oblivious to the world, and senses no passing of time. It is as if the person never existed.

Karma Law 35. Reincarnation can place people into different bloodlines

It is no secret that some people are born into a more pleasant, wealthy, or regal bloodline than their more impoverished peers (enjoying the fruits of nepotism). There are two possible reasons for this. One, the person is reincarnated into a more pleasurable state of being, to make up for their losses in their previous life (through Tier 2). Two, the person is simply accruing vice points and negative karma, irrespective of reincarnation (through karma buildup). The reverse would be true for impoverished peoples, or those born into bloodlines of disrepute.

Karma Law 36. Humans can be reborn into animals in certain situations

It is rare, but it will sometime happen, that a person may be reincarnated as an animal. These bold karmatic consequences are usually reserved for very special situations that require very special considerations, and only when other avenues to restore the pain/pleasure continuum have been exhausted. To wit, suppose that a shepherd or farmer was known to be cruel to their herds or livestock. In this situation, a person may be reborn as the animal they once mistreated and abhorred. As they will not carry existential memories of their past lives, they will still carry the scars that come from seeing the world through a tortured living creature's eyes (or perhaps ones that were treated excessively well).

Karma Law 37. Humans are never reborn as plants

Although flora is living tissue, plants have naught to do with experiencing pain and pleasure. Therefore, these are often treated almost as if inanimate objects in the eyes of karma lords. It is considered unethical for a karma lord to turn a human into a plant, almost as much so, as a human being reborn as a rock or a boot.

Karma Law 38. Humans must not retain any residual memories of their previous lives

Karma lords must exercise a great deal of caution that humans never maintain any memories of their previous lives. This could be disastrous, as such supernatural and metaphysical occurrences cast far too much suspicion on the mysterious and spiritual fabric of the universe. If a person retained existential memories of their former self, the very idea of reincarnation would be conspicuous and considered plausible. To maintain anonymity of karma lords, this must never happen, under any circumstances. Scrubbing must be done carefully and completely.

Karma Law 39. Reincarnation is not about learning lessons (at least not yet)

Learning life lessons is laudable, and can save work for karma lords, but this is secondary to Karma's primary mandate, which is fairness, justice, rewards, and punishments. When feasible, it behooves karma lords to have certain persons reborn as their enemies, to "see life from the other side." After all, this is an efficient way to maintain restorative justice while also protecting anonymity. Any lessons learned (or knowledge from former lives) must occur posthumously when decedents are allowed to gaze into the Krystal Kube to see pieces of the truth.

Karma Law 40. People can be reincarnated back in time

Reincarnation isn't always about being "reborn." It can also be about being "first born." A person may be reincarnated as a person in a past and bygone era, to experience life from a different zeitgeist.

APPENDIX C:
A CODE OF KARMATIC JURISPRUDENCE

Tier 3 and the Province of Afterlife (Fate Rifle and the Cabinet of Four)

Karma Law 41: Karma rule follows a three-tier chain of command

When the laws of nature, the laws of the land, and the rules of reincarnation are not sufficient for restorative justice, the matter gets passed to Fate Rifle, the Lord of the Spirit Realms and the Cabinet of 4, couched in Tier 3.

Karma Law 42: Tier 3 is conducive to "Mirrored Consequences"

Unlike the laws of nature or reincarnation, the punishments or rewards doled out in the spirit realms can be matched and re-experienced exactly as felt and experienced within the original events themselves. The laws of the spirit realms can allow a person to experience "an eye for an eye," as it happened, without the need to mitigate the gains or losses through adjusting the frequency, duration, latency, or intensity of the consequence. This is a true "mirrored consequence," and only Tier 3 can create them.

Suppose a person kills two or more people in the visible world. Tier 3 would see to it that he or she would "experience the death" of each person murdered, in the very same manner, and just as many times, as the people they killed. If a person killed fourteen people via the guillotine, he or she would be immured in a special virtual reality prison, and must lose their head, no less, and no more, than fourteen times. And at that time, they would be atoned, as if they never killed anyone at all, and be privy to whichever treasures the afterlife had to offer.

Karma Law 43: Infinity is draconian

As with the laws of nature and reincarnation, the punishments doled out in the afterlife must never exceed the crime. Ipso facto, eternal suffering is considered the epitome of all that is draconian and heavy handed. After a person "pays for" the crime, they are said to be absolved or atoned, and proffered clemency and forgiveness, even in the spirit realms.

Karma Law 44: Humans cannot comprehend the afterlife or the sixth dimension through their existing five senses

After a person has been punished or rewarded in the afterlife, they experience an energy state of equilibrium where pain = pleasure. Since everyone in the spirit realm has the same energy signature, karma is at a constant state of equilibrium. There is no "pain" or "pleasure," karma buildup, leakage, or displacement. As such, there is no cause for jealousy. And while humans might assume this to be cause for boredom, time does not exist in the sixth dimension. There is no "time" to be bored (besides, boredom is a form of pain, which is not experienced in the afterlife). Also, there are additional senses other than the basic five. Humans cannot comprehend the sixth dimension.

Karma Law 45: Karma accounts for "anticipation anxiety"

As used here, latency is taken to mean the anticipation anxiety that occurs as you wait in anxious anticipation of an aversive stimulus to be administered. Sometimes the anticipation of something painful hurts more than the painful event itself. This is a major bottleneck in human crime and punishment systems, as many a person has sat on death row in fear, waiting for the aversive stimulus to be applied. In many cases, such an arrangement might technically constitute a draconian punishment that exceeds the original crime, especially in situations where the victim of the original crime died quickly, unexpectedly, and painlessly (the very three prerequisites of what could be called a "comfortable death"). Tier 3, being conducive to mirrored consequences, can ensure that anyone can experience such "anticipation anxiety" for themselves through virtual reality.

Karma Law 46. Acts of vice or virtue have a "hurt radius" or "help radius"

This is a universal karma law that applies to all three tiers (and will be explained here). When person A hurts person B, intentionally or otherwise, other people also get hurt. This is called a "hurt radius." Similarly, if person A helps person B, intentionally or otherwise, other people get help. This is called a "help radius." In the former, if an inebriated driver kills someone, even if the person killed experienced minimal pain, the latter's family will undoubtedly experience intense psychological duress (essentially being punished for someone else's crime via karma displacement). This can be handled by all tiers in various ways.

Tier 1- the person who committed the crime might take on restitution to the victim or to the victim's family (through man-made systems of law). Or, the karma lords might reward those affected with unexpected and pleasurable situations to make their coping with the loss more tolerable.

Tier 2- the intoxicated driver may be reincarnated into a situation where he or she either loses a family member to drunk driving, or becomes the victim of a drunk driving accident, dying in a similar manner as their victim.

Tier 3- In situations like this, it's plausible that the "perpetrator" (intoxicated driver) might actually suffer exponentially more than the "victim" (who may have been killed quickly, unexpectedly, and painlessly through a "comfortable death"). It is not unusual for the surviving "perpetrator" to wish he or she could trade places with the person they killed. Tier 3 can mitigate the shortcomings of the man-made legal system and ensure that fairness and mirrored consequences are guaranteed in the afterlife. If a person should harm a myriad of personages, such as through genocide, the hurt radius might be too large to mitigate through Tier 1 or Tier 2 (especially when also acknowledging the pain experienced by the surviving family of the deceased).

Karma Law 47. Karma sometimes produces "blessings in disguise" or "curses in disguise"

When doling out consequences, something might seem like a punishment at first, but later end up being a blessing in disguise. It is futile for humans to attempt to make meaning out of world events, and trying to ascertain the true intentions of karma lords might prove dire. It might take some time before a human can truly figure out if a situation is really a "good thing" or a "bad thing." Similarly, humans must also be cautious of "curses in disguise (when something seemingly good happens, but turns into something quite negative). This is where "false hopes" come into play. And competent (and ethical) karma lords are very astute, and they are careful to administer blessings in disguise or curses in disguise at the perfect moment (or perhaps the most inopportune).

Karma Law 48. Karma acknowledges judgment and forgiveness.

This is a universal law and can apply to any of the three tiers. Judging someone can inflict psychological pain, and can accrue negative karma. Holding such judgment towards others could also be painful to the self. If a person judges someone, they can expect to be judged in return. This can happen in various ways and handled by any of the various tiers. The comeuppance might come naturally through Tier 1 ("If you are gonna judge me then I will judge you!"). Or it might be better handled more efficiently by Tier 2 (reincarnation) where a person is reborn with a "Scarlet Letter" and must face their own judgement. If the judgment cannot be handled by the first two tiers, it may be taken to Tier 3, where the person will be endowed with an equal amount of judgment posthumously. The opposite of judgment is forgiveness, and this would be handled similarly (but where the person accrues positive karma instead of negative karma).

Karma Law 49. Karma lords accrue positive or negative karma like humans

Not only is the world energy, but the universe as well. And like humans, karma lords (including cabinet members) accrue karma. When they engage in their employments correctly, they amass positive karma. When karma lords are remiss, they develop negative karma.

If any karma Police or member of their cabinet should develop a pattern of being remiss in their duties, the Docent Randii may call an ad hoc meeting with the gods to determine whether the member is fit for post. Examples of unethical behaviors include but are not limited to: unnecessary or frequent disruption, punishments not befitting the crimes, rewards not befitting the virtuous deeds, ineffective scrubbing, threats to anonymity, inappropriate mass disruption, over-extending hurt radius, taking on matters not appropriate to one's Tier or purview, peeking into the sixth side of the Krystal Kube, showing favoritism towards certain humans, etc. If the level of negative or positive karma is great enough, a karma lord or cabinet member can expect to be punished or rewarded by the gods appropriately (via Tier 4, which only the gods are aware).

Karma Law 50. Invoking "Divine Armistice"

In rare circumstances, an issue might fall in the purview of all three tiers. As a very last resort, due to the sheer magnitude of energy involved, all three karma police might invoke "divine armistice." In these cases, the whole is much greater than the sum of its parts, essentially creating an alternate world-line. By joining their forces, the karma lords of all three tiers join forces to create a parallel universe in the space/time continuum. A person can then become "reborn" into another dimension. This new life has elements of Tier 1 (natural laws just like Earth), Tier 2 (reincarnation), and Tier 3 (afterlife via a new dimension). This new life or "rebirth" can occur either posthumously after the person dies or concurrently with the already existing "self" already in existence in the original world-line. This requires extensive amounts of energy, and should only be used in the most rarest of occasions.

APPENDIX D:
KARMA POINTS

How many "karma points," on average, various "good deeds" and "bad deeds" are worth (data adjusted based on pain/pleasure readings acquired during Project Madcap in Duluth, MN)

Part 1: Neutral karma (0 karma points)

A lie that spares someone's feelings
"Bumming" someone a cigarette
Donating to a charity that supports your livelihood
Cleaning the house when company comes
Closing all the windows during a rainstorm
Shoveling one's own walkway
Mowing one's own lawn

Part 2: Positive Karma

Minor Class: Examples of events worth (+1) karma point (on average, +/- 0.5)

Holding the door open for a stranger
Helping one's own kids with their homework
Mowing the lawn or shoveling snow off the walkway for the family
Getting the mail for the family
Answering the phone in a group home and taking the message for a fellow resident

Being the one to go to the door to pick up the delivered
pizza for a group of housemates
Throwing away someone else's pop can on the coffee table
Putting a dollar into the guitar case of a street musician
Returning someone's library book before it's due date
Giving a 15% or 20% tip
Waiting for a gaggle of geese to cross the street before going
any further
Offering a compliment to the cashier at a grocery store
Covering your mouth to prevent one's germs from spreading
to others
Sending a card to a family member or close friend with no
money inside
Not returning a gift if you don't like it (out of respect)

Moderate Class: Examples of events worth (+3) Karma points (on
average, +/- 0.5)

Volunteering to tutor a student at a local university
Helping an old man cross the street
Donating $30 to a charity that doesn't benefit you (or $60 to a
charity that does)
Buying someone lunch
Helping someone do their laundry
Cooking supper for the family
Buying a $20 gift for an acquaintance or a $40 gift for friends or
family
Giving a good reference to an employer on behalf of an
acquaintance
Giving up your spot in a line at a food bank for someone that
needs it more
Helping a stranded motorist change a tire
Purchasing $20 worth of unneeded merchandise from a shop or
door-to-door salesman
Helping a close friend or family member move
Sending a card to a family member or close friend with money
inside
Visiting a friend or close family member in jail or prison
Inviting a close friend or family member over for a meal
Going to a charity event that doesn't benefit you personally

Major Class: Examples of events worth (+5) karma points (on average, +/- 0.5)

> Shoveling the neighbor's walkway
> Mowing the neighbor's lawn
> Helping an acquaintance move that is not a family member
> Working two hours overtime at work (without pay)
> Donating $50 to a charity that doesn't affect you (or $100 to a charity that does)
> Sending a card to a non-family acquaintance with a handwritten note inside
> Visiting an acquaintance in jail or prison
> Working someone else's shift so they can have the day off
> Giving a hitchhiker a ride home
> Inviting a more distant family member over for a meal
> Staying home when indisposed so as to not spread one's cold or flu

Benevolent Class: Examples of events worth (+10) karma points (on average, +/- 1.0)

> Donating $100 to a charity that doesn't affect you (or $200 to a charity that does)
> Helping a complete stranger move
> Inviting an acquaintance over for a meal
> Ten hours of volunteer work (such as a soup kitchen)
> Working the "adopt a highway" program
> Towing someone out of the ditch during a blizzard
> A concerned citizen doing a welfare check on someone
> Forgiving someone for stealing or not paying you back ($100)
> Donating a load of clothing to a thrift shop
> Administering first-aid on someone

Noble Class: Examples of events worth (+50) karma points (on average, +/- 5.0)

> Donating $500 to a charity that doesn't benefit you (or $1000 to a charity that does)
> Working at hospice (50 hours)
> Saving someone's life with CPR
> Donating a kidney to a family member

Magnanimous Class: Examples of events worth (+100) karma points

(on average +/- 10.0)

 Donating a kidney to a stranger

 Rushing into a burning building to save someone (involving moderate danger)

 Working as an unpaid first-responder for a year

 Donating $1000 to a charity that doesn't benefit you (or $2000 that does)

 Working at Hospice (100 hours)

Philanthropist Class: Examples of events worth (+ 1000) karma points (on average, +/- 100)

 Taking a bullet for someone in certain danger

 Giving up your life raft for someone else on a sinking ship

 Donating $10,000 to a charity that doesn't benefit you (or $20,000 that does)

 Working at hospice (1000 hours)

Part 3: Negative karma

Minor Class: Examples of events worth (-1) karma points (on average, +/- 0.5)

 Butting in line at the grocery store

 Antipathy towards a co-worker (without mean-spirited acts in concert)

 Not answering the phone in a group home or public setting

 General littering or loitering

 Simple road rage

 Shouting at a telemarketer

 Intentionally standing on the grass when a sign clearly says "do not step on grass"

 Smoking in a no smoking zone

 Carelessness that leads to small negative repercussions

 Making someone spend an hour cleaning up a mess you made

Moderate Class: Examples of events worth (-3) karma points (on average, +/-0.5)

 Not canceling an event due to inclement weather

 Shouting at someone

 Sending a mean-spirited text

 Gossip

Moderate teasing a classmate

General lying

Cheating on a test

Theft ($30)

Passive aggressive behaviors (such as the silent treatment or sarcasm with ill-intent)

Forgetting a partner's anniversary or birthday

A white lie that is detected by others

Making someone spend three hours cleaning up a mess you made

Major Class: Examples of events worth (-5) karma points (on average, +/- 0.5)

Slapping someone in the face

Telling someone he or she is unattractive

Telling someone he or she is lazy

Gaslighting

Rejecting or excluding someone

Major teasing a classmate

Theft ($50)

Standing someone up

Spreading one's cold or flu to others

Getting caught in a lie that hurts another

Act of omission: not donating to a charity when asked

Making someone spend five hours cleaning up a mess you made

Malevolent Class: Examples of events worth (-10) karma points (on average, +/- 1.0)

Theft ($100)

A lie that leads to moderate emotional or physical injury

Doing $100 worth of damage through vandalism or destruction of property

Act of omission (such as not helping a stranded motorist or delivering first aid)

Act of omission: Looking the other way when you see someone else stealing

Making someone spend ten hours cleaning up a mess you made

Discordant Class: Examples of events worth (-50) karma points (on average, +/- 5.0)

    Theft ($500)

    Unhealthy lifestyles that affect a baby during gestation

    Unprotected sex when you know you have an STD

    Negligence (not calling off school due to inclement weather causing multiple injuries)

Ignoble Class: Examples of events worth (-100) karma points (on average, +/- 10)

    Negligence (that leads to someone's serious injury)

    Non-lethal hit and run

    Theft ($1000)

    Marrying someone for looks or money alone

    Punching someone in the face, leading to injury

    Threats that cause serious fear

    Playing a part in someone's suicide

Contemptible Class: Examples of events worth (-500) karma points (on average, +/- 50)

    Playing a major role in driving someone to suicide

    Negligence (leading to death)

    Robbing a bank with guns (but not firing them)

    Theft ($5000)

    Lethal hit and run (accidental)

Abhorrent Class: Examples of events worth (-1000) karma points (on average, +/- 100)

    One murder (crime of passion or pre-meditated)

    Torturing someone via painful means

    Careless negligence that leads to three deaths

    Theft ($10,000)

Note: These are data collected during Project Madcap in one closed system or microcosm (Duluth). As such, these values may or may not be generalized to other locations. Values have been adjusted from original pain/pleasure readings over time and from what could be considered "karma buildup" (although this hypothesis has not been verified)

GLOSSARY OF TERMS AND CONCEPTS

(the ones denoted with an "F" are fictitious, the others represent actual psychological phenomena)

Abyss: A term sometimes used by Frederiech Nietzsche and Nihilists. It is used here to represent the "great unknown" or the mysteries surrounding our inevitable demise or the futility of mortality.

Amrak (F): a vigilante who is famous (or infamous depending on who you ask) for taking the law into his own hands. To date, he has killed over a hundred people, over twenty alone in 2019. He tends to target ex-murderers who eventually get out of the prison system or who have averted the death penalty. His "Karma is a bitch" death flags have been located all over the country, making it difficult to pinpoint his location. He has only been spotted once, and he was wearing a beekeeper's outfit to protect his identity. Every year he uses a new riddle to see who can predict when and where the next person will be killed.

Anodyne Research Institute (F): While the research grant proposing the study of re-animation at Anodyne Hospital was scholarly and recondite, it was scoffed at by peer academics in Canada. However, when Dr. Svenson successfully re-animated a young man following flatline heart failure, the project piqued curiosity and was par for investment. Since then, one other elderly woman has been successfully re-animated, but only for less than thirty minutes.

Apophenia: seeing or reading too much into something and finding patterns that are not really there (including positive coincidences or negative signs, portents, or omens). Seeing patterns in license plates that are not really there is one example of apophenia.

Azwald, Palatio (F): One of the 12 preserved cadavers of the Pantheon. A man of the people, he was an emissary of Ancient Earth who started out as a diplomat for the "lesser men" but eventually traded in his olive branch for a military branch. He was revered by many and hated by just as many others. His platform often involved taking from the rich and giving to the poor, much like Robin Hood. He was assassinated by the hit man Jin Tamps during one of his many lavish political rallies. Palatio is most fondly remembered for his "Compassion Act" which mandated 10% of a person's wages be tithed into funds for the poor and infirm.

Barnum Effect: refers to how a skilled fortune teller can take vague information and formulate it in such a way where it appears they have foresight or clairvoyant abilities.

Behavior Modification: A subsection of psychology that generally does not concern itself with "behaviors" that are not observable, tangible, or measurable (such as thoughts and emotions). Behaviors can be measured by their duration, frequency, latency, and intensity. Specific examples include Operant Conditioning (the use of reward or punishment) or Classical Conditioning (learning by association). The well-known studies of Pavlov's Dogs are a mainstay example of Classical Conditioning.

Benford's Law: This makes predictions about the actual prevalence of numbers (i.e. leading digits) in nature or the real world where resources are limited and you cannot assume no friction. For example, the number "1" is more likely than "9" (due to natural laws of accumulation, object permanence, and inclusion). In other words, you have to count to "1" before you can count to "9," but you don't have to count to "9" before you can count to "one."

Bertzuffe (F): One of the twelve preserved cadavers of the Pantheon. He was a political anarchist whose sainthood and position of power were largely de facto and unofficially recognized by his devout followers. He was beheaded for treason, and his head was re-joined to his body after taxidermy.

Birthday Paradox: this refers to how the likelihood of two people sharing a birthday in a group of people is far more likely than most people might initially realize. For example, the chances of two people in a large room of twenty-three sharing a birthday is actually over 50%, and is not as coincidental as one might think.

Blocking (F): This occurs when a person's goals are unexpectedly interrupted by karma (either naturally or through a karma lord's active disruption).

The Body Keeps the Score: A classic book by Bessel Van Der Kolk, largely about the effects of psychological trauma on the body.

Buildup (F): This is when a person has accrued a large surplus of positive or negative energy (pleasure or pain). When this surplus reaches a certain threshold, the excess energy may leach out into random acts of violence or random acts of charity (until equilibrium and equilibrium are once again established).

Butterfly Effect: the idea that the smallest decision can have drastic consequences in terms of cause and effect. Something as menial as dropping your groceries might lead to a chance encounter with a stranger, which could further lead to these people getting married in the future and bearing children. The classic example of the Butterfly Effect is the theory that if Adolph Hitler was accepted into the Vienna School of Fine Arts, the Holocaust could have been averted. The Butterfly Effect is also important in terms of karma, as any act of kindness or act of aggression can lead to many ripples in the cause and effect continuum.

Carrot and Stick Principle: a concept in psychology for the basic idea that humans are motivated to seek rewards (carrots) and avoid pain (sticks). It is often used as a quick metaphor for operant conditioning or the pleasure principle.

Causality: There are three conditions that must be met before one can say that "Event A caused Event B." First, Event A must come before Event B in space and time. Two, Event A and Event B must be positively or negatively correlated and co-vary together. Three, any other phenomenon that could explain the correlation between Event A and Event B must be ruled out. Also, according to the Covariation Model, the stimulus, circumstance, or people themselves involved in an event can have an impact on why a certain behavior transpired.

Change Talk: Mental health professionals are often trained to listen for and validate "change talk" when they hear it from their clients. When a client acknowledges positive change they are offering "change talk." This is a concept pioneered by Rollnick and Miller and discussed in their book "Motivational Interviewing."

Cognitive Dissonance: occurs when a person's moral values are in conflict with his or her behavior. When faced with this mismatch, a person generally feels anxiety, and will either modify their moral code to accommodate their "lackluster" behavior, or they may change their "lackluster" behavior to be more in line with their moral values. One common example of this is when a person rationalizes unhealthy behavior by telling themselves "I am just following orders" or "it's just business and nothing personal." In this way, they can assuage their guilt while engaging in questionable behaviors.

Cognitive Distortion: These are biases or thinking errors. One example, "catastrophizing," is when a person assumes the worst or expects the shoe drop at any given moment. The idea that life is fair is called the "myth of fairness." While erroneous, these distortions can provide a protective function and false sense of security, at least in the short term. Other examples include: Just World Hypothesis, Fundamental Attribution Error, Dunning Kruger Effect, Restraint Bias, Halo Effect, Rationalizing Cognitive Dissonance, Sunk Cost Fallacy, Emotional Reasoning, Heuristics, Bandwagon Effect, false dilemma, and many others.

Coin-Age (F): A magazine for hobbyists and collectors of rare coinage and bills.

Comfortable death: A death that is 1) painless, 2) unexpected, and 3) fast

Compounded Karma (F): when one large event plays out in two smaller events. For example, if a person broke someone's nose in a bar scuffle, he might not only sprain his ankle on the curb the following Tuesday, but also get the flu a week after that. The combination of pain from the two smaller events might equal the pain of the larger event, in a sort of additive justice.

Construct Validity: Construct validity refers to the extent to which a measurement tool or assessment actually measures what it purports to be measuring, in an accurate and precise manner.

Death Hag: While not a highly common term, "Death Hag" is slang jargon for someone who is fascinated by death and enjoys perusing pictures or watching videos of people dead, about to die, or in the process of dying.

Degrees of Freedom: a concept from statistics. However, it also serves as a useful metaphor for how much freedom of movement a person might have over life's challenges, including social or genetic determinants of behavior.

Deinstitutionalization: This refers to the influx of people leaving the asylums and mental hospitals in the 60's, 70's, and 80's as mental health care became more community-based and rehab-focused, prioritizing community integration, person-centered care, and "least restrictive environments."

Deterrence Theory: This is related to learning theory and Operant Conditioning. According to DT, learning is more likely to occur when a consequence is delivered immediately (celerity), consistently (certainty), and with sufficient intensity (seriousness). Also, it appears that the threat of punishment (such as incarceration) is less of a deterrent for "crimes of passion" that occur in the heat of the moment. For a useful read on Deterrence Theory, see: Do Criminal

Laws Deter Crime? Deterrence Theory in Criminal Justice Policy: A Primer by Ben Johnson, from MN House Research.

Differential (F): This relates to how karma is often a zero sum game. If person A steals from person B, person A gains (+1) while person B loses (-1). Person A is left in a two-up position, and the Karmatic Differential would be "2."

Displacement (F): This is when it appears that the wrong target is being rewarded or punished in relation to the acts of vice or virtue of another. Karma lords try their best to keep displacement to a minimum.

Disruption (F): When a karma lord interferes the natural order of things to set things on a proper course (maintain the pleasure/pain balance). Karma lords try not to interfere with the natural order of things unless they have to, as this requires energy and resources. When a karma police disrupts too often, they might face a reprimand from the Docent Randii.

Dwyer, Bud: A Pennsylvania politician who killed himself on live TV in 1987.

Eighty/Twenty Principle: This is an idea from the ambit of mate selection theory that says that about 20% of males (the alpha males) will copulate with 80% of the most attractive females. This can lead to karma buildup and resentment, as 80% of men (and 20% of women) are left sexually frustrated. This less-than-desireable state of affairs makes it difficult to establish equilibrium in the pain/pleasure continuum.

End of the World: A line of role playing games by Fantasy Flight Games that use the EDGE system. Instead of taking the role of a fantasy character like Elf or Mage you play as yourself in one of four apocalypse situations: zombies, aliens, gods, or machines.

Escape Room Fire Tragedy: This is a reference of a tragedy in Poland where five people died when an "Escape Room" caught fire. Although this event actually happened somewhat later in 2019, it was included here in this story, as it represents horrific and ironic bad luck of a catastrophic proportion.

Face/Vase Illusion: The "face-vase" illusion is a well-known Gestalt illusion, where looking at it from one perspective reveals a picturesque vase. But another perspective yields two faces staring at each other, when foreground and background trade places.

Farmer's Dilemma: A logic puzzle where a person is challenged to consider how best to transport a fox, chicken, and sack of corn to the other side of a river using a small raft.

First Law of Thermodynamics: Also called Conservation of Energy. Energy cannot be created or destroyed but it can change forms. This can apply to karma and the pain/pleasure continuum as well.

Flatliners: A film from 1990 (and rebooted in 2017) about people trying to flatline to see if there is life after death.

Frey Effect: refers to a psychological phenomenon where audible sounds can be induced, perceived, and experienced via the emission of electromagnetic radiation or modulated radio waves, even if no sounds were actually present. The Frey Effect is a point of contention among academics, and conspiracy theories abound as to how the Frey Effect has been exploited as a tool for mind control or subliminal advertising. The characters "V2K" are code-speak for "Voice to Skull" (referring to secret messages being implanted in the brain). The Frey Effect was said to be first observed during WW2. The mechanism for the Frey Effect is believed to occur through the expansion of the Cochlea.

Fundamental Attribution Error: A self-serving bias where we tend to rationalize the cause of other people's misfortunes or shortcomings as being "their own fault" (i.e. blaming the person, not the situation). A similar bias is the "actor-observer" bias when we blame our own faults or shortcomings on the environment or situational factors.

Gambler's fallacy: After a stint of bad luck, a person might expect their luck to eventually sway in their favor (despite the fact that the odds of heads vs. tails on a fair coin will always be 50%). People who ascribe to karma may not consider it a fallacy per se, as nothing is random in their eyes, including a simple flip of a coin. And according to karma, a gambler might be rewarded or punished with a winning or losing streak.

Ganzfeld Experiments: these were conducted during the mid to late seventies and early eighties, apparently showing significant results and a moderate effect size for the existence of ESP. The typical experiment consists of a "sender" and "receiver" in separate rooms. The "sender" attempts to mentally transmit one of 4 stimuli into the mind of the "receiver." If done successfully, there should be a "hit" rate significantly higher than 25%. These experiments were also mentioned in the DS game Gavin was playing *"9 Hours 9 Persons 9 Doors."*

Halo Effect: when a person's overall impression of someone is skewed based on one or a few criteria. For example, a person might display more favoritism or more sympathy towards an attractive person vs. an unattractive one.

Hawthorne Effect: This is a psychological phenomenon that occurs when a person's task performance or productivity increases due to being aware of being evaluated by an observer. This also leads to non-genuine behavior.

Heart Math: Researchers at the HeartMath Institute (HMI) believe that the heart can exhibit subtle clairvoyant qualities and can even predict the future up to 14 seconds ahead of time.

Help radius (F): How far and wide a person's helpful actions can affect others in a closed system, across systems, or through karmatic leakage.

Hope is the Thing with Feathers: A famous poem by Emily Dickinson written around the time of the mid 1800s.

Hurt radius (F): How far and wide a person's hurtful actions can affect others in a closed system, across systems, or through karmatic leakage.

Impression Management: How a person wants to be perceived by others. When people try to "create a good impression" or "keep up appearances" they are engaging in impression management.

Innocent Bystander: A myth according to the Butterfly Effect and karmatic theory. To think about just how connected all people are, consider person A who lives in Madagascar and person B who lives in Oregon. Technically speaking, person A could call person B on the phone at any time. Whether person A calls person B or not, his or her actions have a direct bearing on person B either way. Complacency is an action, and the choice to not act is still a decision. Even people from different time periods can continue to influence other people hundreds of years later posthumously (such as when a tome from the 1700s continues to inspire and be influential in a modern zeitgeist).

Ironic lucrative factor: These are seemingly tragic events with fruitful consequences (blessings in disguise).

Ironic tragic factor: These are seemingly innocuous events with dire consequences (related to the butterfly effect).

Johari Window: A conceptualization of the four selves, created by Joseph Luft and Harrington Ingham in the fifties. They define the four selves as: public self, private self, other self, and blind self. One theory suggests that the more dissonant the private self is from the public self the more stress the person will experience due to feeling disingenuous or phony.

Just World Hypothesis: A concept from the ambit of Cognitive Psychology, a bias where people assume "good things happen to good people" and "bad things happen to bad people." This bias can lend itself to victim blaming.

According to karma, this may not always be a bias.

Karmatic Leakage (F): When information leaks out of a closed system. For example, if a scientist were studying karma in America, a person watching the BBC is being affected by Great Britain (i.e. karmatic leakage).

Krystal Kube (F): The "Krystal Kube" has clairvoyant properties like a crystal ball, but it has six sides. It is a tool that can be used by the karma lords (although they are strictly forbidden from looking into the sixth side). It is said that it was originally gifted to the docent from the very gods themselves. The "K" represents not only karma, but in the original dimension in which the Krystal Kube was forged, the word "crystal" was originally spelled with a "K" instead of a "C." The square shape reveals multiple realities, including the fourth, fifth, and sixth dimensions. Unlike many experiments in human psychology, the Krystal Kube can generate an authentic and identical control group and treatment group for true experiments.

Law of Large Numbers (also known as Regression to the Mean): This is not to be confused with "Law of Averages," a cognitive fallacy. The Law of Large Numbers is the idea that over time and across many trials (such as dice rolls or coin tosses), scores tend to hover and return to the mean, despite the occasional outlier or anomaly. Despite being a law of probability, just as with the Normal Curve, there are other theories that acknowledge the role of metaphysical forces or even karma.

Learned Helplessness: This occurs when a person comes to believe they are less capable than they really are, due to low confidence. This is not to be confused with "playing the victim," where a person intentionally and purposefully adopts and exaggerates the posturings of a victim in order to reap its inherent benefits.

Least Restrictive Environment: This is a value system adopted by community-based human service professions. The idea is that humans should be treated with "just the right amount" of service intervention. Used here, karma police aim for a similar "hands off" approach and only tamper with the human condition when absolutely necessary.

The "Lesser Men" (F): This is a slang term for the "Society for the Preservation of Non-Preservation," a group of traditionalists that abjure the idea of taxidermy for humans. Their umbrage regarding taxidermy is well-known and promulgated widely in the periodical *Get Stuffed*.

Linus Blanket: this is a reference to the blanket Linus carried for a sense of safety and security in James Schultz's *Peanuts*. In the world of mental health, and Terror Management Theory in particular, a "Linus Blanket" is often used as a metaphor for a defense mechanism or "comfort zone." People cope with the mysteries and existential stress in the human condition in myriad ways, via their belief systems, political affiliations, addictions, thoughts, feelings, behaviors, or other more tangible security objects.

Locus of Control: A principle of psychology. People with an "internal" locus of control tend to feel they are in control of their life and their decisions have consequences. People with an "external locus of control" tend to feel more helpless and powerless in the world's wake (like a pinball being knocked around).

Lubbock, Christina: A news reporter who killed herself on live TV in 1974. The footage has become a sort of "Holy Grail" in the Death Hag community. It is said that every last copy in existence is missing or discarded.

Maslow's Hierarchy of Needs: a theory proposed in the early 40's by Abraham Maslow, where human beings are motivated to meet their physical needs (food, water, shelter, safety, etc.) before their emotional needs (sense of belong, self-esteem, identity, etc.).

Mataafa: Another name for the "Great Storm of 1905." It was also the name of one of the steam ships out at sea. The storm resulted in massive damage to ships and over thirty lost lives, leading to the construction of Split Rock Lighthouse.

Marin, Michael: A lawyer who killed himself in a videotaped court hearing soon after his guilty verdict was read in 2012.

Mate Selection Theory: a component of "Evolutionary Psychology," popularized by scientists like David Buss (author of *The Evolution of Desire*). According to this theory, males tend to be judged by their prowess, status, and earning potential, where females tend to be judged by their beauty and appearances. In general, "love" as we know it can be reduced to an existential illusion or bribe to entice the human race into procreation and the spreading of genes. This also explains how a fleeting moment of passion can translate into caring for offspring for about eighteen years.

McHale, Evelyn: A New York bookkeeper who killed herself by jumping off the top of the Empire State Building in 1947.

Meta Mass (F): refers to subjective weight. According to Project Madcap, the world has an "objective reality" and also a "subjective reality." Emotions are difficult to measure, but they still have weight and gravity (as in the "gravity" of the situation). And while that weight cannot be measured in grams per se, they have meta-mass and are every bit as real as a tangible object in a room. The subjective "weight" of one Vice or Virtue Unit in the "subjective world" is the metaphysical equivalent of one gram in the "objective world." These grams are sometimes called "meta grams." Meta mass with a (+) valence is pleasure, and meta mass with a (-) valence is pain. Meta mass could be likened to a kind of energy, where E=MC(squared).

Microcosm: a closed system of interacting people (such as Duluth). A microcosm theoretically allows the ebb and flow of karma to be easily monitored via the interactions of relevant parties (much like studying migration habits of tagged geese flying south for the winter). As Mark's devices are equipped with Wi-Fi and GPS technology, they can also access all the city residents' demographic and genealogical information from various databases. These microcosms can be studied to see how a small group of people interact with each other, and how the "ripple effects" of pain and pleasure can spread throughout the closed system. One could also attempt to test the "zero sum theory" of karma, and see if the aggregate total of pain equals the aggregate total of pleasure within the closed system (as per Conservation of Pain and Pleasure).

Milgram, Stanley: Known for the Milgram Shock Experiment from the early 1960's that tested blind obedience, and the extent to which humans would follow orders even in the face of behavior that might otherwise seem unethical. It turned out that humans would administer (what they perceived to be) painful electric shocks to subjects at the behest of the experiment's command.

Mirrored Consequence (F): This is when a punishment for a crime is identical in every way to the crime itself (for example, a person who breaks someone's right leg would also get their right leg broken, in as similarly a manner as possible). This would be the most literal interpretation of "an eye for an eye." According to karma theory, Tier 3 is the easiest milieu to conduct mirrored consequences as it's easier to create virtual realities in the afterlife.

Monty Hall Problem: refers to the game show "Deal or No Deal." Behind one of the three doors there is a prize. After choosing a door, the host reveals an empty door from the two doors not initially chosen. The host then asks the contestant if he/she would like to change doors. Many people think whether you opt to change doors shouldn't matter, and the probability of selecting the prize will always be 1/3. However, this is not the case. Since the host revealed an empty door, it's actually better to switch doors. The odds of winning actually increases from 1/3 to ½.

Motivation: There are two basic kinds of motivation. Intrinsic motivation is when a person's internal drives and values guide their behavior (such as going to work because you enjoy it). Extrinsic motivation, on the other hand, is when a person's behavior is guided by external rewards or punishments (such as going to work solely to earn a paycheck).

Natural karma (F): When appropriate rewards or punishments are produced naturally in the environment (such as a hangover for drinking too much wine or the increased likelihood of others doing you a favor if you pay it forward).

Nazca Lines of Peru: Ancient runes that are difficult to ascertain up close but can be seen from afar. Some of them are animals, such as a monkey, spider, and hummingbird.

Newton's Third Law of Motion: Every action has an equal and opposite reaction. This can apply to Karma and the pain/pleasure continuum as well, especially as a result of "karma buildup."

Normal Curve (or the "Bell Curve"): this is at the crux of the field of statistics, showing scores or values along the X axis (of a certain variable like human height). Frequency of occurrence is depicted along the Y axis. The standard normal curve shows the mean, median, and mode at the center, where the highest frequency of scores occur. Some variables do or do not approximate a normal distribution. Early mathematicians pondered whether the normal curve had an almost spiritual aspect, as it seemed to suggest a certain predictability, symmetry, or order to certain variables or the universe itself. A true standard normal curve is symmetrical. Many experiments in psychology are based on the normal curve.

Object Permanence: This is a concept coined by developmental psychologist Jean Piaget. Object permanence is a developmental milestone when infants understand for the first time that just because something is hidden from view it doesn't mean the object literally disappeared. Object permanence is said to develop around the time a child is half a year old.

OCEAN Model of Personality: This refers to the "Big 5" theory of personality, where any given person's personality can be reduced to variability along five dimensions (Openness to experience, Conscientiousness, Extroversion vs. introversion, Agreeableness, and Neuroticism).

Quantz, Merryella (F): an iron-fisted dignitary who identified as a political moderate. While she did not believe in government entitlements or subsidies, this was mitigated by her diligent work to channel those monies instead into vocational and academic pursuits for working class citizens with academic potential. While she detested handouts, she favored a high minimum wage. Claiming to be a Mayan deity, she was a victim of many death threats by groups who favored a fiscal safety net. Her ongoing claims of being descended from a Mayan goddess eventually granted her asylum (and not the political kind).

Paplior, Barbara: A casualty of a tragic accident on the Aerial Lift Bridge in Duluth on June 10, 1990.

Parkour: A sport where athletes known as "traceurs" attempt to traverse from one location to another in the most efficient and fastest means possible. It is sometimes known as free-running, and the sport can be very dangerous, and has led to numerous deaths.

Phonautograph: The device predates the phonograph, and was an early sound capture device invented by Edouard-Leon Scott de Martinville around the time of 1851. Unlike the phonograph, the phonautograph "records" sound, in a sense, via a tactile medium and produces the 'sound,' in a sense, via a visual medium. The phonautograph does not record sound directly from soundwaves, but rather captures the vibrations caused by the soundwaves and transcribes them as wavy lines on a special surface. Scott is credited by some to have produced the very first audio record of recorded sound around the year 1860. However, the actual message was supposedly never heard and played back until well over a hundred years later.

Pleasure Principle: a Freudian idea that human beings are motivated by the selfish "Id" to seek pleasure and avoid pain. However, there were others prior to Freud that had similar conceptualizations regarding human motivation. Some schools of thought reject the idea that altruism even exists, as there always seems to be a self-serving gain in almost anything we do.

Problem of Multiple Murders (F): Since a person can only die once, how can they truly atone for their crime when they kill more than one person, according to karma? While Tier 1 (Nature) or Tier 2 (Reincarnation) can sometimes handle this problem, usually this gets passed onto Fate Rifle and Tier 3 (Afterlife) as it's easier to set up the conditions for mirrored consequences and virtual realities.

Project Madcap (F): Mark's invention and life's work. He initially invented the device to measure pain and pleasure like a thermometer measures temperature. Over time he also thought about how such a device could be used to measure karma in a closed system.

Pygmalion Effect: This has to to with how people's expectations can affect thoughts, feelings, or behaviors in themselves or others. This is a type of self-fulfilling prophecy. As the theory goes, if a teacher treats a student "as if" the student were highly intelligent, the higher expectations placed upon the student might translate into higher grades as opposed to if the student were treated with low expectations. Applied here, if a person "expects" an event to be particularly painful or pleasurable, this expectation might affect how much pain or pleasure they actually feel.

Razors: In philosophy, these are things to keep in mind when making a scientific argument (or detecting flaws in others' arguments). The ones that start with "H" are especially relevant to this story: Hitchen's Razor, Hume's Razor, and Hanlon's Razor.

Regal Sort (F): An experienced and resilient player of the game of "life." A useful metaphor might be a role playing game where level 1 characters are expected to fight level 1 enemies and level 8 characters are expected to fight level 8 enemies. The actual (subjective) challenge level of each skirmish is comparable, but the latter is a more regal, elite, and respected affair, as the battle illustrates the skill and prowess of a high-level protagonist. The metaphor here in real life is that a karma police (i.e. Game Master) must never pit a person with low resilience (i.e. level 1 character) against a level 2 or higher challenge. Similarly, it is unethical for a karma police to pit a person with a moderate resilience (i.e. level 8 character) against a level 9 or higher challenge. Karma lords are also careful to not put characters up against challenges that are too easy either.

Restraint Bias: When we overestimate how well we would show restraint in someone else's position in the face of temptation. We often assume we would have handled it "so much better" than someone else did, failing to take into account all the variables at play.

The Riddle of Goldilocks's Dilemma: This is a riddle or "Easter egg" hidden in the very pages of this book (The Fairgrounds Book 1). By noticing this term in the glossary you are already part-way to the solution. The message revealed is the bane of Madeline's existence. This number is the key: 4412321234334.

Romero, Jordan: He shot himself on live TV after a high speed police chase in 2012. Considered a significant media blunder, the tape kept rolling during the unexpected and tragic turn of events.

Ross, Elizabeth Kubler: a psychiatrist who conceptualized the five stages of grief in her classic book *On Death and Dying* in 1969. The stages include: denial, anger, bargaining, depression, and acceptance.

The Scarlet Letter: A reference to Nathaniel Hawthorne's 1850 book of the same name.

Scrubbing (F): This occurs at the Tier 2 of karma (reincarnation) when a person's memories of their past life is erased before being given a new body and identity in which to live a second life.

Smite, Brocker (F). Considered a fear monger by some, his followers thought of him as a moralistic dreamer. He was known by various epithets, including "Diamond in the Rough" and "Pearl Before Swine." He aimed to create law and order through Goldilock's Dilemma by inventing a religion. He lost credibility when it was later discovered that he invented the religion himself, even forging dusty tomes and claiming they were written by spirit hands. While his name has since fallen into disrepute, some still claim that his intentions were good, even if his methods were folly. Even after falling from grace, he still maintained a small but loyal group of followers until his death.

Stimulus Response Chains: In psychology, human behavior is often broken down into S-O-R chains. The "S" represents the environment stimulus, the "R" represents our reaction or response to the stimulus or trigger, and the "O" represents the organic or human factor that exists between stimulus and response. For example, a person with a spider phobia might feel anxious (response) when seeing the spider (stimulus) due to previous negative experiences with spiders (O). Some academics believe all human interactions can be reduced to complex strings of S-O-R chains.

Tabula Rasas: This is the idea that humans start out as "blank slates" and the accumulation of life experiences ultimately shape our personalities. This metaphor has often been credited or associated as far back as Aristotle.

Terror Management Theory: A theory in psychology from Greenberg, Soloman, and Pyszynski. It was inspired by Earnest Becker's "The Denial of Death." It proposes that humans are inherently afraid of their mortality and carry the weight of the world's hidden origins on their shoulders. As such, they create psychological defenses in the form of social constructions or identities that provide life with a false sense of control, meaning, security, and safety in a world devoid of quantifiable objective truths. Politics, religion, and self-esteem are said to provide a vague sense of comfort and safety, much like a "Linus Blanket." The idea of "Mimento Mori" is consistent as well, as it's a constant reminder that nobody lives forever.

The Thinker: The famous statue by Auguste Rodin depicting a man deep in thought as he ponders the meaning of life and existence.

Twenty Four: An educational math game where a person tries to figure out how to get the number "24" when given 4 numbers. You can add, subtract, divide, or multiply the numbers to get twenty-four. Used here, Sandy uses this math-game to represent computer hacks in her role playing game. If a player successfully figures out the puzzle, they successfully "hack" the computer in the role playing game.

Type One and Type Two Errors: These are also statistical concepts. A "Type 1 Error" is a "false positive" (claiming that a treatment has an effect when it actually doesn't) and a Type 2 Error is a "false negative" (claiming that a treatment has no effect when it actually does).

Valence (F): Pleasure has a positive (+) valence and pain has a negative valence (-).

Venn Diagram: A visual aid that shows how two or three "different" concepts or ideas can still share certain common aspects. They are usually shown as overlapping non-concentric circles.

Weltschmerz: A German word for a state of melancholy and despondency related to bearing witness to the current sufferings of the world. It's a type of "compassion fatigue" or "survival guilt" where a person finds little joy in life knowing that so many other people have suffered, are suffering, or have yet to suffer, over the course of centuries.

Who would you rather be dilemma (F): Human systems of law and order often appoint one party as the victim and the other party as the perpetrator in a polarized manner, without always considering who actually has the better lot. Consider "person A" that accidentally killed "person B" in a drunk driving accident. Who truly has the worse lot, Person A who has to live with the guilt of killing someone, in addition to spending years in jail? Or person B, who died suddenly and painlessly? If you were forced to choose, who would you rather be, the "victim" or the "perpetrator?"

Why Zebras Don't Get Ulcers: A book by Robert Suppolsky. It discusses the health ramifications of psychological stress on the body. The short answer to the question the book poses, is that humans tend to over-react and over-use their bodily stress response, causing unnecessary wear and tear on the body. The idea is that animals are more stimulus-bound and present focused, and tend to deal with stress in the "here and now" and move on after a stressor comes and goes.

Yongning, Wu: A young adult stuntman who fell from a skyscraper over sixty stories tall on November 8, 2017. It was reported this would have been his final stunt before retiring.

Zero Sum Game: one where for every winner there is a loser. The scoring system of Othello is a great example. Every time a white coin turns to black, Player White gains a point and Player Black loses a point (which translates into a two point differential). Certain aspects of the stock market is akin to a zero sum game (although not in all respects). And while karma is not about "winning and losing" per se, pain and pleasure are two sides of the same coin. A person cannot know pain without pleasure. And when a person harms another, the former gains while the latter loses. In the "dog eat dog" world of humans, the "game of life" is often a zero sum game.

About the Author: Blake Alb is a writer with a passion for stories that stray from the beaten path. He has an MS in psychology and works as a mental health professional. He attributes his psychology degree as playing a significant role in providing a wellspring of ideas for storytelling. He is a big fan of all things geeky, with a penchant for anime, fantasy, science fiction, and video games. He also enjoys British Comedy and improv. He also wrote "Snowcrow" for World Castle Publishing (shown).